THE COLDEST GIRL IN COLDTOWN

IS THE **HOTTEST** BOOK AROUND!

An Amazon Best Teen Book of the Year

An NPR Great Read of the Year

A *School Library Journal* Best Book of the Year

"A dark, violent, **edge-of-your-seat** read."
—*Entertainment Weekly*

 "This **superior**, dread-soaked tale will satisfy…all ages."
—*Publishers Weekly*, starred review

 "It's dark and dangerous, bloody and brilliant." —*Kirkus Reviews*, starred review

 "Quick paced and **thought-provoking**."
—*SLJ*, starred review

★ "With rapid-fire dialogue, lavish details, and a wildly imagined world, this **will enthrall** Black's fans from start to finish."
—*Booklist*, starred review

"A **chillingly believable** mix of prison camp and old-Vegas glamour." —NPR

"It's good, **so good**….Full of action."
—*USA Today Happily Ever After* blog

The
COLDEST GIRL
in COLDTOWN

The
COLDEST GIRL
in COLDTOWN

by HOLLY BLACK

LITTLE, BROWN AND COMPANY

NEW YORK BOSTON

Copyright © 2013 by Holly Black
Excerpt from *The Darkest Part of the Forest* copyright © 2014 by Holly Black

Little, Brown and Company

Hachette Book Group
1290 Avenue of the Americas, New York, NY 10104
Visit our website at lb-teens.com

Little, Brown and Company is a division of Hachette Book Group, Inc.
The Little, Brown name and logo are trademarks of Hachette Book Group, Inc.

The publisher is not responsible for websites (or their content)
that are not owned by the publisher.

First Paperback Edition: August 2014
First published in hardcover in September 2013 by Little, Brown and Company

Library of Congress Cataloging-in-Publication Data

Black, Holly.
The coldest girl in Coldtown / by Holly Black.—First edition.
pages cm
Summary: When seventeen-year-old Tana wakes up following a party in the aftermath of a violent vampire attack, she travels to Coldtown, a quarantined Massachusetts city full of vampires, with her ex-boyfriend and a mysterious vampire boy in tow.
ISBN 978-0-316-21310-3 (hc) — ISBN 978-0-316-27755-6 (int'l) — ISBN 978-0-316-21309-7 (pb)
[1. Vampires—Fiction. 2. Love—Fiction.] I. Title.
PZ7.B52878Co 2013
[Fic]—dc23
2012043790

10 9 8 7 6 5 4

RRD-C

Printed in the United States of America

For Steve Berman, who inspired the story that inspired this novel

⤙ CHAPTER 1 ⤚

Nothing can happen

more beautiful than death.

—Walt Whitman

Tana woke lying in a bathtub. Her legs were drawn up, her cheek pressed against the cold metal of the faucet. A slow drip had soaked the fabric on her shoulder and wetted locks of her hair. The rest of her, including her clothes, was still completely dry, which was kind of a relief. Her neck felt stiff; her shoulders ached. She looked up dazedly at the ceiling, at the blots of mold grown into Rorschach patterns. For a moment, she felt completely disoriented. Then she scrambled up onto her knees, skin sliding on the enamel, and pushed aside the shower curtain.

The sink was piled with plastic cups, beer bottles, and askew hand towels. Bright, buttery, late summer sunlight streamed in from a small window above the toilet, interrupted only by the swinging shadows made by the garland of garlic hung above it.

A party. Right. She'd been at a sundown party. "Ugh," she said, her fingers on the curtain to steady herself, popping three rings off the rod with her weight. Her temples throbbed dully.

She remembered getting ready, putting on the jangling bracelets that still chimed together when she moved and the steel-toed oxblood boots that took forever to lace and were mysteriously no longer on her feet. Remembered the way she'd lined her foggy blue eyes in shimmering black and kissed her mirror for luck. Everything got a little blurry after that.

Levering herself up, Tana stumbled to the faucet and splashed water on her face. Her makeup was smudged, lipstick smeared across her cheek, mascara spread like a stain. The white baby-doll dress she'd borrowed out of her mother's closet was ripped at the sleeve. Her black hair was a tangled mess that finger-combing didn't do a lot to fix. She looked like a dissipated mime.

The truth was that she was pretty sure she'd passed out in the bathroom while avoiding her ex, Aidan. Before that there'd been some playing of a drinking game called The Lady or The Tiger, where you bet on whether a tossed coin would come up heads (lady) or tails (tiger). If you picked wrong, you had to do a shot. After that came a lot of dancing and some more swigs from a bottle of whiskey. Aidan had urged Tana to make out with his new sulky-mouthed, strawberry-haired girlfriend, the one who was wearing a dog collar she'd found in the mudroom. He said it would be like an eclipse of the sun and the moon in the sky, a marriage of all things dark and light. *You mean an eclipse of the sun and moon in your pants*, Tana had told him, but he'd been doggedly, infuriatingly persistent.

And as the whiskey sang through her blood and sweat slicked her skin, a dangerously familiar recklessness filled her. With a face like a wicked cherub, Aidan had always been hard to say no to. Worse, he knew it.

Sighing, Tana opened the bathroom door—not even locked, so people could have been coming in and out all night with her *right there*, behind the shower curtain, and how humiliating was that?—and padded out into the hall. The smell of spilled beer filled the air, along with something else, something metallic and charnel-sweet. The television was on in the other room, and she could hear the low voice of a newscaster as she walked toward the kitchen. Lance's parents didn't care about his having sundown parties at their old farmhouse, so he had one almost every weekend, locking the doors at dusk and keeping them barred until dawn. She'd been to plenty, and the mornings were always full of shouting and showers, boiling coffee and trying to hack together breakfast from a couple of eggs and scraps of toast.

And long lines for the two small bathrooms, with people beating on the doors if you took too long. Everyone needed to pee, take a shower, and change clothes. Surely that would have woken her.

But if she *had* slept through it and everyone was already out at a diner, they would be laughing it up. Joking about her unconscious in the tub and whatever they'd done in that bathroom while she was asleep, plus maybe photos, all kinds of stupid stuff that she'd have to hear repeated over and over once school started. She was just lucky they hadn't markered a mustache on her.

If Pauline had been at the party, none of this would have

happened. When they got wasted, they usually curled up underneath the dining room table, limbs draped over each other like kittens in a basket, and no boy in the world, not even Aidan, was bold enough to face Pauline's razor tongue. But Pauline was away at drama camp, and Tana had been bored, so she'd gone to the party alone.

The kitchen was empty, spilled booze and orange soda pooling on the countertops and being soaked up by a smattering of potato chips. Tana was reaching for the coffeepot when, across the black-and-white linoleum floor, just on the other side of the door frame to the living room, she saw a hand, its fingers stretched out as if in sleep. She relaxed. No one was awake yet—that was all. Maybe she was the first one up, although when she thought back to the sun streaking through the bathroom window, it had seemed high in the sky.

The longer she gazed at the hand, though, the more she noticed that it seemed oddly pale, the skin around the fingernails bluish. Tana's heart started to thud, her body reacting before her mind caught up. She slowly set the pot back on the counter and forced herself to cross the kitchen floor, step by careful step, until she was over the threshold of the living room.

Then she had to force herself not to scream.

The tan carpet was stiff and black with stripes of dried blood, spattered like a Jackson Pollock canvas. The walls were streaked with it, handprints smearing the dingy beige surfaces. And the bodies. Dozens of bodies. People she'd seen every day since kindergarten, people whom she'd played tag with and cried over and kissed, were lying at odd angles, their bodies pale and cold, their eyes staring like rows of dolls in a shop window.

The hand near Tana's foot belonged to Imogen, a pretty, plump, pink-haired girl who was planning to go to art school next year. Her lips were slightly apart, and her navy anchor-print sundress rode up so that her thighs were visible. She appeared to have been caught as she was trying to crawl away, one arm extended and the other gripping the carpet.

Otta's, Ilaina's, and Jon's bodies were piled together. They'd just gotten back from summer cheer camp and had started the party off with a series of backflips in the yard just before sunset, as mosquitoes buzzed through the warm breeze. Now dried blood crusted on their clothing like rust, tinting their hair, dotting their skin like freckles. Their eyes were locked open, the pupils gone cloudy.

She found Lance on a couch, posed with his arms thrown over the shoulders of a girl on one side and a boy on the other, all three of their throats bearing ragged puncture marks. All three of them with beer bottles resting near their hands, as if they were still at the party. As though their white-blue lips were likely to say her name at any moment.

Tana felt dizzy. The room seemed to spin. She sank to the blood-covered carpet and sat, the pounding in her head growing louder and louder. On the television, someone was spraying orange cleaner on a granite countertop while a grinning child ate jam off a slice of bread.

One of the windows was open, she noticed, curtain fluttering. The party must have gotten too warm, everyone sweating in the small house and yearning for the cool breeze just outside. Then, once the window was open, it would have been easy to forget to close it. There was still the garlic, after all, still the holy water on the lintels.

Things like this happened in Europe, in places like Belgium, where the streets teemed with vampires and the shops didn't open until after dark. Not here. Not in Tana's town, where there hadn't been a single attack in more than five years.

And yet it had happened. A window had been left open to the night, and a vampire had crawled through.

She should get her phone and call—call someone. Not her father; there was no way he would be able to deal with this. Maybe the police. Or a vampire hunter, like Hemlok from TV, the huge, bald former wrestler always decked out in leather. He would know what to do. Her little sister had a poster of Hemlok in her locker, right next to pictures of golden-haired Lucien, her favorite Coldtown vampire. Pearl would be so excited if Hemlok came; she could finally get his autograph.

Tana started giggling, which was bad, she knew, and put her hands over her mouth to smother the sound. It wasn't okay to laugh in front of dead people. That was like laughing at a funeral.

The unblinking eyes of her friends watched her.

On the television, the newscaster was predicting scattered showers later in the week. The Nasdaq was down.

Tana remembered all over again that Pauline hadn't been at the party, and she was so fiercely, so selfishly glad that she couldn't even feel bad about it, because Pauline was alive even though everyone else was dead.

From far away in the guest room, someone's phone started to ring. It was playing a tinny remix of "Tainted Love." After a while, it stopped. Then two phones much closer went off almost at the same time, their rings combining into a chorus of discordant sound.

The news turned into a show about three men who lived together in an apartment with a wisecracking skull. The laugh track roared every time the skull spoke. Tana wasn't sure if it was a real show or if she was imagining it. Time slipped by.

She gave herself a little lecture: She had to get up off the floor and go into the guest room, where jackets were piled up on the bed, and root around until she found her purse and her boots and her car keys. Her cell phone was there, too. She'd need that if she was going to call someone.

She had to do it right then—no more sitting.

It occurred to her that there was a phone closer, shoved into the pocket of one of the corpses or pressed between cold, dead skin and the lace of a bra. But she couldn't bear the idea of searching bodies.

Get up, she told herself.

Pushing herself to stand, she started picking her way across the floor, trying to ignore the way the carpet crunched under her bare feet, trying not to think about the smell of decay blooming in the room. She remembered something from her sophomore-year social studies class—her teacher had told them about the famous raid in Corpus Christi, when Texas tried to close its Coldtown and drove tanks into it during the day. Every human inside who might have been infected got shot. Even the mayor's daughter was killed. A lot of sleeping vampires were killed, too, rooted out of their hiding places and beheaded or exposed to sunlight. When night fell, the remaining vampires were able to kill the guards at the gate and flee, leaving dozens and dozens of drained and infected people in their wake. Corpus Christi vampires were still a popular target for bounty hunters on television.

Every kid had to do a different project for that class. Tana had made a diorama, with a shoe box and a lot of red poster paint, to represent a news article that she'd cut out of the paper—one about three vampires on the run from Corpus Christi who'd break into a house, kill everyone, and then rest among the corpses until night fell again.

Which made her wonder if there could still be a vampire in this house, the vampire who had slaughtered all these people. Who'd somehow overlooked her, who'd been too intent on blood and butchery to open every door to every hall closet or bathroom, who hadn't swept aside a shower curtain. It would murder her now, though, if it heard her moving.

Her heart raced, thundering against her rib cage, and every beat felt like a punch in the chest. *Stupid*, her heart said. *Stupid, stupid, stupid.*

Tana felt light-headed, her breath coming in shallow gasps. She knew she should sit down again and put her head between her legs— that was what you were supposed to do if you were hyperventilating— but if she sat down, she might never get up. She forced herself to inhale deeply instead, letting the air out of her lungs as slowly as she could.

She wanted to run out the front, race across the lawn, and pound on one of the neighbors' doors until they let her inside.

But without her boots or phone or keys, she'd be in a lot of trouble if no one was home. Lance's parents' farmhouse was out in the country, and all the land behind the house was state park. There just weren't that many neighbors nearby. And Tana knew that once she walked out the door, no force on earth could make her return.

She was torn between the impulse to run and the urge to curl up like a pill bug, close her eyes, tuck her head beneath her arms, and play the game of since-I-can't-see-monsters-monsters-can't-see-me. Neither of those impulses were going to save her. She had to *think*.

Sunlight dappled the living room, filtered through the leaves of trees outside—late afternoon sun, sure, but still sun. She clung to that. Even if a whole nest of vampires were in the basement, they wouldn't—*couldn't*—come up before nightfall. She should just stick to her plan: Go to the guest room and get her boots and cell phone and car keys. Then go outside and have the biggest, most awful freak-out of her life. She would allow herself to scream or even faint, so long as she did it in her car, far from here, with the windows up and the doors locked.

Carefully, carefully, she pushed off each of her shining metal bracelets, setting them on the rug so they wouldn't jangle when she moved.

This time as she crossed the room, she was aware of every creak of the floorboards, every ragged breath she took. She imagined fanged mouths in the shadows; she imagined cold hands cracking through the kitchen linoleum, fingernails scratching her ankles as she was dragged down into the dark. It seemed like forever before she made it to the door of the spare room and twisted the knob.

Then, despite all her best intentions, she gasped.

Aidan was tied to the bed. His wrists and ankles were bound to the posts with bungee cords, and there was silver duct tape over his mouth, but he was *alive*. For a long moment, all she could do was stare at him, the shock of everything coming over her all at once. Someone had taped garbage bags over the windows, blocking out sunlight. And beside the bed, gagged and in chains, amid the jackets someone had swept to the floor, was another boy, one with hair as black as spilled ink. He looked up at her. His eyes were bright as rubies and just as red.

✦ CHAPTER 2 ✦

*We all labor against our own cure, for
death is the cure of all diseases.*
—Sir Thomas Browne

When Tana was six, vampires were Muppets, endlessly counting, or cartoon villains in black cloaks with red polyester
linings. Kids would dress up like vampires on Halloween, wearing
plastic teeth that fitted badly over their own and smearing their faces
with sweet syrup to make mock rivulets of cherry-bright blood.

That all changed with Caspar Morales. There had been plenty of
books and films romanticizing vampires over the last century. It was
only a matter of time before a vampire started romanticizing himself.

Crazy, romantic Caspar decided that unlike decades of ancient,
hidebound vampires, he wouldn't *kill* his victims. He would seduce
them, drink a little blood, and then move on, from city to city. By the
time the old vampires caught up with him and ripped him to pieces,
he'd already infected hundreds of people. And those new vampires,
with no idea how to prevent the spread, infected thousands.

The first outbreak happened in Caspar's birthplace, the smallish city of Springfield, Massachusetts, around the time Tana turned seven. Springfield was only fifty miles from her house, so it was in the local news before it went national. Initially, it seemed like a journalist's prank. Then there was another outbreak in Chicago and another in San Francisco and another in Las Vegas. A girl, caught trying to bite a blackjack dealer, burst into flame as cops dragged her out of a casino to their squad car. A businessman was found holed up in his penthouse apartment, surrounded by gnawed corpses. A child stood at Fisherman's Wharf on a foggy night, reaching up her arms to any adult who offered to help find her father, just before she sank her teeth into their throats. A burlesque dancer introduced bloodplay into her act and required audience members to sign waivers before attending her performances. When they left, they left hungry.

The military put up barricades around the areas of the cities where the infections broke out. That was the way the first Coldtowns were founded.

Vampirism is an American problem, the BBC declared. But the next outbreak was in Hong Kong, then Yokohama, then Marseille, then Brecht, then Liverpool. After that, it spread across Europe like wildfire.

At ten, Tana watched her mother sit at her mirrored vanity and get ready to go to the party of an art buyer intent on lending her gallery a few pieces. She had on a pencil skirt with an emerald-colored silk shell top, her short black hair gelled tightly back. She was fastening on a pair of pearl drop earrings.

"Aren't you afraid of the vampires?" Tana had asked, leaning bonelessly against her mother's leg, feeling the scratch of tights against her cheek and inhaling the smell of her mother's perfume. Usually, both of her parents were home before dark.

Tana's mother had just laughed, but she came back from the party sick. *Cold*, they called it, which at first sounded harmless, like the kind of cold that gave you the sniffles and a sore throat. But this was another kind of Cold, one where body temperatures dropped, senses spiked, and the craving for blood became almost overwhelming.

If one of the people who'd gone Cold drank human blood, the infection mutated. It killed the host and then raised them back up again, Colder than before. Cold through and through, forever and ever.

According to the Centers for Disease Control and Prevention, there was only one cure. The victim had to be kept from drinking human blood until the infection was flushed out of the system, which could take up to eighty-eight days. No clinic provided such a service. In the beginning, hospitals had heavily sedated Cold patients, until a middle-aged and very wealthy woman came out of her medically induced coma to attack a doctor. Some people managed to take the edge off the craving for blood with booze or drugs; nothing worked for others. But if the police found out about a potential case of infection, that person would be quarantined and relocated to a Coldtown. Tana's mother was terrified. And so, two days in, once the shakes had gotten bad enough and the hunger came on, she agreed to be locked up in the only part of the house that would hold her.

Tana remembered the screams rising from the basement a week later, screams that went on all day long, while her father was at work, and then all through the night, when her father turned up the television until it drowned out every other sound and drank himself to sleep. In the afternoons after school, between bouts of screaming, Tana's mother would call for her, pleading, begging to be let out. Promising to be good. Explaining that she was better now, that she wasn't sick anymore.

Tana, please. You know I would never hurt you, my beautiful little girl. You know I love you more than anything, more than my own life. Your father, he doesn't understand that I'm better. He doesn't believe me, and I'm frightened of him, Tana. He's going to keep me imprisoned here forever. He'll never let me out. He's always wanted to control me, always been afraid of how independent I was. Please, Tana, please. It's cold down here and there are things crawling on me in the dark and you know how much I hate spiders. You're my baby, my sweet baby, my darling, and I need your help. You're scared, but if you let me out, we'll be together forever, Tana, you and me and Pearl. We'll go to the park and eat ice cream and feed the squirrels. We'll dig for worms in the garden. We'll be happy again. You'll get the key, won't you? Get the key. Please get the key. Please, Tana, please. Get the key. Get the key.

Tana would sit near the door to the basement with her fingers in her ears, tears and snot running down her face as she cried and cried and cried. And little Pearl would toddle up, crying, too. They cried while they ate their cereal, cried while they watched cartoons, and cried themselves to sleep at night, huddled together in Tana's little bed. *Make her stop*, Pearl said, but Tana couldn't.

And when their father put on chain mesh gloves, the kind chefs use to open oysters, and big work boots to bring their mother food at night, Pearl and Tana cried hardest of all. They were terrified he would get sick, too. He explained that only a vampire could infect someone and that their mother was still human, so she couldn't pass on her sickness. He explained that her craving for blood was not so different from how someone with pica might crave chalk or potting soil or metal filings. He explained that everything would be fine, so long as Mom didn't get what she wanted, so long as Tana and Pearl acted normal and didn't tell anyone what was wrong with Mom, not their teachers, not their friends, not even their grandparents, who wouldn't understand.

He sounded calm, reasonable. Then he walked into the other room and downed half a bottle of Jack Daniel's. And the screams went on and on.

It took thirty-four days before Tana broke and promised her mother that she'd help her get free. It took thirty-seven days before she managed to steal the ring of keys out of the back pocket of her father's tan Dockers. Once Dad left for work, she unlocked the latches, one by one.

The basement smelled damp, like mold and minerals, as she started down the creaking, wooden stairs. Her mother had stopped screaming the moment the door opened. Everything was very quiet as Tana descended, the scratch of her shoes on the wood loud in her ears. Her foot hesitated on the last step.

Then something knocked her down.

Tana remembered the way it felt, the endless burn of teeth on her skin. Even though they weren't fully changed, the canines had still bit down like twin thorns or like the pincers of some enormous spider. There had been the soft pressure of a mouth, and pain, and there had been another feeling, too, as though everything was going out of her in a rush.

She'd fought back, screaming and crying, kicking her chubby little-kid legs and scrabbling with the nails of her pink child fingers. All that had done was make her mother squeeze her more tightly, make the flesh of her inner arm tear, make her blood jet like pumps from a water gun.

That was seven years ago. The doctors told her father that the memory would fade, like the big messy scar on her arm, but neither ever did.

❖ CHAPTER 3 ❖

Death is the dropping of the flower,
that the fruit may swell.
—Henry Ward Beecher

Aidan's eyes were wide and terrified. He strained against the bungee cords, trying to talk through the tape. Tana couldn't make out the words, but she was pretty sure from the tone that he was begging her to untie him, pleading with her not to leave him. She bet he was regretting that time he'd forgotten her birthday and also the way he'd dumped her via a direct message on Twitter and, almost certainly, everything he'd said to her last night. She almost started giggling again, hysteria rising in her throat, but she managed to swallow it down.

Sliding her fingernail under the edge of the duct tape, she began to peel it back as gently as she could. Aidan winced, his caramel eyes blinking rapidly. Across the room, the rattle of chains made her stop what she was doing and look up.

It was the vampire boy. He was pulling against his collar, shaking his head, and staring at her with great intensity, as though he was trying to communicate something important. He must have been handsome when he was alive and was handsome still, although made monstrous by his pallor and her awareness of what he was. His mouth looked soft, his cheekbones sharp as blades, and his jaw curved, giving him an off-kilter beauty. His black hair was a mad forest of dirty curls. As she stared, he kicked a leg of the bed with his foot, making the frame groan, and shook his head again.

Oh yeah, as if she was going to leave Aidan to die because the pretty vampire didn't want his snack taken away.

"Stop it," she said, louder than she'd intended because she was scared. She should climb over the bed, to the windows, and pull down the garbage bags. He'd burn up in the sun, blackening and splintering into embers like a dying star. She'd never seen it happen in real life, though, only watched it on the same YouTube videos as everyone else, and the idea of killing something while it was bound and gagged and *watching* made her feel sick. She wasn't sure she could do it.

Stupid. Stupid. Stupid, said her heart.

Tana turned back to Aidan, her hands shaking now. "Stay quiet, okay?"

At his nod, she pulled the tape free from his mouth in one swift rip.

"Ow," Aidan said. Then he lunged at her teeth-first.

Tana was reaching for the bungee cord restraining his wrist when it happened. His sudden movement startled her so much that she stumbled back, losing her balance and yelping as she fell onto the pile of jackets. His blunt canines had grazed her arm, not far from where her scar was.

Aidan had tried to bite her.

Aidan was infected.

She'd made a noise loud enough to maybe wake a nest of sleeping vampires.

"You asshole," she said, anger the only thing standing between her and staggering panic. Forcing herself up, she punched Aidan in the shoulder as hard as she could.

He let out a hiss of pain, then smiled that crooked, sheepish smile that he always fell back on when he was caught doing something bad. "Sorry. I—I didn't mean to. I just—I've been lying here for hours, thinking about blood."

She shuddered. The smooth expanse of his neck looked unmarked, but there were lots of other places he could have been bitten.

Please, Tana, please.

She'd never told Aidan about her mother, but he knew. Everyone at school knew. And he'd seen the scar, a jagged mess of raised shiny skin, pale, with a purple cast to the edges. She'd told him how it felt sometimes, as if there were a sliver of ice wedged in the bone underneath.

"If you just gave me a little, then—" Aidan started.

"Then you'd die, idiot. You'd become a vampire." She wanted to hit him again, but instead she made herself squat down and root among the jackets until she found her own purse with her keys. "When we get out of this, you are going to grovel like you've never groveled in your life."

The vampire boy kicked the bed again, chains rattling. She glanced over at him. He looked at her, then at the door, then back at her. He widened his eyes, grim and impatient.

This time, she understood. Something was coming. Something that had probably heard her fall. She waded through scattered jackets to a dresser and pushed it against the door, hopefully blocking the way in. Cold sweat started between her shoulder blades. Her limbs felt leaden, and she wasn't sure how much longer it was going to be before she couldn't go on, before the desire to curl up and hide overtook her.

She looked over at the red-eyed boy and wondered if a few hours before he'd been one of the kids drinking beer and dancing and laughing. She didn't remember seeing him, but that didn't mean anything. There'd been some kids she didn't know and probably wouldn't have remembered, kids from Conway or Meredith. Yesterday, he might have been human. Or maybe he hadn't been human for a hundred years. Either way, he was a monster now.

Tana picked up a hockey trophy from the dresser. It was heavy in her hand as she crossed the floor to where he was chained, her heart beating like a shutter in a thunderstorm. "I'm going to take off your gag. And if you try to bite me or grab me or anything, I'll hit you with this thing as hard as I can and as many times as I can. Understood?"

He nodded, red eyes steady.

His wax-white skin was cool to the touch when she brushed his neck to find the knot of the cloth. She'd never been this close to a vampire, never realized what it would be like to be so near to someone who didn't breathe, who could be still as any statue. His chest neither rose nor fell. Her hands shook.

She thought she heard something somewhere in the bowels of the house, a creaking sound, like a door opening. She forced herself to concentrate on unknotting the cloth faster, even though she had to do it one-handed. She wished desperately for a knife, wished she'd been clever enough to pick one up when she'd been in the kitchen, wished she had something better than a pot-metal trophy covered in gold paint.

"Look, I'm sorry about before," Aidan called from the bed. "I'm half out of my head, okay? But I won't do it again—I would never hurt you."

"You're not exactly someone who's big on resisting temptation," Tana said.

He laughed a little, before the laugh turned into a cough. "I'm more the run-toward-it-with-open-arms type, right? But really, please believe me, I scared myself, too. I won't do anything like that again."

Infected people got loose from restraints and attacked their families all the time. Those kinds of stories weren't even headline news anymore.

But vampires weren't all monsters, scientists kept insisting. *Theoretically, with their hunger sated, they are the same people they were before, with the same memories and the same capacity for moral choice.*

Theoretically.

Finally, the knot came apart in Tana's hand. She scuttled back from the red-eyed boy, but he didn't do anything more than spit out the cloth gag.

"Through the window," he said. His voice had a faint trace of an accent she couldn't place—one that made her pretty sure he was no local kid infected the night before. "Go. They're swift as shadows. If they come through the door, you won't have time."

"But you—"

"Cover me with a heavy blanket—two blankets—and I'll be tucked in tight enough against the sun." Despite looking only a little older than Aidan, the calm command in his voice spoke of long experience. Tana felt momentarily relieved. At least someone seemed to know what to do, even if that someone wasn't her. Even if that someone wasn't human.

Now that she was out of his range, she set down the trophy carefully, back on the dresser, back where it belonged, back where it would be found by Lance's parents and—Tana stopped herself, forced herself to focus on the impossible here and now. "What got you chained up?" she asked the vampire.

"I fell in with bad company," he said, straight-faced, and for a moment she wasn't sure if he was joking. It rattled her, the idea that he might have a sense of humor.

"Be careful," Aidan called from the bed. "You don't know what he might do."

"We all know what you'd do, though, don't we?" the vampire accused Aidan in his silky voice.

Outside, the sun would be dipping down toward the tree line. She didn't have time to make good decisions.

She had to take her chances.

There was a comforter on the bed, underneath Aidan, and she started yanking on it. "I'm going for my car," she told both of them.

"I'm going to pull up to the window, and then you'll both get in the trunk. I have a tire iron. Hopefully, I can snap the links with that."

The vampire looked at her in bewilderment. Then he glanced toward the door and his expression grew sly. "If you free me, I could hold them off."

Tana shook her head. Vampires were stronger than people, but not by so much that iron didn't bind them. "I think we're all better off with you chained up—just not here."

"Are you sure?" Aidan asked. "Gavriel's still a vampire."

"He warned me about you and about them. He didn't have to. I'm not going to repay that by—" She hesitated, then frowned. "What did you call him?"

"That's his name." Aidan sighed. "Gavriel. The other vampires, while they were tying me to the bed, they said his name."

"Oh." With a final tug she pulled the blanket free and tossed it over to *Gavriel*.

Her heart thundered in her chest, but along with the fear was the reckless thrill of adrenaline. She was going to save them.

There was a sudden scrabbling at the door, and the handle began to turn. She shrieked, climbing onto the bed and hopping over Aidan to get to the window. The garbage bag ripped free with one tug, letting in golden, late afternoon light.

Gavriel gasped in pain, pulling the blanket more tightly around him, turning his body as much behind another dresser as he could.

"Lots of sun still!" she shouted between breaths. "Better not come in."

The movement outside the door stopped.

"You can't leave me here," Aidan said as Tana shoved at the old farmhouse window, swollen by years of rain. It was stuck.

Her muscles burned, but she pushed again. With a loud creak, the window slid up a little ways. Enough to get under, she hoped. The cool, sweet-smelling breeze brought the scent of honeysuckle and fresh-mowed grass.

Looking over at the lump of comforter and jackets and shadow where Gavriel was hiding, she took a deep breath. "I won't leave you," she told Aidan. "I promise."

No one else was going to get killed today, not if she could save them. Certainly not someone she'd once thought she loved, even if he was a jerk. Not some dead boy full of good advice. And she hoped not herself, either.

Leaning forward, she ducked her head under the window frame, ignoring the splinters of worn gray wood and old paint. She tossed out her purse. Then she tried to shimmy a little, to get the swell of her breasts over the sill and cant her hips so that she could grab hold of the siding and pull herself forward enough to drop down headfirst into the bushes. It was a short, bruising fall. For a long moment, the sunlight was too bright and the grass too green. She rolled onto her back and drank in the day.

She was safe. Clouds blew across the sky, soft and pulled as cotton candy. They shifted into the shapes of mountains, into walled cities, into open mouths with rows and rows of sharp teeth, into arms reaching down from the sky, into flames and—

A sudden gust made the branches of the trees shiver, raining down a few bright green leaves. A fly buzzed in the grass near her shoulder, making her think suddenly of the bodies inside, of the way flies would be landing on them, of the opalescent maggots that would hatch and tunnel, multiplying endlessly, spreading like an infection, until black flies covered the room in a shifting carpet. Until all anyone could hear was the whirring of their glassy wings.

Tana started to shake like the trees, her limbs trembling, and was overcome by such a wave of nausea that she was barely able to twist onto her knees before she was sick in the grass.

You said that you were allowed to lose it, some part of her reminded herself.

Not yet, not yet, she told herself, although the very fact that she was renegotiating bargains with her own brain suggested things had already gotten pretty bad. Forcing herself up, Tana tried to remember where her car was parked. She walked across the sloping lawn, toward a line of cars and then past each, touching the hoods, feeling as if she was going to vomit again every time she noticed stuff inside—books, sweaters, beads hanging off rearview mirrors—the small tokens of people's lives, the things they would never see again.

Finally, she got to her own Crown Vic, opened the door with a creak, and slid inside, drinking in the faint, familiar smell of gasoline and oil.

She'd bought it for a grand the day she turned seventeen and sprayed its scrapes with a can of lime-green Rust-Oleum, making it look more like a vandalized cop car than anything else. She and her dad had rebuilt the engine together, during one of the few periods when he came out of his fog of misery long enough to remember he had two daughters.

It was big and solid, and it drank gas with an unquenchable thirst. When she slammed the door shut, for the first time since she walked out of the bathroom, maybe for the first time since she arrived at the party, she felt in control.

She wondered how long it would be before even that slipped through her fingers.

CHAPTER 4

Why fear death? It is the most beautiful adventure in life.

—Charles Frohman

Tana's secret, the secret she never told anyone, was that she had a recurring dream. Sometimes months passed without her having it; sometimes she had it night after night for a week. In the dream, she and her mother were together, undead, dressed in billowy white gowns with ruffles at their collars and at the hems of their skirts. They ran through the night together in a darkling fairy tale of blood and forests and snow, of girls with raven's wing hair and rose-red lips and sharp teeth as white as milk.

The way they became infected was slightly different each time, but usually it went like this: Tana was the one who went Cold first. The details of that part were always elided, the hows and whos of the attack never asked or answered. The dream usually began with her father dragging her to the basement door and telling her he would never let her out again, never, ever, ever. Tana might howl and weep and plead in an orgy of grief, she might shower him with tears, but his heart was hard as stone. Eventually, he got tired of her weeping and pushed her down the stairs.

She hit her head against the wood slats and grabbed for the railing to break her fall. But although her nails scrabbled at it, she couldn't catch hold. She wound up at the bottom with her breath knocked out of her.

There she sat, on the cold floor of the basement, as spiders crept over her hands and beetles clacked, as mice padded from shadows to squeak and steal strands of her hair for their nests, as she listened to her mother argue for her release and her sister cry. But every time her mother called her father cruel, he put another lock on the door, until there were thirty brass locks with thirty brass keys. Day after day, he had to open each lock to leave Tana a bowl of water and a bowl of porridge on the very top step. Then he had to lock her up all over again.

Finally, Tana learned the music of the locks and crept up the stairs just as the keys began to turn. There, she waited for him. He had been careful, but not careful enough. When the door opened, she sprang up and bit him. They would tumble down the stairs together in a blur. And when she woke, she was a vampire and her father was unconscious beside her.

Then her mother came down and hugged Tana in her soft arms and told her that everything would be okay. They were going to leave very soon, but first Tana had to bite her mother. Her mother would be very insistent, saying that she couldn't bear to worry about Tana out in the world alone and that she wanted to be with her always. Sometimes Tana's mother would even beg.

Please, Tana, please.

Tana always bit her. When Tana was younger, in her dreams, blood tasted like fizzy strawberry soda or sherbet. If you drank it too fast, you got brain freeze. When she was older, after she'd licked a cut on her finger, the taste of that became the taste in her dreams: copper and tears.

After Tana's mother was infected, she bit Tana's father while he was unconscious, because she needed human blood to complete her own transformation, and biting him was fine because you couldn't go Cold from being bitten by infected people. After that, they would put him to bed; he was probably tired.

He slept peacefully while Tana and her mother told Pearl that they would be back for her when she was older. Then they put on long gowns and went out into the night, mother vampire and child vampire, to hunt and haunt the streets together.

They'd be the good kind, like the devoted scientists who'd infected themselves to study the disease better; like the vampire bounty hunters who hunted other vampires; like the vampire woman in Greece who still lived with her husband, making all his meals at night and leaving them for him to reheat while she slept the day away in a grave of freshly turned earth under the root cellar. Tana and her mother would be like that, and they would never kill anybody, not even by accident.

In the dream, everything was convenient, everything was perfect, everything would be fine forever.

In the dream, Tana's mother loved her more than anyone or anything. More than death.

I don't want to be a vampire, she told herself over and over again. But in her dreams, she kind of did.

✦ CHAPTER 5 ✦

He whom the gods love dies young.

—Menander

Driving across Lance's lawn, Tana ran over a coiled length of hose and crushed the daffodil patch that his mother had planted. Then she threw the Crown Vic into reverse and pulled up to the window as tightly as she could. As soon as her bumper hit the wall, she got out, climbed on top of the car, and tried to wriggle back through the window, this time holding a tire iron.

It took several tries and a lot of jumping and scrambling and kicking. When she did make it in, her calves and hands scraped, she realized that the room was darker than it had been. The shadows were lengthening as afternoon turned inexorably toward evening. It was probably after six already, maybe after seven. The smell of death hung heavy in the air.

"Tana," Aidan said as soon as he saw her. "Tana, they're going to come in as soon as it's dark. They told us." He looked pale and frantic, worse than she remembered him looking when she'd left. "We're going to die, Tana."

"*Condamné à mort*," a voice rasped from the other side of the door. She could hear the creatures whispering to one another in the hall, shifting hungrily, waiting for the sun to set.

Her hands shook.

She whirled on Gavriel, who was watching her with those eerie garnet eyes, huddled in the corner like a black crow. "What does that mean?"

"There are so many odd dappled patches of sunlight here," he called to them from his pile of blankets and jackets, ignoring her. "Come in. I long to watch your skin blister. I long to—"

"Don't say that!" she cut him off, panicked. If the vampires pushed their way in, she had no idea what she would do.

Run, probably. Abandon them.

Aidan pulled against his bonds. "They keep talking to him in a whole bunch of languages. A lot of French. Something about the Thorn of Istra. I think he's in trouble."

"Are you?" Tana asked.

"Not exactly," said Gavriel.

Tana shuddered and looked back toward the window and her car with longing. The *Thorn of Istra*? She'd once seen a late-night special called *Piercing the Veil: Vampire Secrets from Before the World Went Cold*. On-screen, two guys in tweed jackets talked about their research into how vampires had stayed hidden for so long. Apparently, in the old days, a few ancient vampires held sway over big swaths of territory, like creepy warlords, with more vampires who were basically their servants. Vampires took victims who wouldn't be missed, killing after every feeding. But if a mistake was made and a victim survived long enough to drink blood, it was a Thorn's job to hunt down that newly turned vampire and to kill anyone it bit during its short, savage life. Being a Thorn for one of the old vampires seemed to be half a punishment and half an honor.

On the program, the tweedy men had chuckled over how desperate those Thorns must have been once Caspar Morales started his world tour, all of them scrambling to put down an infection that had already spread out of control.

The Thorn of Istra had, apparently, been driven mad by it. The special showed a grainy video of a meeting beneath the Père-Lachaise Cemetery in Paris. And while elegantly dressed vampires conducted business around him, the Thorn had been in a locked cage, his face and body streaked with blood, laughing. He'd laughed even harder when they found the videographer and dragged him up to the cage, howling wildly just before he bit out the man's throat. She'd seen the expressions on the pale faces of the other vampires. He'd frightened even them.

"The Thorn of Istra's *hunting* you?" Tana asked. The thought of the Thorn out of his cage was chilling. "But that's no problem?"

Gavriel was silent.

Maybe she should leave him. Untie Aidan and get the hell out of there, even if it meant leaving one chained-up vampire to fend off however many were on the other side of the door. Even if it was unfair.

She took a deep breath. "Last chance. Are you in need of rescuing?"

His expression turned very strange, almost as if she'd struck him. "Yes," he said finally.

Maybe it was that nearly everyone else was dead and she felt a little bit dead, too, but she figured that even a vampire deserved to be saved. Maybe she ought to leave him, but she wasn't going to.

She walked over to Gavriel, her gaze tracing the configuration of his heavy chains. One was looped around the foot of the bed frame. His wrists had been manacled together in front of him with thick iron cuffs, those chains linked to the ones attached to another pair of cuffs, these on his ankles.

The easiest way to free him would be to lift the bed, something he could probably have done if his arms weren't restrained, but she wasn't sure she could do it. She was certain she couldn't do it with Aidan still lying on the mattress, weighing the whole thing down.

"Do you think you can keep from biting me?" she asked him.

Aidan was silent for a long moment. "I don't know."

Well, at least he was being honest.

She grabbed Gavriel's gag from a heap of things on the floor and climbed onto the edge of the bed. "You're not so far gone yet. Try," she told him. Bending down, she tied the cloth around Aidan's mouth as quickly as she could, double-knotting it on the back of his head so that it would take a while to work free. At least she hoped it would.

He stayed still and let her. When she was done with the gag, she started unhooking the bungee cords restraining his legs. That went fast, at least; there were no knots. It did involve climbing over him in the bed, and despite the fact that he was Cold, despite the fact that they were in danger, Aidan still managed to cock an eyebrow at her.

She was about to say something quelling when, on his left ankle, she found twin puncture marks with slight bruising around them, the blood itself taking on a bluish tone. She inhaled sharply but didn't say anything, didn't touch them. They seemed horribly private.

Then, because there was no way around it, she untied Aidan's arms. He sat up, pushed himself back against the headboard, and rubbed at his wrists. His chestnut hair hung in his face, tousled, as if he'd just woken up.

Get them in the car, she told herself. *Lock them in the trunk, get away, and figure out everything else from there.*

"If you try to take off the gag, I'll hit you with this tire iron," she warned him, fetching it from the floor and waving it in what she hoped was a menacing way.

Since Aidan couldn't talk, he made a sound that Tana hoped was agreement.

"Okay, now you're going to help me detach Gavriel's chains from the bed," she said.

Aidan shook his head vigorously.

"We don't have time to argue," she told him.

His shoulders lowered and he sighed through his nose. She gave him a long look, and then he moved reluctantly to brace his hands against the footboard. Tana knelt down so that when Aidan lifted the bed, she managed to pull the heavy chain free. She scooted out and Aidan let go. The frame crashed back down, shaking the floorboards.

The vampire shifted, links pulling, the whole rattling thing making an eerie sound that reminded Tana of medieval dungeons on late-night movies.

He lifted his arms, his cuffs still attached.

Aidan tried to say something, but the words were muffled by the gag. Tana guessed that what he had to say was sarcastic.

"There's a roll of the garbage bags that were taped up on the windows," she said, poking around the floor at the collection of things the vampires had abandoned. "Maybe if we wrap some of those around you, then even if the blanket slips, you won't burn. We can duct-tape it together. As long as you don't mind looking ridiculous."

The vampire smiled a closemouthed smile.

Tana passed the black bags and the tape to Aidan. Squatting down in the shadows, Aidan began half assing together some makeshift plastic armor for Gavriel. It looked as silly as Tana had promised, even before the blankets.

"If I'm hurt," Gavriel said as Aidan worked, "you must be very careful."

"We'll be careful," she told him. "Don't worry."

"No, Tana, you must listen," he said. "You must be careful of me."

It was the first time he'd used her name, and the sound of it in his mouth, said with his odd accent, made it unfamiliar.

"We won't let you get burned," she said, turning away to open handbags and stick her fingers into the pockets of jackets, hoping against hope that one of her friends carried a knife. "Even though you're a vampire and you probably deserve it."

I'm sorry, she said to each of the dead as she unzipped and unfastened their things. *I'm sorry, Courtney. I'm sorry, Marcus. I'm sorry, Rachel. I'm sorry, Jon. I'm sorry I'm alive and you're dead. I'm sorry I was asleep. I'm sorry I didn't save you and now I'm taking your things. I'm sorry. I'm sorry. I'm sorry.* There were no knives or stakes. The only things she found were a length of cord with several religious symbols from around the world knotted on it, including a large evil eye that glittered with crystals, and a small stoppered bottle of rose water with a piece of thorn-covered vine floating in it.

Tana could use all the protection she could get. She took the water and the cord, stuffing them into her purse. Then she picked up Rachel Meltzer's cell phone. She dialed 911 and chucked it onto the bed.

Outside the door, a floorboard creaked.

"Little mouse," a voice said through the keyhole. "Don't you know the more you wriggle, the greater the cat's delight?"

Aidan made a soft whining sound behind his gag. Tana felt a wave of terror roll over her. It was all-consuming animal fear, vast and incomprehensible. There were things that could think and talk, and they *still* wanted to kill her and eat her. For a long moment, she couldn't move.

Then, pushing through the weight of her terror, she looked toward the window, where the first orange streaks of sunset were turning the trees to gold. The dark was coming.

"We have to go," she told Aidan. He wasn't as done with covering Gavriel as she would have liked, but they'd run out of time. She lifted the tire iron and swung it at the window, smashing the pane and the wood rails and stiles.

Glass fell around her in a shimmering pile.

"We're going now!" she yelled. "Now! Aidan, come on. Get Gavriel over here."

The operator was calling from the phone on the bed, her tinny voice sounding very far away. *"What is your emergency? Hello, this is 911. What is your emergency?"*

"Vampires!" Tana shouted, throwing down her boots and tossing the tire iron after them.

Aidan helped Gavriel up, wrenching him to his feet. He was wrapped like some modern mummy, shining strips of duct tape holding together garbage bags and blankets, lurching toward the window. Tana had no idea if it was enough to keep him from being burned, but it would have to do. Already, she was trembling with the urge to abandon all plans and just escape, slither out onto the lawn, and run—

"Aidan, you go out the window first," Tana said, cutting off her own train of thought, shoving down her fear. "Someone's got to be down there to take Gavriel's feet."

Aidan nodded and swung his leg over the sill. He looked back at her for a moment, as though trying to decide. Then he jumped, landing badly on the roof of the Crown Vic.

Behind Tana there was the sound of splintering wood, as though something very large had hit the door. "No," she said softly. "Oh no. No."

"Leave me," said Gavriel.

Something struck the door again and the dresser fell over, crashing against the bed. Forcing herself not to turn, she pushed the wrapped body against the window.

"Shut up or I might," she told him. "Now sit, swing your legs over, and drop."

He shifted his body, and Tana braced herself to act as a counterweight and to keep him from falling before he was in position. Aidan stood under the window, catching his feet. Taking a deep breath and hoping the duct tape and blanket shroud would hold, she let him go.

Aidan eased Gavriel onto the top of the trunk.

The door of the room cracked open behind her.

Keep going, she told herself. *Don't look back*. But she looked anyway.

Two creatures stood framed by the doorway—one male and the other female. Their faces were puffy and pink, bloated from all the blood they'd consumed. Their mouths and sharp teeth were ruddy, their eyes sunken, clothes stiff and stained dark. They weren't the slick vampires from television; they were nightmares and they were coming at her, wading through the jackets, flinching from waning pools of light.

Tana scrambled for the windowsill, her body shaking, her hands trembling so ferociously that she almost couldn't get a grip on the wood frame. Going up on her knees, she threw herself forward, missing the car entirely and falling onto the lawn.

Fingers clamped down on her calf, pulling her back. She kicked hard, dragging herself forward with her arms. Teeth scraped against the back of her knee just as she pulled free and toppled away from the window. Behind her, there was a high, keening cry of pain. She hit the dirt, falling onto her back, the air knocked out of her. Dazedly, she turned to one side, looking out at a lawn sparkling with shattered glass, as though someone had tossed handfuls of diamonds in the air after a heist.

"Jesus!" Aidan shouted, hands in his hair. "You should have seen how that thing's arm got scorched. He nearly got you."

She staggered to her feet. The fresh scrape on the back of her leg burned and she started to shake all over again. "I think he did get me."

"What?" Aidan took a step toward her and Tana shook her head.

"Not now," she said. The car was right there. They were almost free. "Help me with the trunk!"

Rolled up in the blanket, Gavriel looked like a body that a pair of murderers were planning to dump somewhere. He was lying on his side, body bent so that his back was turned to the sun. Together, Aidan and Tana heaved him up and off the car. But as they tried to carry Gavriel, Tana stumbled and pulled the wrong way. The bags ripped, the cloth falling open. She slipped, tumbling onto the grass. For a moment, she saw his side and hand blackening in the sun, light seeming to eat away the flesh. Before she could think to do anything, Gavriel rolled over, turning his body so that the exposed part was pressed against the dirt, hidden from the light.

"Gavriel?" Tana said, scrambling up, wrapping the blankets back around him.

He tried to stand.

Stumbling and exhausted and not very careful, they managed to open the trunk and dump Gavriel heavily inside. Aidan slammed it shut, donning his bad-boy-about-to-do-a-bad-thing grin.

"*Aidan*," she said, taking a step back, her voice coming out half as if he'd annoyed her and half as if she was afraid, which she was. "Aidan, we don't have time. You have to get in there with him. I can't drive with you wanting to attack me."

"Have you looked at yourself?" he asked her, his voice odd, almost dreamy. "You're covered in blood."

She glanced down and saw that he was right. Her skin was dappled with shallow cuts, welling and streaking red down her arms and legs. A smear on the back of her hand where she'd wiped her face. It must have been fragments of glass from the window.

"We have to go, Aidan."

"I'm not getting in the trunk with a vampire," he said, looking at her hungrily, his eyes black with desire, the pupils blown. "See, I'm controlling myself. You're bleeding and I'm controlling myself."

"Okay," she said, pretending to believe him. "Get in."

As he walked toward the passenger side, she picked up the tire iron and her boots. She knew what she should do—hit him in the back of the head and hope it knocked him unconscious—but she couldn't. Not with a house full of dead kids behind them. Not when she wasn't sure he would survive the blow. Not when she was shaking so hard she was about to shake apart.

She took a deep breath and made her decision.

"No, on the other side," she told Aidan. "You're going to drive."

He turned back to her, brows knitted in confusion.

"It'll give you something to concentrate on other than biting me. And I can keep an eye on you." She held up the tire iron. "And we head where I say—understand?"

"I've been good," he complained.

"Get in!" she shouted, and somehow that, of all things, seemed to work. With a sigh, he walked around the front of the car. She got in on the other side and passed him the keys, holding the metal bar up with her other hand to show she'd use it if she had to. It was solid and smelled faintly of oil and hung comfortingly heavy in her grip.

Aidan took a quick look at her face and turned the key in the ignition.

"Go," she said under her breath, like a prayer. "Go, go, go, go."

He pulled across the lawn toward the road. In the rearview mirror, the house looked like an ordinary clapboard farmhouse, except for the broken window and the bit of curtain fluttering through it, a lone and lonely ghost.

CHAPTER 6

On the plus side, death is one of the few things that can be done just as easily lying down.
—Woody Allen

A idan had been the worst boyfriend in the world.

They'd met in art class, which Tana had taken only because her friend Pauline had promised her it'd be easy and full of other slackers. Pauline was more or less right. Their teacher spent the time painting trompe l'oeils of arched windows leading into darkness-soaked rooms or somewhat grisly still lifes of rotting fruit, flies, and spilled honey. He sold the paintings in a gallery three towns over and told the class at length about how he needed the money since teachers' salaries sucked, especially in these dark times.

Basically, so long as everyone worked on some kind of project more or less quietly, he didn't bother any of them.

Pauline decided that she was going to cut up yearbooks and glue tiny pieces to stiffened linen so that she could make a bra out of the heads of the boys in class. She planned to frame it in a shadowbox and sneak it into the award cabinet once it was done.

Tana was mostly doing nothing, drawing idly with charcoal, and talking to Aidan.

He was just a cute boy in class back then, one with floppy brown hair that fell in front of his eyes when he talked, who wore clean band shirts with hoodies zipped over them, bright red Chucks, and a black-and-white-checkered belt. He smiled a lot and laughed at his own jokes and told Tana lots of stories about the unfathomable girls he seemed to find himself dating. He seemed hapless and good-natured. He was always in love. He smelled like Ivory soap.

Pauline teased Tana about him, and Tana just laughed. She got why girls fell for him. He was *charming*, but he was so upfront about trying to charm her, so obvious, that she was sure she was immune.

Aidan's project was a life-size papier-mâché version of himself, posed as if he were asleep in class. He badgered Tana into measuring him for it, and she rolled her eyes as she wound the tape around his upper arms and across the width of his chest.

When he grinned down at her, raising his eyebrows as though they were sharing a joke, she realized she wasn't immune after all.

He asked her out soon after, not on a real date or anything, just to hang out with some friends. And she went and had a few beers. When he kissed her, she let him.

"You're not like other girls," Aidan said, pressing her back against the cushions of the couch. "You're cool."

Tana tried to be cool, tried to act as if it didn't bother her when he flirted with anything that moved—and, that one time, when he was really drunk, with a coatrack. She'd heard all his stories about the possessive girl who texted him over and over again when he was just out with his cousin or the dramatic girl who sent him ten-page letters, the writing smudged with her tears. She didn't want to be the star of another "crazy girl" story.

And it didn't bother her, not really, not in the way Aidan seemed to expect. Sometimes it hurt to watch him with someone else, sure, but what she really minded was that he always seemed to be monitoring her for signs that she was going to scold him. She minded going to parties, where she made awkward conversation, drank a lot, and pretended that everyone wasn't waiting for her to pick some kind of giant fight with Aidan. And she minded not knowing the rules, because any time she asked him about them, he just stammered elaborate conversation-ending apologies.

When she suggested he go to parties alone, he would make an exaggeratedly sad face. "No, Tana," he'd say. "You have to be there. I hate going to things by myself."

"You could go with friends," she'd suggest, laughing at him. Because it wasn't as if he was ever alone. He knew everyone. He had lots of friends.

"I want to go with *you*," he'd say, his eyes big and pleading, his mouth quirked in a little half smile, as though he was acknowledging how ridiculous he was being. And it worked. It always worked, that combination of flattery and little-boy silliness and, underneath it all, that fear Tana had that she wasn't as cool as he thought she was.

So she went to parties and pretended nothing bothered her. And the more Tana didn't say anything, the more outrageous his behavior got. He would make out with girls in front of her. He would make out with boys in front of her. He would wink at her from across rooms, daring her to criticize him.

That's when things got kind of fun.

She schooled herself to even greater nonchalance. She'd walk over to Aidan after he seemed to be finished kissing someone, curl her arm around his shoulder, and ask to be introduced. She'd assign points for style and take away points when he'd struck out. No matter what he did, she never let him see it bother her.

"You're playing some kind of game of sex chicken with him," Pauline told her, pushing back a mass of tiny braids. "Who cares which one of you flinches first?"

"Sex chicken," Tana said, snickering. "Too bad we don't know anyone in a band—that would be a good name."

Pauline whacked her with the magazine she was reading. "I'm serious. You know what I mean."

Tana couldn't explain why she kept on with it, couldn't put into words the nihilistic thrill that came from suffering a little or the satisfaction of playing Aidan's screwed-up game by his screwed-up rules and still winning. She was *cool*, and she wouldn't be uncool no matter how much he goaded her. While Aidan sometimes seemed annoyed that she didn't hassle him, there were other times he told her there was no other girl like her. No other girl in the world.

"You can't win when someone else makes all the rules," Pauline warned her. Tana didn't listen.

Then one night, at another party, Aidan motioned her over and introduced her to the boy sprawled on the couch beside him. The boy's mouth was pink, and he looked a little drunk from the bottle of tequila in front of him and from the drowsy kisses he'd been sharing with Aidan.

"This is my girlfriend, Tana," Aidan said. "You want to kiss her?"

"Your *girlfriend*?" The boy looked momentarily hurt, but he hid it well. "Sure," he said. "Why not?"

"How about you?" Aidan asked her, challenging her. "Are you game?"

"Sure," Tana said, her daring so tangled up with her determination that she wasn't sure which one made her agree. Her heart hammered against her chest. It felt scary, as if she were stepping across some invisible boundary, as if she might not know herself afterward. As if she were becoming the self she'd always thought lurked just underneath her skin. Her coolest possible self.

The boy's lips were very soft.

When she looked up at Aidan, the shock on his face went to her head like a shot of strong liquor. She was giddy with power. And when the boy kissed her back hungrily, she was giddy with that, too.

Aidan leaned forward, and his expression had changed—he had a smile on his face, like they were sharing a joke, just her and him, as if he got that all the parties were games of check and checkmate—as though Aidan knew they were both doing this in the hopes that the adrenaline might blot out every shitty thing that had ever happened to them and he was glad she was with him, that they were together.

It made her think of a year before, when she'd stood alone on train tracks and waited until the train was barreling toward her, until she could feel the heat of it, until her blood sang with fear, before she jumped out of the way.

It made her think of another day, when she'd pressed the gas pedal down on her car and gone skidding through the night streets, slicing through icy rain.

He smiled at her as though he really believed she was special. As though only she had ever really understood what it was to take a dare for the sake of being daring.

But none of that turned out to be true, because Aidan dumped her three weeks and a half-dozen parties later, with a message that said only, *I think we're getting too serious & I want to take a break.*

After that, she wasn't sure what the game was or if she'd imagined it. All she knew was that she had lost.

✦ CHAPTER 7 ✦

Death is a shadow that always
follows the body.
—English proverb

Tana directed Aidan to pull the car into a gas station about an
hour after they'd left Lance's house. There were no other cars in
sight, and these days all twenty-four-hour marts had bulletproof-
glass cashiers' booths, so she thought it'd be safe to stop. Full dark
had fallen, her arm was starting to ache from holding the tire iron,
and she was pretty sure she wasn't going to be able to keep it together
much longer. Exhaustion was creeping up on her, her cuts stinging
and her head throbbing. She hadn't eaten anything since she'd
woken—hadn't even thought of eating—and each time her stomach
growled, Aidan looked over at her as though her hunger reminded
him of his own.

It was hard to stay alert, hard not to be distracted by images of
the farmhouse, of bodies, rising up behind her eyelids when she

blinked, everything drenched in red. And along with that, the memory of the vampire's teeth scraping the back of her leg, his hand clamped on her calf.

She'd watched programs in health class talking about the spread of infection. There'd been an illustration of the human mouth and the vampire mouth side by side. She thought of it, illustrated in blue and yellow, pink and red. Vampire canines grew longer than their human counterparts', with thin channels that let the creature draw blood up through its teeth and into the back of its throat. When a vampire bit down, a little of its own fouled blood was pushed into the human bloodstream, causing infection. There'd been cases like hers before, cases where the teeth didn't fully penetrate. Sometimes people were fine, sometimes they weren't. If she didn't go Cold in forty-eight hours, she'd know her luck had held.

Aidan pulled up to one of the pumps. "We can't keep driving without a plan. We've got to go *somewhere*."

"I know," she said, her panic-fogged mind going round and round, every possible move seeming worse than the last. She had no idea what to do next. All she knew was that she felt about ready to jump out of her own skin.

As he opened the car door, a lock of hair fell into his eyes. He pushed it back, the way he'd always done. It seemed like such a normal gesture, when everything else was so not normal, when he wasn't normal, that she had to swallow past the lump in her throat.

He reached for the pump, selecting regular unleaded.

Tana felt as though everything was happening much too slow and too fast, all at once. During the drive, she'd been afraid to talk, because if she started, she wouldn't be able to hold how she felt inside. She wouldn't be able to make him believe she was in control.

"We'll get a map and make a plan," she said, hoping he wouldn't see how tired she was. If she seemed weak, she might seem more like prey. She made her voice as steady as she could. "I'm going to the bathroom to get cleaned up first, though. I'll meet you in the mart after you're done with the gas."

From the trunk she heard a soft thump. Gavriel was back there, waiting to be freed. But what would he do then? Were they supposed to just dump him by the side of the road and hope for the best?

"We'll be right back," Tana called, and though she tried to control it, her voice quavered.

Slinging her handbag over her shoulder and grabbing her boots, she walked steadily away from Aidan and the car until she got to the corner of the mart, then ran the rest of the way to the bathroom, slamming the door behind her and locking it. Before she could help it, she started sobbing. She cried and cried until she choked on her tears. She slid down the wall, crying so hard she could barely catch her breath. She slammed her fists against the loose linoleum tile of the floor, hoping the pain would shock her into calming.

Shock, Tana thought. *I'm in shock.* But she didn't really know what that meant, only that it was bad and that it happened in the movies. In movies, people got over it quickly, too, usually with a slap to the face.

Standing, she slapped her own cheek and watched it become rosy in the mirror above the grimy bathroom sink. She didn't feel any different.

After long moments of standing there, staring at her reflection, she remembered that she'd said she was going to get cleaned up. She washed her arms in the sink, splashed water on her legs to rub off the blood. She couldn't see the scrapes on the back of her knee very well, but from what she could see, they looked not much different from her other scratches and cuts. They didn't seem swollen or discolored. They didn't seem deep. They didn't seem like anything at all, much less something that could turn her into a monster. She cleaned them with the antibacterial soap in the pump and shaking fingers, hoping that could kill any infection before it spread. Then she stood up, leaning against the locked door, and started lacing up her boots, pulling the ties tight.

When she was done, she called Pauline.

Dialing the number was automatic, giving in to the temptation of momentary escapism. She couldn't think as the phone rang; her mind felt empty of everything but the feeling that if Pauline answered, then she was going to be all right for a little while. Tana didn't know what she was going to say, didn't even know how to put together words to explain where she was or what had happened. She'd been operating on instinct and impulsiveness at Lance's farmhouse—get everyone out and worry about the consequences later. But later had come. It was waiting for her outside the door. She could only forestall it.

"Hello?" Pauline's voice was loud and in the background. Tana could hear music playing.

"Hey," she said, like everything was normal. It felt good to pretend. Muscles along her shoulders relaxed minutely. "What are you doing?"

"Hold on, I have to go in the other room. So much is going on."

A door shut on the other end of the line and the music dimmed. Then Pauline started telling Tana the news about David, her kinda sorta boyfriend at drama camp. He had a girlfriend back home—a girl he'd been with since middle school—but he'd been giving Pauline mixed signals all summer. Intense conversations and made-up excuses to touch each other during improvs, followed by agonized hand-wringing. His girlfriend was coming to visit Tuesday, but just that night David had kissed Pauline. She was freaking out.

Tana felt relief wash over her along with the familiar drama. She sagged against the door frame, tipping her head back and closing her eyes. She could have interrupted Pauline, could have told her about the nightmare drive through the dark with the tire iron in her hand, told her about the vampires and the carnage and the scrapes of teeth. But if she did, she would have to think about those things again.

So she listened to Pauline tell her the story, and then they rehashed it a bit, and when Pauline asked her how she was doing, Tana said that she was fine.

She was fine and the party had been fine and everything was fine, fine, fine.

"You sound weird," Pauline said. "Have you been crying?"

Tana thought about asking Pauline to find an abandoned place with a door that could be barred and lock her inside with a few gallons of water and granola bars. Pauline would do it for her; Tana knew she would. And a week later, when Tana begged and howled and screamed to be let out, maybe Pauline would do that as well. It was too big a risk.

So Tana insisted that she was really, really fine. Then Pauline had to go because she had a nine o'clock curfew and was leaving the common room to head back to her dorm.

For long minutes after Tana hung up and put away her phone, she tried to hold on to the feeling of normalcy. But the more she stood there, the more her stomach cramped with fear, the more she was aware of how her skin felt hot and cold at once.

She had to not be infected, that was all. She had to not be infected so she and Pauline could move to California after graduation as they'd planned. They were going to rent a tiny apartment, and Tana was going to get a boring, steady job—like maybe be a waitress or work the front desk at a tattoo parlor or at a copy shop, where they'd get discounts on head shots—while Pauline went to her auditions. They were going to do each other's makeup like pinup girls from the fifties and wear each other's clothes. And they were going to swim in the Pacific Ocean and sit under palm trees while the warm breeze off the water ruffled their salt-crusted hair.

Finally, Tana realized that she couldn't stay in the bathroom any longer. She opened the door, braced for an attack, braced for one of the vampires from the house to have followed her somehow, but there was no one and nothing—just a concrete lot and woods, lit by the flood lamps over the gas pumps. The night was sticky warm, and in the distance she could hear the singing of cicadas. Not caring if it made her a wimp to hate the dark, she ran back toward the brightly lit mart, only slowing when she was at the door. She jerked it open, wishing she hadn't left her tire iron in the car, even though she was sure they didn't let people bring stuff like that into regular businesses.

From behind the bulletproof glass, a clerk grinned at her like a man who wasn't too worried about his security. He had a mass of red hair sticking up from his head in gelled spikes.

There was a small television, mounted high up on one wall, showing a feed from inside the Springfield Coldtown, where Demonia was introducing viewers to the newest guests at the Eternal Ball, a party that had started in 2004 and raged ceaselessly ever since.

In the background, girls and boys in rubber harnesses swung through the air. The camera swept over the dance floor, showing the crowd, a few of which had looping hospital tubes stuck to the insides of their arms. The lens lingered over a boy no older than nine holding out a paper cup to a thin blond girl. She paused and then, leaning down, twisted a knob on her tubing, causing a thin stream of blood to splash into the cup, red as the boy's eyes and the tongue that darted out to lick the rim. Then the camera angle changed again, veering up to show the viewer the full height and majesty of the building. At the very highest point, several windowpanes had been replaced with black glass, glowing, but designed to keep out the kind of light that could scald certain partygoers.

Tana's scar throbbed and she rubbed it without thinking.

"Hey," Aidan said, touching her shoulder and making her jump. He was carrying a bottle of water, but he stared at the screen as if he'd forgotten about everything else. "Look at that."

"It's like the Hotel California," Tana said. "Or a roach motel. Roaches check in but they don't check out."

All infected people and captured vampires were sent to Coldtowns, and sick, sad, or deluded humans went there voluntarily. It was supposed to be a constant party, free for the price of blood. But once people were inside, humans—even human children, even babies born in Coldtown—weren't allowed to leave. The National Guard patrolled the barbed-wire-wrapped and holy-symbol-studded walls to make sure that Coldtowns stayed contained.

Springfield was the best known and the biggest Coldtown, with more live feeds, videos, and blogs coming out of there than from Coldtowns in much larger cities. That was partially because it was the first and partially because the Massachusetts government made sure that people trapped inside had power and communications sooner than those in the others. The outbreak in Chicago had been contained so fast that the quarantined area never had a chance to evolve into a walled city-within-a-city. Las Vegas was Springfield's rival in live-streaming vampire entertainment, but blackouts were common, disrupting feeds and making regular viewing unreliable. New Orleans and Las Cruces were small, and the Coldtown in San Francisco had gone dark a year after its founding, with no one broadcasting anything out. There were people in there; satellites could track their heat signatures at night. That's all anyone knew. But Springfield wasn't just the best known and the biggest, Tana thought, looking at the screen. It was also the closest.

"It'd be a good place to hide out," Aidan said, with a sly look at the car and the trunk with the vampire inside.

"You want to turn Gavriel in for a *marker*?" Tana asked him. There was one exception to the whole not-being-allowed-to-leave thing, one way out of Coldtown if you were still human—your family had to be rich enough to hire a vampire hunter, who would turn in a vampire in exchange for you. Vampire hunters got a bounty from the government for each vampire they put in a Coldtown, but they could give up the cash reward in favor of a marker for a single human's release. One vampire in, one human out.

Even amateur hunters who turned in a vampire could get a marker. If Aidan got one, then he could go into Coldtown and, if he stayed human, if he beat the infection, he could get out again.

"Not for a *marker*," Aidan said, his eyes still on the screen. "For the *cash*. We could get some serious money from the bounty on a vampire. Enough for me to hole up for a couple of months in some crappy hotel and ride this thing out."

"I think I got—not bit, exactly." She blurted the words that she couldn't tell Pauline, that she'd been afraid to say out loud. He needed to know if they were going to make real plans. "Scraped. With teeth."

That made him look at her, really look at her, his eyebrows drawn together with actual concern. "And you don't know if you're going to go Cold."

"I have to assume I am." She tried to not let him see how scared she was, how her heart thundered to say the words. "*We* have to assume."

He nodded. "It'd be enough money for both of us to hole up for a while. Two rooms, two keys. We could pass them under the door to each other when we were done. But we've got to do something. I'm hungry, Tana."

"Gavriel helped us—" She stopped herself, unsure. The farther they got from the farmhouse, the more Gavriel seemed like a monster all on his own. She thought of his eyes, red like spilled garnets, red as poppies, red as the bright embers of a fire. She thought of what they taught in school: *cold hands, dead heart*. Plenty of vampires had forgotten how to feel anything but hunger. He'd helped her, sure, but that didn't mean she could trust him not to turn on her now that they were out of danger. Vampires were unpredictable. "At least that gives us a direction to head in. I'm going to grab some food. You should try to eat, too, and see if it cuts down the craving."

She waited for Aidan to make some comment, but he turned to watch more images from Coldtown on the tiny television, his lips slightly apart, his cheeks flushed.

If she was a good person, she'd take him there. In case he gave in to the hunger. He might. And if he did, he'd be ageless, eternal. He'd be charming girls with his flipped hair until the earth crashed into the sun.

If she was a really good person, she'd take herself there, too.

Tana walked around the store, picking up a map with numb fingers. There were notices tacked to a board near the coolers: photos of teenagers with MISSING underneath and phone numbers, advertisements for guaranteed homeopathic remedies to ward off vampires, kittens free to a good home, and one notice reading only CALL MATILDA FOR A BAD TIME.

Tana grabbed a root beer and then a bottle of water for later. At the deli case, she selected the least scary-looking sandwich—turkey and yellow cheese on white bread—and picked up two of them along with half a dozen packets of brown mustard, an apple, and a bottle of ibuprofen. Then she made herself a jumbo-size coffee, emptying in a packet of hot chocolate for good measure.

Dumping her feast in front of the guy behind the bulletproof glass, she paid for that and the gas. She had about forty dollars left, the remainder of her last paycheck from her part-time job at the movie theater concession stand. Forty dollars and a very sketchy plan.

Tana wasn't sure how much Aidan knew about what going Cold was actually like, but if he was picturing himself in a hotel room, watching television, and sweating through it as if it were some kind of drug withdrawal, then he was picturing it all wrong. Once he was in the grips of the hunger, he'd break down the door if he could. They'd attack each other. And then they'd attack other people, maybe even kill them. Spread the infection even further.

But if they weren't going to go to Coldtown and they weren't going to hole up somewhere, their only choice was to turn around and go home. Drive Aidan back to his house. Talk to his mother, a small, quiet woman in a housedress who had made Tana cups of tea when she came over and never commented on any of the outfits she or Aidan wore. Tana would have to explain that her son had gone Cold. Talk to his father, whom Tana had never even met. Tell them—and then what? Were they really ready to confine Aidan somehow and ignore his screams, knowing that if he got loose, someone would get hurt and they'd get arrested? Or would they ship him off to Coldtown anyway and pretend there were never any other choices?

And what about her? Where could she go to sweat out the infection? Not the basement, where her screams would echo off the walls as her mother's had. Not the basement, where Pearl could hear her.

"Okay," Tana told herself with a sigh, taking a big swig from her mocha. "Time to go."

Outside, the cool breeze blew back her hair and the bag of food swung from her hand. She was looking forward to sitting down and eating. Then, after she felt a little less light-headed, she would decide on a route.

As she headed across the station to her car, she noticed that the trunk of the Crown Vic was open.

"Aidan," she said, her voice hushed.

Slowly, dread in her step, she crossed the asphalt.

The locking mechanism had been torn off and one of the hinges seemed loose, as though bent. Chains were coiled in a pile where Gavriel should have been, along with the remains of the blankets and black garbage bags.

"How did he—" Aidan started, then stopped himself.

"He tore them," Tana said, pointing to a metal link, warped out of shape, stretched and broken on one end. "If he did this, then he could— he could have always gotten free. Back at the house. He played us."

"Maybe they're weaker during the day," Aidan said. "Like, this one time, I found a bat just sitting on the side of the bank in town in the middle of the afternoon. It was tiny and looked really miserable, so I stuck it in my shoe and brought it home. I thought it would be cool to have a pet bat, so I kept it in this old birdcage and it just chilled out. Until night. Then it wasn't docile anymore. It got out somehow and started flying around like crazy. When it spread its wings, it looked like this giant, massive—"

"*Aidan*," Tana said. "He's not a bat." She stared at the mauled metal of the trunk and the way the chains were torn like tinfoil instead of steel.

He shouldn't have been able to do that. Vampires were stronger than humans, but not *that* strong.

"There's a reason people used to say they turned into bats," said Aidan cryptically.

She sighed. Maybe he was right—in a way. Maybe like the bat in the birdcage, Gavriel had been waiting for dark, waiting to get out of the chains, drink Aidan's blood, and escape. But when she showed up, he figured he could use them for a ride through daylight, so long as he seemed harmless enough to need saving. A chill crept up her spine.

"Well, he's gone now. It's just you and me." Aidan grinned lazily at her. It was the exact expression he always wore when he was about to talk her into something.

"Yeah," said Tana. He kept staring and his expression shifted. She didn't think he was seeing her anymore. He was seeing skin and bone and blood. She took a step back. The tire iron was on the passenger-side seat where she'd left it. She'd never reach it in time. "So let's get back in the car and keep going. Maybe find a hotel like you said." She was just talking, trying to say something that would distract him. "Hole up, like you said."

"Or we could give in to temptation." He shook his head slowly, coming closer. "Think about it."

"You don't mean that," she told him.

"Why not?" he asked, advancing. "It could be fun. There's people out there who'd kill for what we have."

"I don't want to be a monster," she said, stumbling away from him. Out of the corner of her eye, she noticed the gleam of a security camera mounted on the aluminum siding of the mart above the door. "Let's get in the car. You can try to convince me. I promise I'll give it serious consideration."

"Oh good," Aidan said, and lunged at her.

She'd been half expecting it, given the way he was talking, but the attack still caught her off guard. He was her friend, and no matter how much she knew he wasn't safe, all her instincts pushed her to trust him. She threw the mocha she'd been holding, hoping the hot coffee would scald, and ran. His legs were longer, though, and he was faster. He tackled her, his weight bearing her to the asphalt. She felt his cool breath on her neck, and her knees and palms stung where she'd scraped them falling. The bag of food fell next to her, cracked root beer bottle frothing as the tide of liquid spread to soak the skirt of her baby-doll dress and mingle with spilled gasoline, washing away the spent stubs of cigarettes.

This is it, she thought, *this is where I'm going to die*. And it's going to be on film, watched by the clerk from behind his wall of glass, taped on camera and maybe broadcast later for her father and sister.

Aidan made a sound like a gurgling scream, and Tana winced, waiting for the inevitable pain. But instead of the blunt burn of teeth, she felt him releasing his grip on her and heard him shout. She rolled onto her back, one hand reaching for the broken bottle, the only weapon available. Her fingers closed on it and she swept it out in a wide arc, hoping to hit skin.

Then she gasped.

Gavriel was standing in front of her, his arms around Aidan's chest, his mouth on Aidan's neck, his eyes shut. There was a terrible peace in his face as he lifted Aidan off the ground, a terrible pleasure as his throat moved, drinking down swallow after swallow of blood. Aidan's eyes were half open, heavy-lidded, and focused on nothing. He wasn't struggling anymore, his mouth hung open in sensual bliss, his body shuddering with sensation.

For one long moment, Tana couldn't move. It was more than the fear of drawing attention to herself, more than the fear of being hurt. She ought to be horrified, but she found herself mesmerized instead.

Aidan moaned, low in his throat. Gavriel's fingers tightened, pulling Aidan's body against his.

Slowly, painfully, Tana pushed herself to her feet. Blood and gravel stuck to her knees and palms. Her once-white dress was filthy.

"Gavriel," she said as firmly as she could manage, and prayed her voice wouldn't shake. She thought of the way you were supposed to talk to wild animals, the way you couldn't let them know you were afraid. "Gavriel! Let him go."

He didn't move, didn't even seem to notice.

She grabbed his arm, half expecting him to whirl on her. "Please let Aidan go. He's going to die!"

The vampire pulled back his head, eyes shut, fangs red, and mouth split in a wide grin. Then his eyes did open, bright as torches, and she stumbled back, terrified. Aidan's body sagged from his arms to the pavement.

From the way Gavriel was looking at her, she wondered if he was thinking about the blood rising to her cheeks, of the way it pounded along with her speeding heart, the flush of it on her skin and the way it colored her lips.

It came to her, all of a sudden, the words he'd said to her in Lance's house.

If I'm hurt, you must be very careful. No, Tana, you must listen. You must be careful of me.

He hadn't been worried he was going to get hurt. He'd been worried that he was going to hurt someone else.

"Don't," she said, shrinking back, the jagged bottle stem she still had clenched in her hand seeming hopelessly inadequate, a bright piece of glass and nothing more. "Please."

Gavriel wiped the blood from his mouth with the back of one hand. "Come, Tana. The night is young and your friend is very tired. We should make him a bed—*a cap of flowers and a kirtle, embroidered all with leaves of myrtle.*" His voice sounded odd, abstracted.

She bent down to where Aidan was lying and touched his chest. It rose and fell as if he was, indeed, only sleeping. "Is he going to—will he live?"

"No," said Gavriel. "No chance of that. He wants to die, so he will. But not tonight and not because of me."

"Oh," Tana said. "So he's okay?"

Under the floodlights, Gavriel's skin looked nearly white, his mouth stained red despite his rubbing it. It was the first time she'd seen him standing and again she was struck by the incongruity of him—tall, bare feet, jeans, and a black T-shirt turned inside out, messy black hair, chains gone, looking like the shadow of a regular boy, a boy her age, who wasn't a boy at all.

And there was a body slumped at his feet.

"Yes," he said, reaching out a hand. "But you're hurt."

She looked down at herself, at the mess of her dress and the mess of her knees and the mess of everything. "I haven't had a very good day. I think I might still be hung over and everyone's dead and my root beer's gone." Horrifyingly, she felt her eyes prick with sudden tears.

He bent down and picked up Aidan, slinging him over one shoulder. "We'll get you another day," Gavriel said, with such odd sincerity that she had to smile.

✦ CHAPTER 8 ✦

*Our dead are never dead to us, until we
have forgotten them.
—George Eliot*

Sometimes there are stories in the news about little kids who do
bad things because they don't know any better. Like playing with
loaded guns that go off and kill brothers, or lighting matches that
accidentally set fire to a whole house.

It's not the kid's fault.

Except that it is, really, only no one wants to say it. Who else is
there to blame? The kid is the one who disobeyed, the one who stole
the keys and unlocked all the locks and almost let the bad thing out.

What really happened in the basement of Tana's house wasn't
like any of her happy dreams where she and her mother frolicked
together. After she'd gone down the stairs, a monster had attacked
her, mad with hunger, teeth gnawing with such ferocity that the vein
in her arm was severed, gobbets of flesh sliding down its throat.

She had shrieked and shrieked for her mother, but her mother was already there. Her mother was the monster.

When Tana woke up, she found out that it was her father who'd saved her. He'd used a shovel to hack off his wife's head. Then he'd made a tourniquet from a strip of his shirt and taken his disobedient daughter to the hospital, where doctors sewed up her arm.

No one said it was her fault. No one said they hated her. No one said it was because of her that her mother was dead.

No one had to.

❖ CHAPTER 9 ❖

And what the dead had no speech for, when living, they can tell you, being dead: The communication of the dead is tongued with fire beyond the language of the living.
—T. S. Eliot

Tana could barely keep her eyes open. Gavriel was at the wheel, having taken the keys from Aidan's pockets after depositing him in the backseat. Tana should have protested, but she'd let him get in on the driver's side, let him turn the key in the ignition. She'd gathered up the bottle of water and the two sandwiches, still wrapped in plastic, brushed off the grit, and eaten them while they sped along the road, headlights picking out the dark shapes of trees and houses. The windows were down, and Gavriel's hair blew around his face like frayed black ribbons.

She didn't know where they were going, only that they were driving away from her former life and into a distorted fun-house-mirror version of it.

After the food, she felt as sleepy as if she'd been drugged. It was the adrenaline draining away, she was pretty sure, the terror receding. She tried to convince herself that she wasn't safe, that she was in a car with a vampire who, in addition to being a *vampire*, was talking like a crazy person, but her body didn't seem to have any more fight in it.

She blinked a few times, trying to stay awake. "What was going on back at the house? Those chains—why didn't you get out of them before, if you always could?"

"I killed someone—a vampire—and I was exhausted and—" He stopped and looked at the road for a long moment. She studied his features, the androgynous, exaggerated beauty of his wide mouth and lashes so heavy they made him seem like he was wearing eyeliner. "My mind is—not as it was. There is a madness that comes over us when we're starved and carved, a madness that can be cured only by feeding—but such things they have done to me that it would take a river of blood to wash away all my wounds. I struggle for my most rational moments. I could have gotten out of the chains, yes, but it would have cost me."

Which meant it had cost him, later, in the trunk of the car, when he was already burned.

"You don't seem crazy," she said. "Well, you don't seem *that* crazy."

The side of his mouth lifted in a half smile. "Some of the time,

I'm not. But the rest of the time is most of the time. And when I am, unfortunately, I am all appetite.

"They left me there with the tied-up boy, saved for the following night, like a sweet on the pillow. I was still waiting for it to get closer to dark when you came in."

Tana watched the shadows shift across his face along with the lights from the road. She wondered if he could smell her blood, drifting from her pores along with her sweat.

She guessed that he'd planned on draining Aidan before he escaped, even if he didn't say so out of some sense that it was bad manners.

She wondered if Gavriel thought about biting her—his face, turned to the road still, was as calm as a statue of a saint in a cathedral, but she had seen him with Aidan. She had seen the way his fingers dug into Aidan's skin and how the muscles in his neck strained, and when he'd looked at her, mouth painted with blood, his gaze hadn't tracked. She wondered what it would be like to be infected and to give in, to let herself be turned, to be ageless and frozen and magic and monstrous.

There were so many girls and boys running away to Coldtown, who would do anything to have the infection burning through their veins the way it burned through Aidan's. The vampires inside were incredibly circumspect about biting people—that's why all the pictures of them feeding inside Coldtown showed them feeding from tubing and shunts. More vampires were a drain on the food supply. What Aidan had—what she (maybe) had, too—was rare and desirable. There was a girl Tana had met, a friend of Pauline's, who cut thin lines on her thighs with razor blades before she went out to clubs, so that a vampire might be drawn to her.

When she looked at Gavriel's mouth then, it was still stained carmine along the swell of his lower lip. Maybe because he'd saved her at the gas station and she was feeling grateful or because she was so tired, she found herself fascinated with his mouth, with the way it curved into a sinner's smile. She knew she was looking at him like a boy, like a gorgeous boy whose smile could be admired, and that was dangerous and stupid. She didn't even know if he thought of her as a girl at all.

She needed to stop thinking about him like that. Ideally, she should stop thinking about him entirely, except as something dangerous. "Why were they after you—those men and the Thorn? Was it bad, what you did?"

"Very bad," he agreed. "An act of mercy that I regret—endlessly, I regret it. I had a tutor once who wanted me to believe that mercy is a kind of sorrow and that since evil is the motive of sorrow, evil is also the motive of mercy. I thought that my tutor was old and cruel, and maybe he was—but now I think he was also right."

"But that doesn't make sense," Tana said, leaning against the cushioned headrest. "Mercy can't be evil. It's a virtue—like kindness or courage or..." Her voice trailed off.

He turned to look at her. "This is the world I remade with my terrible mercy."

She shook her head. "That doesn't make sense, either." Then, helplessly, she yawned.

He laughed, sounding like any boy from her school. She wondered what color his eyes had been long ago. "Go to sleep, Tana. Lean back your seat. If you let me borrow your car for tonight, I promise I will repay you."

"Oh yeah?" she asked, looking at him, with his bare feet and plain, dark clothes. "With what?"

The smile stayed on his lips. "Jewels, lies, slips of paper, dried flowers, memories of things long past, useless quotations, idle hands, beads, buttons, and mischief."

She was almost sure he was joking. "Okay. So where are we going?" she asked, her head nodding against the window.

His voice was soft. "Coldtown."

"Oh," she said, blinking herself awake again.

"I must. But if Aidan comes through the gates with me, he'll be safer, and you'll be safer without him. They'll hunt for him out in the world. And he's likely to start hunting, too."

"But what if he doesn't want to be a vampire?" Tana asked. As soon as the words left her mouth, she realized that he would want it—*of course* he would want it. Didn't he say as much before he attacked her? Being a vampire would get him all the glory he could ever imagine—he wouldn't just be known as the guy at a party most likely to seduce someone else's girlfriend or the small-town boy yearning for a big city. In Coldtown, he would be drowned in attention—and the massacre at the farmhouse would make his story only more tragic. More romantic.

Plus, Aidan was hungry.

She was the one who didn't want to be a vampire. And she was afraid that as time went on, she'd become less and less sure of that.

"The fever is in his blood," Gavriel said. "He looks for no cure but one. I think he is decided in his heart, but who can confess to such a decision?"

"It's hard to fight the infection," Tana said, her voice coming out harsher and more despairing than she'd intended. She didn't want to talk about her mom. She didn't want to tell him that the fever might be in her blood, too. In a few hours, she could be as bad as Aidan. "They *can't*. You don't understand. It takes them over and they can't think straight."

He said nothing in return. In that silence, she realized how stupid she was being. He must have been infected once, must have given in to it, must know better than she did how it felt.

"If you go to Coldtown," she said, hoping to change the subject, "you won't be able to get out. Are you sure whatever you're going there for is worth it?"

"What's that?" he asked suddenly, one hand leaving the wheel to touch her arm.

"What?" she said, looking down.

His long fingers traced the outline of the scar just beneath the crook of her elbow, his expression unreadable. Her skin felt too warm against the coolness of his touch, as though she were feverish. "These are old marks," he said finally. "You were just a child."

"Should it matter?" Tana asked. She was usually careful, but she must have pushed up the sleeves of her dress.

"Why should death discriminate between age and youth, you mean?" he asked calmly. "Death has his favorites, like anyone. Those who are beloved of Death will not die."

She was relieved he hadn't asked her any of the awful, stupid questions she'd grown used to: *Who bit you? I heard that it doesn't hurt when you're bitten—does it hurt? Did you like it? Come on, you're lying, you did like it, didn't you?* But then, he must know most of the answers. "Seems like Death came back for me."

He grinned, a subtly odd grin that somehow made her smile back. "You drove him off again. Sleep, Tana. I will guard you from Death, for I have no fear of him. We have been adversaries for so long that we are closer than friends."

"I'll just close my eyes for a minute," she said. "It's not even really that late."

There was something else that she wanted to say, something that she was sure she was on the verge of saying, but the words were swallowed up by the night.

Tana awoke to the sound of voices. She was alone in the car, spread out across the front seat, head pillowed on her arm, one of her booted feet kicked up against the glass of the driver-side window. The pleasant scent of coffee in the air mixed with car exhaust. And she felt chilled through, as though she'd kicked off a blanket in the middle of winter.

For a moment, waking up seemed like a nice thing to do. She remembered a party and being worried about going alone, where she was sure she was going to run into Aidan. She heard his voice outside the car, though, so it must all have worked out. Except for memories that seemed to be part of a nightmare—stuff that couldn't be real. Blood and empty eyes and a shimmering rain of shattered glass.

Then everything came back to her in a rush and all her muscles clenched with instinctive alertness. Her heart sped and she scrambled in her seat, kicking the wheel in her eagerness to be upright.

Her Crown Vic was parked in a lot, far from the central cluster of cars and trucks. In the distance she saw a large, sprawling building, blinking bulbs and glowing floodlights announcing it as DEAD LAST REST STOP OPEN 24 HOURS. The sheer gaudy brilliance of it made the outer edges of the lot seem even darker by comparison.

She'd never been there before, but she knew the place, the same way she knew South of the Border. Kids at school wore T-shirts emblazoned with the logo or plastered its bumper stickers on their cars. The Dead Last Rest Stop was as flashy and famous as it was because of its proximity to the first Coldtown.

They'd come a lot of miles while she'd slept.

Gavriel was sitting on the hood of her car, a paper bag and a steaming cup resting beside him. His head was down and, shadowed as his face was, he looked like a pale human boy and not a monster at all. Aidan stood with his hands in his pockets, talking to two people she didn't know. He must be reeling with infection, but he seemed to be hiding it well, his voice only a little unsteady. The pair were a girl and boy, their hair dyed the vibrant azure blue of butterfly wings and gum balls. They looked so alike that Tana thought they must be twins.

"You sure you can give us a ride? I mean, thanks, of course, but I just want to make sure you're serious," the boy was saying. His hair was razor-cut in the back and sprayed into a shaggy, teased mop, with longer pieces framing spiky bangs. His eyes were lined with kohl, and a single silver stud shone just above the right side of his lip, like a beauty mark. "Out here in the dull world, we're just a couple of kids without any cash, but inside it's all about barters and favors and who you know. Midnight is tight with lots of people through her blog, so we're going to be set up when we get to the city. We brought plenty of stuff to trade and we've got a plan. So we could help you if you help us."

Aidan smiled. "Definitely." He looked back at the car, toward Tana. She wasn't sure if she should get out. It was bad enough that he was promising people rides.

"Heading to Coldtown was kind of an impulse for us," he said. "So we could use a guide."

The girl—Midnight—touched Aidan's shoulder. "Reckless," she said, as if there were no higher compliment. Her hair was much longer than her brother's, parted on one side to hang in her face, falling completely over one eye. She wore skinny jeans with a blue velvet top and grubby, home-dyed ombré blue ballet slippers. Two rings threaded through her lower lip and the one in her tongue clacked against her teeth as she spoke. "We're part of this online network for people who are planning on going to Coldtown. We used to post all the time about meeting our destiny. Claiming all the stuff that normal people don't want. We'd talk and talk and talk, but how many of us actually did anything? We say that you've got to be willing to die to be different. I bet you believe that, too."

The boy pointed a painted fingernail at Aidan. "You don't even know him, Midnight. He could be doing this on a total whim. He might not be serious. He could be high. He could balk. Look at him. There's something wrong with his eyes and he's sweating."

Midnight rolled her eyes, sarcasm in her voice. "That's a nice thing to say about someone who's offering us a ride." She looked at Aidan. "Don't mind Winter. He's overprotective."

"So *are* you willing to die to be different?" Aidan asked them, and Tana heard the hunger in his voice.

"For sure," she said. "I wanted to go last year, but Winter didn't want to be sixteen forever and I had to admit it was kind of lame. So we compromised. We're going to be eighteen in a month and that seemed old enough to go."

Midnight and Winter, Tana thought. She knew that the names had to be fake and that the way they looked was an elaborate artifice, but they wore their strange beauty like war paint. They made an intimidating pair.

Winter looked down at his calf-high boots, buckles running back and forth over the length of them, frowning as though he wanted Midnight to give Aidan a different answer. A long metal chain ran from his belt loop to his back pocket; he twisted it around one finger idly, in the same fidgety way that his sister bit her lip rings.

"I'm going to blog the whole thing," Midnight said. "That's how we're going to pay for stuff after our trade goods run out. I've got a tip jar on the site, and there are ads and stuff—my readership was already pretty good, but it's gone through the roof since we ran away. A hundred thousand unique visitors are watching Winter's and my adventure. We made a promise to each other—and to them."

"No more birthdays," they recited more or less at the same time, then flushed and laughed a little. It was a vow, a piece of a chant, their scripture, something they took so seriously that saying it aloud embarrassed them.

"Because you're planning on dying and rising again?" Gavriel said from atop the car hood. They glanced at him in surprise, as if they'd forgotten he was there. His face was shadowed enough to hide his eyes, but his unnatural stillness should have unnerved them.

"I just posted about our Last Supper," Midnight said, taking her phone and holding it out to Aidan, leaning closer than she had to. "It's kind of a tradition. Before you go through the gates, you eat one last meal. All your favorites. See, Winter had pizza with olives, ketchup chips, and bubble tea? And here's the picture of mine—steak and eggs with a slice of apple pie. I was so excited that I only took a bite of each. You know, like how you get one last special meal of your choosing before you go to the electric chair."

Last meal. Because they were hoping to die, Tana realized.

She saw how Aidan's gaze drifted over Midnight's skin. She really was beautiful, with large black eyes and all that blue hair, with earrings in the shape of daggers swinging from her earlobes. He grinned as if what she'd just said was very funny.

He was going to bite her.

Tana got out of the car, slamming the door behind her. They all looked over, Midnight frowning at having her conversation interrupted.

"Aidan," Tana said warningly. "Everything okay?"

He turned toward her, a strained smile relaxing into a real one as she got closer. He shrugged and threw an easy arm over her shoulder. "Midnight, Winter, this is my girlfriend, Tana."

Midnight took a step back from Aidan. Winter looked at Tana in a way that told her just how bad she must appear in her ripped and filthy dress, hair sticking up all over the place.

"I'm not—" Tana started, pulling away from him.

But Aidan was still smiling. "And she's worried because I'm sick. I'm Cold. She's worried I'm going to bite you, and she should worry, because I want to bite you. I want to real bad."

At that, Gavriel looked up again, his gaze catching Tana's. She couldn't read his expression, but she could tell he wasn't pleased. One of Midnight's hands flew up to cover her mouth, chipped silver nail polish and onyx rings on her fingers.

Winter studied Aidan's face. "You really are, aren't you?"

"He was bitten last night," said Gavriel, leaning forward, black hair hanging in his face. "He can control the hunger now, for short periods, more or less, but it will become worse. He has maybe another day or two before he ought to be restrained."

Tana expected Aidan to give some response, but he was quiet. Maybe he hadn't realized it would get worse. Tana thought of her mother screaming up from the basement and shuddered.

She thought of the way her skin had felt chilled when she'd woken. She wasn't sure why Aidan hadn't said anything about the possibility of her being Cold—whether he was being nice or whether he figured they would be less impressed if it wasn't him alone who was dangerous—but either way she was grateful.

"Can I interview you?" Midnight asked Aidan, pulling out her phone and fiddling with it, opening some app. "For the blog? Can you describe what it feels like—the hunger?"

"Careful," Winter said, putting his hand on his sister's arm.

Tana could see that Midnight wasn't listening. Her mouth was slightly open, fascinated, a mouse in love with a snake.

"Come on," Midnight said to Aidan, losing her cool affect entirely. She bounced on her dirty ballet flats. "Please. I've never talked to anyone experiencing what you are. I am so curious—and my readers would be super curious, too. It must be amazing to have all that power running through your veins."

"It's like you're hollow," Aidan said, looking into the camera as if he was ready to devour all the viewers, looking as if he were an understudy for one of those online vampire celebrities. "Hollow and empty, and there's only one thing that matters."

"I can't believe this is happening," Tana said, walking over to Gavriel.

He held out a cup to her, the one she'd seen beside him on the hood when she woke. His black shirt was stretched tight against his chest, and he had a crumpled paper bag resting beside him. "They say a long sleep is the best cure for all sickness."

She took a long swallow of the coffee. It was too sweet and choked with cream, as though it had been mixed by someone who had no idea what it was supposed to taste like—someone who hadn't tasted food in a long while. She reached for the bag. "What's in here? Doughnuts?"

He turned away, as though he didn't want to watch her open it. "Take it. That's for you as well."

The bag turned out to hold a necklace of Bohemian garnets clustered together like pomegranate seeds, with a huge garnet-studded locket the size of a fig hanging from the center point. The gold clasp on the back was broken, as though it had been ripped from someone's throat, and the locket itself was empty. It rested on a bed of loose bills, some ink-stained, some smeared brownish-red, some single dollars and some twenties mixed in with a few euros, all jammed together in a messy pile.

"Where did you get all this?" she asked.

At that moment, Midnight screamed. Tana whirled toward them and felt Gavriel's cold hands closed around her. Frozen fingers dug into her skin just below her rib cage. His grip was so firm it was like being held by a bronze figure.

Midnight was on the ground, her phone tossed to one side, her hands scrabbling to push Aidan away. He crouched on top of her, pushing her velvet shirt off her shoulder. Winter had hold of one of Aidan's arms and was trying to pull him backward.

Tana's feet kicked out ineffectually against the car bumper as she was dragged up into the air. She felt Gavriel's chest against her back, smooth and chilled as stone. She felt the icy curve of his jaw where it rested against the top of her head.

"Hush, Tana," Gavriel said, sliding his cheek downward over her hair, so that he could murmur against her throat. Terror overwhelmed her, vast and animal. Her body took over, twisting and writhing and clawing. It was like being in that dark basement again, her mother's cold lips giving her one final kiss.

"Hush," he said. "It's almost over."

"No!" Tana shouted, struggling uselessly. "No, no, no. I have to help him. Get off of me."

Then, suddenly, he did, hands sliding free of her. She staggered away, nearly falling to her knees.

Winter had let go of Aidan's arm in preference for pulling him away from Midnight by his hair. Aidan's head lashed back and forth,

Midnight's hand up under his jaw, pushing him away from her. But he was close, close enough for his teeth to snap just above the bare skin of her arm. His fingernails raked at her shoulder, making bloody runnels.

Her screams spiraled up into the night air.

For a moment, Tana's mind was blank. Then she rushed over, crouching down, so she could dig her hands into Midnight's armpits and haul her up.

Aidan looked at Tana, and for a moment, it was clear he thought she would help him. Then she scuttled away, pulling Midnight as hard as she could, and he snarled in comprehension.

Aidan went for Midnight's legs, but she was fast enough to kick him in the chest, hard. Even though she was wearing only slippers, he stumbled to one knee, gasping, one hand held out as if to ward off more violence.

Winter locked his arm around Aidan's neck and held him like that. For a moment, Aidan's body went slack, then he brought up his shaking fingers, stained red. He was about to lick them clean. Tana leaped forward, grabbing his wrists and pulling them to her, wiping his hands against her dress. She wasn't sure how much human blood would turn him, but she didn't want to take any chances.

Aidan started to laugh, a choked sound with Winter's arm against his throat.

Midnight sobbed softly, red soaking her torn shirt, turning the blue velvet to black.

Tana looked at Gavriel. He was watching her with half-lidded eyes of glittering scarlet, an intent and covetous stare.

"You didn't do anything," she accused, pointing a trembling finger.

He swayed slightly toward the scene of carnage, like a tree bending in the wind, as if she had beckoned him. "You could have stopped him and you just let it happen."

"It's dangerous to go to Coldtown infected but not yet turned." His voice was distant, but something in the way he moved his mouth, some languorousness, showed that the blood in the air and feel of her struggle against him had ignited his desire to feed. "It would have been safer if you'd just let it happen. Every new vampire born in Coldtown compromises the blood supply. There are only so many donors."

"It's dangerous to be infected anywhere," Tana said. "I just don't want him to die."

"One way or another we all wind up dead," Gavriel said, his eyes on Aidan.

But then he bent and picked up the coffee cup from the ground, bringing over the remaining liquid to wash off Aidan's fingers. Tana knelt on the cool asphalt of the parking lot, carefully scraping Midnight's skin from underneath Aidan's nails with her own.

"Buzzkill," Aidan said, low. Cold sweat dampened the bangs of his forehead. He grinned up at Gavriel, his head lolling against Winter's arm now, as though there was no more fight in him.

"You owe me," Tana told Aidan. "I hope you know just how much you owe me."

Leaning over them, Gavriel's face was no longer shaded, his eyes catching the blinking lights of the rest-stop sign, his skin too pale to belong to a living human.

Winter stood abruptly, freeing Aidan and backing away from the vampire.

"Something the matter?" Gavriel asked him.

Aidan stretched out, looking up at the stars.

Midnight pushed herself to her feet a little unsteadily, wiping tears off her face and smearing her black mascara. She saw Gavriel and froze as her brother had.

"Red as roses—yes, those are my real eyes. Am I not what you've been looking for?" Gavriel's smile was all teeth. "I have been here all along waiting for you to notice. I can give you what you want. I can give you endless oblivion."

"Stop it," Tana said, hitting him on the shoulder, continuing to pretend he was a regular person who wasn't scary in the hopes he'd forget, too, continuing to pretend she had any power at all in this situation. "Stop it *right now*. I've had enough of everyone attacking everyone."

Her words seemed to break the spell he'd had over Winter, who put his hand on his sister's unhurt shoulder. "We should get you to an emergency room."

"No hospital," Midnight said groggily. "I just need bandages—we can get them inside."

"*Jenny*," said Winter. "Please. Let's go home."

She looked at him with wide, black, furious eyes. "We have everything we need right here. And don't ever call me that name again. Ever."

Tana looked toward Aidan, still staring dazedly up at the stars. He was breathing faster, as though he couldn't quite inhale fully. One of his hands was pressed to his heart. He barely seemed to notice when she called his name softly.

"Go with them," Gavriel told Tana, sitting down beside Aidan and pushing up the sleeve of his own T-shirt. "Since you wish it, I won't let him feed on the living, but there's no reason he can't drink from the dead. It will curb his hunger. Go, Tana. We'll be here when you return."

She went.

→ CHAPTER 10 ←

When life is woe,

And hope is dumb,

The World says, "Go!"

The Grave says, "Come!"

—Arthur Guiterman

The winter before the sundown party—before Tana went missing and maybe was infected, before Pearl got scared and mad as the days went on without Tana calling to tell them *anything*—there had been an assembly at the high school to discuss vampirism. Even though the seventh and eighth graders were in a different building, they were all, including Pearl, marched over and herded to the very front of the auditorium.

As Pearl went down the steps, she craned her head, looking for her sister. The upperclassmen seemed so much older than she was, loud and intimidating. Some of the senior boys had stubble and the girls dressed as if they were in college. In her denim skirt with leggings under it, with brand-new pink sparkly Converse sneakers and a side ponytail, Pearl had felt she looked cute when she got dressed in the morning. Now she felt like a little kid.

"*Pearl!*" a voice called over the roar of students finding seats and shouting to their friends. Turning, she spotted Tana and Pauline waving to her from about halfway down the auditorium.

Tana cupped her hands around her mouth to make her voice louder. "Come sit with us!"

Pearl looked after the rest of her class, obediently trooping to the front. Then she looked at her sister waving. Finally, she decided and picked her way past the older kids to the seat Tana had saved for her.

"I'm supposed to be over there," Pearl said, pointing to her teacher.

"But we're going to have more fun over *here*," Pauline promised her, smiling a big let's-all-get-in-trouble-together smile. She was wearing a black-and-white-striped dress, bright orange boots, and a vintage pink hat with a veil. Seeing her and Tana together at school was weird—like seeing a part of her sister that was usually hidden.

At home, Tana was the one who made dinner when Dad forgot (which was a lot); who knew only three recipes (spaghetti, salad with a chicken cutlet on top, and burritos); who was good at braiding hair and not pulling too hard (except for when she did French braids); and who could fix almost anything (sinks, toilets, favorite mugs). At school she was obviously somebody else. Somebody who swaggered around in her big boots and black leather jacket, taking auto shop with the boys and glowering at everyone who wasn't Pearl or Pauline as if she wanted to knock them out.

Right then, she and Pauline were leaning back in their chairs, grinning at each other over Pearl's head. It was weird.

"We have a special speaker today," Principal Wong told them in her no-nonsense, embarrass-the-school-and-I'll-make-you-sorry voice, short hair combed tightly to one side and gelled to stay there. "We're going to hear from someone who was trapped inside Springfield when the walls went up. Thank you for agreeing to come and tell your story, Yashira Baez. Let's give her a big Astell Regional welcome!"

Everyone applauded noisily, with a few sarcastic whoops from boys in the back. Pearl leaned down to take a strawberry-scented pen and notebook out of her bag, in case she was supposed to write stuff down.

A small Latina woman stepped onto the stage, wearing jeans and a muted yellow cardigan, looking old enough to be someone's grandmother. "I'm going to tell you this story just like it happened. I was headed into Springfield to get my great-aunt out when the military blockaded the area. She was in an assisted-living apartment complex and she was too old to drive. So when I heard the rumor that the city was going to be closed off, I thought I could get her out in time. Unfortunately, I got trapped in there with her. I lived in the first Coldtown for two long years until I could figure out a way to get enough cash together to buy myself a marker from a bounty hunter. I could never have done it without donations from my church, so now I go around to schools to try to give back to the community.

"People ask all the time whether vampires are like us. I always say that in my two years trapped inside, I played checkers with vampires. I sat on stoops with vampires. And they were a lot like the people they'd been before. But they weren't the *same*. Vampires are predators and we're prey. You've got to never forget that."

She looked out at the audience very seriously. "Circuses tame tigers. Get them to jump through flaming hoops. Those tigers are real nice to their trainers, I bet. Bump them with their big heads. Roll on their backs like house cats. But if they're hungry enough, those tigers are going to eat those same trainers they were so nice to."

A couple of people in the audience laughed nervously. Tana didn't laugh. Pauline looked over at her a little worriedly.

"Now, I never assume that everyone knows the basics, so we're going to go over them again. Infected people—people who have vampire blood in their veins, people who've gone Cold—they can't spread the infection. They're *infected*, but not *infectious*. Got it?"

"*Obviously*," Pauline said under her breath. "Otherwise, the whole world would be buried in vampires."

Ms. Baez went on, going over stuff she considered basic. Pearl knew most of it—or at least she felt like she'd heard it before.

Once a person was bitten, symptoms appeared within twelve to forty-eight hours. Sometimes people were rescued before a bite could be completed and experienced minor symptoms, but didn't actually go Cold.

A very small number of people had immune systems able to fight off the infection. Ms. Baez told the story of an Indonesian bounty hunter who'd been bitten on eight occasions, and even though his skin was mottled by scars from the attacks, he didn't get infected. He swore by the cocktail of snake blood mixed with a drop of infected human blood and plenty of arrack that he drank each morning—his recipe for staving off infection. He considered himself immune until he was bitten for the ninth time and succumbed to the Cold, turning soon after.

Pearl noticed Tana rubbing her arm, where Mom had hurt her. She had a big scar that sometimes she hid and other times she showed off, as though she was daring people to ask her about it. Grandma and Grandpa had taken Pearl aside years ago and told her that Tana was going to be messed up in the head because of Mom and that Pearl was going to have to watch out for her. Pearl wasn't sure what that meant except for times like right then, when she leaned over, took Tana's hand, and squeezed.

Tana squeezed back.

What Grandma and Grandpa didn't understand was that Tana wasn't messed up because of Mom; she was messed up because of Dad. If Dad had just given Mom some blood, instead of locking her up, none of the bad stuff would have happened. Mom wouldn't be dead and Tana wouldn't be scarred and no one would be sad. Maybe they'd all live in Coldtown now, or maybe they would have emigrated to Amsterdam or something, where it was still illegal to be a vampire, but no one cared.

"It can happen very fast," Ms. Baez was saying. "Even before the symptoms appear, the vampire blood is preparing the body for turning—so once that person drinks human blood, they're going to become a vampire. It takes less than an hour to die, and as soon as fifteen minutes they can be back up again, with new teeth, denser muscles, and that newborn vampire hunger.

"Uses up a lot of energy to change the way they do, so until they feed, they're not going to be able to control themselves too well. You got to stay away from the newly turned, no matter how well you knew them in life."

Ms. Baez walked to the edge of the stage. "How about a fun exercise? I am going to teach you a big word. Does anyone know what an apotropaic is?"

Pearl didn't, but some boy called out that it was stuff vampires didn't like.

Wild roses. Garlic, called "the stinking rose." Holy symbols. Running water. Hawthorn. Pearl knew all those already; Hemlok explained them on his bounty-hunting show. According to Ms. Baez, though, some of them didn't work. She'd used a holy symbol twice while she was in Coldtown and neither time did it have any effect.

"I bet they won't let her talk about all the creepy stuff," Pauline said under her breath. "All the people drinking animal blood to stay human, even drinking their own blood. People staying drunk for months to reduce the hunger."

"Is that true?" Pearl whispered back. "Does it work?"

Tana shrugged.

"People even drink *vampire* blood, if they can get it," Pauline went on, low-voiced, talking as though she were telling a ghost story. "They say a couple of the bounty hunters in Europe are pretty much addicted to the stuff. But you don't get better—you just don't get worse. It's like resetting the infection from day one."

"Time for questions," Ms. Baez said from the stage. "I can't promise I have all the answers, but I'll be as honest as I can."

"Why don't they just let people out of Coldtown if they want to go?" a girl asked. "If they're not infected, what's the difference?"

"Money," Ms. Baez said. "It costs the government a lot of money to run Coldtowns and a lot of money to test people for release. That money has to come from somewhere, so it comes from the budget for bounty hunters. Plus, the government doesn't *want* all the people to get out. If they did, what would the vampires eat? Each other? The quarantine would break down."

"Look at Principal Wong," Pauline whispered to Pearl. "She almost blew a gasket at that answer."

"Aren't you mad you were stuck there?" one of the boys asked.

Ms. Baez shrugged. "I left mad behind a long time ago. The world is the way it is. I can only fix my little piece of it. And I choose to do that by telling kids the facts, so they don't believe everything they hear on the Internet."

A pulse of laughter rose up from the teachers at that.

Tana stuck up her hand suddenly. Pearl's heart started to thud, afraid of what she was going to say.

"Yes?" asked Ms. Baez, pointing to her.

Tana stood up. "Can't they drink each other's blood?"

"Excuse me?"

"I mean, if all the humans were dead or if they ate everyone in every Coldtown and they couldn't get out, what would happen? Wouldn't they feed on one another?"

Ms. Baez nodded. "You want to know a secret? Vampire blood is pretty great for vampires. It grants them a piece of the drained vampire's power. So, yeah, they can drink it."

"Why?" one of the teachers burst out. Pearl hadn't heard anything like that before and she was surprised.

"Think of it like the accumulation of toxins in animals. At the lowest level of the food chain, there is a very tiny bit of toxin in each, say, blade of grass. Now, if a mouse comes along and eats lots and lots of grass, all the toxins from those individual blades accumulate in the mouse. Then a raptor comes along and eats a dozen mice, and gets all those toxins, and so on and so on. If you think about toxins like power, then you can see why the older the vampire, the more power it's accumulated and the more power another vampire can absorb by draining it."

"They don't need us at all," said Pearl, under her breath. She imagined a world with only vampires in it, all red eyes and cold skin.

"So long as they can't have babies, they do," Pauline whispered back. "You can't have new vampires without new people. And if you eat all the old vampires, you're going to need new ones ASAP."

"How come they don't, then?" Tana called down, still standing, not bothering to raise her hand again. "Why don't they just eat one another and leave us alone?"

Principal Wong stood up, ready to scold Tana, but Ms. Baez wasn't paying any attention.

"Oh, they do, kid," said Ms. Baez. "They eat one another. They eat us. They eat every damn thing. They'll drink up the whole world if we let them."

❖ CHAPTER 11 ❖

Death is the king of this world: 'Tis his park
Where he breeds life to feed him. Cries of pain
Are music for his banquet.
    —George Eliot

The inside of the Dead Last Rest Stop was huge, bigger than most malls, but with services malls would never have any reason to provide—showers for a dollar; canned goods; a boutique with sepulchral dresses and coats in black and purple and silver; a pharmacy; an interfaith chapel; five restaurants; three bars; a dance club; and even a bag check so that people arriving by bus could pay two dollars to dump their luggage for a couple of hours while they shopped or slept in rentable coffin-shaped pods. Loud Eurotrance remixes of funereal music pumped out of speakers all along the walls, and every store window announced the same thing, whether in big, blinking letters or hand-lettered signs: OPEN 24 HOURS.

Tana felt dazed. It was surreal to be inside of a brightly lit space, safe, when she'd been in mortal danger for the last twelve hours.

The central area was a hexagonal room with polished black floors, ebonized benches, and a central sculpture of what looked like a large red crystal heart with a stake driven through it. Televisions along the walls broadcast popular feeds from inside Springfield's Coldtown. On one, golden-haired Lucien Moreau was teaching a human girl how to waltz; on another, a ginger-haired vampire girl was talking to the camera, describing how her night had gone while a human boy cuddled up to her pale skin, offering her a piece of tubing taped to the needle in his wrist.

Tourists stopped to stare at the feeds. They took pictures in front of the crystal heart, arms thrown over one another's shoulders and too-wide smiles on their mouths.

A tired-looking middle-aged woman stood off to one side, handing out pink flyers to anyone who passed her. "Have you seen my daughter?" she asked, over and over. "She's only twelve. Please, I know she came through here. Have you seen her?"

At first, people under the age of sixteen weren't allowed to go through the gates of the Coldtowns, but then a nine-year-old was turned away because the guards thought she was lying about being bitten. She wasn't. People died. There were tests for infection, but the tests were expensive, making self-reporting critical to keeping the quarantine. Since that incident with the child, anyone was allowed to enter any Coldtown at any age without proving anything.

Tana looked at the woman, at her tired face and at the smiling little girl on the flyer. She thought of Pearl and wondered what that girl had imagined was waiting for her behind the gates.

Midnight walked past the woman without even seeming to notice her and collapsed on one of the benches. Both her hands pressed the velvet cloth of her shirt over the scratches to stop the bleeding.

"I'll get bandages and stuff," said Winter. "You stay right here. And *you* stay with her." He scowled at Tana.

Tana nodded and Winter walked toward the pharmacy, looking back twice. His big boots clopped like hooves on the shiny granite tile floor.

A few passing kids wearing backpacks stopped to stare at Tana in her bloody clothes and at Midnight, with her smeared mascara and the way she was clutching her shoulder.

"What are you looking at?" Tana told the kids, snarling the way Pauline would have, and they hurried off.

Midnight smiled at her lopsidedly.

"I'm so incredibly sorry," Tana said. "About what happened. I'm sorry you got hurt."

"How did you...how did you wind up with them? With Aidan and the other one?" Midnight asked. Her lips looked chapped and bluish under the fluorescent lights.

"There was a party and everyone died," Tana said. She didn't expect it to come out quite like that, quite so plain and awful.

Midnight nodded and closed her eyes, as if the scratches stung. "How bad? It wasn't that thing that was on the news up north...?"

The news? For a moment, Tana was confused. It felt like something too private for the news, but of course that didn't make sense. "I don't know. Maybe."

"It was! Oh my god, I saw all the tweets and the pictures someone leaked of the crime scene. You were really there?"

Tana nodded, not sure what else to say. She had no words for it that were big enough.

"Wow," Midnight said. "And you got away. That's major."

"More or less, we got away," said Tana.

"Hey, do me a favor, okay?" Midnight reached into her pocket with one hand and took out her phone, the face of it scratched from the pavement. "Hold this while I talk. My tripod is in my luggage, but I don't want to bother getting it. This is the real stuff—the stuff I promised to tell everyone. Just try to hold it steady."

"Sure," Tana said, somewhat taken aback. It wasn't as if she hadn't taken video of anyone before—of Pauline so she could see how her auditions looked or of friends acting stupid and goofing around—but she'd never filmed anyone who'd just been attacked and was still bleeding.

"And you could say something, too. You *should*. Everyone wants to know what it's like to be you right now."

Tana shook her head quickly; the idea of talking about what had happened brought back every awful image. The staring dead eyes. The whispering voices through the door. Her back slammed against the ground of the gas station with Aidan towering over her. "I don't know, myself."

"Later maybe," said Midnight, handing the phone to Tana. "How do I look?"

Tana had no idea how to answer that. Midnight looked pale and beautiful, streaked and bloodied. "You look fine," Tana said, as neutrally as possible.

"I guess that's going to have to do." Midnight winced as she pulled on the ripped neck of her velvet shirt, exposing her collarbone so Tana could get a good shot of the gouges. They were grisly, wet with blood, and swollen at the edges. "You know how to use this thing?"

Tana touched her fingers to the phone, hitting the small picture of the video on the bottom corner. "I think so. Aren't you worried your parents are going to see this? Let the cops know where you are? I mean, you're underage runaways."

Midnight snorted. "Our parents don't get what we do online. They're not smart enough. They're *nothing* like us. Trust me, by the time they figure out what happened, we'll be long gone."

"Okay," Tana said, holding up the camera and clicking the button to begin filming. "Ready."

"Hi," Midnight said, an odd intensity coming over her as she gazed into the lens. "It's me, faithful servant of the night, adventurer, poet, and madwoman. And what an adventure I've been on! Lots has happened since I posted last. Winter and I made it to the rest stop outside of Coldtown, so we're less than an hour from being inside. It's exactly like what we always believed—when you're following your deepest, truest, darkest destiny, the universe clears you a path. We met some people who are going to give us a ride. In fact, you might recognize them from the news—but I'll get to that later. First, I have to tell you about what happened to me."

Then Winter returned with a bag of medical supplies. Midnight asked Tana to keep the phone recording as Winter bound up her shoulder, spraying the wounds with antiseptic and taping down gauze bandages. She narrated all the while, eyes on the camera, even when it obviously hurt. When that was done, Midnight gulped down some aspirin and said she wanted to edit and upload the video to her blog before she did anything else.

Listening to her, Tana had to admire the way Midnight was able to turn what happened into a madcap story, into part of the Legend of Midnight. Even the not-so-good stuff was spun on its head to be enviable. Tana could imagine herself watching the video and wishing she was as brave and lucky as the girl in it. But standing in front of Midnight, knowing what actually happened, Tana could see that Midnight wasn't just telling a story to other people, she was telling a story to herself. She was smoothing over all the frightening parts until she wasn't scared. *But she should be*, Tana thought. *She should be scared.*

"There's free Wi-Fi throughout the building—I'm just going to plug into the outlet over there." Midnight pointed toward the food court. Taking the phone out of Tana's hand, grinning, she aimed the camera part at her. The corner light flashed. "Meet me when you're done with whatever. You don't mind, right? You didn't have to say anything."

Tana was sure she looked awful, but a bad picture online was the least of her problems. She felt worn out, cold, and brittle. She could smell Midnight's blood, a metallic scent, and wondered if that meant the infection had finally kicked in. Or maybe it was nothing. Maybe she should stop worrying.

"No, I guess I don't mind." Tana glanced over at a display of logo shirts. "I'm going to pay to take a shower."

Winter gave her an almost friendly smile, the first since Aidan had attacked his sister. "That's a good idea. Who knows how much hot running water we're going to get inside."

Tana wanted to say that she was still making up her mind about Coldtown, but she hesitated too long and then felt foolish. She waved an awkward good-bye instead.

The gift store was kitschy, full of shot glasses, bumper stickers, and T-shirts—baby tees with CORPSEBAIT across the front, big black sleep shirts with dripping letters: UP ALL NIGHT AT THE DEAD LAST REST STOP, I BITE ON THE FIRST DATE, DEADEST GENERATION, NOTHING IS THE NEW EVERYTHING, and I'LL TAKE MY COFFEE WITH YOUR BLOOD IN IT. There were mirrors with cartoonish rivulets of blood running from two puncture wounds silk-screened onto them, so that when you looked in the mirror, it seemed as if you'd been bitten. And there were necklaces, spelling out the word *cold* in looping cursive letters.

An elderly lady with short gray hair was paying for a packet of water-purifying pills and tins of food when Tana passed her at the checkout counter. The lady wore a Chanel-esque black suit and carried a gold-tipped cane with mother-of-pearl roses along the length. Her back was bent, making her seem hunched like a vulture.

"What?" the woman accused the clerk, her rheumy blue eyes steady. "You think dying is just for the young?"

Tana left before she could hear the clerk's reply.

In the next store, the boutique, she thumbed through lacy satin gowns with names like Innocence Shattered and Ruined Blossom and Sliced-Open Apple of Sin. She found a pretty blue dress that she liked and that would have probably fit her, but at a hundred and twelve dollars, it was way too expensive. Tana had the same forty that she'd had at the gas station. She'd left the bag of bills where she'd knocked it, on the ground next to her car. She hoped it was still there. If she was going to hole up someplace and wait out the next forty-some hours to see if she was infected, she'd need more money, no matter its provenance. And she'd need the money even more if she went to Coldtown with the rest of them.

At least there was a sale rack in the back with marked-down clothes. She managed to find a wrinkled gray slip dress about a size too big for her priced at twenty-five bucks. She got that and the cheapest pair of underwear in the store—crimson with ridiculous black lace trim and a silly bow—for an additional ten.

The bored-looking clerk, a man with huge silver studs through his ears and a tattoo of a snake wrapped around his neck like a noose, rang her up and took her money with clear disdain.

She knew she was going to look kind of overly fancy and also a little bit naked in the slip dress, but she wasn't willing to face an actual vampire while wearing a hilarious slogan nightshirt. And all she wanted to do with her current clothes was set them on fire.

She took her purchases in their glossy black boutique bag with purple tissue paper wrapped around each garment and went to the showers. There, she was able to pay a dollar for fifteen minutes in an individual stall and three dollars for packets of body wash and shampoo, a tiny toothbrush kit, and a towel only slightly larger than a washcloth that had to be returned.

A large mirror hung in the hallway outside the stalls, where women and girls sat on benches, lacing up Chucks and rolling on deodorant. Seeing herself, she stopped to stare at her reflection as though the girl in the glass was someone else, someone unknown and unknowable. Her black hair looked wild, with bits of twigs and leaves stuck in it. The skin around her eyes was dark as a bruise, probably half from sleeplessness and half from smeared mascara that she made worse when she'd splashed her face with water. Even her blue eyes looked gray under the harsh overhead lights. Her once white dress was as bad as she'd guessed, brown at the hem where the root beer had soaked into it, striped with dark streaks of blood and dirt. There were at least two visible rips in the fabric, and her high boots were spattered with grime and mud.

But the worst part was her expression. She made herself try to smile, but it came out wrong. She'd once seen a bunch of vintage mug shots in a magazine and there'd been one she'd stared at for a long time. There'd been something off about the girl in it. Now Tana saw that strangeness in herself.

She wasn't okay. She really, really didn't look like someone who was okay.

Going into the stall, Tana hung her pocketbook, towel, and bag of clothes on the hook farthest from the nozzle, unlaced her boots and tied them together, so they could hang with her other things. Then she pulled off her mother's baby-doll dress, her bra, and her underwear and tossed them into a corner. Her muscles felt stiff and sore, her hands fumbling over the most basic tasks.

When the hot water hit her shoulders, it felt so good she groaned out loud.

She washed her hair twice and combed it through with her fingers to get all the twigs out. She scrubbed her skin with her fingernails, not caring if it abraded, caring only that she was clean. The water cut off after her fifteen minutes were up and she leaned back against the tiles. Her heartbeat hammered against her chest in alarm, but nothing was wrong. It was just leftover terror.

She didn't feel chilled through anymore. She didn't want to attack the woman in the next shower stall. She felt exhausted and scared and scraped up, but other than that, she felt pretty much the way she always had. She felt fine.

She thought about Aidan out in the parking lot and about Gavriel's bare arm. If Aidan drank enough of Gavriel's blood, maybe he'd be better for a while, but they were just buying time in scraps and tatters.

It had been almost seven hours since the vampire's teeth scraped her leg. Too soon to let herself hope she'd be okay, but she found herself hoping anyway. She thought of her own bed in her own room and imagined herself curled up there, her cat sleeping on her feet and Pearl doing her homework in the next room. She thought of bright light streaming through the windows and her phone ringing because Pauline wanted to go to the pool hall where the cute guy worked to play game after game of darts as they'd done all last summer, scoping him out between throws. And she thought of how, once Pauline and the guy finally dated, they'd all snuck back in there one night with Aidan and thrown stuff at the board—first kitchen knives, then forks, then even broken pieces of a glass someone had dropped.

It had turned into an oddly surreal night, but not as surreal as this one.

After a few moments, she forced herself to dry off as much as she could with the small towel and to step into her new clothes, tossing the old ones into the boutique bag. Without a bra, the thin fabric of her new dress showed the outline of her nipples, but she couldn't bring herself to put on any piece of clothing she'd been wearing for the last thirty-odd hours, no matter how bare she looked.

She reached into her purse to see if she had a comb and some lipstick—anything to make herself seem less sickly—when she noticed that her phone was flashing. She had six new messages. She must have turned her ringer off at some point at the party and not remembered to turn it back on.

Stepping into the dressing area, she put the phone back into her bag and found a comb to draw the tangles out of her hair. As wavy as it was, it would tangle again fast, but at least she'd look a little less messy. Maybe by some alchemy it would make her feel less of a mess, too. She brushed her teeth in the sink, over and over again until her gums bled.

Then she listened to the messages.

The first one was from her father, giving her hell for not coming home in the morning. The next was from her father again, asking her where she was, saying the police had called. Then there was a message from Pearl, twelve-year-old arrogance dripping from her voice, saying that Dad was worried and that she was sure Tana was *fine*, but could Tana call *please*, because listening to him was *boring*. Then there was a call from a police officer, leaving a number, saying that he understood she'd been at a party the night before and he needed to talk to her. Then her sister again, saying to please, please, please call; this time she sounded frightened.

The last message was from her father.

"The police have been to the house," he said. "They described to me what happened at the party and how only three kids, in all probability you and two others, managed to get away. Since you haven't come home or tried to contact us, I'm assuming that you've been infected." There was a long pause. When her father resumed speaking, his voice was unsteady. "Thank you for staying away, Tana. It's the responsible thing to do, and I hope that no matter what happens, you leave us—especially Pearl—with our memory of you the way it was. We love you, sweetheart, and we'll miss you, but please don't come back here. Don't ever come home."

For a moment, she was tempted to call home anyway, to tell them that she was okay while she still could, to say something cruel to her father to get him back for leaving a message like that, to at least text Pearl.

You leave us with our memory of you the way it was.

Tana deleted the messages and put her phone away.

She'd decided. She was going to Coldtown.

She cleaned off her boots in the sink and laced them onto her feet, wishing she didn't have to. She'd have liked to never touch them again, but she didn't have the money for new shoes. The boots were a little damp, but she thought they'd dry soon.

With the dollar and change she had left, she bought a slice of pizza and ate it, sitting on a plastic chair in the food court. It tasted like sawdust and cardboard. Across the way at a nearby table, some boys in baggy jeans were shoving one another in a good-natured way.

"We should do what other countries do and blow those corpses sky-high," said one of them, leering at two girls with purple pigtails and black lipstick who were passing the table. "Bomb *all* the Coldtowns."

One of the girls turned around and flipped dual middle fingers at him. "Hey, idiot, you want to fight the vampires? Move to Europe. Too bad about the skyrocketing infection rate there."

"Maybe I will. I'll have my own show—*Slade Slays*—and kill every vampire there is. How about that?"

"How about it's called *Slade Dies*," called the girl. "That show I'd watch."

All the other boys at the table started laughing.

Tana got up and threw away her grease-smeared paper plate. Then she walked over to where Winter and Midnight were sitting by the outlets. Midnight had her head bent over her laptop, earbud cords hanging down around her neck. Winter looked up at Tana and blinked a couple of times, pulling off his bulkier headphones, his blue hair flattened where he'd mussed it. She noticed for the first time the T-shirt he was wearing underneath his black jacket— it had the words COLDER THAN YOU across the front in small white letters.

She snorted.

"Wow," he said. "You look much better."

"Thanks." She made a face. "You still want that ride? I'd understand if you decided not to take it."

Winter touched Midnight's arm, making her look up. "We better talk about it. I think maybe—"

"We want the ride," Midnight said firmly, in a tone that dared her brother to contradict her.

He didn't.

CHAPTER 12

Call no man happy till he is dead.
—Aeschylus

Vampires were always more beautiful than the living.

Their skin was without blemish, marble smooth, and pore-less. The older they got, the more their unnatural red eyes grew bright as poppies and their hair became as lustrous as silk. It was as if whatever demon possessed them, whatever force kept their corpses from the grave, had refined them in the blaze of its power, burning away their humanity to reveal something finer. Caspar Morales had stolen the fire from Prometheus, and his children were spreading it.

They looked absurdly gorgeous, glowing from the television like fallen angels. Even from the beginning, that was a problem. People liked pretty things. People even liked pretty things that wanted to kill and eat them.

After the infections started burgeoning and the first walls around the infected areas were built—the crude ones that kept only some things inside—news cameras couldn't get enough coverage. Reporters were always climbing around the rubble, filming, putting their lives in danger.

And it wasn't just television and newspapers. Flickr and Tumblr and Instagram were full of pictures of teeth and blood. In the beginning, an amateur videographer uploaded footage of long-limbed vampire girls feeding on a shock-faced middle-aged man. It got hundreds of thousands of hits in a matter of hours. Gossip columns ran long pieces on vampires who acquired an almost celebrity status, their string of kills only seeming to increase interest.

Vampires were fairy tales and magic. They were the wolf in the forest that ran ahead to grandmother's house, the video game big boss who could be hunted without guilt, the monster that tempted you into its bed, the powerful eternal beast one might become. The beautiful dead, *la belle mort*. And if, after gorging themselves in an orgy of death, they became less lovely, if they became bloated and purple and horrible, then they hid it well.

Everyone was afraid to die and vampires never would. It was tempting to wish to be one, even if not everyone had the courage to try.

But everyone wanted to see one, if from afar.

And no one really wanted them gone.

There were seven hot zones in the United States, seven cities kissed by Caspar Morales, seven places brought over into the dark. Of those cities, six became Coldtowns, and five of those Coldtowns remained operational. All but San Francisco had feeds running out, plenty of them corporate-sponsored and lucrative. Between the reality shows about vampire hunters—most of which had a high rate of cast turnover—and the reality shows featuring vampires—there was a very popular one cut from the live feed in Lucien Moreau's Coldtown parlor—the United States stabilized into an odd détente with vampires.

Coldtowns were jails ruled by their inmates. Within them, vampires were free. But any vampire on the outside—without the protection of those walls, whether hiding, newly turned, or committing massacres—was fair game for hunters and for the military.

And if people argued that the system was flawed, that the infection was still spreading, that romanticizing the dead was making the problem worse, well then, one only had to look at how bad things were outside the United States—and how much money there was to be made by continuing to let things stay just the way they were.

CHAPTER 13

He would make a lovely corpse.

—Charles Dickens

When Tana got to the parking lot, Aidan was sitting in the backseat of her Crown Vic with the door open and his legs out. Gavriel was bent over him, one arm on the roof of the car, talking in a low tone. He stopped speaking when he caught sight of her. A breeze blew his hair back from his face, making it look like the ruffled feathers of a crow.

"Hey," Tana said.

Aidan looked a little less sick—his cheeks were even a slight pink. Gavriel had somehow acquired heavy-looking black motorcycle boots. She wasn't sure if he'd had them on when she'd woken up at the Last Stop, but he hadn't been wearing them at the gas station. She remembered his bare feet and the cracked bottle glass he hadn't seemed to notice.

She wondered what he'd done to get those boots.

Please, she thought. *Please, no more. Please, no more horrors tonight.*

"The gates of Coldtown are close as my own shadow," Gavriel said. His wine-colored eyes studied her in her new dress and combed hair, as if he was trying to memorize the way she looked. It made her conscious that she was wearing barely more than a slip, and she pulled at the hem awkwardly. "You can turn me over to the guards when we arrive. There's a reward for vampires, I'm told."

Tana gave Aidan a look, remembering what he'd said at the gas station. "I wonder who might have mentioned that."

Just then, Midnight came up behind Tana, looking between Gavriel and Aidan intently. "Is he okay?" She tucked blue hair behind her ears.

"He will be," said Gavriel. "He'll be a new creature made from old skin."

Aidan tilted his head toward Midnight. "Sorry about...you know. I hope I can still come to Coldtown with you."

Tana wanted to object to his giving up on getting better, but resisting blood would just get harder with time. He was being realistic. And who was she to tell him to throw away immortality?

Midnight gave him a wavering smile. Winter, behind her, glowered. He had two overstuffed black garbage bags slung over one shoulder and a beat-up suitcase hanging from his other hand.

Since she'd listened to her phone messages, an awful numb calmness had settled over Tana, one that she was afraid to consider too closely, one that fed on bad ideas and adrenaline. She ached to make awful choices, to drown out all her thoughts in a cacophony of *doing*. She wished it was an unfamiliar feeling, that ache, the urge that made her hit the gas when she ought to hit the brake.

She hoped this wasn't one of those decisions.

But she couldn't imagine pleading with her father through the door to let her in, couldn't imagine trying to prove that she wasn't infected—if she even turned out not to be—and didn't want to upset Pearl.

Sometimes it seemed as though all her life was already used up in that dark basement, as if her mother's mouth on Tana's arm was the last thing in her life before this that had felt *real*. Everything else was just prologue and epilogue. A grace period of pretending that her life was going to be like other people's, that the bite didn't mark her as already touched by darkness, fated for darkness, a girl with one foot already in the grave.

"Instead of money, you can get a marker if you're turning in a vampire," Tana said, her mind finally starting to plan a future for herself, one where she came out ahead, one where she could survive. "A marker that lets one person out of Coldtown. We could get one of those. *I* could get one of those, if Gavriel will let me turn him in."

She'd seen pictures of markers, silver and iron disks with symbols around the outer rim, gold at the center surrounding a small hole, and supposedly some kind of chip inside. There was an heiress who ran away to Coldtown; her parents, hoping to lure her out, hired bounty hunter after bounty hunter to get markers for her. She made a necklace out of them and wore it to the Eternal Ball every night until a gang member slit her throat and sold them off to the highest bidder.

If Tana went inside with Gavriel and Aidan now, she'd be going to Coldtown with a way out. If she went Cold and got caught later, she'd be chucked into a Coldtown anyway and then she'd be stuck there.

Her nihilistic plan was actually starting to make sense.

"Tana," Gavriel began. "You should not—"

"Yes, please come, Tana," Aidan said, cutting him off. He grinned in that persuasive way he had, half as if he'd be lost without you and half as if he thought he'd done you a favor by suggesting the thing you secretly wanted. "Think of all the fun we're going to have. Midnight's going to show us around, right? She forgives me, doesn't she?"

"I don't know. That really hurt," Midnight said lightly, a teasing half smile on her mouth. Her gaze was hungry, though, focused on Aidan and Gavriel. Every part of her vibrated with yearning to be as they were. Changed or changing.

"I shouldn't have done that," Aidan said, and his expression was a match for hers, full of greedy desire.

"You know what I want in return," Midnight said silkily. "We didn't tell on you. We proved we're worthy. Your friend's probably hungry and if he wants, he can—"

Gavriel grabbed her chin before she could even gasp, swift and deadly as a shark rising from the depths. "Unless I am much mistaken, you told *everyone*. I saw your phone; do you think I don't know what it does? I should drain you both and leave your bodies as a warning to those who seek death as if it were some hidden treasure."

Midnight's skin was flushed, her eyes bright. It was as though the words rolled past her and all she saw was the nearness of his mouth. Tana took a step closer, despite herself, drawn into the same delusion.

"Let her go," Winter said. He pulled at Gavriel's shoulder, but the vampire boy didn't move.

"Perhaps Midnight and I should show Aidan what it is to truly feed, what it would be like for him if he tasted blood." He spoke the words sweetly against Midnight's ear, as if to a lover. She swayed against him, his arm coming up and tightening, holding her in place. She looked confused then, instinct tinting her expression with the beginnings of panic. "I can hear your heart beating, like a wounded animal hurling its broken body against the walls of its cage. A pretty song."

Tana thought of what Gavriel had said in the car. *There is a madness that comes over us . . . a madness that can be cured only by feeding.* Gavriel had given some of his blood to Aidan—that was what he'd obviously been intending to do when he sent them away. And how else could Aidan be so much better, unless something hadn't taken the edge off his craving?

But that meant Gavriel must be very hungry.

"We don't have time for this," Tana said desperately, trying to sound reasonable despite her frayed nerves. "Gavriel. We have to get to the gate before dawn. There might be paperwork—or a line. It's not safe to stay here anymore."

Gavriel wasn't looking at her. He contemplated Midnight's throat.

"It's definitely not safe to *kill someone* here," Tana said, louder, touching his arm. It had worked in the past, being calm, acting as though everything were normal. She hoped it would work again. "Gavriel, we have to go. Stop being so scary."

At that, he looked over and smiled again, spinning Midnight in his arms as if they'd been dancing. Winter caught her and held her upright.

"I can wait a little longer," Gavriel said. "A very little longer."

"The car keys," Tana demanded, holding out a trembling hand. He fished in his pockets—an utterly normal gesture—then dropped them into her palm ceremoniously. She picked up the bag of cash and jewels from beside the hood of the car, shoving it into her purse.

"I won't always obey you," he said softly. "One night you will ask me for something I cannot give."

She'd started to relax, but his words sent a fresh spike of terror up her spine. Marching to the driver's side, she closed her eyes and took a deep breath, trying to steady herself before she got in, then slamming the door behind her. She was shaking again and mad about it.

"What is it about vampires?" Aidan muttered as he walked toward the car. "Only ever interested in biting people that don't want to get bit."

Midnight sniffed, offended. "He was interested."

"Didn't bite, though," said Aidan, getting into the backseat of the car.

"Midnight." Winter touched his sister's arm. His voice carried in the parking lot. "We don't have to go with them."

She looked at him coldly. "No more birthdays."

Tana turned the ignition, listening to the comforting growl of the motor and inhaling the faint burned-plastic scent of the heater. The clock on the dashboard read a little after two in the morning. Gavriel took shotgun; Winter and Midnight joined Aidan in the back. Winter made sure he got in before his sister, positioning himself in the middle like some kind of chaperone—as if, when the infection kicked back into high gear, Aidan was going to care whom he attacked. Not to mention that Aidan liked boys just fine anyway.

It was easy to get to Coldtown, even without looking at a map. All Tana had to do was follow the path of warning signs. RESTRICTED ACCESS 15 MILES, the first one said, sending her turning onto an empty four-lane road riddled with potholes. They passed abandoned industrial parks, large dirt lots with the burned-out remains of cars, scrub bushes, and shadow.

The original barricades had annexed about a third of a small city, but by the time the towering gates were built, more like half the city was considered under quarantine. The walls of the Coldtowns went up with lots of regular people trapped inside. The rest moved as far away as they could as quickly as they could. Every house they passed was dark inside.

They drove for a couple of miles until Gavriel said, "You're going to have to restrain me."

She looked at him in alarm, her hands jerking the wheel. The car swerved in its lane.

The vampire grinned lopsidedly, showing one sharp tooth. "There's a checkpoint coming in maybe a mile. If I'm to be your captive, I must look the part. Otherwise, I'm bound to make them nervous."

"A checkpoint?" Aidan said, leaning forward in his seat. "Like, cops?"

"Homeland Security," said Winter. "And sometimes the National Guard. He's right. People posted about them on the boards. They're just going to ask us what we're doing here. Probably try to tell us we're not allowed through. But they can't keep us out; they just bluster."

Midnight looked up from her phone. "Gate guards think anyone who wants to live inside is scum." Her tone was acid.

"They're not going to think that, since we've got him with us. They're going to think we're badass bounty hunters," said Aidan.

Tana pulled onto the dirt shoulder of the highway with a sigh. In the distance, behind a stretch of trees and down a slight hill, she could see a McDonald's with all the windows smashed in and graffiti covering the booths inside.

"How did you know about the checkpoint?" Midnight asked Gavriel softly, leaning forward in her seat so that she was asking the question over his shoulder.

"Research," he told her, then turned to Tana. "Once we're there, you must go home. Death has passed you by twice, Tana. Don't court him a third time."

"No, she's *got* to come with us," Aidan said, leaning into the gap between seats. "You are coming, aren't you, Tana? You won't let me go on this adventure alone, will you?"

"There is nothing for her beyond those gates," Gavriel said. "Do you think to bring her along like a talisman to remind you of your humanity? Or do you think sharing your damnation will lighten the burden of it?"

"You seem to like her," Midnight said archly. "Maybe she'll lighten your burden instead of his."

Gavriel gave her a look as though he might reach into the backseat and snap her neck. Then he threw back his head and laughed an eerie, wild laugh. "Clever girl. You play with fire because you want to be burnt."

"*Midnight*," Winter said through clenched teeth.

Tana got out of the car, slamming the door behind her. The trunk was already half open, Gavriel having bent it when he kicked his way free at the gas station; it didn't close right anymore. She fished for the chain beneath Winter and Midnight's garbage bags, willing her breathing to even out.

Gavriel caught her arm, his fingers cool against her skin.

She gasped in surprise, pulling away and taking a staggering step back. She hadn't even heard him get out of the car.

"I didn't mean to—" He stopped, and when he spoke again, he sounded oddly formal. "Tana, I have no skill in this—I am long out of practice at keeping my thoughts clearly ordered and the sort of persuasion that might convince you may be beyond my clumsy tongue." He brought his hand up to touch her hair, the brush of his fingers so light that she wasn't sure if he'd actually touched her at all. "You're brave and you're good, anyone can see that—you dared to save even an unhappy creature like myself, merely because I needed saving. You have parried everything this night has thrust at you. But surely it's enough. Whatever is driving you—please, please let it drive you no further."

"You think I want to die," Tana said. "I don't. That's not what this is about."

He shook his head. "I mean only—do not come to Coldtown. You may love Aidan and you may think you can save him..."

For a moment, Tana was confused. Then she remembered Aidan's arm slung over her shoulders as he, introduced her to Midnight and Winter. "Oh, no, it's not like that. Aidan isn't my *boyfriend*. I know he said he was, but—"

Gavriel's red eyes narrowed, but she couldn't read his expression. She stumbled on. "He *used* to be and he just said that because—because that's the way he is." Tana peered into the backseat of her car, where Aidan and Midnight were talking. Winter sat between them, fitting a cigarette into a long, pretentious holder, his body hunched forward. Tana sighed. "He didn't mean anything by it. I think he thinks about *girlfriend* like some kind of honorary title, like the way that every president is still 'President So and So,' no matter who's currently in office."

Gavriel started to say something else, but Tana held up her hand to stop him. She was babbling, but she wanted to see her babbling through. "Listen, back at the farmhouse, on my way out, one of the—" *Monsters*, her brain supplied. "One of them got me on the leg. It's not deep or anything, but—but it was his teeth. He was trying to bite me. He *did* bite me—a little." Saying it out loud made it real all over again. She could feel herself start to shake.

He looked at her with alarming intensity, his red eyes like hot coals. "Where?"

She turned a little, to show him the back of her leg. The dress was short enough to show the bottom edge of the scrapes.

He crouched down, pressing cool fingers just above her knee. Her breath caught in surprise. He pushed up the hem of her skirt slightly, hands gliding over her skin, making the tiny hairs stand up all along her thigh.

She threaded her fingers together, pressing her hands against the front of her dress, against her stomach, to keep them from trembling, to keep the rest of her from moving. She wanted to laugh, nerves jangling. It was so strange to be touched so gently by a creature like him—a creature who looked just like the kind of boy who you might let touch your thigh for a totally different reason. "So you see, it's not like I have a death wish or I'm into some kind of adventure tourism or I knocked my head too hard when I hurled myself out that window." She realized that she'd started babbling again, but she didn't know how to stop. She thought about how she hadn't shaved her legs since Saturday night and there was probably stubble. "If the cops catch up with me, they'll dump me in some place for observation. And if it turns out I'm infected, then I get sent to Coldtown anyway. This way, I can get a marker and have a way out—if it turns out I don't get sick or even if I do and I make it through somehow. And I won't have to go in alone. So, you see, it all makes sense. . . ."

"There's a very small puncture," he said, moving his fingers again. She bit her lip to keep from making a sound. "Just one—and the scratch his teeth made dragging over your skin."

"Deep?" she asked.

He let the skirt of the dress fall and braced his hands on his knees, looking up at her. His hair was black as crow feathers and falling across one of his eyes. "I can't tell. There's a bluish tint to the scab."

For a moment, she couldn't breathe. Blue meant poison. Blue

meant that like some family curse, she was going to wind up just like her mother—hungry and sick and screaming. Blue meant the worst was likely happening.

"Tana, you might yet be well," he said, but she didn't believe him. He was just being nice.

She heard the door of the car open and Aidan laugh. "What are you guys *doing*? I mean, she has good legs and all, but is this really the time?"

Gavriel stood up slowly. Embarrassed over any possible guesses about what she'd been doing and sick with the thought of the poison in her blood, Tana started to busily dig under Midnight and Winter's garbage bags to pull out the chains. She tried to look busy, hiding her face from Aidan. Grabbing the coiled metal, she rubbed her thumb over a link and realized that the steel was wound through with wild rose vine.

Even upset as she was, her brain noted that was one of the things vampires aren't fond of. Soon, maybe, she'd find out for herself what was true and what was just left over from a thousand scary stories that weren't ever supposed to happen.

"Hey," she called back to the car, her voice coming out unintentionally harsh. "Anyone have a lock?"

Midnight slid out. "I think there's one back there. We brought it in case we needed to secure a squat. Let me look." She got closer to Tana and then stopped, studying her face. "Everything okay?"

Tana nodded, wiping her cheek with the back of her hand. She hadn't even realized her eyes were wet.

Midnight looked over at Aidan and Gavriel, then back at Tana, as though trying to read something in their faces. "We can tie him up," Midnight said, finally. "If you want. You don't have to do it."

"No," Tana said, dragging the chain toward Gavriel. "I'm fine."

"Fine, fine, everyone's fine," said the vampire, a mad gleam in his red eyes, crossing his arms over his chest as Bela Lugosi did in black-and-white films. "Fine as scattered pieces of sand."

She wondered how much effort it had taken him to talk to her the way he had—to, what was it he'd said? *Keeping my thoughts clearly ordered*—and how crazy he was going to be now, as a result of that strain. She thought about him talking to the border guards and shuddered.

She couldn't imagine herself changed into a being such as he was. He seemed as alien and remote as a distant star in the sky.

Gavriel let Aidan and Tana drape him in chains and let Midnight lock them tightly around him with Winter's old bicycle lock. Then he shuffled back to the passenger door and dropped himself heavily into the seat, cocooned in silvery links.

They all got back in, Midnight maneuvering so that she was in the middle of the backseat, meaning Aidan was next to her. Winter gave her an exasperated look, which Tana caught in her rearview mirror.

She felt strange as she pulled back onto the highway, her hands unsteady on the wheel. Somehow, *knowing* that the scab was bluish convinced her that she could feel the swelling of the skin of her thigh around the wound, that she could feel the Cold in her, icy sludge moving through her veins.

It was kind of a relief to know that the inevitable had come, though. She didn't have to be afraid anymore. What was happening inside her didn't care whether she was scared.

The car rounded a curve, and the checkpoint came into view. It was just a few cones and a single police car with lights flashing.

"Tell them I'm like you," Gavriel said as they began to slow down.

Aidan laughed. "I think they can see you're not like us anymore."

"No," he said. "Tell them you know me. That I'm like you, one of you. From the party. Tell them."

"Wait," said Winter. "Wait. Is he saying he *wasn't* at the party? Did you meet him by the side of the road? Did you pick up a hitch-hiker who coincidentally turned out to be a *vampire*?"

Gavriel fixed his gaze on Winter. "You know me," he said, and a chill went up Tana's spine. "You've known me since outside the rest stop, when I turned and the light hit my face."

"What does he mean?" Midnight asked.

"I don't know," Winter said in an odd voice. "Nothing."

"We'll call him Maynard McSmollet and he can be from two towns over," said Aidan, snickering. "No one really knew him that well, kept to himself, but he was crashing the party because he could never resist a kegger—or how about Roderick Spoon? Roddy. The Rodster. He was in band and played electric keyboards but got kicked out of several schools for setting small fires. Yeah, that's better. What do you think, Gavriel?"

And then there was no more time for suggestions, because the car was pulling up to the officer. A gloved fist tapped a heavy black Maglite against the window. Tana lowered the glass, heart thudding dully.

The guard was middle-aged, his short military-cut hair peppered with gray and his uniform not the kind that local cops usually wore. He had craggy skin and looked down at her with a lip curl of disgust.

"You kids can't be out this way. No sightseeing. Go on, turn around and—" The guard shone the light in the car, stopping when it reflected Gavriel's garnet eyes.

Gavriel grinned, teeth bared.

"See? We're not tourists," Winter said from the back.

The guard stepped back. "You kids are crazy. Did you catch that thing?"

"He was—he's our friend," Tana said, hoping she sounded convincing. "Just turned. We're taking him to the gate."

"You better get on out of the car," said the guard, reaching for his belt and detaching something from it—a weapon, Tana was pretty sure, until he brought a radio to his mouth. "I'll take things from here. Jesus, you didn't even muzzle him."

"That's okay. We'll drive him ourselves." Tana looked ahead of them at the dark stretch of road. Bad things happened in places like this. She glanced at Gavriel, his gaze fixed on the guard's throat.

"Come and muzzle me," the vampire said, his voice like honey.

"Step out of the car," the guard ordered. "All of you. Move! Now!"

She jumped, startled.

If she slammed her foot on the gas, she'd hit a cone and maybe the side of the guard's car, but she could get them past the stop. She took a deep breath and got ready. The Crown Vic was a heavy car—not the best acceleration, but once it got going, it stayed that way. And they'd have a head start. Maybe they'd even make it to the gate before they were arrested.

But before she did anything, Winter leaned forward in his seat. "Hey!" he shouted at the guard. "We've got rights. According to the law, we have the right to the bounty on him, so if you think you can scare us into giving it up, try again."

Tana looked at Winter in surprise.

"Damn," Aidan said under his breath. "You think he's going to shoot us now? I'd really rather he didn't shoot us."

"Your friends, huh?" the guard said with a sneer, leaning his head through the window and narrowing his eyes at Gavriel. "You know what those friends of yours are planning? They're gonna sell you. We don't get a lot of corpses going in willingly."

Tana saw Gavriel's fingers moving, subtly shifting chain. He wasn't tied particularly carefully. In a moment, he'd work his arm free. In a moment, he'd grab the guard, drag him across Tana's lap, and sink his fangs into the man's throat. She saw the way it would play out, the shock, the screaming, the geysering red running down the inside of the windshield.

Maybe she was closer to going Cold than she'd thought, because picturing it didn't horrify her. Instead, she wondered what it would feel like if it were her fingers closing on the guard's neck, her teeth tearing his skin. She imagined she could smell him, his stale cigarette breath, the brine of his sweat, and underneath all of that, welling up through his pores, the unique scent of his blood.

Then the guard leaned back from the window, out of danger, and clicked a button on the radio. He spoke into the static. "Yeah, I've got a car of kids here with a corpse. Say they're going to claim a bounty on it. Yeah, it seems in on the joke. I know, world's full of crazy."

Tana blinked herself out of her dazed imaginings to find that they were being waved through the checkpoint.

→ CHAPTER 14 ←

POST BY: MIDNIGHT

SUBJECT: THE TEN MOST IMPORTANT THINGS
TO BRING TO COLDTOWN

---

1. Cash and lots of it. You can barter for lots of things inside, but cash is still the most important tool for bribing guards and getting what you want. You've been saving up, right? Bring every last penny. It's not like you're coming back.

2. Batteries, chargers, extension cords, small solar generator, phone, video recorder—plus your laptop, of course. You might have to bootleg your energy source to get your feed up and running, but then you'll be able to share your adventures with the rest of us and hear us pining away to join you. Having an effective way to communicate with the outside world might turn out to be profitable, too. Lots of Coldtown stars were just like you when they started.

3. Clean cannulas (hollow needle and length of tubing) and means of sterilization for venipuncture (rubbing alcohol, hydrogen peroxide, bleach, matches, or lighter). Think about putting this in a pretty case that you can bring to clubs or parties and show off. Sure, it would be great if you didn't have to use any of that, but most Coldtown vampires aren't going to bite you straight off. They only turn people they really care about.

4. Your stuff. Clothes, shoes, shampoo, perfume, jewelry, makeup—only bring the things you really love, because once you're through the gates, you're going to be on foot and traveling light, but also remember that everything's harder to come by in Coldtown. Dragging a bigger suitcase might be worth it when you're trying to find that perfect outfit. Think about the person you want to be—and the person you want to impress—and dress for them.

5. Stuff for trade—good booze, good weed, cans of luxury food, fresh produce, clothes, and medicine. (Antibiotics, aspirin, and other painkillers are especially valuable.) All this stuff will help you hold on to your cash reserves a lot longer—and maybe even increase them significantly.

6. Mace and other means of defense. We know how special Coldtown is and we're such a supportive community online that it's hard to imagine there are people beyond the gate who aren't like us, but with no police or anything, we have to be careful.

Newcomers are considered prey by bands of unworthy wannabes, so don't be taken in by the kids near the gate telling you about great squats or secret clubs. Don't let anyone touch your bags, either, and be ready to defend yourself if necessary.

7. Something to make yourself stand out from the crowd—whether it's your intricate poetry or the parrot-skull necklace that shows your quirky personality or the violin you've been practicing since you were a child—bring the thing that shows off the way you're unique. You want the vampires to see why you deserve to live forever.

8. List of contacts. The great thing about these message boards is that we have friends who've already crossed over that can show us the ropes when we arrive. You'll want to get in touch with them and make a plan to meet up once you're there, so be sure you have information like addresses, phone numbers, etc., printed out in case of electronic failure. Also, sad to say, keep in mind that some people are more willing to share their connections and good fortune than others. If you get a bad feeling about someone, even if you know them from the boards, steer clear.

9. Your sponsors and ways to contact them. It's always possible that you'll run into a snag in your plans, run out of money, get robbed, or even get hurt. If that happens, you need to know the people who you can call on to send cash and extra sup-

plies. Make sure you have the contacts for your parents, grandparents, distant family, friends, online blog followers—anyone who, in a pinch, might be persuaded to give you money. Remember, too, that being inside Coldtown, there are images and experiences that you have access to that you might be able to trade for what you need. It's not ideal, but it's something we all have to think about.

10. A buddy. Trust me, you'll need one.

CHAPTER 15

To die is landing on some distant shore.

—John Dryden

The gates loomed in front of them from several miles away, towering above the tops of trees and bright with floodlights. They'd been built after the outbreaks, at the height of superstitious fervor, and were constructed from planks of sacred oak, ash, and hawthorn— all soaked in holy water and then nailed with thousands of silver devotional symbols from around the world. And beyond that, the tallest of the ruined halls, factories, and church spires were visible inside the walled city, some glowing with flickering light, some overgrown with a heavy carpet of ivy.

It looked nothing like a prison. The gates seemed as if they were the doorway to an ancient temple or the opening to some enchanted country. Tana had seen them before, on the news, but somehow, in footage from helicopter-mounted cameras, they hadn't radiated the same feeling of majesty they did now.

As they rounded a bend in the road, the guard station came into view. It was small and ordinary, resembling a tollbooth. Two guards in heavy flak jackets stood together out front, sharing a cigarette. They looked up at the car when its headlights swung through the gloom, but they made no move to pick up their flamethrowers.

"Pull in over there," Winter said, touching Tana's shoulder and pointing toward a stretch of cracked asphalt curving down into overgrown grass. Other cars were parked haphazardly, some covered in a thick layer of grime. A hand-printed sign nailed to the post of a streetlight read TEMPORARY PARKING ONLY, a corner of it flapping in the wind. Underneath it, another metal sign read RESTRICTED ACCESS AREA. PERMIT REQUIRED.

Tana pulled in and stopped her Crown Vic next to a beaten-up station wagon. She looked at the clock on her dashboard. In less than two hours the sun would be coming up.

"I'm going to walk over there and figure out the paperwork or whatever for bringing him in," she said, turning in her seat. "Winter, you better come with me, since you knew what to say to that guard."

Winter glanced at Aidan warily. Aidan winked.

"Here," Tana said, ignoring them as she pressed her keys into Midnight's hand. "If something goes wrong, just get the hell out of here before sunrise."

"Oh, no," Gavriel said, pulling a hand free and unlooping more chain. "If there's trouble, I would be at its heart."

"The sun's coming up soon," Tana reminded him. "And stop messing with the chains—you need to keep all that on until we get inside. You're still supposed to be our prisoner, remember? This is *your plan.*"

He shook his head. "You bid me to bide, but if I'm to burn, then surely you will let me put that fire to some use."

If his lazy, crazy half smile and the gleam in his garnet eyes were any indication, he meant every word he'd just said. He wanted trouble. But why he thought she could let him or stop him from doing anything, she had no idea.

Midnight grabbed for Tana's fingers and squeezed them. "Just don't take any crap from those guards, okay? Get that marker. No matter what happens, it's worth a lot. We're going to storm into Coldtown like heroes, you know that? People are going to talk about us online for months."

"Careful," Winter told his sister, nodding toward Aidan, who gave him a look of wide-eyed innocence in return, and then toward Gavriel, who was staring out into the darkness, thinking whatever thoughts blood-starved vampires who liked to quote Shakespeare had.

"Oh, no." Midnight sounded giddy. "We left *careful* back home, along with *uptight* and *normal.*"

Tana got out of the car, taking a deep breath of air, leaving the twins to bicker. It was odd to be in such a desolate place and be able to hear the distant hum of music amplified by speakers and smell cooking on the other side of the gates. Not just cooking, either. The scent of wood smoke and burned plastic drifted to her nose from the city beyond, along with another smell, a sweet foulness that took her a moment to recognize as rotten flesh. It made her think of sitting on the rug in the living room of the farmhouse with her friends' bodies around her.

"Winter," she said. "Come on."

For a long moment, he stayed where he was, staring at his sister, having an argument entirely consisting of things unsaid. Midnight played with one of her lip rings, turning it nervously. After a moment, Winter sighed and slid out of the car, slamming the door behind him.

"The faster we get back, the less can happen," Tana said, hoping that would reassure him. She was nervous, too.

"You're really going to Coldtown with us?" he asked, falling into step beside her as she crossed the empty black road.

"Yeah, I guess." She took a deep breath; it was unfair not to warn them of the situation they were putting themselves in by traveling with her. "I'm infected—I think. I mean, probably. I've got a few hours before I'll be sure."

Winter looked over at her in surprise. "Probably?"

"It's not a good thing," she said. "Don't act like it's a good thing."

He took out another black cigarette from his silver case, fitted it into his cigarette holder, and lit it. The air smelled like lemongrass and incense. "You want one?" he asked, his expression growing calculated. "They're herbal."

Tana shook her head. She didn't want anyone to see the nervous tremble of her hands.

The guards watched them walk closer. One was smoking, leaning against a flamethrower about the size and shape of a rifle. The other pointed his weapon directly at Tana. Both looked bored.

"Everything okay?" the guard asked.

"Um," Tana said. "Yeah. We want to know how to turn in a vampire for the bounty. The guy at the checkpoint called ahead...?"

The guard flicked his cigarette onto the concrete and stomped on the butt. "You kids have a vampire?" He and his partner shared a significant glance.

"Maybe," Winter said, taking a long drag on one end of the lacquered holder.

The guard dropped down the barrel of his weapon and then leaned on it, mirroring his partner. He cocked his head to one side, evaluating them. "Okay. So if I were to go across the street—"

"Just tell us how it works," Tana said. "We're going through the gates—all of us—and we want a marker."

"Oh yeah?" the other guard asked. "A bunch of kids want to go into the quarantined area with all the freaks and ticks? You get dropped on your head too many times? Your mommies not understand you?"

"You say the company in there is bad." Winter tapped on his cigarette holder, causing a line of ash to fall to the dirt, and gave the guards his most sneering, contemptuous stare. "Seems like the company out here is even worse."

The guards chuckled.

"The office is that way," one of them said, pointing toward the administrative buildings to one side of the gates, built of stone, with a single window and a cheap, flimsy door. "You want to kill yourselves, go right ahead. Just fill out the forms first. And if you've got a vampire, well, congratulations. Just be sure he's not some kid with red contact lenses." They laughed again at that, clearly filing Tana and Winter into the slot of no threat at all.

"Thanks, wow, you sure are helpful," Tana called back with clipped sarcasm, turning and walking in the direction they'd indicated.

On the other side of the wall, she heard a high-pitched wail that sounded more animal than human. She shuddered. Winter looked back at the car and took a deep, shaky breath.

After a few moments, it died away. Winter slowed his stride. "Why does he do what you say? The vampire."

"Gavriel?" Tana shrugged. "I have no idea."

"There must be some reason." Winter ground the stub of his cigarette against the wall.

"He was chained up when I found him. The vampires—Aidan heard them say that the Thorn of something or another was hunting for him. It's a Russian city—my brain's fried and I'm blanking on it. You know the guy, though—the one who killed that journalist in Paris. Gavriel is in some kind of trouble with him."

Little mouse.

"An enemy of the Thorn of Istra," Winter said, an odd expression on his face. "That's what he told you?"

"He helped me back at the house," Tana said, not sure why she was feeling defensive. Winter and his sister were supposed to love vampires so much they wanted to *be* vampires; why should he sound as if she were demented for unchaining one? "He's still helping us, remember?"

"But why?" Winter asked. "No offense. I just don't get it. I'll bet he's been a vampire a long time—before the world went Cold, even. Those old vampires hate humans, and they hate people like me and Midnight, specifically—any vampire turned in the last decade and anyone who wants to be a vampire. And here he is, letting us restrain him, voluntarily surrendering to imprisonment in a Coldtown. It doesn't make sense."

I struggle for my most rational moments, Gavriel had told her when they were driving. She'd seen the strain of it since then—moments when he seemed lost and others when he seemed lethal. "I don't know," she said. "He wanted to come to Coldtown, though. He's not doing it for us."

Winter took a moment to digest that, then wrenched open the door to the office. A bell jingled overhead. He held it wide for Tana. She slipped past him and went inside.

As she did, Tana thought of what Gavriel had said to Winter earlier. *You know me. You've known me since outside the rest stop, when I turned and the light hit my face.*

Who was he that Winter could know him? She had a moment of anxious panic that Winter was playing her in some way, but she couldn't think how.

Fluorescent lights overhead bathed the whole room in a harsh, blinding glare that made Tana blink several times. A counter of cheap laminate was covered in sloppy stacks of multicolored forms. Two pens, each attached to dirty string with even dirtier tape, dangled down from either side of the counter. Behind the counter were four metal desks. Only one of them was occupied. A large woman in a bright dress with big abstract poppies on it stood up slowly, as though her knees hurt. Her gray hair was piled into an impressive danish-size bun on the back of her head.

She looked at Tana and Winter for a long moment, then walked over. "What do you kids want? It's four in the morning. Shouldn't you be in bed?"

"We want to claim the bounty on a vampire," Tana stammered.

She was unprepared for how much the way into Coldtown looked like a shoddily run DMV.

The woman's eyebrows went up. "You some kind of baby bounty hunter?"

Tana sighed. "We just need forms for going inside, and we want to turn in a vampire for a marker."

"De-registration?" Now the woman shook her head. When she spoke, she sounded tired. "Don't be stupid. You don't want to go into Coldtown. Take your bounty for the vampire and live another day. One marker isn't going to get the both of you out anyway."

Tana looked at the clock. "There's four of us, not counting the vampire, so please just get us the paperwork. We know what we're doing."

The woman sighed. "Everyone's always in such a hurry to rush off to their own death. Well, hold your horses a minute. We had a woman and her three children—can you imagine!—through two nights ago, so I know the packets are around here somewhere. I just need to find my notary seal."

While she rustled around at her desk, Winter circled the room, stopping in front of a bulletin board with a sea of posters tacked up, one stapled over the next. Most advertised higher bounties for particularly famous or dangerous vampires. A few were from parents looking for someone to take on a commission to buy back their child with a marker—and begging for a hunter who'd charge them a price they could pay. Some promised rewards other than cash: cars, property, old engagement rings, stocks, and even the vaguely ominous ANYTHING WE HAVE, ANYTHING YOU MIGHT WANT, ANYTHING AT ALL.

"Did you ever see the Matilda feed from a couple of years back?"

Winter asked suddenly, looking toward Tana. The spikes of his blue hair had wilted, and his eyeliner was a little smeared under one eye, as though maybe he'd rubbed it without thinking.

Tana shook her head.

"There was this vampire, Matilda, who came to Coldtown. She infected another girl by accident—well, the girl *wanted* to be infected— but anyway, Matilda detoxed her and filmed the whole crazy twelve and a half weeks. And the part that was really fascinating was that sometimes she would sit in front of the camera and talk about what it was like being a vampire. She told us about the people she killed, what blood tasted like, how her vision was different, how *she* was different. She wanted to warn everyone, she said, that being turned wasn't how the Eternal Ball or the Coldtown feeds made it look. It wasn't glamorous or special or anything."

Tana watched his face as he spoke. "And you still want to be a vampire? I mean, that's why you're both going inside?"

"Yeah." Winter's voice was firm, but there was something in his eyes—fear and a kind of awful, drowning look, like a man who is slipping deeper and deeper into quicksand and knows that struggling will just make things worse. "Messed up, right? But somehow Matilda made it seem real—like since it *wasn't* glamorous and special, then maybe I *could* have it. But I know it's what every wannabe coming here wants. Most of them are going to die without getting it. Get used for blood or get turned and find out they're not any better at their new life than they were at their old one."

Tana didn't say anything.

"You think we're going to wind up like them, but we're not."

"I don't think anything," said Tana.

He sighed as if he was annoyed but kept talking anyway. "Midnight was obsessed with it before me—immortality, the dark gift—you should have seen the walls of her room when she was twelve. Scrawled with poetry about eternity and piled with animal teeth, pastel candies in the shape of coffins, pages torn from Edgar Allan Poe books and pasted over her dressers and spattered with her blood. But I was the one that started going on message boards and meeting other kids who wanted to run away to Coldtown. After a while, Midnight wanted us to make our own board, so we could talk about the real stuff—and eventually we realized that it was time to put up or shut up. So we know what we're doing and even if you think—" He stopped speaking abruptly, ripping a page off the wall.

"What is it?" Tana asked.

The woman walked back to the counter, nodding to herself and muttering. She put down a couple of forms in different colors. "This isn't something you do on a lark. Or because you're sad. Or because you're young and stupid. It's forever."

"Thank you for the warning," Tana said coldly, gathering up the papers.

"You kids don't really have a vampire, do you? That's nothing to joke around about—you put down false information and that's a crime. You'd need to present the vampire or, if it was a kill, you need to have preserved the head."

"Oh, we have a vampire all right," Winter said distractedly, darting a glance toward the door. "In fact, why don't I go get everybody? You can start the paperwork, Tana."

"Okay," she said, puzzled.

On his way out, he shoved a piece of crumpled paper into her hand, the same page he'd pulled off the wall.

"I didn't know, honest I didn't," he whispered. "I thought maybe— but I swear, I wasn't sure."

She tried to focus as the gray-haired clerk explained acceptable forms of identification and where Tana would have to stand to get her photo taken and the dotted lines on which she needed to sign, but it was difficult. She kept getting distracted and looking back at the poster she was smoothing out, as though the image on it might change.

The paper promised a $75,000 bounty for the kill or capture of the Thorn of Istra. But it wasn't the amount of money that shocked her—it was the picture.

Despite obviously being the blurry copy of a copy of a copy, she knew him immediately. Gavriel looked as though he'd stepped out of the late nineteenth century, in a smart suit on an old Parisian street, a bow tie over the starched white collar and a derby half hiding his black curls. Gavriel, looking directly at the camera with a sneer on his wide lips and eyes that smoldered with banked fire. Gavriel, holding a walking stick in one hand as though he were going to whip the photographer across the jaw with its silvery handle.

Her first thought was, *what a funny mistake.* The Thorn was hunting Gavriel, had broken out of his cage underneath Paris to find Gavriel. And then she remembered, as she stared at the paper, how when Aidan had insisted the vampires whispering through the door were threatening to take Gavriel back to the Thorn, Gavriel had said, *Not exactly.* He'd tried to tell her, but she hadn't been paying attention.

Not exactly.

The Thorn of Istra, the mad vampire. She thought of the grainy video of him she had seen, head tipped back, so covered in blood that she hadn't remembered his features, hadn't remembered him as looking like anything but a monster, laughing, endlessly laughing.

Mad as a dog. Mad as a god.

Gavriel.

CHAPTER 16

Death, they say, acquits us of all obligations.

—Michel Eyquem de Montaigne

All of Tana's holidays were awful. Her mother's parents would come and hug Tana and hug Pearl and talk about what a tragedy it was that their mother would never see how big they got or how pretty they were. Her other grandparents—her dad's parents—would say little digging things about the state of the house and the girls' wrinkled dresses. They would sigh over how the green beans were overdone or the roast was burned. Tana would hear them late at night telling her dad that he owed it to his daughters to remarry—that it would give them stability and self-esteem. That it would help Tana forget.

Their father had grown up in Pittsburgh. He got a fake ID at fifteen so that he could work in one of the two remaining steel mills with his brothers and father. He worked hard and managed to put himself through two years of community college, majoring in business. From there, he got accepted at a state school in Philadelphia, working as a janitor at a hospital to pay his way.

He met Tana's mother on the way back from the fireworks on the Fourth of July. She was swimming in a city fountain while her art school friends only dipped their feet in. She looked like a beautiful nymph from a painting he'd seen in one of his classes. He waded into the fountain in his clothes, grinning like an idiot, and told her so. A few months later, they were married.

He'd loved her more than he'd ever loved anything. She had been wild and full of manic energy, a whirlwind that could sometimes crash into deep depressions. But other times she'd been gloriously full of fun. Without her at the center of everything, he was lost. No matter what Tana and Pearl's grandparents said, he wasn't interested in remarrying. Sometimes he went on dates, but they always ended quickly. He would come home and head into his old bedroom—a place that was left just as it had been since his wife died—for a while, before retreating to the couch in the den, where he'd slept since her death. The holidays stayed miserable.

Tana's father was the kind of man who believed in doing the right thing, no matter what. Working hard, staying as honest as you could, doing what had to be done. Doing the right thing because it was right. And he believed that the right thing was obvious to anyone who took a minute to think about it.

When his wife got bitten by a vampire and her fever spiked and her skin became chilled, when she begged him not to turn her in, he knew what he had to do. He didn't care about the government billboards and TV spots admonishing people to observe the quarantine. The rich bribed private hospitals to lock up their loved ones in very private rooms. And he knew there were plenty of other working stiffs doing what he did: turning their basements into makeshift prisons with reinforced doors and heavy chains.

The way he saw it, locking up his wife when she'd gone Cold was the right thing to do, so he did it.

Saving his elder daughter from bleeding to death was the right thing to do, too. To keep her safe, he had to kill his infected wife, so he severed her neck with a shovel.

He didn't flinch. He didn't hesitate. He had hated it, but he'd done it just the same. Even though it was a terrible thing. Even though he lived in the past now, plodding through life as if against a heavy storm, so distracted by grief that he could barely remember to do the grocery shopping or turn off the stove after he'd warmed some packaged dinner.

Tana wondered if he had a fantasy like hers, one where he had been the one who was bitten, one where he and his beloved vampire wife were still together. One where they hunted the streets and swam in fountains under a fat, bright moon.

Growing up, Tana thought that she and her dad didn't have much in common. Tana wasn't ever sure what the right thing was, but out here on the road, she couldn't help thinking of him. She wondered whether, if push came to shove and she discovered what it was she was supposed to do, she could be like him and be strong enough to do it. No matter what.

❧ CHAPTER 17 ❧

Coming that close to death you get kissed.
—Debra Winger

Winter came back with Gavriel, who was wound in chains and shuffling. Aidan and Midnight stood beside the vampire, helping him keep balance, while Winter dragged the garbage bags and suitcase that made up their luggage. With flamethrowers raised, guards marched the group into the little office. In the bright light, Tana could see that one of the guards was bigger than the other, with a spray of pimples across his chin. The second guard had the patchy peach fuzz beginnings of a blond mustache. They were no longer laughing. They looked alert, and shocked at having to be, as if it had been weeks since they'd seen any action and maybe months since they'd had to deal with a real vampire.

Gavriel had his head down, hair in his eyes, but when he saw her, he looked up and grinned as though he was having an enormously good time. She studied him anew, the black T-shirt that pulled tight across his chest, the way his black jeans hung low on his hips, the steady gaze of his red eyes. Those clothes weren't his, Tana realized. Those clothes didn't quite fit him, because they belonged to someone else—had probably been stolen from someone else. Probably someone dead. None of it was his.

Tana's heart thudded dully. She thought of the necklace with the broken clasp resting at the bottom of her purse, of the random bills and his new boots. How many people had he killed since he escaped from his cage?

The Thorn of Istra, her mind supplied. *That's the Thorn of Istra.*

Lots. He's killed lots and lots and lots.

Midnight was smiling, too, looping her arm through Aidan's, as if they were going to a party. She tossed her blue hair, and Winter looked over at Tana, his lips pressed together as though he was biting back words.

The gray-haired clerk behind the desk took a plastic card from where it hung on a lanyard beneath her shirt. "I'll swipe them into the holding rooms."

"Who's claiming the bounty on the vampire?" the pimple-faced guard asked.

"I guess me," said Tana, half raising a hand as if she were in school. For a moment, she wondered what would happen if she named him, if she claimed the full bounty. It was a lot of money, enough to pay her sister's way through community college. For catching the Thorn of Istra, they might even throw in the marker. Maybe she'd get her own TV show: *Teenage Bounty Hunter*. The thought made her smother a giddy laugh.

"Take her into number six," the other guard told the gray-haired clerk.

"Where are you going to take—" Tana started.

"Worry not," Gavriel said, a smile stretching his mouth as he reached for the door handle. "I like surprises." He closed his eyes. Long, dark lashes dusted his cheeks as he stretched out his arms, the loosely wrapped chains falling to the floor with a loud clanking sound, his lean muscles thrown into sharp relief under the lights. He looked as if he was getting ready for a fight. He looked more tranquil than she'd ever seen him.

Well, so much for his appearing to be anyone's prisoner.

Maybe what would happen if she named him was that he'd declare the ruse to be up and kill everyone, Tana included. Or maybe he'd just shrug a little ruefully and accept the betrayal. Neither was what she wanted.

As a kid, she'd occasionally wondered what it'd be like to meet a vampire that had been alive for a long time. She'd imagined it being like meeting a very old person, someone with a lot of experiences and a bunch of weird stories about walking around during the French Revolution. But spending time with Gavriel, she thought that every day since the one he'd died was not one where he aged, but rather one where he grew away from humanity. He didn't seem older than he must have been when he died; just entirely stranger.

"This way," a guard said in a trembling voice, and nudged the ancient vampire with the butt of his flamethrower. Tana held her breath, but Gavriel did as he was told, disappearing through a doorway.

Tana was led in a different direction and then up in an elevator.

The clerk took her to a small, dirty tiled room, where she sat on a worn wooden bench and waited for a half hour, all alone. She thought about calling Pauline, about waking her up and telling her the truth, but her phone couldn't get a signal. Finally, a new guard came, looking tired, his eyes bloodshot, as though he'd been pulled from his bed in the middle of the night. He smelled like nicotine and mouthwash. His thinning hair was combed over his bald spot and still damp, probably from a hasty shower.

"Okay," he said, sitting down next to her. He had a pen tucked behind his ear and a clipboard. "There was a vampire attack. A bloodbath, up north. A bunch of kids are dead. You know anything about that?"

"I was there." She thought he probably knew it already, since his expression didn't change. It seemed impossible that only a little more than twenty-four hours had passed since those vampires had crawled through the window of Lance's farmhouse, only ten hours since her leg got scraped by their teeth. "I'm lucky to be alive, and Aidan, well, that's where he got infected, but I guess he's still lucky not to be dead."

Immediately, she worried that she shouldn't have said anything about Aidan, but the guard was nodding as if she wasn't saying anything not already in the report.

He nodded. "How about the other one?"

She started to answer, but then she thought of the crumpled piece of paper in her pocket and what Gavriel had said before they were stopped by the first guard. *Tell them you know me. That I'm like you, one of you. From the party.* Of course. He was hiding in plain sight—

that's why he'd come with them, why he was helping them, because he was going to slip into Coldtown as just some newly turned vampire kid. He didn't want anyone to know that he was the murderous legend from the Père-Lachaise Cemetery.

The image of him laughing, covered in blood, came to her again, unbidden, along with the way he'd grinned at her in front of the gate guards. Maybe killing everyone in this building was his idea of fun, but he'd come to Coldtown for some purpose. Some purpose that required that no one knew he was coming.

"Gavriel? He's some private-school kid who was at the party, got infected, drank some of my blood, and turned. We didn't know where else to go, so I drove them both down here."

"It was their idea to turn themselves in?"

Tana nodded. "They don't want to hurt anyone." She wondered if she might be laying it on a little thick.

"And how about Jennifer and Jack Gan? They say they caught a ride with you from the Last Stop rest area."

Tana smiled involuntarily at their names. They were just so . . . regular, so exactly the kind of names Midnight would despise. Knowing them felt like having a powerful secret.

"That's right," she said. "They seemed nice, and they have some message board connections, so they offered to help us to find a place to stay inside if I drove them."

"And you're making the same stupid mistake they are." The guard frowned. "Kid, you're in shock. You've got survivor's guilt in spades. You shouldn't be making any kind of big decisions right now. Why don't we call your parents and get them to come and get you?

You can think about going into Coldtown later, if that's what you really want."

"I'm getting a marker, aren't I?" Tana held her chin up. "It's not like I can't get out again."

"Your friends are dead. I get it. I saw the pictures. It must have been awful. But those things out there—they might remember being human and they might ape being human, but they're not human anymore. It's supposed to be quarantine in there, but it's closer to a zoo. Even with the marker, you'd have to take a blood test to be allowed to exit. No one infected leaves, under no circumstances. No infected and no leeches get out. Ever. *Even with a marker.* And there are lots of folks big enough and mean enough to jump you for that marker, too. There's desperate people in there."

"I know," Tana said.

He cleared his throat, looking sad. "I got a daughter your age. Tell me why you want to go in. Give me one good reason and I'll stop giving you shit."

I'm probably infected, she thought. That would shut him up. But she didn't want to see the way he'd look at her once she said those words, as though she were already dead.

She took a deep breath. "It's not so much that I want to go," Tana said, trying to string together words that could tell some version of the truth, an honest answer she hadn't even given herself. "No, that's not right. There's a part of me that does. My mom got bitten and here I am, following the path of what would have happened if she'd turned. I'm curious. I want to see." She pulled up her sleeve, showing him the scar on her arm, the mottled and discolored skin, the uneven flesh. "I guess that now that I'm here, I feel like I've been heading this way for a long time without knowing it."

And that was all true. It wasn't the whole story, but she hoped that it was enough to convince him that he couldn't talk her out of going.

"Wait here," the man said after a long moment. He stood up and went out the door, closing it hard behind him. She wondered if that was her psych evaluation. She'd heard something about one, about how you had to be sane enough to be able to say where you were going and why for the authorities to let you into a Coldtown. Back in the old days you had to have a driver's license—suspended was okay—or a state-issued ID card saying you were over sixteen, but not anymore.

They made it easier and easier to give up your life so your neighbors could have the illusion of safety.

Tana sat in the little room, looked at her phone, and watched the minutes tick closer to dawn.

When the door opened, the gray-haired clerk from the front office was behind it.

"You carrying any contraband?" she asked, entering the room and patting Tana down the way airport security did if you set off the metal detector.

Tana wasn't sure what the clerk would consider forbidden, but she wasn't carrying much of anything. She shook her head. After a moment, the clerk nodded and handed her a small manila envelope with a band around it.

"There's your marker and the paperwork that says you got the exclusive bounty on one vampire." The clerk turned and motioned for Tana to follow her. "Also, your de-registration materials. Got it?"

"So if I want to leave Coldtown, I just come back to the gates and present the marker?"

The clerk took a long look at Tana. "You're never getting out, honey, so don't you worry about it."

That so unnerved her that she didn't say anything else as they walked together down a short hallway. The clerk touched her key card to a plate near the door and it swung open. Midnight was there, leaning against the wall of another hallway, the straining garbage bag slung over her shoulder and a beat-up suitcase at her feet. Her blue hair was pushed back from her face, a streak of dye marking her ears. The skin around her eyes looked red and a little puffy, as though maybe she'd been crying.

"Both of you, go on through that door," the woman said. "On the other side, there's a camera halfway up the wall. Take turns looking up into it. It's a retinal-scanning device."

They did. The camera was only a small lens threaded through the concrete block walls. Tana stared up at it for a long moment until it flashed with a flare of light, then she walked deeper into the room. Once Midnight stepped in behind her, the door shut with a whooshing sound and then a metallic click. Airtight, Tana guessed. It had no knob or other means of opening from this side, not even a plate for a key card. She studied the room, noting the reinforced door frames and what she guessed was shatterproof glass set in the small windows at their centers. Unlike the run-down front office, this was serious business. For a moment, Tana wondered if the reason the clerk predicted she wouldn't make it out was that a dozen darts were about to shoot from the walls and kill her. But then there was another single, heavy click along the far wall, and the clerk's voice floated down through hidden speakers.

"Please exit through the opposite door, which is now unlocked. You will be walking into a containment chamber inside the quarantined sector. Once you're outside, wait for me to lower you down and unlock the gate. Then you will have three minutes to enter the city. If you do not enter the city willingly during the three-minute grace period, your entry will be accomplished by force."

"Don't worry!" Midnight yelled. "We can't wait to get the hell out of here."

Tana snorted and they shared an exhausted smile. Then she stepped up to the door on the opposite side and pushed, but at her touch the door opened onto a cage suspended high above Coldtown. For a moment, Tana just looked out in amazement. An open cell was in front of her, rocking gently back and forth, thick black bars on all sides but one, where it was attached to the wall with chains. Midnight stepped past her onto the platform, dumping her stuff on the floor and sinking down next to it.

"Come on," Midnight said. "Are you afraid of heights?"

"I am now." Tana took a deep breath and launched herself onto the platform. It swung a little unsteadily, causing Midnight to grab for the bars and look at Tana with wide eyes. Ignoring Midnight, she tried her best not to look over the side. They were at least four or five stories up, and she could see the tops of several buildings from their odd birdcage-like perch. Smoke rose in a few gray ribbons, and multicolored lights pulsed inside what looked to have once been a church. It was a fallen landscape, the magnificent ruination of a city. Overhead, the sky was already lightening, the pale blue and gold of morning tinting the eastern portion, although bright stars still burned in the west.

Dawn was coming fast.

To the right-hand side, in back of the gate, bodies were being laid out in a single, tidy row. Five rested there, most wound in stained sheets. Two boys were dragging a sixth body, spread out on a plastic tarp, into a place at the end. One of the boys looked up at them, but Tana couldn't read his expression from so far away.

With the sound of metal grating against metal, the cage began to slide abruptly downward. Tana's stomach lurched. Midnight made a small cry of surprise. As they came away from the wall, the door fell from the top, closing with a rusty clang. The cage was something she'd never seen before, not in any of the photos from Coldtown. It felt like something from another time.

"This is crazy," Tana said dizzily.

Midnight looked a little awed herself. "It's because they don't want any doors on the wall to open right onto the city."

The streets below seemed mostly abandoned, although a few stragglers had stopped to watch their descent from a distance. Tana looked out at the city. She felt as though she had stumbled into a world alien and yet familiar. She'd seen it on the news, seen it in the background of the vids of runaways and in the photographs of daring journalists. She had seen the blackened, burned remains of old buildings captured in pictures—seen what had once been a row of storefronts, now with spiderweb shatters in the glass, with blankets and plastic bags covering the empty frames of windows, and the jagged outlines of edifices stretching out toward the far walls. Spires whose panes flickered with light. Great domed buildings pulsing with distant music. A landscape gone feral.

"Hey," Midnight said, pointing down the side of the wall. "Look—the boys."

Tana turned slowly, trying not to make the thing sway more than it was. Aidan, Winter, and Gavriel were in another cage suspended beneath theirs—one that swung in a pendulum-like motion, but went no lower. Gavriel stood with his fingers through the bars, looking out at the orange haze in the east with a smile lifting one corner of his mouth. Winter stood next to him, with Aidan on the floor, his feet dangling through the bars.

"I think ours is broken," Aidan called up to them.

"They mess with vampires like that, I heard," said Midnight, softly, nodding to the wall. "They'll wait as long as they can."

In the dim light, Tana saw scorch marks along the cinder block exterior, ones that seemed to have flared up as if something had been very close to it while burning.

"You've got to get out of there," Tana called. "I really think—"

Gavriel tore the gate off the hinges.

Midnight screamed at the suddenness of it. One moment, the vampire had been looking out at the sky and the next he had peeled back the metal with his hands. Now Tana looked at the warped remains of the hinges, pulled like taffy, and then at Gavriel's face, transformed by whatever power let him do that. His mouth gaped open, fangs evident. When he looked up at her, hunger twisted his features, and she was suddenly glad to be far from him.

He jumped down to the dirt below, landing as easily as a cat.

A few moments later, the cage that held Tana and Midnight hit the ground, too, knocking Tana to her knees. There was a loud buzzing and their door opened. Midnight staggered out, pulling her garbage bag behind her as her brother lowered himself on a loose piece of chain.

They stumbled through a section of road that was probably once a roundabout but was now an asphalt courtyard, an island of overgrown shrubs and weeds at its center.

Aidan followed them, falling clumsily. He got up and brushed himself off, looking back at the wall with horror, as though the reality of their situation had just settled over him.

"Quick," Midnight said, pulling her brother to his feet. "Come on. We've got to get out of here."

"Where are we going?" Aidan called as he ran. He reached for Tana's hand. She took it and they raced after Midnight and Winter.

The streets had been paved a long time ago, but they were cracked now, with deep pits. Tana had to watch each step as she moved, fast as she dared, skipping after Aidan. She looked back once to see that Gavriel was still with them, his face blank.

He must be very, very hungry, she thought. *Very, very, very hungry.*

From the windows of houses, from behind drapes and blinds and shutters, they were being watched. Watched as they stumbled past mounds of refuse, past rats that scattered at their approach and gleaming black flies that rose like an oily mist off rotting food and the long-dead body of a dog.

They turned onto a narrow street, Winter and Midnight dragging their garbage bags and suitcase, looking shaken.

Halfway down the block, Midnight leaned over and braced her hands on her thighs, breathing hard. Her hair hung down, the shadows turning it dark. "We have to figure out where we are," she said.

"Dawn's coming," said Tana, letting go of Aidan. She was winded, too, and leaned against the brick wall. The building opposite it was covered in graffiti, elaborate paintings of dragons of which she could make out only a few details in the gloom.

Midnight knelt down and unzipped her case. "Just give me a minute. I downloaded a bunch of different sketches kids uploaded of the streets. They are the only maps we've got."

"It wasn't supposed to be like this," Winter said tonelessly. He wasn't talking to them, Tana could tell. Maybe he wasn't talking to anybody.

Gavriel moved beside Tana. In the dark, she couldn't see him very well. He just looked like a pretty boy, tall and lanky. She thought again of the crumpled paper in her purse and of him, caged beneath a cemetery. How long had he been there? How long had he looked just as he did now? A hundred years? Two hundred? Could he even remember the press of time? Maybe having stepped outside of it would drive anybody crazy.

"I must go," Gavriel said, pushing back ash-black hair and looking at her with the utter sincerity of the drunk or deranged. "You will take care, won't you? This city is hungry."

"You're going now?" Tana asked him. She should have been relieved, knowing what he was and what he was capable of, but she didn't want him to go. The thought of being alone with Aidan and Midnight and Winter filled her with a nameless anxiety. "It's almost dawn. You don't even know where you're going."

He smiled, a real smile, the kind real boys gave real girls. "It's been a very long time since anyone worried for me."

Ahead of them, Midnight was looking at her tablet. Its glow lit her face from beneath, as though she were going to tell a ghost story.

"They have a friend—" Tana began.

"I have a friend, too," said Gavriel. "And I mean to kill him."

"Oh." Tana took a step back. He was on the run, the same as before, even if the reasons were different. She thought of the vampires at Lance's sundown party, who were doubtless planning to drag him back to the Père-Lachaise Cemetery, where they'd torture him until he got even crazier than he was now. Until his mind was so lost that he could no longer hold on to it even some of the time. He'd broken out once, but she doubted he could do it again. She made her voice as firm as possible. "Don't let them catch you."

He hesitated, clearly surprised by her words. Then he smiled again, inclining his head in a shallow bow, acknowledging everything she'd left unsaid. "Traveling with you was a delight worth any delay, but I can delay no longer."

Midnight straightened up. "Okay, I figured out where we have to go. It's not far." She slung her garbage bag back over her shoulder and began to march down the alley. "Come on," she said, looking back at Tana and Gavriel.

Aidan followed closely, with a worried look at the sky. "Is he going to be—"

"Tana," Winter called. "We're moving."

"Remember what you told me in the car?" she said to Gavriel. "Death's favorites don't die."

"I am no favorite." As he said the words, his expression changed. His fingers closed on her shoulder. His eyes glittered like gems as he bent toward her. "But let me have one last thing I do not deserve."

For a moment, she shrank back automatically, thinking he was going to bite her. Then, stunned, she realized that wasn't what he intended to do at all. His lips brushed hers lightly, as though he was giving her the chance to push him away. She squeezed her eyes shut, to blot out the terrible thing she was about to do, and pulled him closer.

She wasn't supposed to want this.

When he kissed her again, she gasped against his cold mouth— her breath held too long since he didn't need to breathe at all—her tongue sliding against his, brushing against sharp teeth. He was careful, but she still felt the drag of their points against her lower lip. The cool press of his body made her skin feel fevered.

He pulled away from her and touched his mouth, his face full of a gentle amazement. "I didn't remember it was like that."

Tana's heartbeat seemed to have moved into her whole body and thrilled it with a single speeding pulse. Everything was a little blurred at the edges and she wanted—she wanted him to feel like she did, like he'd done something forbidden, wanted to give him something he'd like and *really* wasn't supposed to have, something that would feel wrong, something he wanted.

"Kiss me again," she whispered, reaching up, her fingers sliding through his hair. She almost didn't know herself as she moved against him.

He bent helplessly toward her.

She bit her tongue. Bit it hard, the pain chasing through her nerve endings and alchemizing into something close to pleasure. When her mouth opened under his, it was flooded with welling blood.

He groaned at the taste of it, red eyes going wide with surprise and something like fear. His hands gripped her arms as he pushed her body back against the brick of the wall, holding her in place. He'd been careful before, but he wasn't being careful now as he licked her mouth; and it amazed her as much as it terrified her. He kissed her ferociously, savagely, their lips sliding together with bruising fervor. The pain in her tongue became a distant throbbing. Her fingers dug into the muscles of his back, their bodies pressed so close that he must have felt every hitch in her breath, every shuddering beat of her heart. And as scared of him as she had been, right then she was more frightened of herself.

Gavriel reeled back from her, lips ruddy. He wiped his mouth against the back of his hand, her blood smearing over his skin. Gazing at her for a long moment with something like horror, as though he was seeing her for the first time, he spoke. "You are more dangerous than daybreak."

Before Tana could reply, he stepped into the lengthening shadows of morning and was gone.

✦ CHAPTER 18 ✦

I want to be all used up when I die.
—George Bernard Shaw

When Gavriel was young, Russia was nearing the end of her Golden Age. Revolution was coming, but the aristocracy pretended otherwise, swilling champagne and speaking in perfectly accented French in their gilt parlors. The books of the day gloried in the nobility of suicide, willful decay, and romantic melancholy.

At twenty, Gavriel, called Gavriil then, had inherited his grandfather's voluptuous mouth and flashing eyes, but he didn't seem to be living down to that inheritance. He was the middle child, with a little sister called Katya, sparkling and sharp as a diamond in the Imperial Crown, and an older brother named Aleksander, who was constantly in debt to decadence. Aleksander was a drunk, a gambler, and a womanizer: each a costly habit on its own. Combined, they threatened to bankrupt the family.

Their father, the *vikont*, was three years in the grave when their mother begged Gavriel to talk with his brother and coax him to be more reasonable in his debauches. But it was impossible to convince Aleksander of anything that inconvenienced him now that he'd inherited the title and all the land that came with it.

"You are the good brother," Aleksander would say. "There need only be one of those in a family, don't you think? Two is indecent."

"I will switch places with you if you like, Sasha," said Gavriel. "Irresponsibility is a younger son's portion."

Aleksander would hear none of it. And, in truth, Gavriel was too distracted to make much argument. He had fallen in love with a girl named Roza, met through a friend's sister. Roza had amber eyes and a mass of hair the dark blond of buckwheat honey. When she'd glanced shyly in his direction that first time, a half smile on her mouth, he found that he could barely catch his breath.

Later, he couldn't quite remember what they'd spoken of—only that he'd been desperate to charm her. Incredibly, he seemed to have succeeded. She agreed to let him pay court to her. Her father, the stolid owner of a factory, had more than one daughter to settle and seemed to find Gavriel's title and connections enough to make up for the paucity of his finances.

Love took Gavriel as nothing had before. He was drunk with it. He wrote Roza long letters in which he shamelessly stole lines from Tyutchev to describe her eyes. He cajoled his mother into letting him give her a sapphire ring that could have been sold instead. He took a new interest in his clothes, suddenly aware of every worn cuff and hem on his coats.

The longer it went on, the less Aleksander found it amusing. "You're making a fool of yourself over a merchant's daughter," he would say before Gavriel stalked from the table. "It's one thing to marry her for her money, but you do her too much honor by this display."

Maybe that was what prompted Aleksander. Perhaps he wanted his responsible, careful, dull younger brother back. Or maybe he merely thought that since Gavriel couldn't see what a fool he was making of himself, Aleksander would make a bigger fool of him— big enough to *make* him see.

Whatever the reason, Aleksander set out to and succeeded in seducing and debauching Roza. She wept as she explained, sitting on a silk-covered couch and begging Gavriel not to be angry, that she and his brother had never meant to fall in love.

Gavriel sat stock-still. Inside him roiled such turmoil that he feared that should he move, he would smash every piece of furniture in the room, crack every pane of every window, until there was nothing but shining splinters where the parlor had been.

Instead, he leaned back his head and laughed, a long, cruel laugh that did not seem to belong to the boy Roza had known. It blazed up from deep inside him, from some embers he'd always been careful never to stoke.

"You're a fool," he told her, and watched her stumble out of the drawing room, looking back at him as if he were the betrayer.

She'd go to him now, Gavriel reasoned. For long moments he sat, staring at the wall, willing himself to calm. Finally, he got up, intending to leave the house. On the way through the hall, he passed the library, where Roza was kneeling on the floor, massive skirts billowing around her, hands over her face. Alek was heaping scorn on her, telling her he would never marry a girl who'd already proved herself faithless. She'd misunderstood; he'd promised her nothing. He merely wanted to know what kind of wife his brother would choose for himself. It was a terrible thing, the glee with which Aleksander dismantled every one of her romantic hopes. He had ruined her and he was proud of it.

Gavriel waited until she staggered out, racking sobs threatening to rob her of the ability to walk, before he challenged his brother to a duel. His voice was unsteady when he spoke the words. Aleksander looked at him as if he were a puppy trying to show his teeth.

Then Alek walked to a crystal decanter, pouring out a measure of clear liquid. "Don't be ridiculous."

Gavriel knocked his brother's glass to the floor, shattering it. Then, taking a step toward Aleksander, Gavriel slapped him across his cheek, the sound of skin against skin as sharp as a branch snapped in two.

For a moment, Alek staggered back.

Then, throwing up his hands in resignation, Aleksander agreed to meet Gavriel on the grounds of their estate the following morning, an hour before dawn. He didn't seem particularly concerned, touching his reddened cheek with a grin. He'd been in thirteen duels before and had emerged without so much as a scratch. He was an excellent shot. Gavriel had been Aleksander's second, but he had never done anything more than stand around on the grass and make sure the pistols were properly ready.

One of the servants must have overheard and told the *vikontess*, because she came to Gavriel's room that night and begged him not to go. When he refused, she said she would go to Aleksander and persuade him to apologize for the grave offense.

"I will not forgive him," Gavriel told her. "And I still mean to marry her, do you understand?"

"Roza?" his mother asked, her voice shaking. "You cannot."

"Even if I no longer loved her, I would marry her to prove that he cannot take from me what I will not give. I would do it to spite him. But I do love her."

His mother left, wringing her hands.

The sun was already rising, orange flames licking the sky, when Aleksander arrived at the clearing where the duel was set to take place. He was stumbling drunk. Two of his friends held him up.

They found Gavriel alone, pacing through the snow, the shoulders of his long coat dusted with fresh flakes.

"Ganya!" Aleksander cried out, as though nothing could please him more than the sight of his little brother. "Have you been waiting long?"

Gavriel shook his head. "Not long at all."

"You can't go through with this," said a boy named Vladimir, one of his arms around Aleksander, staggering under his weight.

"Go to the devil," Aleksander said, pulling out of their hold. He drew his own pistol and lurched over the snow, getting closer to Gavriel, waving the gun around. "My little brother wants to defend his honor. Let him! I thought he was too much of a coward. Come on, Ganya. Shoot! What are you waiting for?"

"Sasha can barely stand," Vladimir called. "Don't be stupid."

It was just like Aleksander to steal even this from him, Gavriel thought. To treat the duel as a joke, to treat *him* as a joke. Now his only choices were to take aim at a man about to fall over or to bear the shame of crying off. And Aleksander would laugh at him later. *I wasn't so very drunk*, he would say. *And if I was, so what? If you weren't such a milksop, then surely you'd have—*

Gavriel raised his pistol and shot his brother through the heart.

For a long moment there was only the burn of the gun in his hand and Aleksander's blood staining the snow like spilled rubies. No one spoke. Then Gavriel threw down the gun and began walking back to the house.

He felt as cold as the snow.

By evening, Roza had heard of Aleksander's death. Mad with grief, she threw herself into an icy river and drowned. Gavriel's mother, having lost one son, refused to lose another; she gave Gavriel what jewels hadn't already been sold and sent him to Paris, where the Russian authorities couldn't arrest him.

There, in Paris, he fulfilled the promise of his voluptuous mouth and passionate eyes. He fulfilled the promise of his blood. If his brother was bad, he was determined to be worse. He drank absinthe to his brother's wine. He gambled away the boots right off his feet. And if Aleksander had been a rake, Gavriel was determined to best him by never saying no, not to even the crudest, most degrading and vile offers, not to anything.

That was when he met Lucien.

CHAPTER 19

You crave one kiss of my clay-cold lips;

But my breath smells earthy strong;

If you have one kiss of my clay-cold lips,

Your time will not be long.

—The Child Ballads 78: The Unquiet Grave

Eyebrows raised, lips caught in midscoff, Aidan was watching Tana from the mouth of the alley. Midnight smirked, looking into her phone and thumbing something on the screen, while Winter glowered impatiently beside her. The wind caught Midnight's and Winter's hair, which blew like two blazes of deep blue sky.

"Well, that was *interesting*," Winter said, sour-voiced.

Tana rubbed her hand against her face, her thoughts too chaotic to make any sense. All she knew was that she was embarrassed. Her face felt hot and her tongue stung, reminding her of what she'd been doing. "You waited."

Aidan took a step toward her, the smile leaving his face. "Hey. You okay? He didn't hurt you, did he?"

To get that reaction, her expression must be very strange, Tana realized.

Midnight rolled her eyes, as though Aidan was being ridiculous. "I bet you were a good girl back home," she said to Tana. "A good girl all your life until you finally met the trouble you want to get in."

"You obviously don't know her at all," Aidan told Midnight gruffly. Then he turned back to Tana. "Did he bite you?"

She shook her head. The more she thought about it, the more stupid she felt. She was probably infected, but that didn't mean she should have tempted him into making it a sure thing. And, hungry as he was, crazy as he might be, he could have drained her dead, pinned her against the brick wall, and ripped out her throat. She'd been playing with fire, just as he'd accused Midnight of doing.

Clever girl. You play with fire because you want to be burnt.

At that thought, a feeling of vast exhaustion came over her. They'd made it beyond the gates of Coldtown, and Tana was tempted to lie down amid the refuse, close her heavy eyes, and pretend away everything else. She'd done her best to protect the world from what she and Aidan would become, and now that that was done, despair settled on her shoulders.

She didn't want to be infected.

She didn't want to think about the taste of her own blood, or about how, if she sucked hard enough on her own tongue, the taste would bloom fresh in her mouth.

She rubbed the scar on her arm and thought about what it must feel like to press teeth against skin, about what her mother must have had to do to rip open an arm. She stopped herself in the unconscious act of bringing her own wrist to her lips.

Winter sighed and took her by her elbow, steering her down the street. "You sure he didn't bite you? You're acting weird."

"I'm *fine*. I just didn't think, you know," she said finally, stumbling along the cracked concrete sidewalk beside him and smiling a little guiltily. "I didn't think they could even *like* that sort of thing."

Winter's lip curled at the edge. "You sure looked as though you—"

"Okay, okay." She lifted her hands, interrupting him, warding off the words. She remembered looking at Gavriel's mouth, smeared with Aidan's blood, when he got into the driver's side of the car back at the gas station. She'd thought about kissing him then, sure. But it was one of those messed-up fantasies that people have when they're under stress. Sick, but harmless. It wasn't like he was ever going to know.

"Haven't you watched the feeds?" Winter asked her, more gently. "Vampires like anything and everything that keeps them from getting bored. *Anything* and *everything*."

She shook her head again, shaking off the conversation in a motion that turned into a shudder.

"I've got pictures of you two lovebirds," said Midnight in a singsong voice, holding out her phone. They weren't clear, just images of two dark shapes leaned against each other, the outline of cheekbones and his fingers in her hair, the glare from a window above them that had probably messed up the camera's light sensors.

"You should probably just delete those," Tana said, embarrassed, reaching for the phone. "You can barely see anything."

"Oh, no, I don't think so!" Midnight laughed, dancing out of Tana's way, clearly pleased that her teasing had some effect. "While you were busy saying good-bye, I found us a place that's not too far. My friend Rufus has a squat over on one of the renamed streets. Wormwood."

Tana nodded, trying to smile. What she needed was sleep, she decided. Lots and lots of sleep.

"Lead on," Aidan said. His skin had an odd sheen to it, and he looked pale, as though his blood was cooling inside him, as though body warmth would soon be something that could only be stolen from others.

A few cars were parked on the sidewalk. One sheltered a woman bundled up in a comforter in the backseat among bags of garbage. Was she alive? Tana couldn't see the blanket rise or fall. Another car burned merrily, sending acrid black smoke up into the sky.

Tana passed two girls holding each other up, clearly coming from a party. One had green glitter sparkling in her hair, and the other was wearing the torn remains of a gold-sequin dress. They were barefoot, seeming to have lost their shoes. Both had bruises and needle marks all the way up their calves to their thighs, disappearing beneath the hems of their dresses. Both had identical expressions of dazed contentment as they staggered along.

A few blocks away, someone began to scream. A moment later, that scream was joined by another and another. Three voices, each distinct, each rising and falling in a continuous cry that made up a hellish melody. The barefoot girls stumbled, looked in the direction of the sound, and then kept on walking, one speaking softly to the other.

Midnight bit her lower lip, sucking the ball of a silvery ring into her mouth. She shook her head.

Aidan closed his eyes, seeming to drink in the sound.

"Come on," Tana said, turning down a garbage-strewn alley, heading in the direction of the screams before she thought better of it. *This is exactly what's wrong with me,* she told herself as she walked. *If there's trouble, I go straight for it.*

"Are you sure?" Winter asked, but followed her anyway.

Several blocks later, they came to a crossroads with a large courtyard. A crowd of humans had gathered around the edges, some of the people carrying white flowers. Three vampires knelt at the very center of the road, underneath a defunct stoplight—a man, a woman, and a young girl—screeching up at the sky as the sunlight scorched them. Their hair flamed. Flesh was blackening and flaking off, like paint from the planks of an old house. Underneath, their skin looked raw and red, as though they were made of embers instead of muscles and ligaments. In moments, their cries had grown guttural, and then the noise diminished. Two people from the crowd inched closer to the bodies, and the woman vampire jerked upright. Tana saw a flash of fangs before the vampire collapsed again in a heap of black smoke and steam. Gasps rose from the crowd, and a few people stepped farther away.

"I know what this place is," Winter said under his breath. "Suicide Square."

For a moment, Tana was sure she hadn't heard him right. She felt dizzy with horror.

"If you've seen videos of vampires burning in the sun on You-Tube, this is where most of the footage comes from." He pointed up at a camera mounted outside a window. Then he nodded to the audience. "People come out to watch them die—happens every morning. Citizens hope to get infected or for the vampire to give out money or information—sometimes they can be generous right before they die, I hear. Or other times they'll kill a bunch of the crowd, just for spite."

"But why do they want to die?" Tana asked.

Midnight looked at the dying vampires. Her lip curled with contempt. "Most of them never wanted to go Cold in the first place. They can't hack drinking blood or being stuck in Coldtown. A lot of them can't deal with the things they did when they were freshly turned. Not everyone's worthy."

Not everyone's a monster, Tana thought. It should have made her feel better, more proof that vampires weren't so inhuman that they didn't feel pity or fear or regret. Instead, it just reminded her that sometimes there were no good choices.

"Or they get super bored," Winter said. "That's why the old ones die. Eventually, they don't care enough to feed and they starve."

Midnight gave him an unfriendly look and he stopped talking. She drew herself up, and Tana could see her willing him to remember his role. They had an image to project—two beautiful, condescending creatures who needed nothing but each other, who walked in each other's shadows automatically. But Tana could tell that Midnight didn't like Winter's talking about some future where even if they were vampires, they still might not be happy.

"You can ask Lucien Moreau about it personally," Midnight said, as though reminding her brother of something he should already know. "We're going to crash one of his parties."

Aidan had moved into the shadows of a building, as if the sun bothered him. Tana wondered if he was trying to imagine himself as one of them, wondering if he could hack it, wondering if he was worthy.

"But why die like this?" Tana asked softly, to herself, not really expecting an answer. Two of the vampires had stopped moving, but the little girl—now almost entirely cinders—moved occasionally, spasmodically, causing what was left of her to crumble. People had begun to throw the white blossoms, pelting flowers at the girl in particular.

"Tradition?" Winter shrugged, turning away from the spectacle. He was trying to play it off as if he were apathetic about what was happening, but he looked pale and sick. Watching the vampires burn up in front of him wasn't like watching it on video. It was different to hear their screams echoing across the square. It was different when, with every breath, you sucked in the smell of scorched skin and hair.

"Now at least we know where we are on the map," Midnight said. There was a light in her face that Tana hadn't seen before, a beatific calm, as though, perhaps for the first time, she felt sure about everything. "It should be easy to find Rufus's place."

Tana took Aidan's arm, lacing her fingers through his, ignoring how cold they felt. His gaze seemed to snag on people from the crowd and follow them for a bit, before moving to study another, a cheetah surveying a herd of gazelles for stragglers.

They marched a few more blocks in the dawn light, Winter and

Midnight in the lead, looking for the right street. Some had regular names like Orange or Dickinson or Mill Road. But others had new names scrawled along the fronts of buildings or pasted over the original signs, proclaiming them Way of the Dragon or The Nonsense Court of Endless Alley or Butcher's Boulevard. The confusion was made worse by house marks that were even stranger—some numbered in random order, others in hammered cuneiform, or even random letters of the alphabet. There was a series of houses scrawled with what seemed to be a combination of stick-figure drawings and mathematical code.

The area they walked through mostly consisted of row houses; a few brick industrial buildings; and the odd church, one with its stained-glass windows smashed and its door spray-painted with the word ROTTERS in bright neon green. The streets were quiet, but sometimes Tana thought she saw someone watching them from a window. They passed a brown lawn with what looked like a body collapsed in a wilted bush. The reek of it, a heady mix of decay and spilled wine, persuaded her to stay back and to pull Aidan's arm—hard—when he started over.

"The hunger's bad," he said. "Clawing at my stomach. For a while, I was okay, but I don't think I am going to be okay for much longer."

She nodded. She wasn't sure how long she was going to be okay for, either.

As they walked on, she noticed a dark-haired boy watching her from the vantage of a peaked roof. He was shirtless, his brown arms covered almost entirely in colorful tattoos. An albino crow sat on his arm, its snowy head and bone-pale beak tipped to one side. Even from the street, she could see the glint of the creature's pink eyes.

"Hey," Winter said. "There. That's the house."

Tana turned to observe Midnight walking toward a set of steps, her garbage-bag luggage resting by the side of the street. The place was three stories in height with what looked like a rotted-out balcony on the third floor. The sides had been painted a deep gray but had chipped and bubbled off to reveal pale blue underneath. There was very little lawn out front, and what grass grew there was scrubby and brownish.

Tana glanced back toward the roof on the other side of the street, but the boy with the crow was gone.

"Do they know about us?" she asked, hesitating on the stairs. "Me and Aidan? We're not exactly...safe to be around."

Midnight narrowed her eyes at Tana, then knocked her fist against the wood frame. "That's not going to be a problem," she said over her shoulder.

Then the door opened a crack, a chain keeping it from opening farther. Midnight said something. The door shut and then, latch removed, swung open wide.

A boy was standing in the doorway, looking like a pirate or a prince. Half his head was shaved, and he wore layered clothing of leather and flowing cotton, with rings on each of his fingers and long necklaces of silver and bone hanging one over another at his throat. He waved them inside with a grand sweep of his bejeweled hand.

Tana followed the others into a house that had long ago fallen into disrepair. Mildew discolored the ceiling, and flickering candles cast strange shadows on the smoke-stained walls of the curtained room. A tall girl with honey-blond hair wearing a vintage pale pink gown almost the color of her flesh sat on an old Victorian settee with the stuffing hanging out. Next to her, on a threadbare divan, was a dark-skinned girl, her hair dyed bright red and twisted up with a stick, wearing black jeans and an army coat. The room was coated in a perfume of herbs and alcohol so raw that it scorched Tana's nose to breathe. Against one wall, cans were stacked up, next to cardboard boxes. She could read them from where she was: PEACHES IN SYRUP, PEAS AND CARROTS, CORNED BEEF HASH.

"This is my friend Rufus, the one I was telling you about," Midnight said, seeming thoroughly delighted, touching the shoulder of the boy with the half-shaved head. He smiled at her.

"Welcome, everyone," Rufus said. "Get comfortable."

Midnight walked over to the couch and reclined on it like an evil queen. She reached out a slippered foot to slide it up the tall girl's knee and then pointed her toe toward the other. "This is Christobel and Zara. Zara and Christobel, meet Tana and Aidan."

Aidan grinned at the girls but stayed near the door.

Winter went back outside to bring in the rest of their stuff. He dragged in Midnight's garbage bag and dumped it on the floor heavily beside his and then set down their suitcase beside the bags.

"Thanks for putting us up," Tana said warily.

"Is this house yours?" Aidan asked. Very deliberately, he walked to the stairs and sat down on them, clenching his hands into fists.

"It's ours now," said Christobel. "There's plenty of abandoned places. You just pick one out and break in."

"Bill Story lives next door," said Zara, hunching forward. "He's been streaming feeds since the city was quarantined."

"I've always wanted to meet him," Midnight said dreamily. "The intrepid reporter."

Even Tana had heard of William T. Willingham, a comic-book writer who'd been caught behind the gates, given up fiction, picked a catchy name, and turned to documentary-style reporting about what was really happening inside the quarantine. His literary friends tried to get him out, but he gave the two markers they'd sent away—one right after the other—to people he said were more deserving and who had no chance otherwise of being released.

Cynics claimed he'd never been as famous as he was in Coldtown and was going to milk it for all it was worth. According to them, he was shopping an autobiography. Fans said he was the perfect example of how brave regular people could really be when life turned out differently than expected. Tana had seen footage of him once, a regular-looking guy in glasses.

I can never decide if I'm lucky or not to have seen this, he'd said.

Tana thought about the marker in her purse and couldn't imagine giving up her only chance to get out—not for anything. She wondered how long Rufus and Christobel and Zara had been in Coldtown, breaking into houses, posting about their adventures, and not worrying about the future. She wondered if there was something about the city that made you want to stay, despite everything.

Of course, since most people were stuck here, it didn't matter whether they wanted to stay or not.

She thought of Pauline, sleeping in her bunk at drama camp.

Was she up yet? Eventually someone from back home would call her to tell her what happened. Or she'd go online and see pictures, read reports. Then she'd realize that Tana had called her *after* the massacre—called her and lied. For a moment, the weight of everything that had happened in the last day settled on Tana's shoulders.

Winter crossed the room and sat down on the floor beside Midnight, resting his head on her knee. They looked like a matched set of elegant punk rock figurines.

"You're both just like I thought you'd be," said Rufus, eyeing them appreciatively. "Just like in your videos. You're not scared at all, even in the middle of this place, are you?"

Midnight shook her head, posing deliberately. "I feel like after a long journey, we've finally come home."

The others giggled, but Tana could tell they were impressed by her.

Christobel looked over at Tana and patted the seat beside her. "You look so tired. Come in, sit down. You're safe here."

Tana crossed the floor and perched on the end of the divan. It smelled like dust, and the smell was oddly comforting, reminding her of used bookstores, of browsing the racks and finding old mysteries with funny covers. She let out her breath in a rush and tipped her head back, looking up at the chandelier painted a messy red and black, the original brass showing through in patches. It hit her suddenly that they'd made it. They were inside Coldtown, they were still human, and they even had a place to sleep.

Zara got up from the couch. "You all must be starving. We don't have much food, but let me bring out what we do have."

"Grab some booze while you're out there," Rufus said.

"Grab it yourself," she told him, and stalked off. He laughed, calling something after her that Tana didn't quite catch.

Tana smiled up at the chandelier, listening to them banter.

She imagined herself lying on her bed in her own bedroom, with strings of fairy lights hanging above her and kitschy stenciled-over paintings from Goodwill on the wall. She thought about Pearl in the other room, watching terrible television with the volume turned up too high. Her dad would come home and then they would have dinner together. It made her feel very strange to imagine herself back there—comfortable and claustrophobic at once, as though she'd grown larger when everything else had stayed small.

Her father had warned her to leave Pearl alone, but she had to say some kind of good-bye. After a moment, she went to the window and took a photo of the view of the walls from the inside in the early morning light. Then she composed a text to go with it: *Coldtown is crappy & I love you & I'm fine.*

Hopefully, Pearl would like that. Hopefully, Pearl would understand.

A few minutes later, Zara came back with a big silver tray, piled with a fairly random assortment of things: black olives, mandarin orange slices, pickled beets, baby corn, smoked oysters still in the tin, a block of misshapen cheese, and a hunk of stale and slightly burned bread. Tana popped three olives into her mouth, along with a stalk of vinegary baby corn.

Rufus got out a bunch of little glasses from a cabinet and a bottle of yellowish and slightly cloudy liquid. He poured with his back to them and then brought the shots over to everyone, like a butler. She thought abruptly of the drinking game she and Aidan had played at the farmhouse, The Lady or The Tiger. She didn't remember who'd come up with it, only that their friends had been playing it since freshman year of high school, after they'd read the story in English class. What she did recall was Pauline standing unsteadily on the granite island in Rachel Meltzer's house, red Solo cup in hand, declaiming a limerick of unknown provenance:

There was a young lady of Niger
Who smiled as she rode on a tiger;
They returned from a ride
With the lady inside,
And the smile on the face of the tiger.

"What is it?" Aidan asked, holding his glass up to the light and frowning at it.

"You know how in prison they make Pruno?" said Zara. "Well, this is our Coldtown specialty—our very own moonshine. Regular old white sugar, baker's yeast, and water. We run it through a still, bottle it, and sell it."

Tana sniffed hers. It seared her nose hairs. *Tiger*, she chose silently and drank. Immediately, she began to cough.

Aidan raised his eyebrows. "What's it supposed to taste like?"

"Satan's balls," Rufus said, and they all laughed. He raised his glass. "To bravery, because you've got to be brave to drink this!"

Christobel and Zara threw theirs back, then Aidan, then Midnight and Winter. They all winced, and Zara howled with laughter.

"Burns all the way down," Rufus said.

"And keeps burning," Aidan put in, but he was smiling.

For a moment, Tana felt light-headed. A cold shudder went through her body, and she was reminded of the infection lurking in her blood. *I have the opposite of a fever*, she thought, and shook it off.

The food was weird, but it was food. She stuffed herself with it, gnawing on the bread and spreading mandarin slices over it as if they were jam. The shots got easier to knock back, too, although the more she drank, the dizzier she felt.

After the third, she forced herself to stand. "I think maybe I better lie down. I don't feel so good."

"Well, on that note," said Rufus, a smile stretching his mouth. "Let's show everyone to their rooms."

Christobel and Zara stood, too, glancing covertly toward Aidan.

In that moment, Tana knew something was definitely wrong. What she saw passing between them was more than laughing behind someone's back; it was scheming.

"Come with me," Christobel told Aidan, her silky gown skimming over her body as she walked toward the stairs. He started after her when Tana grabbed his hand.

"Wait," she said, her mouth feeling numb enough that she wasn't sure she could get the words out. "Wait."

He looked back at her, confused and very drunk.

But once she had his attention, she couldn't think of a single thing to say that would prove something bad was about to happen. "Maybe we shouldn't bother them—I mean, they said we could just break in anywhere, right? We can go find our own place."

Aidan frowned, looking at Christobel and then back at Tana, as though he was trying to puzzle out her meaning. "I don't want to go anywhere. I feel weird," he said, and she realized why it was so hard to think.

They'd been drugged.

Tana watched helplessly as he climbed the stairs, Christobel in the lead and Zara following, pushing him along. She didn't know how to save Aidan; she turned toward the open door, toward escape and the cool morning air that might clear her head. She took two faltering steps. Rufus kicked the door shut.

"Going somewhere?" he asked.

Midnight started to laugh from the couch. "Your face!" she said. "Oh my god, Tana, I wish you could see your face! I should have recorded it. Don't be scared—I mean, really, you'd think after traveling with a *vampire*, you wouldn't let us rattle you."

Stupid, Tana thought. *I am so stupid. I got tired and distracted and sad. I stopped paying attention.* "What are you going to do to us?"

"She's infected, too, you know," Winter said. "We should put them in together."

"Really?" Rufus looked over at Midnight for confirmation. "Her?"

She stretched out her skinny-jean-covered legs on the couch. Her velvet top slipped to one side, showing the bandage. "I guess we'll see."

"Come upstairs," Christobel called to Tana.

With Rufus and Winter leading her, she had no choice.

The windowless bedroom contained a mattress and a few blankets piled haphazardly on it. A brass chandelier. A scratched old skylight with water damage at the corners showed a small patch of blue sky and a lot of brown leaves. The door was big and old, with an electronic cat hatch in it.

Now, when it was too late, she had a moment of terrible clarity. *Two infected people. Eventually, we snap and attack each other, taste human blood. Then we're not human anymore. Then we'll be willing to bite them. Of course, that's what they want.*

She heard locks turn, one after the next. On the other side, someone started giggling.

Thirty brass locks with thirty brass keys. Like in her dream. Fury pierced her then.

She punched the door, kicked it, threw her whole body against it, but she was weak and everything was getting cloudy. "I'm going to kill you!" she yelled through the opening, her voice coming out slow and strange. "Open this door so I can kill you."

Aidan tried to rise and collapsed heavily onto the mattress, chuckling, obviously not understanding half of what was going on. "You never give up, do you?"

With her last bit of strength, she crawled onto the mattress, which smelled like cigarettes and old perfume. Curling up next to Aidan, with daylight streaming down from above, she passed out before she could answer him.

CHAPTER 20

Death gives us sleep, eternal youth, and immortality.

—Jean Paul Richter

The Monday morning after Tana went missing, Pearl woke up early. Her father was at the kitchen table, head pillowed on his hands, sleeping in the same clothes he'd worn the night before. A half-finished coffee rested next to him, a filmy ring formed around the inside of the mug.

Most days on summer vacation, Pearl had gone over to a friend's house to swim in their pool, or shop for cheap earrings at the mall, or imitate dance moves from YouTube videos, but today she didn't want to go anywhere. Her stomach felt sour with nerves.

She poured herself a bowl of Cheerios and added milk. Carrying it into the living room, she set it down on the coffee table and switched on the TV from the couch, flicking through channels until she came to a show she recognized—*Hemlok: Vampire Bounty Hunter.*

All the neighborhood kids had been super into Hemlok when they were younger. For the last three whole summers, Pearl had played bounty hunters and vampires with them, running through backyards with a branch in her hand, holding it up like a stake. She'd even dressed up like Hemlok one Halloween, although Mike Chavez told her that it wasn't a good costume for a girl. But in the last year, Hemlok had been on at the same time as another show that she liked better, so she hadn't seen any of the new episodes. And this summer, boys and girls didn't play with each other anyway.

But right then, the familiarity of the show was reassuring, so she left it on.

"The thing about vampires," Hemlok said from his equipment room, strapping stakes carved from rosewood and hawthorn onto a bandolier, their tips capped with plastic so they didn't go blunt during travel. "They're all messed up in the head. They're hungry all the time. We gotta think like they do, think like predators, and outsmart them at their own game. They might be faster and stronger, but we're still human, and that's what makes us better, that's what counts."

The show cut to him sitting in his truck with his assistant, Jeana. She was drinking from a Big Gulp, in white jeans and a cutoff shirt studded with rhinestones, her hair teased so big that it hit the roof. They were parked in front of a strip club, loud music pumping from the speakers. A rerun, Pearl realized; an okay one, but not super great.

"We think we've spotted her inside that building," Jeana said in her exaggerated camera-friendly whisper. "There's a door around back, so we're going to have to get one of us on either side of the building and see if we can't flush her out."

Before he started vampire hunting, Hemlok used to be a wrestler. He quit (although some people say he was thrown out of the league) after an opponent died in the ring. Pearl knew all this from the Hemlok fan club she'd joined when she was nine, around the same time that Hemlok started going on talk shows and telling the story, weeping as he explained that the death of that man was the moment he realized he needed to change his life.

Looking at the screen, Pearl wondered for the first time if the vampire was scared.

Before, she'd always figured that good vampires went to one of the Coldtowns or someplace they were supposed to be and that bad vampires stayed behind to attack people. But now that it was Aidan, who'd always been nice to her, and her big sister, Tana, out in the world, sick or newly turned, she couldn't think of things that way anymore.

Of course, there were bad vampires like the ones who'd killed those kids in Tana's class. Maybe the vampire that Hemlok was hunting was like that. But how could he tell?

Back on the show, Hemlok was getting extra supplies out of the back of his truck.

"There's three ways to kill a vampire and be sure it's dead," Hemlok said. "You put wood through its heart, you set it on fire, or you chop off its head. Anything else is fighting a gunslinger with an openhanded slap. 'Course some people stand by bleeding them out, but to me, that's like a silver nail in the head: might hold them for a while, but ain't permanent."

"And don't forget sunlight, baby," said Jeana, zipping herself into a chain mail shark suit. "Sunlight sure kills 'em."

He rolled his eyes. This was a big part of the show, the relationship between the two of them. "Nobody looking to kill a vampire is going to be like, oh, yeah, I guess I better get out some sunlight. That's no weapon."

"It kills 'em." She tossed her hair. "That's all I'm saying. Kills 'em good."

He grunted and picked up a clear bottle, screwing off the top. "Now some of you been asking about which holy waters or wild rose waters to use on stakes or why I use holy water at all, since there's been a whole bunch of hubbub about how it doesn't really do anything. Well, first of all, I always use oil, not water, 'cause it seeps into the wood better and stays there. And I use rose oil that's been blessed, so that's double duty.

"And for all you people who say holy whatever doesn't help take down vamps, I'm out here in the field—so who are you going to believe, me or some scientists?"

Leaving that question hanging in the air, he hefted up a giant crossbow, its body carved into a crucifix. "Now, another common viewer question is which of my weapons is my favorite." A wooden stake sat cocked and ready in place of a quarrel. "That's this baby. She can drop a vampire from thirty feet."

"It's time to start killing," Jeana said, tapping a white ceramic watch.

He smiled at the camera. "Okay, let's roll."

Pearl felt along the couch for the controller. They were almost to the part where the vampire came out from the bar. There was a chase after that, and Jeana almost got bit on the arm, but her chain bodysuit protected her. Hemlok wound up shooting the vampire with the crossbow and sawing off her head for the bounty.

Pearl didn't want to see it. Not right then, after all the stuff the police had said about her sister, not when her dad had come back from the hardware store with wild rose vines for the lintels and a big blowtorch he didn't explain. She clicked off the television and opened her laptop, booting up the feed for Lucien Moreau's party.

Her dad hated that she watched stuff like this, where the vampires weren't portrayed like villains, but today she didn't care.

She brought another spoonful of cereal to her mouth as the inside of his mansion came on the screen. It looked like something out of a fairy tale, with its gold damask wallpaper and candles on sconces jutting out from the walls. Elisabet, Lucien's consort, was on the screen, her beautiful dark hair pulled back into a chignon and the front of her dress wet with blood. Her red lipstick made her fangs seem even brighter when she smiled. Lucien Moreau, elegantly dressed in cream, his hair like spun gold, caught her up in his arms, whirling her around. His mouth was stained equally bright when he brought it to hers.

Pearl smiled.

That was where her sister was going. Tana was going to live like that, like a princess in a faraway city. Maybe, someday, Pearl could even join her. And once she did, she just knew that everything would be perfect forever.

→ CHAPTER 21 ←

Dying is a wild night and a new road.
—Emily Dickinson

When Tana woke, the sky overhead was just beginning to
darken. She could smell onions frying and heard music playing. People shouted to one another on the street, laughter in their
voices. All the kind of stuff she might have expected to find in every
city except this one.

Aidan was sleeping beside her, his jaws slightly apart.

She stretched, feeling the stiffness of her muscles. She was still
groggy and for a moment imagined putting her head down and just
sleeping on and on. But if Aidan opened his eyes and saw her like that,
all curled up and delicious, like a blood-filled muffin, she doubted
he'd resist biting. She pushed herself to her feet. The more she remembered where she was and what had happened, the more fear pushed
away the last dregs of drugged lethargy.

Her purse was still slung across her body and she unclasped it, pushing aside everything that wasn't the small manila envelope. Panic sped up her heart and made her almost too afraid to look. But the marker was still there, tucked away safe. No one had taken it. For a moment, she actually thought nice things about Midnight and Winter—they might not care if she died, but at least they hadn't robbed her.

She held the marker up to the light.

Just a little larger than a quarter and even lighter than one, it was terrifying to think that this gleaming coin, this object that was supposed to save her life, was small enough to drop through a drain by accident or slip through a hole in a pair of jeans. Bright silver with gold at the heart where the circuits were, surrounded by small, angled cutouts in the metal, it looked like nothing so much as an old-fashioned subway token. She closed her hand into a fist over it, tight, then put it away.

She went over the rest of her inventory. She had the clothes on her back, her boots from home, and her handbag. That held the religious symbols and rose water she'd found at the party, a random assortment of cash rolled up in a brown paper bag, and the garnet locket with the broken clasp that Gavriel had given her in the parking lot.

At the thought of him, she pressed her tongue absently against her teeth, making the bite there sting anew. It throbbed along with the beat of her heart, drumming in her ears. When she realized what she was doing, shame heated her face. It was bad enough that she'd kissed him *like that*, but it was the same impulse as hitting the gas on an icy road, and she couldn't let herself forget it.

He wasn't going to save her. He didn't even know where she was, no less that she needed saving. They weren't going to sneak out of Coldtown to have mad, bad adventures together where he recited lots of poetry and they visited Pauline at drama camp. If he liked her in some strange, savage way, it wasn't the way humans liked one another and it wasn't the way people in storybooks liked one another, either.

Stop being stupid, she told herself, even though it was much too late for that. She'd been a hundred kinds of stupid already.

"Tana." Aidan rolled over on the mattress. His face was gentle with sleep, his hair messy, but his eyes watched her with a disturbing intensity. He slowly shifted into a sitting position, and she noticed that his lips had taken on a blue tint. He gave a long, shuddering sigh. It was almost forty hours since he'd been bitten, and he was looking ever worse as the hours ticked by. "What do you think Rufus and Midnight and those other psychos are going to do now?"

"Wait," she said grimly, and after a moment, he seemed to realize what she meant. She said it again, though, just to be sure. "They're going to wait."

"I won't—" he began, then stopped himself. The words were hollow anyway. They both knew he would.

"Don't worry about it. We're going to get out of here," she told him, although there was a flatness to her tone. Even she wasn't sure she believed it.

Leaning back against the wall, he didn't seem ready to attack her yet, but she wondered how long she had. He was still just waking up. "Haven't you ever thought about it—being a vampire?" he asked.

"*Everybody's* thought about it," said Tana.

"I mean, what with your mom and all—" He stopped abruptly, as though he'd just realized he'd stumbled into dangerous territory. He gave her one of his old, charming half smiles, a teasing one. "And you *kissed* a vampire. That's crazy. That's not usually what they do with their mouths, you know. I'm kind of jealous."

"Oh, come on," she said, rolling her eyes. "Like you care what I do. You dumped me, remember?"

"First of all," Aidan said, giving her his most insouciant smile and holding up a single finger, "I never said I was jealous of *him*. Maybe I was jealous of *you* for getting all his attention. He's not a bad-looking guy, if you don't mind a side serving of lunatic raving. Good mouth."

That made her laugh, a real, relaxed laugh, like in the old days.

"Secondly," he said, holding up another finger, "you scared the hell out of me when we were dating, Tana. I was used to having girl-friends who'd yell at me or get upset about the stupid stuff I did, or try to save me from myself. You weren't like that. Sometimes I felt like you were a better me than I was."

"I didn't know what we were doing a lot of the time," she pro-tested. "I didn't even—"

There was a rustling sound at the door, cutting off her words. A girl's hand snaked through the plastic flap, a dozen silver rings on her fingers and fresh glossy green polish on her nails. She was holding a wooden bowl. A bowl filled so full of red liquid that setting it down caused some to spatter over the floorboards, sinking into the grooves of the wood. The scent of it was iron and basements and losing baby teeth so her big-girl teeth could come in. It was skinned knees and Gavriel's mouth on hers. It was smeared walls and staring eyes.

Tana scrambled to her feet.

Blood.

For a long moment, she and Aidan looked at the bowl. Tana felt hypnotized by the sight of it. The slick redness was as dark and deep as a pool of melted garnets.

If she drank it, she would turn into a monster. She let herself imagine that for a moment, imagining her new monster body and monster eyes and monster thirst. She imagined Midnight and Winter, Rufus and Christobel and Zara opening the door to the room and finding a monster-girl inside.

And if she didn't drink and Aidan did, he would die and wake again—newly turned, ravenous, and alone with her.

"See?" An unfamiliar girl's voice came from the other side of the door. Probably Christobel or Zara. "We don't want anyone to get hurt. We didn't want to have to lock you up. We donated that blood, all of us together, pulled it out of our veins with needles. And now we can't go to the clubs tonight, but see? We're worthy. Drink it and you can come out of the little room. Drink it and we'll all be friends again."

Thicker than water. That's what people said about blood. It looked it, too, viscous and syrupy. Tana could imagine the silky texture of it on her tongue, the warm saltiness, how it would stain her lips and teeth.

"Maybe we should," Aidan said, his voice going low, seductive and seduced. He took a step toward it. "We could do it together, like a suicide pact. Except we'll never die, Tana."

Walking quickly across the floor, her heart hammering, she

picked up the bowl and flung it as hard as she could against the wall. The wood cracked, two halves bouncing off the floor where they fell. Bits of plaster rained after it.

"I can't believe you did that," Aidan said in a tone of pure astonished frustration. He walked toward the wall as though drawn.

Tana slumped, sliding down to the floor, where she sat staring at the blood painting the wall. The stain seemed to make a shape like a great bird, feathers dripping down as it flew up into the sky.

She couldn't quite believe she'd done it, either.

"I'm not going to get any better." His voice rose, staring at the red. "I'm so Cold, Tana, and I am only going to get Colder."

She slammed her hand against the floor, trying to focus her thoughts. "Gavriel let you drink his blood, right? Back at the Last Stop. And it helped. All we need is more."

He laughed, but not as though he thought it was funny. Not as though he thought it was a possibility, either. "The most precious stuff in Coldtown and you're going to just *ask* for some…like you're borrowing a cup of sugar?" He reached out a hand to the wall, streaked with blood. "Give up. I came knowing I was going to be a vampire. What's the point of waiting? We're not going to be fine, Tana. We're never going to be fine ever again."

She wondered what it was like to bite someone. She thought about the expression on Gavriel's face when he'd sunk his teeth into Aidan, the way his mouth had moved on Aidan's throat and his fingers had dug into Aidan's skin. It was as though some serene frenzy had come over him. He looked transcendent, a dreamer not yet awakened.

Her stomach clenched just thinking about it, a combination of desire and dread that made her wonder if it was a symptom of the infection. She shouldn't find the memory of that anything but horrific. But putting aside what she should feel, oh yeah, she got why Aidan might be embarrassed at the memory of drinking from Gavriel's wrist.

That thought wouldn't leave her head as she watched Aidan brush his fingers over the wall and bring them—painted red now—to his mouth.

"*Aidan*," she said softly, hopelessly, just before he licked them clean, one by one.

He made a sound in the back of his throat and knelt down, pressing his lips to the wall, laving it with his tongue. Already, he seemed inhuman, a creature feeding instead of a boy she'd known.

Tana inched away, putting as much distance between them as the small room would allow. A shaky breath escaped her mouth, sounding like a sob.

"Okay!" she shouted, her voice coming unsteadily. "Midnight, are you out there? Okay, he did it. He caved. You can let us out now. You can let him out."

She heard only the sound of murmuring voices floating up from the rooms below.

There was a commercial that ran sometimes on television, especially during daytime soap operas when moms might be watching. It showed chicken nuggets on a plate in front of a human boy and a blood milk shake in front of a slavering vampire girl tied to her chair with ropes. The human messily gorged on the nuggets in the time the vampire just got started on her milk shake. Then voice-over guy said, "Shipton's nuggets will make your kid hungrier than a newborn vampire."

The joke's on you, she told herself, remembering. *Nothing is as hungry as a newborn vampire.*

He was going to die. And before he came back to life as a vampire, if Tana wanted to live, she was going to have to kill him just like her dad had killed her mom. Kill him before he attacked her with all that new strength.

Her best bet was probably the wooden bowl. It was already split in half, and maybe she could chip off a splinter big enough to work like a stake.

But just the thought of it, of pressing it into his chest deep enough to puncture his heart, made her sick.

Aidan sat down heavily, his back to the bloodstained wall. His lips were red. "I'm sorry," he said miserably, and she couldn't help wondering if he wasn't just apologizing for what he'd done, but for what he would inevitably do. "I'm sorry, Tana."

She nodded. "I know. Me, too."

They sat like that, on opposite ends of the room, watching the river of light move across the floor as early morning stretched into afternoon. Aidan began to shiver, his gaze going again and again to the wall. Occasionally, he would turn to look at her with a wild light in his eyes and then turn away, breathing heavily as though he was in pain.

Think, she told herself, *think*.

She got up, pacing the room, forcing herself to look at the trim of the door frames and baseboards, to consider what could be pried loose and used to kill him. Of course, there was another way.

If she took a little blood, his still-human blood or blood from the wall, so long as she was infected, she'd change, too.

Haven't you ever thought about it—being a vampire?

It would be good-bye, Pearl; good-bye, Pauline; good-bye, dream of Los Angeles and palm trees and bright blue ocean. Good-bye, lying on a towel in the backyard under the summer sun, ants crawling across her foot, slippery cocoa butter gleaming on her skin. Good-bye, beating heart and burgers and having blue-gray eyes.

Kill Aidan or die herself. Die and rise.

We'll never die, Tana.

She looked at the wall where the bowl had struck, considering the small hole halfway up the plaster, and had a sudden, desperate thought.

Crossing the room, she kicked the blood-soaked wall, just above the baseboard. Even in her steel-tipped boots, her toes hurt, but she'd cracked the plaster. She kicked again, widening the hole. Maybe she didn't have to make a terrible choice. Maybe she could put off being a monster for another day.

"What are you doing?" Aidan said, looking up at her.

"I don't know," she said. "It might not work."

She walked to where a sharp-looking piece of the bowl had fallen and picked it up. Then she closed her eyes, gritted her teeth, and slammed it midway between the first hole and the dent.

Dust coated her skin and clothes.

Then, wedging her boot in the first hole, she reached up through the second to the slats, gripped the wood, and started climbing. It was hard to balance, and harder, with her foot pressing down, making more plaster crumble, not to slip. And then, hardest of all, to slam the piece of bowl into the wall from that position so that she made another hole and kept climbing.

"Tana?" Aidan asked. She looked down, realizing he was standing beneath her. He had a hungry expression on his face. His mouth was slightly apart, his pink tongue pressing against one of his canines speculatively, as if testing it for sharpness.

"I think I can make it to the skylight," she said. *Normal, normal, keep acting like everything's normal. I'm climbing a wall as if I'm the lamest superhero in the world and you're dying and everything's normal.* "If the chandelier holds me and if I can actually jump on it."

Tana was reminded of a similar exercise they did every year in gym class. Last time, she'd gotten halfway up the climbing wall before jumping off and landing on one of the mats in exhaustion. Pauline, who'd conned an ice pack out of the school nurse for her unhurt wrist so she could sit on the bleachers and avoid the whole thing, had called her a sucker for even trying that hard.

Now, she wished she'd tried a lot harder. She wished she'd practiced climbing that wall every day.

"You're going to leave me here?" he asked her.

Tana shifted her weight, muscles straining. "When I get up onto the roof, I'll see if I can find some way to get you out—"

He shook his head, his voice oddly flat. "It's too late for that. I can feel it."

There was nothing she could say. His skin was pale enough to be nearly translucent, the flesh around his eyes blue as bruises. She wondered if he could feel his heart slowing, if the catch in his voice was because he was finding it harder to breathe.

"I'll get you out tonight, then, once you're changed," Tana told him.

He didn't answer, just watched her grunt as she pulled herself higher. She wished she were stronger, wished she hadn't woken up exhausted. Sweat started at her brow and her thighs. Her arms burned. She ignored everything and concentrated on not falling.

High up the wall, she looked out at the chandelier. What had seemed a short distance to jump from the floor now looked impossible.

Beneath her, Aidan paced the floor like some kind of large, hungry cat. If she fell, if she twisted her ankle or broke her leg, she would look a lot like prey.

Jump, she told herself. *Jump*.

But she was too scared. Looking down, she felt off-balance, all her limbs shaking. She didn't think she could do it.

Taking a deep breath, she gave herself a little pep talk: *Get over your fear of this or get over your fear of murdering in cold blood someone you care about, because those are your choices.*

It was, admittedly, a pretty crappy pep talk. But it worked.

She jumped.

Her legs hit the brass arms of the chandelier, hands grabbing for the central column. She barely made it, one leg hooked over, the other dangling down, fingers flailing for a grip. Her purse strap pulled against her throat.

Plaster fell from the ceiling, dusting her in a rain of white. The chain slipped a little, and she slipped, too, one of her hands sliding from the chandelier. Her head banged against one of the lightbulbs as the whole thing swung dizzily.

It's going to pull free from the ceiling, she thought. *I'm going to fall.*

Straining with her remaining arm and leg, she tried to heave herself back up. She felt a sharp tug, and the strap of her purse pulled against her throat tight enough to choke. Then there was a snapping sound and the leather slid free.

Looking down, she realized that Aidan had her purse in one hand, holding it out as if he was proud of himself. He'd bitten the strap.

"Give that back!" she yelled. "Why did you—"

"Be careful," he told her, a smile in his voice. "You don't want to fall."

He had the marker. But if she let go now, with the chandelier half ripped free from the ceiling, there was no way it would hold her a second time, from a second jump.

She had to focus on getting up and getting to that skylight, even if what she wanted to do was cry.

Hands shaking and head ringing, she pushed herself back to a more secure position on the chandelier. Every time it hitched lower, she was sure she was going to fall. Every time it swung, she was even more sure she was going to fall. But she managed to get herself into an upright position, one foot balancing on an arm of the chandelier while she stood.

Reaching up, shaking and sweaty, she grabbed hold of the lever. The window pivoted inward. A drizzle of dirty water rained down, along with a few leaves.

"Now what?" Aidan called up. Then he started to cough.

She was going to have to pull herself up. It was going to be all arm strength and desperation that got her out, if anything got her out at all.

She extended her hands as far as she could and grabbed hold of the sill. Then she launched off the chandelier, scrabbling to get her chest over the edge of the skylight. That moment, when her feet had only air underneath them and she was breathing in gasps, trying to haul herself up, pure terror sparking like acid in her veins, was awful. And when she made it, upper body resting on the tiles of the roof, she stayed that way for a long moment, afraid she was too tired to even pull up her legs.

Finally, dragging herself forward, she looked back down at Aidan. The chandelier hung between them, on an angle, electrical cords ripped loose from the ceiling.

He was grinning. "Wow. That was amazing."

Panting, exhausted, she said, "Please, please give me my purse back. I don't know why you took it and I don't care. Just give it to me."

"Sorry, Tana," he said, unzipping it and rooting around inside, pulling out the small envelope. With pale, unsteady fingers, he took out the small silver disk with the computer-chip center and held it up in the growing light. "I wanted to make sure you *have* to come back. I'm scared."

"I won't leave you here," Tana said, low, looking directly into his eyes, so he could see that she meant what she was promising. "You don't need any proof of that. You know me. I'm crazy—crazy enough to come back, marker or no marker."

"Then it doesn't matter, right?" And he flashed her one of his exasperating puppy-dog looks. "I'll give you the rest of the bag, just let me keep the marker. It's my dying wish."

Please, Tana. Please.

"No," she said.

"Too bad." Aidan closed her bag and threw it to her. She snatched it out of the air, angry and even angrier that he was giving her something to be grateful for.

"You better not lose that marker," Tana said, stomach churning, resigning herself. "You better not give it to some hot kid you want to impress. It's still mine."

"I won't," he said, bringing it to his mouth and kissing it with his dried-blood-stained lips. "Come for me after it's dark."

Tana rolled onto her back, lying on the roof and looking into the faded blue of the sky. She was exhausted, her mind supplying only the words *I'm tired, I'm tired, I'm tired* over and over, a chant that felt more true every time she thought it.

She blinked and a shadow fell over her. She sat up to see a Latino boy walking toward her across the peak of the roof. She yelped in surprise.

He was the same boy she'd seen that morning. He had short, cropped jet hair, multicolored tattoos snaking up the dark skin of his arms, and bright gold hoops in both his ears, but no bird this time. "You okay?" he asked.

She nodded.

He walked over to the skylight and looked down into it. "They locked you in there with that kid? What's wrong with him?"

She nodded. "Aidan's infected. They fed him blood. He's going to turn."

The boy shook his head. He seemed piratical enough to fit in with Rufus and Zara and Christobel, and he'd known they were a *they*, but he hadn't called out to them that morning from the rooftop. She really, really hoped they weren't friends.

He stuck out his hand. She took it, letting herself be hauled onto her feet. The gentle slope of the roof made her steps unsteady, but she didn't think she was in any danger of falling unless she tried to go fast.

"I saw you," she said. "With the bird."

"I live around here," he told her. "Lived here since before the quarantine. It's safer higher up. My name's Jameson."

Tana looked around at the sea of rooftops, some connected and some not. "If you show me the way to the street, I'll buy you dinner."

"The sun's going down," he said. "They call that meal breakfast around here."

She looked up at the clouds, painted with the scarlet and gold of dusk. "Breakfast, huh?"

Jameson shrugged, walking toward the peak of the roof. "Welcome to Coldtown. Breakfast at dusk. Lunch at midnight. Dinner at dawn. And don't expect everybody to be as nice as me. C'mon."

Hesitating, Tana glanced back at the skylight. "He's dying down there. By himself."

"Everybody dies alone," Jameson said, and kept going. "Not everybody wakes up right after. Come on."

After a moment, not knowing what else to do, she followed him. He led her from rooftop to rooftop, until they came to a fire escape, which they clanked down noisily.

Coldtown was a city running upside down, where day was night and night was day. As they got closer to the town center, the streets filled with shopkeepers and street vendors setting up for the coming night. Kids on torn blankets selling dented canned goods for a quarter apiece called out to her as she passed. There were other makeshift stalls, one full of small generators that ran on solar power and operated by hand crank; another with an array of dresses and coats on racks; and a third with chickens and rabbits in cages. A woman stoked a fire underneath two enormous soup pots while a man on a stool stirred them furiously; a sign behind the couple promised a ladleful of vegetable broth at half price if you brought your own bowl. A man in a top hat and red suspenders called out gleefully from behind a smoking barbecue grill, "Rat on a stick, better get 'em quick, crispy and sweet, meat for a treat!"

Tana's stomach growled, but she wasn't sure she could bring herself to eat. She wondered if it was the infection, if it was finally going to steal her hunger for anything other than blood. At that thought, her stomach churned worse than ever.

By the time she got to High Street, her head was spinning.

"Go grab a seat," Jameson said, gesturing to a place with small, grubby plastic tables and mismatched chairs. "I'll get us something. You can pay me back."

She wondered what his game was, but since they were in a public place and running off might land her in a weirder or worse situation,

Tana sat. He returned a few minutes later with two plates filled with what looked like scrambled eggs with chives, a couple of warm tortillas, and two mugs of black coffee with a film of grounds on top.

"Okay," Jameson said. "I helped you out *and* I bought you food. Now maybe you could tell me a little about the Thorn of Istra."

Tana just stared at him. "How come you think I—"

He took out his phone, thumbed a few buttons, and pushed it across the table toward her. She didn't understand what she was looking at for a moment. It was a blog post with a blurry photograph that Tana recognized as the one Midnight had taken with her camera phone. She must have messed around with it in Photoshop before posting, though, because the picture was brighter. Tana's and Gavriel's faces were recognizable, tipped toward each other in a moment before their mouths touched. His eyes were closed.

"And before you ask why I think he's the Thorn of Istra, it's because the post says so. The girl claims you and your friends— including the Thorn—picked up her brother and her at some kind of crap tourist place."

Tana stared at the phone.

"You can read it yourself if you want." Jameson forked up some eggs. "But basically it says you survived a massacre, where you met the Thorn. He didn't tell anyone who he was, but her brother figured it out at the gate when he saw a wanted sign. Let's just say that lots of people were interested in her post." Jameson's voice was neutral, his tattooed arms resting on the table. She studied them—words in large, ornate script that disappeared under a white T-shirt, roses winding on green stems, and moths of pale brown-and-white wings. "Particularly Lucien Moreau."

She nearly choked on her eggs. "The vampire on TV?"

Lucien Moreau. Pale gold hair and a face like a pre-Raphealite painting. Ancient and ageless, he showed up during the quarantine, waltzing into the city, taking over the biggest house he could find, and installing cameras everywhere. The parties that raged on in his house were as famous as the Eternal Ball, but more elegant and more deadly. You could watch them online and on certain late-night local channels, but no mainstream station would ever broadcast them unedited. Tana didn't watch, but Pearl and her friends did. She'd heard them whisper about what they'd seen: the blurry outlines of velvet capes, the tangled limbs, and Lucien, charming as ever, talking to you right through the camera, promising you with the curve of his mouth and the brightness of his eyes that no matter how loudly you screamed, you'd like whatever he did, and you'd never be the same once he was done.

"I have a friend who lives in Lucien's house. She does errands and stuff for him. She was supposed to be keeping an eye on the gate. Apparently, ever since the Thorn broke out of his prison in Paris, Lucien's been scared he's coming here."

"Why?" Tana forced herself to pick up the mug, ignoring her unsteady hands. She took a sip of the coffee, the hot liquid steadying her enough to take a bite of the eggs. At the first taste, she realized she was hungrier than she'd imagined.

Jameson leaned forward in his plastic seat. "Lucien is the reason the Thorn was locked up. Apparently, your friend Gavriel let Caspar Morales slip through his fingers. Lucien, or maybe Elisabet, or probably both of them together, told some ancient vampire called the

Spider what Gavriel had done, which is how the Thorn of Istra spent the last decade being tortured somewhere under the streets of Paris."

Tana thought about what Gavriel said in the car after they'd left the gas station. The words had seemed nonsensical at the time, but now it seemed to Tana that they were a riddle.

This is the world I remade with my terrible mercy.

An act of mercy that I regret—endlessly, I regret it.

Tana's head was spinning again. "How do you know all that?"

"I told you," he said. "My friend lives with Lucien. Did the Thorn say anything about what his plans were? Did he talk strategy?"

I have a friend, too. And I mean to kill him.

"There's somebody he wants dead." Tana scraped a pile of eggs onto a tortilla and lifted it to her mouth. After the third bite and another swig from the mug, she started to feel a lot better. "I don't know anything other than that. I wouldn't have even believed that Gavriel was the Thorn of Istra if Winter hadn't shown me this." She took the crumpled flyer from where she'd jammed it into her purse hours and hours before, unfolding it on the table, pressing out the creases. Seeing his black curls, the silver-topped cane, and the violence in his eyes, Tana was surprised all over again at the memory of his mouth's softness. "He didn't act like—I mean, he was terrifying, but he was weirdly kind, too. Not how you'd think."

Jameson peered over at the paper and whistled at the amount of the bounty. "How come you didn't turn him in at the gate?"

Tana shook her head. "He helped me out. That would be a pretty crappy way of paying him back. But I don't understand—why would Lucien and Gavriel even know each other?"

"Lucien is Gavriel's *maker*," Jameson said.

"What?" She couldn't imagine it. Couldn't imagine Gavriel, whom she thought of as half the boy who'd promised her another day and half the screaming creature underneath Père-Lachaise Cemetery, having anything to do with slickster Lucien Moreau, who had sold licensing rights to his image so that posters of him could be sold at malls across the country. "Look, obviously I don't know much of anything. All I can tell you is that Gavriel's traveling alone, and there were some vampires hunting for him. He let us assume they were sent by the Thorn of Istra, but I guess they belonged to this Spider person. The massacre Midnight mentioned in her post, that was because of them."

A white thing streaked down from the sky, surprising Tana into nearly toppling off her chair. The crow spread its albino wings and alighted on the table, regarding her with its ruby eyes. It stalked across the plastic surface, cawing once and then picking at a few fallen curds of egg.

Jameson started to laugh as the bird hopped up onto his shoulder. Flapping its wings, it flew up to his head. "This is Gremlin," he said, swatting the crow back to the table.

Tana put out her fingers tentatively and was surprised when the bird scampered over and rubbed its beak against her skin. She smiled a little, relaxing. There was something about an animal that made it hard not to feel like the person who kept it was basically decent.

"Let me explain something about Coldtown," Jameson said. "Mostly, we're an ecosystem that works. The vampires need lots of living people to supply them with blood, willingly, through the shunts. If they had to go around attacking people, they'd risk spreading infection and losing their food supply. But when something shakes Coldtown up, we descend into chaos very quickly. Whether it's human terrorists breaking the windows of the Eternal Ball and setting themselves on fire or turf wars between rival vampire gangs, things can get heated pretty fast. So if Gavriel's here to stir things up, there are a lot of vampires and humans who already hate Lucien and who would join him—"

She tried to imagine Gavriel's recruiting anybody and shook her head. "I think whatever he's going to do, he'll be alone. He's not really . . . he's kind of crazy."

Jameson looked faintly relieved. "I'll tell my friend to try to get away from Lucien's for a few days, but I doubt she'll go."

Tana took a last swig of the coffee, drinking down the grounds, feeling the caffeine sing through her blood. The sky above them had turned dark, and she thought of Aidan, back in the house, dead and risen, and waiting for her to return. "Why's she with him in the first place if he's so awful?"

Jameson looked away from her. "She's a vampire," he said quietly.

The way he'd said it, as if he was embarrassed, made her wonder what it was like to have grown up here human. What did it mean to never have made the choice to come to Coldtown, to never want something from the vampires? What would he do for a marker like the one she'd lost? And how would he feel if he knew about the infection bubbling in her blood?

Reaching over, Jameson stroked Gremlin's white feathers. "Did you know that crows get to like the chemical in ant bites? Formic acid, I think. Anyway, they start to get so addicted to it that they'll spread out their wings on top of anthills. I think that she—my friend—I think she knows that Lucien's horrible, but she's gotten to like it."

Tana shuddered at the image. "Maybe she's just used to it."

"Maybe," Jameson said, but he didn't sound convinced.

"My turn to ask you for something," she said. The thing about Jameson was that he seemed so oddly normal. Tough-looking, with a shadow of stubble over his jaw and the wiry muscles of someone who spent a lot of time climbing across rooftops, but he'd helped her and hadn't asked for anything much in exchange. "If you know a place where I can buy some stuff like clothes and maybe a weapon, I'd love some directions. I didn't exactly come prepared."

"I know somebody with a pretty decent pawnshop. I could walk you over." Jameson raised both his eyebrows, waiting.

"Thanks again," she said, and he stood.

Tonight, she was going to have to find her way back to Aidan and retrieve her marker. And once she did, she was going to have to find herself a new prison, one where she could hole up and wait out the infection with enough food and water and blankets to get her through eighty-eight days of torment.

Eighty-eight days, starting with this one.

→ CHAPTER 22 ←

One has to pay dearly for immortality; one has to die several times while one is still alive.

—Friedrich Nietzsche

The night that Gavriel was bitten for the first time, he woke to freshly starched sheets and an unfamiliar high-ceilinged room. He stank of liquor; even his sweat smelled faintly of Chartreuse, and he thought he might still be drunk. When he sat up, his head spun such that he had to lie back down. Outside the windows, the gas lamps of Paris burned beneath a moonless sky.

"Drink this," a man's voice said, bringing a glass to his mouth.

He gulped what turned out to be water. He felt odd, hot and cold at the same time, as though a fever was coming on. He was used to waking in filthy rooms, used to shame on the face of the person or persons who'd brought him there, used to walking back to his tiny apartment with a sour stomach and rumpled clothes in the late afternoon, scandalizing his landlord.

What he wasn't used to was finding himself in an opulent hotel with a blond man standing over him wearing a wicked grin. Vaguely, he remembered a piano playing and a sting at his throat, as though a cobra had struck him, and some great pressure against his neck. But he'd spent most of the evening in one of the more raffish *haut bohème* salons, and while he'd heard it said that places like that were frequented by snakes, no one meant it literally.

"I ought to go," Gavriel said muzzily, trying to sit up again. "I'm not well."

"Some sicknesses are worse than their cure," said the man, pinning Gavriel in place with the press of a single hand. In the dim light, the irises of his eyes appeared to be spilled-blood red. Gavriel stared up at him, too amazed to be afraid. After courting the devil's attention for so long, it seemed that at last the devil had come for him.

"When it's done, we'll be like brothers," said the devil.

"I already have a brother," Gavriel slurred. "He's dead."

The devil loomed over him, his grin widening to show off sharp teeth. "As am I."

Gavriel opened his mouth to shout, but drunk as he was, he began to laugh instead.

When Gavriel woke again, light was streaming through the window, making his memories of the night before seem ridiculous. A particularly silly and indulgent nightmare, brought on by too many drinks and too much misery. No man loomed over him, ready to strike. No blood stained the bright white sheets. The hotel room was empty, his shirt and shoes resting on a nearby settee. On a low table, a fresh bottle of Chartreuse was set out, beside a cut-crystal glass and a plate of baked oysters.

He blinked at the bed, at the rumpled sheets. He brushed fingers over his neck. They touched tender skin, as though he'd been bruised. That gave him pause, making him nervous enough to gather up his things and leave the room quickly, heading for home.

He felt light-headed as he made his way past the gambling dens and pawnshops that studded the Ninth Arrondissement around the Folies Bergère Music Hall. He walked inside a *boucherie* without even really deciding on it. There, he spent what meager coins he had on calf liver and ate it raw, straight off the brown paper in which it was wrapped, on the steps of his building.

Gavriel slept through most of the day, waking at night with a creeping chill in his bones. Outside his apartment, he heard all the sounds of night in Paris—people hawking wares, whether food or flesh. Someone was playing dice in the back alley below his window; the sound of them on the cobblestones made him think of a skeleton rattling in its coffin.

He found that he did not want to be alone. Fortunately, in Paris, he could find low company at any time. In a cabaret where a dark-haired girl performed the shocking *danse du ventre*, he met up with a few of his acquaintances. He knew little about any of them, really, except for their appetites, which were prodigious. Still, their laughter chased away the dreams of the night before—at least until Gavriel found himself studying the throat of Raoul de Cleves, a *comte*'s son prone to gambling and deep in debt. As the night wore on, Gavriel became more and more aware of the movements of blood under de Cleves's skin, of the way his heart sped it along, fresh and hot. It would be so easy to slice open flesh and release that red stream, bright as claret. It would be so easy to get him alone, to promise him the loan of some money and then press him against the wall of the alley and—Gavriel pushed away the thought of what came next. He tried to watch the girl onstage, but when she rotated her hips, making the bells on her skirt tinkle, all he could think of was the artery that ran down the inside of her sweat-slicked inner thigh.

He staggered home, drunk as he could make himself. When he opened the door to his room, a fire was burning in the grate and the devil sat in a threadbare chair, as elegantly dressed in a dove-gray coat with covered buttons as if he'd come straight from Versailles.

"I'm Lucien Moreau," the devil said, eyes bright with hellfire. "I imagine you have questions."

Gavriel stood in the doorway, frozen.

"*I feel so strange,*" said Lucien in a falsetto, a smile stretching his mouth, clearly much entertained by his own performance. "*What's happening to me? How could you make me have these terrible desires? Satan, avaunt!*"

Gavriel came inside, closing the door behind him. "I apologize," he said. "I am very drunk and not likely to be as clever in my inter-rogation as you imagine. I confess I am discomposed, but you may stay as long as you please. I have been searching through the streets of Paris for damnation, and now that damnation has come to sit by my grate. Who am I to turn it away?"

He was not as cool as his words made him appear, but Lucien's mocking rendition of his thoughts had put him on his mettle: He refused to let the creature see how afraid he was.

Lucien inclined his head in thanks. "You never do quite what I expect. To me, surprise is a quality precious above rubies." He held up his hand, and Gavriel could see that one of the silvery rings he wore covered the length of his finger like some kind of armor, with a wicked hooked talon at the end.

He drew that across his wrist, letting blood well. It was darker than the blood Gavriel remembered spattering his brother's chest, darker and with an unusual blue tint. The smell of it seemed to fill the room, a hypnotizing scent, like ozone rising after a lightning strike, and he lurched forward without meaning to.

"Drink," Lucien said. "This is what you thirst for. Come and drink."

And as Gavriel bent his head, falling to his knees, fingers shaking as he closed them around Lucien's wrist, some part of him knew that before this moment, he had only been playing at wickedness. He had never done anything in Paris so terrible that he could not have returned to the man he had once been.

Then the flavor of Lucien's blood washed over him and he was lost. He sucked at the wound, tongue pushing into the slit skin of Lucien's wrist, a low sound starting in the back of his throat. He forgot about Aleksander. He forgot about his mother and father and sister. He forgot about the sound of the gun firing and the smell of the powder and the way his brother's body had sprawled in the snow. There was only this.

And when he woke in the late morning, with blood staining his lips and teeth, blood smeared on the pillow where he'd rubbed his mouth against it in the night, all he thought of was getting more.

Before, Gavriel had been full of self-loathing and conflicting desires, but now his days had a singular focus. He waited for night and for Lucien to drink from him and then feed him from his wrist. Nothing else mattered very much. He drifted through his days, no longer caring about salons or cabarets, no longer caring about drink or degradation.

At first, the feedings exhausted him, but then the blood seemed to have worked some strange alchemy. His hunger abated. He walked through the streets during the day, feeling stronger, swifter, and more alert than ever before. He could snap a poker in half and catch the reins of a frightened horse, jerking it to a halt, without even exerting himself. In his room, alone, he threw a knife at the wall again and again, perfectly able to control where it struck. His canines grew longer and sharper, making his gums bleed. He was delighted, running his fingers over their points absently when he was alone, to prove to himself they were really there.

And as Gavriel hunched over Lucien's wrist, new teeth making neat little holes in his skin, Gavriel felt as far from himself as he could have ever wished to be.

On the seventh night, when Gavriel returned to his apartment just after dusk, Lucien was there, lounging in a chair, wearing a dinner jacket with a shawl collar. He had a girl with him, sitting on one of the arms, in a thin, stained shirt and heavy-looking brown skirt. Dirt rouged her cheeks, darkened her throat, and gloved her hands. A box rested on the table, apple-green satin spilling out.

"I told her that she could take a bath here," said Lucien. "Is that all right?"

Gavriel nodded numbly, his heart speeding as he took in the scene. "Of course, if she wishes."

"She wishes," said Lucien, and gave the girl a little shove. She stood obediently. "I told her she had to be quite thoroughly clean before she could put on the dress you bought her."

Gavriel glanced over at the box of green satin and then back at the girl. She was looking at the fabric with longing fierce enough to make her foolish. He remembered his sister's closet full of such dresses, and he thought that it was such a small thing to want, but of course, for her, it wouldn't be.

Run, he thought, but didn't say aloud. *You know you ought to run. Please run.*

He pointed toward the back of his apartment and watched her as she lifted the box and walked slowly toward the tin bath in his bedroom, the jug of water he'd left there along with a square of lye soap. She moved lightly, and there was a sway to her step that made him think of the dancer he'd seen just days before. He imagined pressing his mouth to her neck, her heartbeat fluttering like a bird's wings, and shuddered.

"Why is she here?" Gavriel asked.

"Oh, don't be tiresome," said Lucien. "Surely you can guess both her provenance and her purpose. There is no mystery."

"Lucien," Gavriel said, cautioning him, "what do you mean to do with her?"

"She's not for *me*," Lucien said. "My blood has made you ready, but the final transformation is before you. Tonight is your last night as a living man. Drink from her and be born anew. Her death buys you life eternal."

Gavriel shook his head, backing away.

"Oh, come now. You can't pour wine back and forth between two vessels forever," Lucien smirked.

"I have enough innocent blood on my hands," Gavriel said. "Enough and more than enough."

Lucien laughed. "So that's what you're running from, is it? Oh, my dear boy, very soon it will be as nothing to you, I promise. There will be rivers of blood to drown in, and one single drop will be as meaningless as a single star in all the tapestry of the sky."

"I won't do it," Gavriel told him, stalking toward the door. Lucien grabbed for his arm, but Gavriel pushed him away with all the stolen strength of his blood. "I don't care what I do to myself, but I won't be the cause of suffering for another."

"You will," Lucien said, red eyes shining, lips curled into a mocking smile.

Gavriel escaped into the night, the echo of Lucien's laughter following him.

Lucien found him a week later. Gavriel had taken the stagecoach away from Paris and found himself a small hostelry outside Marseille. He had lain down the night before, sweating and shaking, hearing the heartbeats of humans like drums through the walls. Cold crept deeper and deeper into his skin until it finally froze his heart.

When Lucien opened the front door and saw the common room streaked with scarlet, the bodies of the innkeeper and his wife, the barely grown children who worked in the kitchens and stables, he smiled. Gavriel, crouched over a body, looked up at him with a despair so deep that it was barely a feeling at all.

Of course, Lucien had killed the girl Gavriel had tried to spare. He told Gavriel all about it on their ride back to Paris.

CHAPTER 23

Death has made

His darkness beautiful with thee.

—Alfred Tennyson

The streets after dark were stolen by vampires. They strode along, their ruby eyes flashing and their coats flapping. Some had Mohawks and nose rings, making faces at everyone they passed; some ran through the streets, arm in arm, flowing white dresses fluttering behind them; some twirled ebony walking sticks, strutting in velvet jackets, with long, dandyish hair; some were surrounded by a crowd; and some strolled alone.

Tana stuck close to the buildings, ducking under awnings to stay out of their way. Her heart raced, and she couldn't tear her eyes from their unnatural pallor and easy grace, couldn't stop staring at their hellish eyes.

"You get used to them," Jameson said, but she noticed that if a vampire got too close, he'd crouch and his hand would twitch toward something in his boot.

Finally, Jameson stopped at a metal-barred window displaying earrings in the shape of scarabs, a purple raincoat with a matching umbrella, and several wigs in bright colors. A sign crafted from glass beads and broken bits of mirror over the door read: ODDMENTS & LOST THINGS.

The door had a metal speakeasy grille set into it. Jameson pulled a bell.

A few moments later, a girl opened the grille. The moment she spotted Jameson, she broke into a wide grin, although her smile dimmed slightly at the sight of Tana.

She flipped the locks on the door and opened it, letting them into the dimly lit building.

The girl was tall, with long, tawny hair, like a lion's mane, loose around her shoulders, and eyes the bright green of bottle glass. Gold was dusted over her cheeks and painted on her eyelids. She was wearing a kimono-style robe, looking as though she'd just gotten up.

"Hi," Jameson said, smiling shyly. He looked a little dazzled by her beauty.

"Hi," she said back. She seemed to be holding her breath, waiting for him to do or say something. Whatever it was, he didn't do it.

Gone was the breezily confident boy who'd taken Tana to breakfast and explained Coldtown politics. "You can get most anything here," he said to Tana. "Valentina's got a magical power to recall where an old box of the exact thing you're looking for was put a year ago."

The girl—Valentina—smiled. "I wasn't working here a year ago," she protested.

His lips curved, but he didn't look at her. "That's why it's magic."

Tana glanced at the racks of clothes against one wall, with open suitcases near them, each one overflowing with shirts and coats. A few mannequins had been arranged to look as though they were tied up, and those wore an assortment of sparkly dresses and hats. Oil lamps burned on several surfaces, making shadows dance.

A woman descended the stairs, her heeled shoes loud on the wood. At the sound of her arrival, Valentina pulled away from Jameson. The woman was the oldest person Tana had seen so far inside the gates, with long, gray-streaked hair, fine enough to look like spiderwebs where it caught on her black gown. A heavy rose-gold medallion hung around her neck, and she wore bright blue earrings almost the exact color of her eyes.

"Well, don't just stand there, Valentina," she said to the girl. "Lock the doors behind our customers. We want everyone to have the safest possible shopping experience."

Valentina took a few steps toward the door before Jameson caught the knob.

"So I'm going to go," he said, turning it and stepping out into the street. "Good luck, Tana. Bye, Valentina. Bye, Ms. Kurkin."

"Oh, stay," said Ms. Kurkin. "Have a cup of tea with us."

"I can't," Jameson said. "But Tana is new to town. She could probably use one."

Ms. Kurkin smiled. "Always with the strays."

Valentina turned the locks behind Jameson with a single glance out through the barred speakeasy window. Tana wondered at his quick departure, wondered if he hated being locked in as much as she did. But given that she was the one who'd been bitten about twenty-six hours ago, she was probably more of a danger to them than they were to her. She was just glad they didn't know it.

"Well," said Ms. Kurkin. "So what can I do for you? Something to sell, I'm supposing. Something you stole from your mother back home? A precious little locket your grandmother gave you when you were a baby? Family heirloom?"

"Mostly I need to buy stuff," Tana said, guessing that Ms. Kurkin didn't much care for the kids who trooped through her store. But then Tana thought of the garnet necklace with the empty locket that Gavriel had given her, the one rattling around in the bottom of her purse, the one that made her shudder when she considered where it must have come from. She reached into her bag and pulled it out, setting it down on a glass counter that held various sparkling items, from earrings dripping with rhinestones to diamond rings. The garnets shone dully, like dozens of punctures welling with blood. "I do have one thing to sell, actually. The clasp is broken, though."

"Hmmmm," Ms. Kurkin said, walking behind the counter and pulling out a jeweler's loupe, holding it in front of her left eye.

"These are Bohemian garnets—from the Latin *granatum*, for pomegranate, because of their resemblance to the seeds. Probably from the Czech Republic, although the setting is Russian. You can see the symbol for gold." She picked the necklace up, weighing it in her hand. "Quite lovely. Old. Sturdy. I could give you six hundred dollars for it—half cash, half credit—although it'd be worth four times that to the right buyer."

Tana sucked in her breath abruptly enough that it made a sound.

"Unfortunately," Ms. Kurkin continued. "You're not likely to find the right buyer inside Coldtown."

An antique necklace from Russia. How likely was it that the Thorn of Istra had pulled that off the throat of someone in a parking lot and it had—totally coincidentally—come from the country where he was born? But if he hadn't stolen it, then it had been something that belonged to him, something he'd brought with him all the way from Paris, something he'd owned long before that.

And he'd given it to her.

The woman gave Tana an odd look. "Or for thirty dollars, I could fix the clasp while you shop and you could wear it out on the town tonight. It's a beautiful piece. You don't have to sell your soul right away."

Nodding mutely, Tana reached into her purse and handed the woman behind the counter two twenties from the odd assortment of stained bills Gavriel had given her. And like a normal shopkeeper at a normal shop, the woman tapped a few keys on the register and counted out ten dollars in change.

"I'll start on it now," the woman said. "Valentina will show you the rest of the store while you wait."

Valentina smiled at Ms. Kurkin's tone of imperious command and then shrugged at Tana. She waved her toward the steps and the second floor, where more clothes were to be found, piled up on worn wooden tables and hanging in mirrored armoires. True to Jameson's word, Valentina did seem to have a crazy ability to understand the pattern of the mess and fish out beautiful things from unlikely places.

"So where did all this come from?" Tana asked, pulling on a pair of black stretchy skinny jeans that were only a little too tight. They were marked five dollars. "It's a lot of stuff."

"Ms. Kurkin started this place after the quarantine as a place for people to come and swap what they didn't need for what they did. Soon after, scavengers started bringing her things they found in abandoned houses, hoping for cash. And then others came, looking for baubles and gowns. A lot of people come to the city and not that many leave. It's a pretty good business." Valentina pulled a leather jacket, the elbows a little worn, down from a hook and held it out to Tana. "This looks about your size."

Tana shrugged it on, liking the weight. Wearing it felt like being armored. "It's perfect."

Valentina smiled at her. "This is a city with a very particular dress code."

Tana laughed, bending to look through a pile. She found a T-shirt with a fanged happy face, another shirt that said DESPERATELY SEEKING DEATH, cutoff shorts, pajama bottoms covered in a pattern of steaming teacups, and a filmy blouse of the palest ivory with a high collar and little, faux pearl buttons fastening it up the back and at the cuffs. "So how about you? How did you wind up here?"

Valentina's expression changed subtly, as though she was trying to determine what Tana was really asking. Then she sighed and flopped into one of the overstuffed chairs, ignoring the clothing she was sitting on. She had a long, lean body, like a model's, with large, expressive hands. Her nails were painted the same gold that dusted her eyelids. "Jameson brought me to Ms. Kurkin, told her that I was worth trusting to help her with the store. Her last employee disappeared—which happens around here—so she needed to find someone new. I can't decide if Jameson was trying to be incredibly nice or just getting rid of me. Maybe both."

"Have you known him long?"

Valentina shook her head. "I came to Coldtown with a friend about a year ago. We were both from the same small town. We didn't fit in, and we thought we were going to run away to a place where everyone was like us and we'd be transformed and…"

Valentina paused as if at a loss for the next word. Tana nodded, urging her on. It was nice to talk. There was nothing she could do for the next couple of hours, while Aidan was newly turned and desperately thirsty. Her best bet was to go back and get the marker closer to dawn, after they'd fed him. Until then, she might as well enjoy the clothes and the company.

"Turns out, we were idiots. My friend almost got killed by the first vampires we met. He went off alone with these three red-eyed girls and, I mean, he didn't even like girls. Next thing I know I find him in an alley with the vampires crowded around him, slicing his skin. They licked the blood off him like it was candy, and they were so careful never to bite him, the bitches. He would have died if Jameson hadn't come along then."

Valentina had a faraway look in her eye as she went on. "He had this huge, honking flamethrower, the same kind the guards use. There aren't a lot of rules in Coldtown, but one thing vampires get really cranky about is when someone appears to be hunting them."

"Was he?" Tana asked.

Valentina shrugged. "I don't know, but he crisped all three of them and took us home like we were feral cats or something." She sighed. "He brought us to a squat, up in the eaves of a church, where other kids were living, some of them really little and some of them older. The place is empty now, but we lived there awhile. Jameson is a little bit of a folk hero around here."

Tana thought of the clothes in piles and asked, "Where are the other kids who lived there?"

"Two of them became Rotter hangers-on, including my friend," Valentina said. "It's a vampire gang, basically anarchists, and they'll turn people who prove they're psychotic enough to impress them. My friend's still human, but hopeful. One of the little kids got turned by a vampire and lives with her now. Another one went out one day and never came back. Jameson looked and looked, but sometimes people just disappear in the city."

Tana spotted a nice-looking knife, long and sharp, resting in a jar with a few feathers and a fountain pen. "Jameson must have a complicated relationship with vampires."

"Jameson? Yeah, I guess. His girlfriend's one."

Tana looked up at Valentina in surprise. "Oh, right," she said after a moment, remembering what he'd told her at breakfast. "She must be the friend he was talking about. The one from Lucien Moreau's."

"Don't say anything if you see him, okay? He's never told me about her, but it's a small town. I hear things. And I saw them once, up near Velvet Road, arguing. She was gorgeous. And I definitely don't want him to think I care. He knows what I used to be, so it might be awkward for him."

"What you used to be?" Tana echoed, frowning in confusion.

"I wasn't born a girl," Valentina said, shifting her long, elegant limbs to stand. "At least not on the outside. He knows I came here because I couldn't afford surgery. If I was turned, I figured at least I could keep looking like I do now. At least my face wouldn't change. But things haven't exactly worked out."

For a moment, in her mind, Valentina's features took on a masculine cast. But then Tana blinked and saw only the girl in front of her.

It was a reason that Tana had never even considered for wanting to be young forever.

"I won't say anything," she promised. "I barely know him anyway."

Valentina smiled, a little wryly. "Coldtown's a small place, and it's getting smaller all the time. You'll know everybody soon enough."

Tana wound up buying the long dagger, the jeans and leather jacket, three T-shirts, and four pairs of underwear that Valentina promised had been bleached and then washed. She figured she'd need the clothes—although forty-eight hours were almost up, even if she didn't go Cold, she'd have to wear something on her way out. She got the knife because she'd been wishing for one for a while. She also bought a big, ugly, rust-colored poncho that looked warm and would be easier to carry than a blanket; bolt cutters; a screwdriver; nylon rope; a solar cell phone charger; and a backpack to put it all in.

All of it together cost her $132. She still had money left—at least another hundred and maybe more—but she didn't want to count it right then, in the shop.

Valentina looked down at the knife as she rang up Tana. "You know how to use one of these?"

"I'm hoping that it will look scary enough that if I wave it around, people will back off."

Valentina raised her eyebrows wordlessly.

Then Ms. Kurkin came back with the locket necklace and its new clasp. Tana hid it away in her bag and went over to one of the large antique mirrors against the wall, braiding her hair tight to her head and tying it with a piece of string. She looked at herself in the wavy glass, trying to convince herself that she was tough enough to face whatever else was in the little room where Aidan waited. Then she said good-bye to Valentina and Ms. Kurkin and headed out onto the street, retracing her steps all the way back into danger.

Climbing up onto the roof was easy, but once Tana got up there, it was an unfamiliar landscape, especially in the dark. She went slowly, making sure to place each foot carefully on the asphalt shingles. Following Jameson, she'd been too preoccupied to notice, but now that she was alone above the city, she realized that someone had recently constructed much of what she was using to cross between buildings. Ladders and boards, soldered in place or nailed down, bridged the gaps, making a maze high above the streets.

It took her a while to find the skylight in the dark. As she searched, she was sorely tempted to stop looking and find a place to hole up for the rest of the night. Sleep a little more. Maybe that would give Aidan a chance to get used to his new self. Maybe by the time she showed up, a day or two later, he'd be able to control his hunger and eager to show off his new red eyes.

Of course, maybe he would have sold the marker by then, too. Maybe she'd have gone Cold.

Or maybe he'd be dead. The story of an infected kid in the Midwest had been all over the news a couple of months back. He'd confessed to his girlfriend that he'd been bitten and wanted her to lock him in an old shed on her family's property to get through the infection. She'd promised she would, but instead she got together a bunch of friends from school to tie the boy up, carve him open, and drink his blood—not understanding that infection couldn't be passed on like that, that because he wasn't yet a vampire, his blood couldn't make her and her friends go Cold.

But Midnight was smart enough to wait until Aidan was a vampire if she wanted to carve him up. She'd know she could bottle that stuff and sell it to the highest bidder.

Tana shuddered, wishing that she was like Jameson with his flamethrower, wishing that she had something better than a big knife, a pair of bolt cutters, and a tough-looking leather jacket. She wished she were a local legend.

Finally, by moonlight, she was able to make out the skylight she'd come through. It was still open, the chandelier as messed up as she'd left it.

A few bright green leaves spiraled down into the dark room.

The door was ajar, letting in light from the hallway. Light that showed the room was empty.

"Aidan," she whispered, but there was no one to hear her.

Looking around, she saw a chimney nearby and wrapped one end of the rope around it, wishing that she'd gone to Girl Scouts. Didn't they learn how to tie knots?

She climbed down into the room. Down was easy, except that it was hard to go slow, when her rope was just rope, with no interval knots to brace her feet against. Halfway down, Tana slipped and fell onto the floorboards, making a sound that everyone inside must have heard.

Stupid, stupid, stupid. She braced for the sound of running feet, but the only thing she heard was a low moan from somewhere deep in the house.

Tana crept into the hallway.

A man in a bowling shirt, jeans, and sandals sat against the wall, his head tipped back and his eyes open. He had short hair the brown of rabbit fur and wore a pair of large, round silver-rimmed glasses, the lens of one mottled with bloody fingerprints. His arms were outstretched and his wrist had been ripped open, a mess of torn skin and pink insides. The floor was washed in a sticky pool of red that the rug had begun to soak up, blackening it along one edge. Much too much blood and more still bubbled lazily from his veins.

The other wrist was marked with two small puncture holes.

One of his legs twitched spasmodically. He looked at her with his glazed-over brown eyes. The smell of blood rose up, breaking over her like a wave, rich and hot. Her tongue pressed against her teeth eagerly. Bile rose in the back of her throat.

"Ru-un," he said between rapid, heaving breaths, and then just stopped, like a toy that had been switched off. A rattling sound came from deep inside his rib cage.

Tana's heart was thudding in her chest, beating like punches from a fist.

In that moment, she realized she'd seen him before—a picture of him, anyway. He must be the neighbor they'd talked about. Bill Story, the one who'd been chronicling life inside the walls, the one who'd refused to leave even after his friends sent him a way out. She was sure that however he imagined dying, it wasn't like this.

She carefully removed Bill's glasses. Then she pressed her fingers to his eyelids, closing his eyes and hoping they'd stay closed. Then she crossed his hands over his chest, the way that dead pharaohs posed on their sarcophagi.

No matter what warning he'd whispered with his final breath, she couldn't run. She couldn't go anywhere without the marker. Carefully, she slid the long knife out of her boot.

Edging along farther, she turned a corner and saw Christobel standing by a window with a can of paint and a brush. She was blackening the panes and crying at the same time, her thin shoulders shaking and her eyes red-rimmed. She looked at Tana and started to cry harder.

"What are you doing?" Tana whispered.

"Getting everything ready for tomorrow." Her makeup streaked her blotchy cheeks in tracks of glittering gray and silver. Her voice sounded vague and dreamy, almost singsong. "We're going to be vampires, and the house has to be ready for us. It wasn't supposed to be like this. You shouldn't have left. Why did you leave?"

Since Tana had been their prisoner, she'd assumed that if she was spotted sneaking back into their fortress with a big knife, it would be cause for alarm. But Christobel was looking at her as if she had gone out for groceries and taken too long getting back and now their whole dinner party was ruined.

There was another low moan from behind a door down the hall and the sound of frantic hushed voices. Christobel looked nervously in that direction and then back at Tana.

"After you left, we thought—when we didn't hear you anymore, it seemed like Aidan had fed on you. So we thought it was safe. We were sad, but—"

Tana nodded and gestured for her to go on, to speed past that part. She knew why she'd been locked in the room with him, even if not everyone on the other side of the door was willing to admit to it.

"Midnight and Zara fought over who would go first. Zara said it was her house and so she'd go, so she went and he—he drained her."

"Oh," Tana said, thinking of the human Aidan she'd known. Aidan, who was silly and selfish, but who could never have been a murderer.

"I know he didn't mean to." Christobel started crying even harder, dropping the paint can and kicking it with her foot. The black paint spattered the wall and ran in rivulets, like rotten blood. "He was so upset after. But it was supposed to be you who died, not Zara. It's not fair. We did everything right. We gave him you to eat, as the sacrifice for the newly risen vampire. It was supposed to be *you*."

"Where is he now?" Tana asked, trying to keep from slapping the girl. "Down there?" She'd pointed toward the room where the sounds came from, and the girl nodded.

Is it safe? she wanted to ask, but she didn't think that Christobel was going to give her an honest answer. With Bill Story and Zara dead, it was hard to imagine that Aidan was still hungry, but what did she know about newborn vampires? At the farmhouse, those creatures had fed until they were swollen like ticks.

Tana walked farther down the hall, her footsteps tracking more black paint as she went. When she glanced over her shoulder, Christobel was looking out the window, even though she'd painted it so thickly that there was nothing to see.

It was supposed to be you.

In that moment, with her hand on the doorknob, Tana wished that life were like a recording where you could fast-forward past all the scary parts where everything got turned upside down to whatever came next, no matter how bad. Taking a deep, ragged breath, she pushed the door open. Then the tableau revealed itself and there was no more wishing.

Aidan crouched on the floor with inhuman stillness. That and the unnatural pallor of his skin made it clear that he was changed, even before he looked up at her with his new scarlet-tinted eyes. Beside him rocked Midnight, back and forth, holding her brother's body.

Winter's blue bangs hung in his face, and his mouth looked chalky and chapped, the way Pearl's mouth sometimes did when she'd brushed her teeth and hadn't wiped all the toothpaste away. Two bright pinpricks marred his throat, one leaking a thin line of blood. Winter's eyes were closed, but Midnight's eyes were open and red as coals in the heart of a fire. At the sight of Tana, she made a horrible keening sound and clutched her brother closer.

Rufus hunched in a corner of the room, wearing only pajama pants. A tiny video phone rested next to him as though he'd dropped it and forgotten it was there. The blinking light showed that it was still recording.

CHAPTER 24

Any relic of the dead is precious, if they were valued living.

—Emily Brontë

Pearl sat in front of the television, like she had all day, laptop open as she ate spaghetti with lots of sprinkle cheese. Her father was in the kitchen, cleaning the stove. He'd been cleaning since Tana left—doing laundry, scrubbing the inside of the microwave, even pulling out the refrigerator and getting down on his knees to wash the tiles by hand. He'd been at it so long that although it was after ten, he still hadn't eaten dinner. The only times he stopped were when the phone rang with calls from Homeland Security and, later, Aidan's parents.

On her laptop, Lucien Moreau's party was just kicking into high gear. Three vampire girls were dancing on a table with a boy who might have been a corpse. On the television, a news anchor in a blue suit stood in front of the logo TEEN BLOODBATH with a big red spatter over the letters.

"Now for the latest update on the sundown party turned trag-edy," she read off the teleprompter, "we go to Mitch Evans at the gas station off Highway Ninety-Three where a trio of teen survivors of the tragedy were spotted late Sunday night. Aidan Marinos and Tana Bach, along with an unidentified third young person, were caught on video, isn't that right, Mitch?"

Then the screen flashed to a newsman with an ill-fitting toupee standing in front of a gas station and holding a microphone on a bewildered-looking kid. "Absolutely, Tiffany," the man in the toupee said. "We're here with Garrett Walker, who's been working behind the counter at Global Gas for nearly a year. Can you describe what you saw last night?"

Pearl scooted forward on the sofa. "Dad!" she yelled. "Dad, they're talking about Tana on television."

"Sure I can," the kid with big red spikes in his hair, Garrett, said. "Two kids came into the mart. She was all scratched up, and the boy looked a little shifty, so that made me keep my eye on them. I thought maybe they were going to steal something."

"What do you mean, *shifty*?" Mitch Evans asked on the screen.

Garrett shrugged. "He was looking at things too long. Staring right through you."

"And how about the girl?" asked the reporter.

Garrett squinted at the sky, as if he was trying to remember. "She bought a sandwich, I think. Nice blue eyes. Short skirt. Honestly, I didn't pay much attention to her until after what happened out by the pumps."

Pearl reached out and picked up the cell phone resting beside her on the leather cushions of the couch. She'd looked at it about a hundred times since she'd seen the text from her sister that morning: a photo of a normal-looking street just after sunrise and the words *Coldtown is crappy & I love you & I'm fine.*

Every time Pearl looked at it, she could hear Tana saying the words, could hear her exact tone of voice. She even knew what they meant, because sisters spoke a certain kind of language so deep it was almost code. They meant that Coldtown was okay and not too scary, but also that Tana was teasing her for thinking of it as a romantic place. They meant that Tana wasn't a vampire yet, because she could take photographs of sunrises. They meant that Tana was trying to hide how she really felt, which wasn't fine at all.

Pearl's dad walked into the room, sponge in hand. "What are you yelling about?"

She pointed at the screen. "Watch. They're talking about Tana."

"Turn it off," her father said, his voice hard.

"No, they're talking about Tana," Pearl repeated, because he must not have heard her.

"The police already explained what happened at the gas station. Now, do what I say and turn it off." He sounded stern, but Pearl didn't care. She wanted to hear.

On the screen, Mitch Evans looked very serious. "Tell us about that. You could see the whole thing?"

"Yeah, and I never saw anything else like it, neither," said Garrett. "The one boy looks like he's going to rip her throat right out when another boy comes out of nowhere. The new boy lifts the first one up into the air and bites down on his neck. Bites right down on it like no muss, no fuss. Just like on TV. The girl's lying there—doesn't even try to run. Then finally she gets up, brushes herself off, and the vampire—he must have been a vampire, right?—loads up the boy into the back of the car and they all drive off like nothing happened."

None of it sounded like Aidan, who was funny and nice and used to tease Pearl until she laughed. None of it sounded like Tana, who would have run or fought or something.

"The girl got into the car voluntarily? Was she cooperating with the vampire?"

"Looked like," said Garrett.

After she'd noticed the text that morning, Pearl had gone out to the kitchen and taken a picture of their dad, asleep at the kitchen table, and another picture of her mostly empty cereal bowl and sent those to Tana along with a message: *Everything weird and boring here. U better have fun fun fun and send pix so i can be jealous.*

She hadn't gotten any reply.

"Pearl," her father said warningly.

"No!" she shouted, hurling her plate of spaghetti at him, the sauce spattering across the wood floor and the plate shattering. "No! I want to hear about Tana."

"And you couldn't tell if the girl was Cold?" asked Mitch Evans on the television.

Some of the spaghetti stuck to the wall and other pieces fell. They all looked like worms.

"I couldn't tell nothing. You saw the footage, didn't you?" asked Garrett, the gas station guy.

"Unfortunately the police haven't released the video to the public yet, but we hope to show clips of it to our viewers soon. But I can say that Tana Bach, Aidan Marinos, and their unidentified companion are the only survivors of the massacre that left us with forty-eight teens dead, snuffed out at a party that should have marked one of the happiest times in their lives. The police are left asking how did three teenagers escape, what horrors did they endure during the seventeen hours they were held captive in that farmhouse, and where are they going now?

"Viewers, we want you to call the number flashing at the bottom of the screen if you see anyone matching their descriptions or spot a gray 1995 Ford Crown Victoria with green patches. Remember, do not approach them. At least one has already been turned, the other two are probably infected, and their state of mind is unclear. They are considered highly dangerous. Back to you, Tiffany."

They returned to the newsroom. "Thank you, Mitch," said Tiffany with a stiff smile. "And remember, if you do come into physical contact with a vampire, you are legally obligated to report yourself to the authorities. Do not attempt to wait to see if you've become infected. Do not attempt to self-quarantine. Call 911, explain the nature of the attack, and wait for further instructions.

"Next up, we'll hear from an expert who will go over the best way to vampire-proof your house, and after that we have an exclusive interview with a bounty hunter who claims to have details on one of the three vampires who perpetrated this slaughter. But first, a word from our sponsors."

Her father hadn't moved from where he was standing in front of the television. Even though he'd told her to turn it off, he'd watched until the end.

Pearl thought about finally saying the words she hadn't said all day long, ever since she saw the message from Tana: *I know where she is, Dad.*

But she didn't say those words or any others. She picked up the remote, solemnly clicked off the television, grabbed her laptop, and went upstairs to put on her pajamas for bed.

CHAPTER 25

Man dies of cold, not of darkness.

—Miguel de Unamuno

Tana's fear was a living thing, clawing at her throat, as Aidan's red eyes focused on her. She swallowed terror down as best she could without choking. Not meaning to, she took a step back, the knife coming up. It seemed a flimsy thing against two monsters.

"You came back," Aidan said a little dazedly, holding out his hand, as if he didn't even notice her weapon. He looked relieved to see her, relieved and hopeful. "I thought it would be—I don't know— not like this. I've done bad things, Tana."

Still holding the knife, she crouched down and gripped his fingers with her other hand. Even though his skin was cold, she squeezed in what she hoped was a reassuring way. "It's going to be okay. Let's get out of here."

He didn't move. "Everything looks different, silvery and blurry, like watercolor smears and...I can hear your heart, Tana. Your blood, your heat. It's blowing off you—bright and red and sweet as anything. But that's not—I know that's not how you look. I can't see things right anymore."

"Lots of stuff looks different to me, too, right about now," said Tana, trying to act like he wasn't terrifying her.

Aidan's mouth had changed, his canine teeth grown a little longer and sharper. But he had that same persuasive way of talking. "It was an accident. She was going to turn Winter, but she took too much. Now he won't wake up. But if we just let him rest, then..."

Tana's gaze went to Midnight, with Winter's body in her arms. That was the accident he was talking about, not Bill Story or Zara.

"You know that's not true," Rufus said, sounding a shade short of hysteria. "It doesn't work like that."

"Shut up!" Midnight shouted. Fangs gleamed in her open mouth. "Shut up, shut up, shut up!"

"There's a dead man in the hallway." Tana tried to make it sound as if she were perfectly calm, but the quaver in her voice betrayed her.

"Bill had never seen it, a person dying and waking up a newborn vampire. He wanted to record what happened. We *all* did." Rufus's voice kept its manic edge. "Things just got out of control."

"He brought over some of his equipment to film me biting her," Aidan said. "I didn't want to do it. I was afraid I'd hurt her the same way that I—" He stopped talking abruptly.

Midnight pressed her lips to Winter's pallid cheek and whispered words against his skin.

"What went wrong?" Tana asked, to keep them talking. She was trying to think through the fear, trying to plan. If she wanted the marker, she was going to have to get Aidan alone. It wasn't safe for him to hand it over in front of them.

"Midnight finally convinced Aidan that it would be okay," Rufus said. "We waited awhile, until we figured the infection was in her system, and then used the venipuncture stuff she brought to draw some blood from Winter. Sterilized it with a lighter, which I know isn't great, but they're brother and sister, so whatever. She drank the blood and waited. Then she died."

"She *died*," Aidan said. "Just like I did. She died and we watched her. We even filmed it. It took forty minutes before it was over."

Tana shuddered, thinking of Aidan alone in the room, listening to his heartbeats count their way down to dead. There was something changed about him, something that turned his familiar face into a mask. She could see a newly born thing looking out of his eyes.

"It was horrible," Rufus said. "But that's what she wanted. It's what she told us to do, and she kept yelling at us to keep going, to keep filming."

"And when she got up, she was really hungry." An odd expression passed over Aidan's face, as though he was remembering that hunger, as though it was waking anew inside of him. "She was burning up with it."

"Bill got too close and she *lunged* at him," Rufus said, lowering his voice, as though that was going to help.

"He tried to get away from her," said Aidan. "But it only made the wound rip open wider. I grabbed her and tried to pull her off him. I *tried*. But then the smell of the blood was too much for me and I..."

Tana remembered the wounds on Bill's other wrist and thought she knew what he meant. She wondered if being turned had wrought some inner change on Aidan or if this was his true self, his true self without any reason to hesitate.

"We didn't mean to," Midnight said, looking up abruptly. "It's still gnawing at my gut. The hunger. All I can see is blood. All I can smell is blood." She shook Winter, and his head flopped back and forth, a marionette with his strings cut. "Wake up, Winter. No more birthdays, remember? It happened just like we said and all you have to do is wake up."

Tana sucked in a breath. She felt as though everything teetered on a razor's edge.

"Winter volunteered to be the first one turned, after," Rufus was saying, and Tana tried to focus on him, on what was happening then and there. "He trusted her. And then she just didn't stop feeding— she went on and on and we didn't know how to stop her. Winter seemed lost, swooning in her arms. He had been making these breathy sounds, and they just got quieter and quieter. Christobel realized that something had gone wrong before any of the rest of us did. She tried to get Midnight to let Winter go."

"And what were you doing all this time?" Tana asked Rufus.

He swallowed hard. "I was still filming. I hadn't realized..." He stopped talking before explaining exactly what he hadn't realized. *That Midnight had gone crazy? That Winter was dying?*

"So what happened after that?" Tana prompted, and Midnight's mad eyes found hers.

"They want to take Winter away from me," Midnight said. "We're not supposed to be parted."

"Do you know what happens to corpses?" Rufus yelled. "They bloat. They get blowflies and they stink. The longer we wait, the worse it'll be."

Tana wondered how many bodies he'd seen before, how many he'd moved, and how many had belonged to people he'd once cared about. He sounded entirely practical, but there was something in his face that belied that indifference.

She wondered where Zara's body was, whether he'd buried her already or taken her to the gate or if she was waiting, rolled in a blanket in another room. Tana wondered if he'd done whatever it was himself or if Christobel had, before she'd started painting.

Most of all, she wondered if either of them still wanted to be vampires.

"I'll help," Tana said, letting go of Aidan's hand and standing. If they moved around, maybe she could talk with Aidan alone. And if that was impossible, then she still had to get out of the house, marker or no marker.

"Winter stays with me," Midnight told them, stroking her brother's hair.

"That's disgusting," Aidan said.

She flashed him a terrible look. "He's mine!"

"Fine, we'll leave him," Rufus told her, walking toward the door. Tana followed, holding her breath as she went through, gripping her knife tightly in her palm, waiting for cold hands to seize her and pull her back. When that didn't happen, she looked over her shoulder at Aidan and raised both her eyebrows. "You, too. We're going to need help lifting the bodies."

It turned out that even as a vampire, Aidan liked being bullied a little. But not enough to give her the marker.

"When you get back," he promised her, quietly, in the hall, "I want us to talk."

And so, she helped wrap and carry Bill Story and then Zara. Her body had been resting on the divan in the front room, posed as though she were a mannequin about to come to life.

Every night, in every Coldtown, people die. People are fragile. They die of mistakes, of overdoses, of sickness. But mostly they die of Death.

Death drinks down their warmth until their veins are dry. Death forgets restraint. The older vampires might grow dusty and careful, but those freshly made want to glut themselves and sometimes, foolishly, they give in to Death and do.

And so, each morning, the denizens of Coldtown who remain must bring out their dead. They're brought in front of one of the guard towers, and in the afternoon, the guards come from the safety of the wall and hammer two silver nails into the corpses—one in the head and one in the heart. If the bodies are still there the next day, spoiling in the sun, they're shipped home to their families.

By the time Tana and Rufus and Christobel had wrapped Zara and Bill in sheets and set them down beside the other bodies, the sun was high in the sky, hot and unforgiving. The three of them walked back through the too-bright streets, littered with the night's leavings: several kids slumped together in an alley, wrapped around one another for warmth like bears in a cave; a scattering of feathers and sequins in a gutter; stubbed out corn silk and clover cigarettes with blue lipstick smudging the filters; broken bottles of whiskey; and withered white flowers. They stepped over it all without speaking, too tired to do anything else. Distant bird noises and petals blown from rooftop gardens filled the air with daylight sounds and smells. Tana wanted to sleep, but this was the most vulnerable that Aidan was likely to be. And after dragging bodies he'd killed through the street, she wanted that damn marker.

She wanted it back and she wanted to punch him in the face.

Aidan was sitting on a bare mattress in a room upstairs, one with windows covered in garbage bags in a disturbing echo of the one she'd found him in at Lance's party. He was thumbing through a yellowed paperback he'd gotten from somewhere around the house. Dylan Thomas. Aidan looked up at her, grinned, and tossed the book to one side. She remembered Bill's slack, changed face and bluish skin in the unforgiving light of day. Bill, whom she didn't know at all, but who would have still been alive if not for Aidan. Aidan, with his constant need to please everyone around him, who had changed a girl into a monster to make her happy.

And Zara, beautiful Zara, with two puncture marks on her neck. She'd pinned up her hair and picked out a beautiful dress to go to her grave. Zara, whom they'd had to throw out as if she were garbage.

Aidan, who was partly responsible for the deaths of three people. Aidan, who was a monster.

"I can't stay," Tana said, hovering in the doorway.

Aidan shook his head, squinting against the indirect light of the hall. It obviously bothered him, but he didn't seem to hurt. "She's watching the footage that Rufus recorded over and over again. She's watching me bite her and listening to herself talk about exquisite pain and transmutation and 'this is my body this is my blood.' Watching herself kill Winter. Over and over and over. With Winter's body still right there, decaying next to her. I can't take it. And I keep thinking about Kristin dying and how horrible I am and I just can't stop." He hit his hands against his head three times like he was trying to drive the demons out. "I saw her die and it was the worst thing I'd ever seen, her dying with the others, all of them dying—I mean it was the absolute worst, unimaginably bad. But now, when I think about it and I remember all the blood, it's awful and yet I want to lick it all up, lick the walls of the party, and I can't stop, Tana, I can't—"

"Kristin?" Tana said, but then it came back to her that that had been the name of his new girlfriend, the strawberry-haired one who'd worn the dog collar at Lance's party. Tana sat down on the edge of the mattress and put her hand against his back, feeling his shirt slide over his chilled skin. "It'll get better. You're not used to being what you are yet, that's all. It takes time, but you have endless time, Aidan."

"I don't want to get used to it," he said.

Tana thought about the three vampires in the square, burning up in the sun, and what Winter said about their not being able to handle what they'd become. She'd heard distant but distinct screams that morning, too, as they walked through the streets. "You *have* to,"

Tana said, making her voice firm. "And you have to give back what you were holding on to for me."

"Because you don't trust me," he said.

"You're not used to what you are yet," she told him. "That's all. Friends don't blackmail each other."

"You can't leave me here, Tana," he said. "Promise me that you won't leave me."

After a long moment, she said, "I'll be here for eighty-eight days at least. I'm infected, remember? That's a lot of time." She wasn't sure she *was* infected, not anymore, but she figured that it'd be safer if he thought her being Cold was certain.

Safer, because if there was any way to, she was leaving him. She was going home, home to hide under covers that smelled like bleach and violets and to sleep until she forgot the last three days. She wanted to take a shower so hot that it gave her a sunburn. She wanted to cry until she didn't have any tears left, until the salt of them dried on her cheeks and blew away.

"We could find him again—*Gavriel*," Aidan said, making the name into a taunt, but not a mean one. He sounded like Pauline did sometimes when she was teasing Tana about a boy, the way she'd once sounded when she was teasing Tana about Aidan. "I bet we could find him if we looked, and I know you'd like to see him again, even if you won't say so."

Tana let herself smile with relief that Aidan had moved on to a subject that didn't involve dying. He might let her out of the room without a fight, might let her out with the marker. "Okay, sure. Let's look for him."

"I bet he wants to see you, too." With a sigh, Aidan reached into his jeans and took out the manila envelope, then put it in her hand. "We'll start tomorrow. You trust me now, right?"

She wanted to open it up and look, but she didn't want to take her gaze off Aidan. She could feel the weight of the marker, could trace her finger around the outline of it through the paper. That would have to do. She slipped it into one of the zip pockets of her jacket while he watched.

"I trust you," she said, and stepped into the hallway.

The dim slashes of sunlight through the painted windows were little comfort. As soon as she'd walked a few steps, she started to run down the stairs. She was tired through and through, tired from adrenaline, exhausted from being drugged the morning before, and worn down from fear so deep it seemed to live in her bones. She forced herself to walk out the front, down the street, and seven blocks in a random direction before she let out her breath. Then she looked for a house with boarded-up windows. Using the bolt cutter to force her way inside, she searched it as thoroughly as she could in her exhausted state, climbing her way to the topmost room. There, she pushed a dresser against the door, made a nest of the dusty curtains, and curled up in their center, happy for the warmth of the sun on her face, happy for it to burn away everything about the night before.

It was full, black night when Tana woke. She came out of sleep like a thunderclap—waking from dreams so deep and dark that she couldn't remember anything but dirt and hands pulling her down into graves with cities inside them. She was covered in sweat, as though she'd slept through a fever.

Outside her window, the lights of Coldtown were glowing like luminous jellyfish floating on a vast sea—candles in some windows and electric lights in others, generators pumping and wind turbines whirring. Tana's clothes were stiff and rusty with dried blood. She stripped them off and wrapped herself in the poncho like a robe.

It had been two days ago, around sunset, when the vampire had scraped the back of her knee with his teeth. Which meant that forty-eight hours had passed since then, had passed while she was asleep. That was Sunday night and it was Tuesday night now. Which means that her body must have shaken off the infection. If her symptoms hadn't gotten worse yet, then, against all odds, she'd beaten it.

She wanted to scream for joy and jump up and down. She settled for spinning around the room, not caring that she was wearing only a weird poncho, not caring about anything except that she was going to stay human. She was going to be fine.

It felt almost dangerous that something so good had happened. But if she got ready fast, she could be out past the gate and on the road before dawn.

The upstairs of the house had several bedrooms, most of which had been stripped of furniture. She found the bathroom at the end of the hall, and when she turned the taps on in the bathtub, water flowed. It was dark at first and stank of iron, but after she let it run a little while, it became clear. She showered under the icy spray—the water heater having probably stopped functioning years back—

finding an ancient, cracked lump of soap and rubbing her skin with it until she got the blood off her knees and out from underneath her fingernails. Then, with nothing else to wear, she put her jeans back on along with her new underclothes and shirt.

Back in her room, she tugged on her jacket, slipping one hand into the pocket.

The envelope was still there. With trembling fingers, she opened the flap and took out a folded-up page ripped from the Dylan Thomas book. *My hero bares his nerves along my wrist.* Over the poem, Aidan had written in red marker: *I'm not ready to let you leave me.* Tipping up the envelope, a quarter slid out into the middle of her palm.

The weight had been right, and the shape—it was just the object that was wrong.

He must have written those words as she carried bodies through the streets, knowing what he'd say when she got back. Knowing the whole time that he was going to con her. Tana punched the wall, not caring that her knuckles split. She hit it again, punching it over and over until blood smeared the wallboard.

Never again, she promised herself. *No matter what, she was never going to let anyone get the better of her ever again. No more mistakes.*

Rufus looked more somber than she'd seen him, when he opened the door. He blinked in surprise at the sight of her. He was wearing plain jeans and a T-shirt instead of his usual finery. His eyes were bloodshot.

"Aidan and Midnight cleared out about an hour ago," he said, leaning against the door frame. "With Winter's body." Behind him, she heard Christobel calling down sleepily, asking who was at the door. He ignored her, but a little bit of snark bled back into his voice when he spoke again, one brow raised. "I guess they don't need us anymore. Zara's dead and it was all for nothing. But Midnight, she was wearing her best, most tattered finery, planning on presenting herself to Lucien Moreau."

Tana slammed her hand into the wall again. "Damn it!" she shouted up at the sky. The stars winked down at her as if they were laughing at how silly she'd been. "Well, I guess that's where I'm headed."

"You can't go to Lucien's dressed like that." Rufus sounded apologetic. "If you're not a vampire, the only way to get in is to dress as deliciously as possible—like a raw, quivering, little pork chop—and stand around with all the other humans, hoping you look good enough to get picked. Unless you know somebody who can get you on the very exclusive list."

Tana didn't know anyone who could get her into a fancy vampire party. But she could think of a person who might be on the list, one boy with a vampire girlfriend, who must visit her sometimes, maybe even without climbing across a rooftop.

Tana kept looking up as she walked through the streets, hoping to spot Jameson's white crow or some sign that he was around. The chance of her actually lucking into finding him was low, but since she didn't have any other way to contact him, she figured she'd go past places he'd taken her, eat at the cart they'd eaten at before, and ask Valentina at Oddments & Lost Things if he'd brought any other strays past.

She bought coffee at A Shot of Depresso, where crushed beans were stirred into boiling water in massive copper vats, and the proprietor stood on a stool to ladle some into a cup. For fifty cents extra, you could get a squirt of fresh goat milk from a sleepy goat chewing on a patch of clover near a stall filled with bright green bottles marked LAUDANUM.

Standing in line, she noticed that very few of the people in front of her paid in cash. Some seemed to be racking up a tab, giving their name and getting a note put down on a ledger. Others bartered tomatoes, a skinned rabbit, a bundle of weed tied with string, and even a handful of aspirin for their serving.

In addition to the coffee, Tana bought a giant glass of cold mint tea and two squirrel-meat burritos, which were surprisingly good. The *queso* was fresh-made, and the red sauce was spicy and delicious, coating the stringy and kind of gamy meat. She sat in the moonlight at the edge of a clearing where a mismatched group of tables and chairs rested and ate until she felt full and was pretty sure Jameson wasn't coming. Kids bundled in layers of clothes shared cigarettes back and forth and scrounged in their pockets for stuff to trade. An old man with white hair and red eyes sat beside a chessboard, inviting anyone with a shunt in their arm to play him for the price of dinner.

When she was done, she wiped her hands on her jeans and stood, telling herself she was going to remember to eat more than one meal today.

Then Tana made her way over to Oddments & Lost Things, knocking on the door and peering in through the grate. She heard the metal shift of the locks and then Valentina was there, ushering her inside.

"Tana, right?" she said, smiling. Today she wore a peacock-blue slip dress with green flats, her hair pulled back in a high ponytail.

Tana inhaled the perfumed dust of the store and looked around with fresh eyes. She hadn't realized how tired she'd been the day before, waking from being drugged and then exhausting herself with terror. Now she felt angry and wide awake and a whole lot better.

"Yeah," Tana said, pushing the stray hairs that had come out of her braid behind her ear. "You wouldn't know where to find Jameson, would you?"

Valentina shook her head. "Sometimes he just shows up out of the blue with something he found—a sack of decent coffee beans or, once, a girl's ring he thought might fit me—but it's not like he comes by a lot or anything. He has a cell phone, or at least he did. He gave me the number, but I've never called it."

"Can we try?" Tana asked.

Valentina opened the worn wooden drawers of the desk, sifting through the detritus. She pulled out a cell phone, the face of it cracked and the plastic scratched. When she pressed a button, though, the screen came to life. She tapped a few more keys, and Tana heard the faint sound of ringing on the other end. Valentina brought it to her ear. After a moment, she shook her head and hung up. "Voice mail."

Tana sighed and took the phone from her, copying the number down. "He has that girlfriend at Lucien Moreau's, so I was hoping he could help me get into the party. But if I can't find him, at least you can help me find a really hot dress, right?"

Valentina gestured to the wall, where dozens of gowns hung, overlapping one another, silk and chiffon, beaded and spangled. "Absolutely. I hear Lucien likes bright colors that show up well on television. But are you sure you want to go *tonight*?"

Tana shook her head. "It has to be tonight. Why?"

"New vampires. A bunch of them." Valentina went to a garment rack in the back and returned with three dresses on hangers—one white, one gold, and one red.

"What do you mean?" For a moment, Tana thought of Aidan and Midnight. But surely two new vampires weren't enough to draw any notice.

Valentina dumped the clothes over a chair and pulled a heavy laptop from behind the counter. It was covered in stickers and hooked up to a weird-looking device with strips of metal. "You really didn't see? Oh, you probably didn't bring a laptop."

"I didn't bring much of anything," Tana said, moving around the counter to watch. Valentina's background screen came on—a picture of a bunch of friends in graduation robes. Tana looked for Valentina among them, but before she could pick her out, Valentina opened her browser.

"Here, look, this is a site that compiles the best links from all Coldtowns—and this is the page for ours." She clicked through, bending over the screen, her ponytail spiraling over one cheek. "Springfield."

She clicked on a link and a screen sprang to life. It was inside a theater, but someone had taken out most of the seats and there was a party going on. People got up onstage, declaiming poems and swigging from bottles, lace dripping from the cuffs of their billowing poet shirts.

Valentina hit the fast-forward button, speeding through two more performers, before a boy in black climbed onto the stage. She tapped the key to return it to normal speed, and Tana saw Gavriel grinning out at the audience, garnet eyes shining, black curls wild around his face, looking as mad as he'd been caged beneath a Paris cemetery.

He took an extravagant bow, one arm flung out with a flourish. Then turning, he dragged a single chair onto the stage. The stuffing had been ripped out of it, the brocade hanging down in tatters. "I have a performance to offer you tonight. It is not a unique talent that I have, but we marvel not over the man who eats a single meal or who does one meager shot of liquor. We marvel over excess. That is what I would give you.

"Come, let me bite you. Have you ever wanted to be as I am? To be immortal? I will turn you. Any of you. All of you, if you like. Tonight. Come to me." He threw his arms wide. "I am thirsty. Let me drink. Let me gorge."

For a long moment, he waited. The crowd had gone hushed. Then a single dark-skinned woman broke from the ranks and started toward the stairs. She walked up the steps slowly, looking back at her friends. She had on a silver-and-black harlequin dress and had painted one of her eyes with a black diamond. Tana could see the fear on her face as she walked slowly to the chair and sat down. Tears glittered in her eyes as she stretched out her long, elegant neck.

Valentina stopped it, freezing the screen as Gavriel bent toward her. "He does it, too. Bites all of them, drinks a ton of blood, and then staggers out. Leaves them alive, every one. They're saying that's the Thorn of Istra."

"He is," said Tana softly.

Valentina looked at her, surprised. "Wasn't his job to stop the spread of infection? Stop outbreaks by *killing* new vampires?"

Tana couldn't seem to stop staring at the frozen screen, at the greedy expression on Gavriel's face. Then she gave Valentina a lopsided grin. "I guess he quit. I mean, that's like a Coney Island–style hot dog–eating contest."

They looked at each other for a long moment and then started giggling uncontrollably.

"So you're still going to Lucien Moreau's?" Valentina asked, walking to a rack and taking down a long black gown with one hand and a golden gown with the other.

Tana nodded, walking over to pet the nap of the velvet. "If Jameson comes in, though, you better show him that video. The reason he told me about his friend being at Lucien's was that he worried she'd get caught in the cross fire if Gav—if *the Thorn* came after Lucien. He wanted to warn her."

She remembered what she'd said to Jameson about Gavriel—that whatever he would do, he would do alone. But then why turn so many new vampires? Maybe she'd been very wrong.

"I think I'll come with you," Valentina said.

"To the party? Didn't you just tell me that it was dangerous?" Tana tilted her head to one side, trying to puzzle out Valentina's change of heart.

"I'm going to warn her," Valentina said. "I saw her that once, so I can find her again. I owe Jameson."

"Well, that's good news for me." Tana bent down and started unlacing her boots. "It's always more fun to show up at a party with friends."

→ CHAPTER 26 ←

POST BY: MIDNIGHT

SUBJECT: SAD VAMPIRE

I thought I would be writing a different post. I know I promised I would tell you guys what it was really like beyond the walls of Coldtown, but I'm not sure I can bear to. In all my imaginings, I never thought it would be anything like this.

Now Winter is dead and I'm a vampire.

I was going to just post the video footage I took and not explain, but that's not fair to you all who have been my real true Dark Family, supporting me through everything, encouraging me to go on this journey. I know that you'd want to hear about what happened, not just see it.

I've posted lots of times about hating how every second I was getting older. You saw all my freak-outs that my cells were dying and my hair was falling out. Every time I woke up with strands on my pillow, I was sure that piece of hair was gone forever and I would go bald and be ugly. Sometimes I thought I could feel the decay inside me, taste the rot in my mouth before I brushed my teeth in the morning. For days before I left for Coldtown, I couldn't eat, because the idea of food disgusted me, the way I could feel it heavy in my stomach.

I know you feel the same way sometimes, like there's something wrong with us because we're not the magnificent monsters we were meant to be. Well, you're right. I can tell you now, from the other side, that we were right. Everything feels right now.

My being bitten is on tape, and I'm going to upload that video as soon as I edit it. It was just as amazing as I had hoped it would be. The pain wasn't so bad. Your skin gets kind of numb around where the fangs go in, and there's this amazing feeling, like someone is pulling all the weakness and rot away to make room for something else.

But here's the part that's hard to talk about. I did a bad thing. A really bad thing.

I'm the one that killed Winter. I didn't mean to. I only meant to turn him, but things got way out of control when my new fangs slid into his vein. Drinking someone's blood is nothing like having your blood taken. Drinking blood is like an explosion of rose petals, it's like honey and milk and every warm thing in the world. It's like drinking pure light.

I held him to me and drank and drank and drank. It was like drowning in him, like being closer than ever, together inside my veins. But now Winter isn't here to laugh with or help me pick out outfits, or to understand me the way no one else ever did. Maybe no one else ever will understand me like that.

I'll never be anyone's twin sister. No one will recognize me as the mortal I once was. The last bits of the girl I gave up being died with him. Now there is only Midnight.

I guess it wouldn't have come to this if I hadn't wanted to be a vampire, if I hadn't wanted to be a marvelous monster and beautiful like the dawn. But even though I will miss Winter every minute of every day for the rest of eternity, I know that he wanted this for me. So, in his memory, I am going to rip out this town's throat.

Oh, and you, my faithful friends and readers, deserve a warning. The videos are disturbing, but we always say that we want to see the real stuff, so here it is.

CHAPTER 27

Verse, Fame, and Beauty are

intense indeed,

But Death intenser—Death is

Life's high mead.

—John Keats

The gates of Lucien Moreau's house stood open, with bouncers choosing guests from a human crowd gathered in front of them. Tana looked around at the girls in glittering red dresses and inky gowns, their eyes shimmering with liner and shadow and fake feathery lashes, and at the boys in their tight coats. Valentina had said it would be hard to stand out, and it was.

Tana had chosen a long ivory silk dress with a plunging neckline, the kind worn by starlets in old movies, with a slit on her thigh that hid the scratch but revealed a lot of the rest of her leg. Unlike most vampire partygoers, she had no fresh holes at the crooks of her elbows, where needles slipped in for venipuncture, no marks except for the old scar on her arm, and she hoped that might be unique enough to get her inside if Jameson's name didn't. Tana had piled her mass of black hair up on her head, secured with two silver combs she'd bought at the pawnshop so that everyone could see that the only thing at her throat was Gavriel's garnet necklace, each stone shining like a single droplet of blood. She hoped she looked fresh and clean, untasted, wrapped up like a dumb little sacrifice.

She'd left her boots, jacket, and backpack at the shop and concealed the rest of her things in a vintage clutch of hammered brass, sculpted into the shape of a gilded lion's head with gluey pits for eyes where stones had once been set. Her knife she'd strapped to her thigh with two leather belts.

It had taken her the better part of an hour to put together the outfit and fifteen more minutes of struggling in front of a cloudy window to get her hair up and staying that way. Then Valentina had made Tana sit in front of a mirror while she brushed her lashes with mascara, highlighted the arch of her brow with silver, and painted her lips a pale shell pink. As she walked up to the gate, the lion clutch banged against her hip from a thin chain, making her change rattle inside it, a hollow metallic sound.

Valentina wore a bronze dress that shimmered with beading. It showed off the long expanse of her legs. Her lion's mane of hair hung around her shoulders, and her golden makeup was brighter than ever. Tana grinned at her as they waded through the crowd to the gate.

The bouncer was a big, muscular man with long hair pulled back in a black velvet ribbon. His gaze stopped on Tana for a moment, but instead he waved in a tall girl, naked except for a mangy mink coat. Tana edged closer as a trio of boys in leather pants slipped past. Then the bouncer chose two girls in matching green silk cheongsams, their hair styled and colored in identical copper bobs so it seemed as if they were twins.

"Our friend is on the list!" Tana yelled over the noise, pointing and hoping the bouncer could hear her.

"Your friend?" he repeated back dubiously. "Really? What's the name?"

"Jameson," Tana said, standing up on her toes, trying to see the clipboard.

"He got any more name than that?" the bouncer asked. A superior smile twisted his lips.

Valentina stepped forward, managing to project an impressive aura of haughty impatience. "You know his name. Jameson Ramirez Alonso. Now, he told us to meet him here, and he told us we wouldn't have any trouble getting in. This is ridiculous."

The bouncer looked as though he wanted to hassle her a little more, but something about her crossed arms and downturned mouth warned him off it. "Fine, go on."

Relief washed over Tana, and then, before she could quite believe it, they were walking past the scrollwork gate with knife-sharp posts and into Lucien Moreau's party.

"Nice job," she said under her breath.

Valentina smiled, chin high. "Good plan. We're like a pair of hot girl spies."

The house was a massive Victorian with a wraparound porch. The building loomed tall and strange, with several roofs of slate and glass. Partygoers stood on the sloped lawn beyond the gates, a few lying in the patchy grass or laughing as they ran in teasing circles. A thick, cloying incense perfumed the air, and the closer she got to the massive door, which stood open atop the steps, the stronger the smell grew. Myrrh and musk, covering up some sweet, foul stench underneath.

She walked up the steps and through the open door into the foyer. There was music playing somewhere, the thin, tortured sound of violins, accompanied by discordant, distant human cries. Her heart started to speed and her breath came unsteadily. She had the immediate sense that this party wasn't for humans, no matter how many were present or who watched the recordings from their homes.

Cameras looked down from the corners of the ceilings, blinking with green lights to show they were on. On the local cable channel back home, from three until four thirty in the morning, there was a show in which a girl called Asphodel, wearing a long purple wig, would broadcast clips of the party she thought were worth highlighting and discuss them with callers. Black bars covered any actual penetration of fangs so as not to offend the FCC. A red-eyed girl in a silver dress passed Tana, spattered with blood, jolting her out of any pretense this was anything but a dangerous fishbowl of monsters, a snake cage full of mice.

A thin, mad giggle threatened to burst from Tana's lips, but she clenched her fingers hard enough for her nails to dig into her palms and waited for the feeling to pass.

"You okay?" Valentina asked. She was looking up the stairs at the people there, holding mismatched champagne coupes in their hands. A vampire in a tuxedo looked down from the landing, his pale hands gripping the wood railing. He smiled like a ferryman come to conduct her to the realm of the dead.

Tana nodded. *Calm down*, she told herself. *Just find Aidan, get the marker back, and get out.*

When she left Coldtown, she decided, she and Pauline would go on a road trip. She wouldn't go straight home, not with her thoughts full of blood and teeth and ruby eyes. They'd go on an adventure instead—a normal one, where nothing very adventurous happened. They could head south until the money ran out. She imagined driving through the day with the windows down, slushies melting in the cup holders, the radio turned up, and Pauline singing along in the passenger seat.

Tana forced herself to move, to walk into the first of a honeycomb of high-ceilinged rooms. It was purple-walled, with a boy spread out on a table that was covered in a white cloth. A few vampires gathered around, licking the thin lines of blood welling up from shallow slices on his arms and legs, his skin already glossy with spit. His eyes were closed, but sometimes they fluttered a little, as if in dreams.

"Do you see her anywhere?" Tana whispered.

Valentina shook her head. She was trying to seem blasé, but she couldn't quite tear her gaze from the boy and the blood. Taking her arm, Tana steered her through to a second room. There, human girls and boys, painted with latex, metal gags covering their mouths, had been manacled directly to the walls, which were covered in a pattern of steel plates to look like picture-frame molding. Tana watched in astonishment as a man walked up to one, grabbed the girl's wrist, and sank his teeth directly into her skin.

"They're infected," said a vampire in a long dress of deep red satin, corseted over her stomach and sewn with pieces of jet. It showed off a long, jagged half-moon of a scar at her shoulder. Her coffee-brown hair was pulled back into a tight, sleek chignon and her lips were painted the same scarlet as her eyes. "It doesn't matter if you bite them. They can't get any *more* infected, can they?"

Tana smothered a gasp at the sight of the woman. She was famous; Tana knew her instantly from watching clips from Coldtown and from dozens of Tumblr gifs showing her sternest expression captioned with OMGWTF? or I'M FREAKING **DEAD** SERIOUS or NOMNOMNOM. She was Elisabet, Lucien's lover, rumored to be far more callous and cruel than he was. She appeared young, barely older than Tana, but her eyes were ancient and cold as lead. And there was something else about her face. . . .

"They'll never get any less infected, either," Valentina said under her breath.

"You ran away with my prize." Elisabet pressed a cool finger over Tana's chin, making her flinch.

"Oh," Tana said, dread shivering up her spine. She realized with a lurch of nausea that she'd seen Elisabet before, in Lance's house, her face so bloated from feeding that until this moment, Tana hadn't realized who she was. She thought of the gore-streaked walls, and there was a ringing in her ears, shock drowning out all other sound.

"Where is he?" Elisabet whispered against her ear, impatient, as though maybe she was repeating herself.

Tana had no idea what to say to that. Fear made her stupid.

"I don't know who you're talking about," Tana forced out, not bothering to disguise her terror.

"My mistake," Elisabet said, lips cool against Tana's skin. "Enjoy the party, sweet girl."

And with that, the vampire spun away.

Still shaking, Tana closed her eyes and let the noise of the party wash over her—the music and the conversation and the moans. Let all her thoughts go, hoping that the fear would go with them.

"What the hell just happened?" Valentina asked.

"Please tell me *she* isn't Jameson's girlfriend," Tana said, and, finally, sucking in a deep breath, opened her eyes.

"Of course not. Are you crazy?" Valentina didn't look ready to calm down. "I thought Elisabet was going to kill you and eat you right in front of me. Let's go."

Tana shook her head vehemently, but she thought of sharks that bumped against their victim several times before they bit down. Maybe Valentina would be smart to get far away from her if Elisabet was just circling. "We both need to find a different person. How about we split up, take a quick sweep, and meet by the stairs? We'll take ten minutes, tops. And if one of us doesn't show, the other goes back to your shop and waits."

"And if one of us *never* shows?" Valentina asked, looking at Tana as if she knew exactly what she'd been thinking.

"Then I guess the other one can feel pretty lucky," Tana said with a halfhearted shrug.

"Be careful," said Valentina.

"You, too." Tana took a deep breath and kept moving through the rooms, only looking back once. She wanted to turn around and tell Valentina that she'd changed her mind. She didn't want to be alone. But it was safer this way.

Find Aidan, she told herself. *Then go, go, go.*

She came to a huge ballroom next, with a ceiling of windows like a massive gazebo, all tinted black. The panes glittered and flashed like prisms with the reflected light of three brass chandeliers, each arm in the shape of a dragon. During the day, the ceiling must flood the room with strange gray light. Tana still hadn't seen Aidan or Midnight, but the crowd was bigger here, so she carefully picked her way through, looking for them.

From behind her, she heard a rasping voice, as brittle as dried leaves.

"*He's here*," it said.

She froze, transported to Lance's party, hearing the echo of the vampires on the other side of the door. She was sure it was one of them speaking—the others were here, too, not just Elisabet. Maybe the one that had scraped her. She had to lean against one of the walls for a long moment, trying not to hyperventilate. Out of the corner of her eye, she saw the vampire who'd spoken. He had white hair and long, jagged fingernails. The other one appeared younger; he was brown-haired, with a pointed chin and freckles that stood out against the pallor of his skin. Both wore matching black suits with mandarin collars.

A visceral, full-body shudder passed through her. She reminded herself that she wasn't the one they were looking for. They were hunting

Gavriel. To bring the Thorn of Istra back to the Spider and to his prison, to pay for letting Caspar Morales go. To make sure Gavriel stayed there, mad as ever, as though the world hadn't changed and the ancient vampires were still in charge, even if nowadays they ruled over what they barely understood. And if Elisabet had been with them, then maybe Lucien was helping the Spider—sending out his own people to make sure Gavriel wound up right back in a cell.

He's here, they'd said.

And it was Gavriel they were looking for, so did that mean he was at the party? She craned her neck, trying to spot him in the crowd.

What she saw instead was Lucien Moreau walking into the room, unmistakable and oddly magnetic. People turned toward him automatically, as flowers align themselves toward the sun. Elisabet was on his arm, looking as remote as she did on the Coldtown feeds.

If her beauty was dark, Lucien's was bright. He was all careless elegance, with tousled blond hair that shone like gold and an ivory suit with the top two buttons of his white shirt undone. The bones of his face were arranged in a way that was both handsome and austere. He had an aquiline nose, finely drawn lips, and a certain gauntness to his cheeks that spoke of greater age or infirmity than the rest of him showed.

Looking past Lucien and Elisabet, Tana finally saw Aidan. He was underdressed, slouching against a wall in a black silk shirt over black jeans. Tana wondered if Midnight had picked out those clothes for him and then wondered if they'd been borrowed from Rufus.

Steeling herself, she walked over to him, giving a wide berth to any other vampire she saw.

"Tana!" Aidan said, looking incredibly pleased to see her right up to the moment when she punched him in the face.

He staggered back, and several people glanced over, tittering. Elisabet was looking her way again, which unnerved her, but not enough that she regretted hitting Aidan. She didn't regret it a bit.

"Ow," he said. "I think one of my fangs knocked into my cheek. That really hurt."

She put her hands on her hips and just stared at him. She knew that he was stronger than her and about a million times more deadly, but he was still Aidan and he still hated it when someone was mad at him.

He rubbed his chin, where her fist had struck. "Come on, Tana. I wasn't going to keep it. I just wanted you to stay a little longer. You know how I hate going places alone."

"You are such a jerk," Tana said. "Seriously. A huge, unbelievable jerk."

"I know," he said, looking both repentant and impish at once. "But you got all dressed up and came to a party, so don't you want to have a good time? I mean, you're already here."

"You've got Midnight to party with." Tana stuck out her hand, palm up. "Hand it over. Now."

"What if we hang out for a while first? I've got stuff to tell you that you're going to want to hear."

"Please." Her anger was draining away, turning to fear. He could keep her in Coldtown forever. She couldn't make him give back the marker. She couldn't make him do anything.

He sighed, watching her expression change, then reached into his back pocket and, keeping his hand cupped over it, put the marker into her hand. "You better be careful not to let anyone see it."

She let out a breath, surprised and indescribably relieved. Despite his red eyes, despite everything, she supposed he was still Aidan, still her ex-boyfriend, still her friend, still a person. The same boy she'd met in art class, the same boy with the floppy hair who was always in love and always sincere, even when he was joking. She shoved the disk into her lion's head purse, but not before sneaking a look to make sure it really was the marker. "Thank you."

"The only reason I took it is because I wanted a chance to talk to you again, when things were less awful. To get you to forgive me for everything I've done."

She didn't bother pointing out that making her even madder in the service of getting forgiveness didn't make a lot of sense. It didn't matter now. "It wasn't your fault. Well, some of it wasn't your fault."

He smiled. "Did you know Gavriel's at this party? That's what I was going to tell you. I saw him before, but I don't think he saw me."

Tana turned her head without really meaning to, but all the faces belonged to strangers. She saw the terrifying vampires in the black suits talking to Lucien and Elisabet, and despite her stupid, hopeless desire to see Gavriel one more time, she hoped that Aidan was wrong. Those vampires were hunting for him. She remembered their whispered voices through the door. She remembered the sting of their teeth against the back of her leg and the dead, staring eyes of her classmates. No matter what Gavriel was capable of, she didn't want him to have to face them.

Aidan nodded. "Yeah. I mean, I was going to say hi and all, but when I got closer, he was gone. I didn't see where he went."

Tana did not want to consider what Aidan might have said to Gavriel about her.

"We should go," she told him. "Is Midnight with you? Because I think this party is going to get very unsafe in a minute."

"She's here looking for a new place for us to squat. She wants to find us a family of vampires. Nestmates or some crap like that, she calls them."

"What about Rufus and Christobel?" Tana asked.

He shook his head. "What about them? She's going to keep killing humans. She says that when their hearts stop, their souls drag you halfway to eternity as they die and for a moment you're like some dark god staring down at the world. She scares the hell out of me, Tana. I don't want her to be the only friend I have here."

She didn't know what to say to that. It wasn't fair that Aidan had become a vampire. He wasn't like Lucien Moreau or the kids who came here hoping to be turned. He shouldn't have had to fight his impulses. No one at the farmhouse should have had to die. Whole pieces of cities shouldn't be walled off like prisons ruled by their inmates. Children shouldn't have to grow up trapped inside, with no way out. None of it was fair, and she couldn't think of a way to fix any of it; and the helplessness was worse than anything else.

"Aidan, you've got to—" Tana started to say.

From one end of the room, from behind Elisabet and Lucien, a silvery knife came flying through the air.

The crowd parted, gasping in a single voice. The freckled vampire from the farmhouse shrieked, the curved dagger stuck deep in his chest. He clawed at it, then began to shrink into himself, like a balloon with all the air rushing out, his skin turning desiccated, dark, and papery.

His white-haired companion stretched a long-fingered hand as if he could possibly help. As if it wasn't already too late.

The suited vampire was curling up, fingers clenching into dried-out claws. He fell to the floor, pieces of him cracking off as if he were made from the fibers of a hornet's nest, a liquid spilling out that looked more like amber than blood.

Every head was turned to watch the spectacle, including Tana's. She'd never seen anything like this, not on YouTube or in documentaries or in Suicide Square. She'd never seen an ancient vampire withering away to his mortal remains before her eyes. They were careful and clever and almost never died, certainly not like this. She was so stunned that she almost didn't catch the whisper-soft sound of an impossibly fleet footstep.

She was able to register Gavriel just before he reached the white-haired vampire. Gavriel had two more knives, one glittering in each hand. Short, cruel, curved blades. He threw his arms around the vampire from behind, pulling him close in what looked like an embrace—before he jerked his arms to the sides, uncrossing the blades, and scissoring off the vampire's head.

Blood gouted, dark and thick as syrup, before he began to wither, too. Lucien's white suit was splattered, the bystanders' faces and elaborate clothing were dotted with blood as if it'd rained down from the sky like a summer storm in a nightmare. Tana felt it on her cheeks, wet and still warm, as though he'd just fed.

The white-haired vampire's face remained frozen in shock or grief, his last expression preserved as his head spun from his shoulders. It hit Lucien's shining marble floor and rolled into the crowd.

Gavriel spun on Lucien and Elisabet. It was only then that Tana realized Lucien had moved, seizing up the dagger from the body of the first fallen vampire.

Elisabet made a small sound of surprise.

"Good entrance, right?" Gavriel asked, and then looked at Elisabet. "And what a delight to see you here with him."

He was as beautiful as he'd ever been, features sharpened by anger. But it was impossible to look at him, spattered with gore, and believe that once his mouth had been on hers. He seemed like something out of a dark hallucination, now, something terrible and unknowable, a trickster god of murder.

"We wondered how long it would take you to arrive," said Lucien, holding the dagger as though it were merely something to gesture with. "You took a circuitous path."

Gavriel shrugged. "It was my own time to take."

"That little feast of yours last night was quite something," said Lucien. "Do you know what kind of chaos you've unleashed, infecting all those people?"

The corner of Gavriel's lip rose. His eyes shone with mad delight. "No idea, but I look forward to finding out."

At that, Lucien laughed. It might have even been an honest reaction. "You've changed."

Gavriel acknowledged the words with a small bow of his head. "In a decade, how could I not have? And what a decade it's been."

Lucien flinched. "You're angry that we betrayed you, and you have every right. That was my fault and my failing. I have regretted it often." He swept his hand through the air. "But look at the world you made. How beautiful and vibrant it is. We were wrong to cling to the shadows and creep through the night. Your mistake has set us all free. Now, at last, you can see what the old vampires feared."

"You left me to rot away in chains," Gavriel said.

Gavriel and Lucien locked eyes.

Gavriel went on in a soft voice. "And you tried to recapture me for the Spider. Do you deny it?"

"My people were afraid. Elisabet worried he'd broken you and sent you to hunt us down. The ancient vampires hate any of us who adapted. They hate me most of all, broadcasting secrets. We tried to capture you, but not for the reasons you think."

"You shouldn't worry over me," said Gavriel. "Not anymore. All the pieces were sewn back together in nearly the right places."

"What can we give you, Gavriel?" Elisabet asked. "What can we do to show you how sorry we are? Whatever it is, we know that you're owed it."

Gavriel licked the blood off his knife, his tongue sweeping to the tip of the blade. "I want to watch both your ashes blow away across the face of a bloodred moon." He sang the next bit, his voice swelling with madness. "*By the light, by the light, by the light of the bloodred moon. I'll be killing you soon.* Do you remember that song? I've altered the words a little."

"So nothing will satisfy you but death?" asked Lucien, clearly uncertain at how to talk to this new Gavriel.

"I came a long way for it. I'd hate to go back empty-handed." He truly sounded crazy, Tana thought. Crazy like some poet or prophet. Crazy and lethal. He shrugged his shoulders and grinned.

"Let us show you how grievously sorry we really are," Lucien said, with the voice that had enchanted so many children hungry for the grave, the voice that mesmerized viewers the world over. He put his hand on Elisabet's shoulder, pressing down lightly. "Let us make a formal apology. We'll kneel and beg your forgiveness. Could you think of any other creature we would kneel before?"

Elisabet glanced over her shoulder at him, as if looking to read on his face whatever he planned, but then, slowly, sank to her knees, her skirt puddling around her. She looked like a beautiful supplicant at a shrine.

Even Gavriel seemed transfixed, staring down at her. His brows drew together, and his chin lifted as though he was trying to wrench himself free of her hold on him.

Lucien moved behind her, stroking her dark hair back from her face. "She took my men and went after you. They wanted to protect me. Isn't that sweet? But I swear to you, I had nothing to do with it."

Elisabet looked up and struggled to rise, but Lucien seized a handful of her hair and jerked her head back. Then, with Gavriel's own knife, Lucien sliced her throat open. The river of her veins parted, blood pouring out like water. He cut farther, severing her head.

The whole room gasped as Elisabet's body slumped forward, Tana gasping with them. Lucien wore a tiny, odd smile as her body began to curl and wizen, her honey-colored skin wrinkling like bark. Her lush mouth withered, and the hollows where her eyes had been grew as sunken as the gluey holes of Tana's purse. Lucien let her head fall.

A moment before, Elisabet had been one of the most dangerous people in the ballroom. Now she was dead. A few partygoers knelt down beside her as if there was something yet to do for her, as though she'd just fainted. A woman with a pierced nose and mermaid braids stroked the vampire's once-smooth cheek. A boy drew his finger through Elisabet's blood and popped that finger into his mouth.

"You're worth more to me than she ever could be, Gavriel," Lucien said, stepping away from her body. "Now that I've punished her for you, perhaps you will see how much I mean that. I loved Elisabet in my way, but you are as a son to me. Forgive a father his sins."

Gavriel took a step back, the shock on his face evident. "Did she really deserve that?"

"You asked for our deaths," Lucien said. "I gave you hers. Ask me for something else, and I will give you that, too. I knew from the moment you broke out of the cage under Père-Lachaise Cemetery that you would come here, either as my prisoner or of your own free will." Abruptly, Lucien raised his voice. "Cut the feeds from this room! Cut them!"

One by one the lights on the cameras around the room went from green to red.

The crowd that had gathered began murmuring. Tana wondered what it meant that Lucien had left the streaming video on while he murdered Elisabet and only now was calling for it to be turned off. What could be worse than that? She edged toward the door, pushing through the crowd.

Gavriel looked incandescent, trembling with readiness.

"We never would have hurt you," Lucien said. "We knew that once we'd captured you, we could begin to plan. Plan a glorious future and a far better revenge than you dreamed, my dear, lost friend. The old ways are dead, and it's time the old ones died with them."

"Starting with you?" Gavriel said, but his gaze kept tracking from Lucien to Elisabet, as though he was still surprised by her corpse.

"You don't really want to kill me," Lucien said. "Look at you, you're even sorry Elisabet is gone. You just want to come home."

"Do I?" Gavriel asked.

"You know why, in films, the villain hesitates before he kills the hero? You know why he explains his whole dastardly plan? Do you know why you're hesitating now?"

Gavriel quirked a smile. "I do know. But I wager you'll never guess."

Lucien plunged on. "Because the villain knows that without the hero to hate, his life would be empty. Once he's murdered his adversary, he's alone."

"So you're the hero?" Gavriel asked.

"Every hero is the villain of his own story, wouldn't you say?" Lucien was speaking to Gavriel, but he pitched his voice to carry to the crowd of partygoers. He knew how to draw them to him and make them hang on his every word.

"I wouldn't." Gavriel looked amused, though, as if this rhetorical style was familiar to him. As if it charmed him—not the show itself, but the memory of Lucien acting this way.

"Isn't every hero aware of all the terrible reasons they did those good deeds? Aware of every mistake they ever made and how good people got hurt because of their decisions? Don't they recall the moments they weren't heroic at all? The moments where their heroism led to more deaths than deliberate villainy ever could?"

Gavriel was staring at Lucien as though fascinated, as though finally one of Lucien's attempts to capture his attention had worked.

"You've been alone for ten years—and maybe longer than that. But you won't be alone anymore. I know you. I know you better than anyone in the world, and if you forgive me, I will serve up vengeance enough to sate even you. Together, we'll kill the Spider."

Gavriel's knife hand sagged.

He was going to do it, Tana realized. He was going to let a man who'd just murdered his girlfriend talk him into making an alliance, with her corpse still on the floor between them. She turned away, disgusted, through a door to the outside.

On the lawn, she felt dizzy from the mingled scents of incense and blood, and her head had started to throb. She leaned her hand against the wall near a collection of trash cans and garden tools, waiting to see if she was going to vomit. Then she'd walk to the front and see if Valentina was still there.

"Tana?" a girl's voice asked. Tana looked up to see Midnight, coming toward her from the front yard in a shiny vinyl dress. Her blue hair hung around her shoulders, and she looked as sweet and calm as if the last two days had never happened. "Is that you?"

"Yeah," Tana said, taking another shuddering breath. "I'm okay. Just give me a minute."

"I'd hoped you'd come to the party," Midnight said, stepping closer. The scent of decay wafted off her. "I wanted to thank you for everything you did the other night."

Tana was about to tell her that she was welcome, when Midnight grabbed for her throat.

CHAPTER 28

How shocking must thy summons be,
O Death!
—Robert Blair

Vienna in 1912 was very different from Paris a mere twenty years before. The streets were full of motorcars and bicycles during the day, and at night the whole city glowed with electric lights. Phones rang and elevators whisked the bourgeoisie up the floors of their rent palaces along the Ringstrasse, where the walls of the old city had once been. Sigmund Freud had published *Drei Abhandlungen zur Sexualtheorie* already and Carl Jung was just about to publish *Wandlungen und Symbole der Libido.* The modern age was well under way, and everyone believed themselves to be marching forward to a better tomorrow. But prostitutes still prowled the ground where gallows had once hung, willing to lie down on top of tombs with a man for the price of a newspaper. Other things prowled there, too. Vienna was a city with its lights on, and no one wanted to acknowledge what happened in the dark.

Lucien Moreau strode through the night streets in his buttoned-up black sack coat, Elisabet beside him in a beaded, high-necked lace dress, all cream and gold and black. Gavriel was on the other side, in a charcoal coat that nearly matched Lucien's own.

They were gorgeous creatures, wholly fascinating, and unequivocally broken, Lucien mused as they walked.

They were also likely to be executed before the night was out, all because of him. A vampire was supposed to seek permission before creating progeny, and Lucien hadn't. He would never have received it, not for either of his offspring, unstable as they were.

Gavriel was half in love with death. He'd lost a lover to it and put his own brother in a grave, so maybe it was no surprise that he stalked murderers through the city streets, sinking his fangs into their jugulars and gulping down their blood. Every night, it was as though he avenged his brother by killing some stand-in for himself.

And one only had to look to see the madness that glittered behind Elisabet's eyes. Lucien had discovered her in Portugal, on trial for the murder of her husband. He'd been impressed with the way she spat on the ground and declared that not only had she done it, but if the Lord raised her husband back up in that very courtroom, she'd do it again. Lucien and Gavriel broke her out of the prison that night; she'd gone with them without a single look back. When she hunted, she used a razor instead of her teeth and attacked her victims with a ferocity that would have been unnerving in a man twice her size.

And now he would have to mourn them. He tried to say amusing things as they walked through the streets, tried to pretend that it was possible for the Spider, ancient and terrible as he was, to let them live, but Lucien knew his progeny would, in all likelihood, be destroyed. Ancient vampires ruled over their portion of the world like feudal lords, favoring the same sorts of punishments. Perhaps Lucien should have told them to run, but he knew that neither Istanbul nor Shanghai nor any other place was far enough to hide from a creature like the Spider, who could pull at his baroque web of connections to cause the fall of the banks in Luxembourg or a revolution in Spain. If they ran, he would track them across the world.

Besides, if they ran, it would get Lucien in a lot of trouble.

Elisabet flashed him a fierce look. "We should kill the Spider," she said. "Kill him and drain him. His blood would grant us all his centuries of power. Even shared, we'd be able to make the rules instead of listening to them."

"Don't be stupid," Lucien snapped, although in truth, he had heard that there was a Spider before this one, killed in the way Elisabet proposed. "If you make a single move against him, we'll all be dead. It's important that you show him that I've taught you the proper respect for your elders."

"Then perhaps you should have," said Gavriel in his soft, self-possessed voice.

Lucien shot him a sharp look. One of the things that had drawn him to Gavriel was that as lost as Gavriel was in his morass of grief, there were times when he was unnervingly clear-sighted. But Lucien didn't like to have that sharp sight turned on him.

He knew what he was, what depths of depravity and cruelty he had plumbed, what ambitions drove him. He prided himself on knowing those things—but that didn't mean he needed anyone else to see them as well.

They made their way to a walled manor in the old city, the facade all carved marble and stone. The gates stood slightly ajar, and Lucien slipped inside, past carefully shaped hedges, toward a large red double door with a brass knocker in the shape of an agonized woman's face. As Lucien lifted it, he realized that the hinge of the knocking mechanism was between her teeth, making it appear like a riding bit.

Gavriel raised both his brows at Elisabet. She rolled her eyes.

It should have pleased him, the way they truly behaved like siblings, but he resented it. It made him feel that, though he ruled over them, they still kept secrets. "He'd like to see you like that, I'll wager," Lucien said, just to watch Gavriel look embarrassed, to watch Elisabet snort, just to show them that everything, even their jokes, belonged to him. Death might steal them soon, but until then, they were his.

A few moments later, a stoop-shouldered woman came to the door. She was wearing a dark-colored dress, her graying hair pulled back into a braided bun.

"*Guten Tag*," the woman said, and ushered them inside. Following her, they passed through many rooms with painted fresco ceilings depicting battles, the dead and dying looking down at them from gilt-lined recesses. Electric globes hung like fruit from chandeliers, reflected in mirrored panels. They passed red brocade couches and tables with carvings as elaborate as the plaster moldings on the walls.

She led them to another courtyard, this one with a single hawthorn at its center. A few of the Spider's personal guards, rather pretentiously known as the *Corps des Ténèbres*, stood around conspicuously in their long robes. Standing beside the tree was a very tall and thin vampire in a charcoal sack coat with a waistcoat and trousers. A watch fob ran from his pocket to underneath his vest, and a red-gold intaglio signet ring, still choked with wax, shone in the glow from the gas lamps. His hooded red eyes regarded them from a saturnine face with a high forehead and a poisoner's mouth. There was no mistaking who he was, despite his ordinary dress and demeanor. He exuded a kind of power that had almost a gravitational pull.

Elisabet was staring at him with a terrible kind of fascination. And Gavriel seemed to be trying not to look anywhere at all.

"Ah, Lucien," said the Spider, walking toward them, taking his hands out of the pockets of his trousers to scorch the end of a cigarette with a bright gold lighter. His fingers ended in long, yellowed, hooked nails like the talons of some great bird, and Lucien wondered how many more centuries it would be before he woke up with hands like that. "So good of you to come."

The servant woman, with a worshipful glance toward her master, withdrew.

"I am ever yours to command," said Lucien with a short bow. He hated the antiquated vampires, hated their silly palaces and their airs and the way they expected one to bow and scrape. Here, among all the trappings of modern Vienna, one might be tempted to think the time of monarchs was past, but whatever revolutions happened elsewhere in the world, none was likely to occur among the shadowy governance of vampires.

The Spider snorted. "You're an apple farmer's son from a little town in Normandy, no matter how much you play at consequence."

Oh, and had he mentioned how much he hated their ridiculous

obsession with ancestry, as though it mattered what blood ran through one's veins when all of it was stolen? He bit his tongue and said nothing.

The Spider turned to Gavriel, pointing at him with one clawed nail, making him flinch. "At first glance, they do not seem so unworthy for you to have hidden them from me, Lucien. Why did you not present them as you should have? Is there some reason I would have forbidden you from turning them?"

Only that one is a psychopath and the other has what Freud would call a powerful death urge? But which one is which?

"I am impulsive," Lucien said, readying himself to make a speech of contrition. "But I meant no harm. I taught them how to hunt and kill, to leave little trace of their passing through the world. They've done nothing wrong save being born—and in that, too, they are innocent. I am their maker. That crime is mine."

"Yes," the Spider said.

Lucien would have said more, but that one word halted him. He'd never thought he would receive any real punishment. He glanced surreptitiously toward the two *Corps des Ténèbres* in plain sight and reconsidered Elisabet's plan. No, still better to run if it came to that.

"Lucien Moreau, I accept your confession. Our power comes from our small numbers, from our secrecy, from our adherence to what few rules we have. Your death is a just one, for it will warn off others like you who are equally impulsive." The ancient vampire set his clawed hand lightly against Lucien's shoulder. Lucien turned and looked into the Spider's face, puzzled for a moment. But then a shudder went through him. Because he saw, in that moment, that all of the Spider's fine clothes and civilized words were just a mask. Beneath it was something ancient and savage, something that feared nothing and only *hungered*. Lucien felt his knees buckle as though some unseen force bore down on him. He went to the floor with a groan.

Gavriel gasped.

"No," Elisabet shrieked, throwing herself down beside Lucien in a sea of skirts and crawling toward the Spider. "No, please spare him. He is our father, our brother, our master. He is the one who gave us life eternal. Please!"

The Spider held up a hand and she subsided. For the first time in a hundred years, Lucien was truly afraid. "Let one of you take his place, then. Will you?"

For a long moment, Lucien's progeny were silent. He closed his eyes, cursing them both in his thoughts.

"It is right and good," said the Spider, "for a parent to die before his child. You are right to leave him to his fate."

"No," Gavriel said. "Wait. I will take his place. Get up, Lucien."

Lucien looked at Gavriel, black curls spilling over his cheeks, and thanked whatever wisdom had made him turn a man who availed himself of every single opportunity to throw his life away. Lucien hoped he wouldn't have to watch the execution.

"You're certain," said the Spider, his greedy gaze boring into the boy, stripping him raw.

Gavriel nodded quickly, clearly steeling himself. He began to kneel.

The Spider shook his head, smiling. "You may remain standing. You're loyal and courageous, two qualities not often found among our kind. What a waste to cut down such a rare creature. No, my sentence is that you will hunt for me—you will hunt others like us. You will be one of my Thorns, and your term of service will be your entire illicitly born life."

"I'm not to die?" Gavriel asked, clearly puzzled. He looked toward Lucien, but Lucien was powerless to speak, possessiveness lighting through him like a flame. Gavriel was *his*, made from his blood, alive by his whim, his to jeer at or adore or destroy. And if Gavriel wasn't to be his, then Lucien would rather he was razed from the earth.

"No." The Spider took a long drag on his cigarette, looking like a very modern sort of monster, despite his years. Despite what Lucien had seen in his face. "Oh, no, you're to give me the gift of all that loyalty."

What Lucien hated the most about ancient vampires, he decided, was the way they had studied cruelty for so long to know just how to hurt you best.

It won't always be this way, Lucien vowed.

And it wasn't.

CHAPTER 29

While I thought that I was learning how to live, I have been learning how to die.

—Leonardo da Vinci

Midnight bore Tana to the ground, her weight and the suddenness of the strike enough to knock Tana off balance. She fell amid the trash cans, the sour stink of garbage all around her. Tana looked up at the sky for an odd, lucid moment, seeing the stars spread out like a carpet over them. Then she kicked Midnight in the stomach.

The vampire girl let go of Tana's throat in surprise, and Tana scuttled back. But before she could get to her feet, Midnight threw herself against her, grasping her arms and sitting on her legs. Pinned, Tana could only try to reach for the wooden shaft of a rake that seemed just beyond her grasp.

"What is wrong with you?" Tana demanded, fingers wiggling through the dirt. "I helped you."

"Helped me? I didn't need you and your watching, judging eyes. You'll try to take Winter away from me again. Leave him in the sun to bake and rot. He's mine. I get to bury him the way I want." Tana didn't know if this manic energy and violence had always been in her or if being turned had made her this way, but right then Midnight sounded like a little girl who'd forgotten to feed her gerbil and then, finding it dead, cared more about decorating its shoe box coffin than about what she'd done. "And now you're trying to take away Aidan, too. It's not fair."

Tana finally caught hold of the rake and brought it down as hard as she could. It smacked Midnight in the shoulder, which wasn't exactly what Tana intended, but it made Midnight recoil, snarling. Tana hit her again. This time the wood struck her head. Midnight grabbed it and snapped it in two, throwing the jagged ends among the trash.

In that moment, Tana pushed free and started to run toward the house, but Midnight caught her, dragging her back through the dirt.

Tana tried to flip over, pushing against the ground. She rose up just as Midnight sunk her teeth into Tana's neck.

Pain seared along Tana's nerves. It hurt, it really hurt. It was like her mother ripping open her arm all over again. But as she cried out, a kind of icy numbness began to spread through her veins, and after that, a velvety, consuming pleasure. It ate away at the edges of her thoughts, pressing on her to fall deeper into its darkness. She still felt Midnight's mouth moving against her neck, still felt the sting of teeth and the pull of her blood being drawn from her, but all those feelings were growing more and more indistinct. Instead, it was as though she were being devoured by cold flame, and each lick of that black fire made her shudder with rapturous agony.

She kicked her feet and scrabbled with the nails of her fingers, scratching Midnight's arms futilely. The vampire held Tana firmly, pulling her closer. Her lion's purse was wedged between her waist and the ground, but that small discomfort barely registered.

It was so hard to push through the feelings and *think*. Everything was getting murkier. The shadows were closing in. When she opened her eyes, all she saw was the blurry blue of Midnight's hair.

Think, she told herself muzzily. *Think*.

She forced her hand to close on the metal shell of the purse and push at the lock, letting her money, the marker, and everything else spill out onto the dirt. She felt among the fallen things, looking for something, but she no longer remembered what she had been searching for.

A wave of blissful weakness washed over her. She was so tired. And her ears were full of a distant thudding that seemed to slow, like a drumbeat in time to music about to end.

Then her fingers closed on an object she recognized. The rose water she'd taken from one of the purses at Lance's party. Pulling off the stoppered top clumsily, she splashed the contents in Midnight's face.

The vampire screamed.

Tana plunged back into reality. She was lying in the dirt, about to die. Panic hit her hard and she scrambled to stand, even though she swayed unsteadily on her feet. She grabbed for what she could find on the ground, holding her pathetic weapon up as she knocked into trash cans and then the wall.

Midnight's face was red along one side, as if she'd been scalded. Drawing back her lips over her teeth, she hissed like a cat and rushed at Tana.

Tana had a sudden, vivid memory of her teacher in art class explaining how understanding anatomy was important to life drawing. He'd borrowed a skeleton from the biology room and started talking about ulnas and tibias, when Marcus Yates, the school's most reliable weed dealer, called out something about stabbing someone so you hit them right in the heart. *Up under the fifth rib*, he'd said.

She didn't have time to count, but she remembered those words as she brought up the stick she'd grabbed—the broken piece of rake—and slammed it into Midnight's side, thrusting it up toward her heart.

Midnight screamed again, thrashing as Tana pushed the weapon in deeper, using it like a spear. Then, abruptly, Midnight went limp. Her eyes were closed, but her mouth hung open, a terrible grimace distorting her features.

Tana slumped back, wiping her bloody hand on her dress, too stunned to quite process what had happened. She sat in the dirt, shaking with horror and cold.

Get up, Tana, she told herself. *Get up and get out of here. You've got the marker. Go.*

Quickly, without looking at Midnight's body, Tana stuffed her things back into her purse and stood, leaning against the side of Lucien Moreau's house. Light streamed out of the tinted glass window, shockingly bright. It seemed to smear in her vision.

Don't think about it. Go. Just keep going slowly until you make it to the gate. You can sleep in your car. Go.

She took four stumbling steps, before she realized the problem with her plan.

Midnight had bitten her. She was infected. And this time it wouldn't be something her body could fight off. There would be no resisting, no control. She'd be like Aidan was, or worse. Tana fell to her knees, all her thoughts a riot of denial.

Then the door opened and two vampires walked down the steps. They were dressed in ratty black jeans and dark jackets. One of them was smoking a cigarette, although he tossed it to one side when he saw her.

"Get up," he said.

She started to laugh, but it came out more like choking. "I can't."

"You murdered a vampire," he told her, pointing to a camera high up on the side of the house. "Lucien sees everything that goes on here. And he doesn't like humans attacking his guests."

"Well, good, then," Tana mumbled, still grinning stupidly, "because that didn't happen." Lucien, being a vampire, might not see it that way. But it was hard to care much when everything hurt.

As the guards took her, she knew she ought to scream or beg, kick or cry, but she had no more fight left. She let herself be lifted and carried back to the party. They took her through an entrance she hadn't seen before into a small hexagonal-shaped room, which was empty except for the built-in bookshelves that covered the walls and for a settee, where they dumped her.

Tana wasn't sure how long she sat there before Lucien Moreau came in. He'd changed his clothes and was now dressed in a blue shirt and loose gray trousers, looking relaxed as ever. Up close, though, Tana noticed a rank smell clung to him like spoiled meat. Crouching down, he seized her jaw between three of his fingers and turned her face one way and then another. He smiled then, baring his fangs. She felt the iron strength in his hand and the terrible indifference of his gaze, as though she were an animal he was considering the best way to butcher.

"You killed a vampire at my party," Lucien told her. He shook his head as though she was in a great deal of trouble and a very naughty girl.

"So did you," said Tana. If she was going to die, she might as well die sarcastic. She'd seen a lot of old movies, and that was definitely the way to go out. As if she were Humphrey Bogart or Clark Gable not giving a damn. She wanted to make Pauline and Pearl and even her father proud when they watched the feed; if she could be a little bit funny before, maybe the dying part would be less horrible to see.

A corner of his mouth lifted, as if maybe he appreciated a little sass from his prey. "It's *my* party."

She thought of the walls of Lance's farmhouse, streaked with blood. She thought of pink-haired Imogen with her pale, staring eyes. "It's all your fault," she said muzzily. "You. You're the reason."

He gave her an odd look. "I like it when you humans don't bother being sorry, but it's a little much to say that it was my fault."

"So what happens to me now?" She remembered the infected girls and boys shackled to the parlor walls, fed on by vampires. Maybe she'd become one of those. Or maybe he'd just kill her. Maybe she could try to kill him right back, if only she could make herself stand up.

Lucien looked at her, as though he was weighing that very question.

Then he slid his hand down from her jaw to her throat, tipping her head with cool precision. Tana took a deep breath, waiting for him to strike, fumbling in the cushions for any weapon. It was almost over, she told herself.

Then his fingers flicked her garnet necklace, and his expression changed. "That's pretty against your throat. Where did you get it?"

She didn't hesitate. "Gavriel."

His eyes widened fractionally, studying her as though he'd never bothered to really look at her before. Lucien stood and went out, slamming the door behind him. Fear washed over her, but she was so tired and dizzy from blood loss that she couldn't even hold on to it. She stood up and then slid to the floor.

She thought of Gavriel as he'd been earlier that night, with his curved daggers and his mad song. She wondered if he would come and sing to her.

Tana fell into an uneasy doze, curled up on the carpet.

She regained consciousness lying on cold stone, something soft piled under her head.

"Get up," Valentina was saying, shaking her shoulder. "Tana, you've got to get up."

She tried to open her eyes, but they felt as though they were glued together and wouldn't move. Her limbs felt so heavy that she thought she might sink right through the floor.

"She's lost too much blood," said an unfamiliar voice, a girl's. It echoed in the room. "It's all over her. There's no way she's going to make it."

"I don't think that's *her* blood," said a boy.

Tana reached out with her fingers and touched steel bars, chilly against her skin. She wasn't sure where she could be. The room smelled damp, with the vaguely mineral smell of basements. *Open your eyes*, she told herself, but she couldn't.

"Somebody!" Valentina shouted. "She's really sick. Somebody, please!"

When she woke again, she was lying in a massive bed in a dimly lit room. Her arm was shackled to the brass headboard and there was a long IV running from her arm to a bag of clear fluid that hung from a picture hook on the wall, over a bedside table. Someone had taken the painting down and leaned its gilded frame against a chair.

She still hurt, pretty much all over.

"When you're in danger, everything becomes clear, doesn't it?" Gavriel said softly, in a tone that made her shiver. He was sitting on her non-IV side, in a leather chair beside a makeup table, his face in shadows. "Everything else falls away. Danger is a terrible addiction, but that's what I like—the clarity of thought it provides. How about you?"

And even though she'd known him for less than a week and plenty of what she did know of him was horrendous, at the sight of him, she let out her breath all at once. She let herself fall back on the bed, boneless with relief.

She knew she shouldn't feel that way about a monster, but right then, she wanted nothing more than a monster of her very own.

"What's happening to me?" she finally asked, then rattled her arm, indicating the line of tubing. Had she dreamed Valentina's voice?

"Would that it were the waters of Lethe dripping into your veins." He leaned forward, so that the dim light of the tinted window showed the curve of his mouth and the way his dark lashes brushed his cheeks when he lowered his eyes. He looked very young and very old at once. Then a corner of his red mouth lifted in a wry smile. "But alas, the answer is merely that you lost a lot of blood and we're giving you saline."

"Like the stuff people with contacts put in their eyes?" she asked, before realizing he probably had no idea what she was talking about.

He picked up her purse from where it rested beside her and shook it gently. "In case you were concerned. All just as you left it."

She nodded. "Thanks. Although I guess whether I'll ever get to use that marker is pretty up in the air right now."

"You should have let me eat her in that parking lot," Gavriel said, raising his eyebrows.

That startled a laugh out of Tana. It wasn't just that what he'd said was funny—it was the waggish way he'd said it, as if he expected her to get the joke, expected her to get that he was joking. It made her feel less bizarre about how comfortable she felt around him, if he felt even a little bit the same way.

"It's not so bad," Gavriel said, standing and coming to sit at the end of the bed. The amusement had gone from his face as he watched his own hand smooth over her bedclothes. "You're younger than I was when I turned and more adaptable than I remember myself to have been. You'll be marvelous."

For a moment, she didn't understand what he was saying, and then she realized, of course, he must know she was infected. Lucien had seen the fight she'd had with Midnight, and Gavriel must have, too, given what he'd said a moment ago. He certainly could see the bite marks on her throat.

"I'm not going to be a vampire," she said, trying to make her voice sound more certain than she was. She remembered the sound of her mother shouting up from the basement, calling for blood, being willing to sink her teeth into her own daughter's arm. She remembered Aidan lunging at her in the guest room of Lance's party when she'd untied his gag. What would Tana do once the infection wormed deep into her brain, so that there was nothing but the need for blood and the willingness to do anything to get it? Once she was entirely Cold, Cold through and through. Then she would scream and threaten and beg for blood.

Her eyes started to water and she blinked back the tears. She hadn't cried since the gas station, and she wasn't going to cry now.

"Tana," Gavriel said helplessly.

"Whose necklace did you give me?" she asked, wiping her eyes with her free hand. "Lucien recognized it."

"It belonged to my sister once," he said, so quietly that she was sure there was more to the story than that. Then he smiled. "But Katya is long dead, and there's no point in my keeping it when I hardly ever wear it."

"Hardly ever, huh?" Tana said. "I bet garnets look good on you."

He smiled distractedly, seeming to think of another time. Whatever it was, it made his features smooth out and his whole face look softer and very young. "She had it on in Paris when she met Lucien and Elisabet. We pretended to drink champagne with her at a mezzo-soprano's salon in Montparnasse. I imagine Lucien remembers that necklace because he stared at my sister's throat the entire evening."

The casual way he said it, with genuine fondness, made her believe that Lucien—and probably Elisabet—had truly been his friend then. Tana thought about how much fun it must have been, once upon a time, to be vampires and have forever stretching out in front of you—an endless carnival of nights. They must have felt as almighty as angels, looking down on the world from their windows, choosing to spare each passerby.

She liked thinking of it, even as her body felt heavy with exhaustion.

"I heard all that stuff Lucien told you," Tana said, forcing her mind back to the present. "You can't really believe him, can you? I mean, you've got to be somewhat skeptical, right?"

"Are you asking if I've guessed that Lucien killed Elisabet because he didn't want her to tell me something? In fact, I have." He stood and came closer, brushed her hair back from her face. "But Lucien and I will sort out our own grudges after the Spider's arrival. And I will tell you all my stories soon; no more deceptions. But now night is coming for you. We have tomorrow and tomorrow and tomorrow."

Tana scrambled to sit up, the restraint on her wrist holding her to the headboard. "No! Later I won't be myself."

"Oh, you will be," he told her softly, walking to the door. "We labor under so many illusions about ourselves until we're stripped bare. Being infected, being a vampire, it's always you. Maybe it's more you than ever before. You, distilled. You, boiled down like a sauce. But it's you as you always were, deep down inside."

She stopped struggling, horrified by the memory of Midnight's face transformed by rage and those teeth sinking into her throat. Horrified by the memory of her mother's voice in the dark. Horrified by the thought that she might be the same or worse and that it would be her, truly her doing those things. But Gavriel must know; he'd been human, he'd been infected, he'd been turned.

Besides, she'd killed Midnight. She'd already done those things, already learned she could.

"Before you go, just tell me one thing," Tana said. "Tell me why you've been so nice to me. I know you're the reason Lucien let me live. He wasn't planning on giving me any saline drip or putting me in some fancy bed before I said your name. And I'm not anybody special. I'm not saying that I'm not smart or a perfectly nice person or anything, but I'm not—"

He'd been halfway across the room when she started speaking and he'd frozen, his face turned away from her. Then he moved to the foot-board of the bed, his hands gripping the brass railing, his face a mask. Finally, he cut her off. "Tana. In all my long life, though there were many times I prayed for it, no one has ever saved me. No one but you."

He was watching her with an expression so intense that she had to look away from it. She could think of no reply. She felt a little bit stupid that she'd asked and a little bit embarrassed by his answer. Maybe it would be better if he left and came back; maybe if she was less sick and less tired, she would feel less vulnerable.

Gavriel walked to her side of the bed. Tana flinched at his approach, suddenly nervous. He seemed like a stranger again. His eyes looked black instead of red in the dim light of the room, and she thought of what he must have been like under gas lamps in a city across the sea.

He took her free hand and lifted it to his mouth, kissing the back as though he were that courtly gentleman again.

"Sleep, Tana," he said, placing her hand back on her stomach, his fingers only a little cooler now than hers. "Sleep while you can."

He looked as though he wanted to say something else but then rose. He walked to the door and this time she didn't stop him. She heard a lock turn on the other side of the wall.

Great, she thought. *Perfect*. Shackled to a bed in a locked room. But at least a locked door might keep out everything else in Lucien Moreau's house. And at least if she was shut in here, no matter how bad the infection got, she wouldn't be able to hurt anyone.

She flopped back with a groan, trying to make her mind blank. Soon she would be sick and then what? She'd scream and cry and beg, and either Lucien would kill her out of annoyance or Gavriel would give her blood. It took eighty-eight days to sweat the venom out. No one was going to protect her from herself during that time. If she wanted to avoid becoming a vampire, she had to get out of here and find someplace to hole up. And to do that she needed to be less tired and sore. Gavriel was right. She needed to sleep, heal, and let the saline work.

She couldn't. Every time she closed her eyes, she thought she could feel the chill of infection creep across her skin. She couldn't stop wondering if she was already going Cold, couldn't stop worrying that when she woke up, she'd already be too crazy to make any plans that didn't involve attacking the first person who came through the door. And when she managed to put that thought out of her head, she thought of Gavriel. It seemed impossible to believe that he'd pressed her back against a wall and kissed her, his body straining against hers, her hands tangled in his hair, his expression that of a man thoroughly lost.

To distract herself, Tana studied the room she'd been imprisoned in.

There were too many things in it for it to be a guest room. The side tables were stacked with books and a glass goblet with a ring of some dark liquid dried at the base. There was a makeup table of burled wood littered with open jars and brushes. Long, shimmering golden earrings set with pieces of jade had been thrown haphazardly into an open drawer, along with a large amulet.

The door to the closet was partially open and the skirt of a black dress was visible. Turning her head, Tana tried to get a better look at the painting that had been set on the floor so that her saline bag could hang in its place. If she strained against the cuff, she could just make out the shape of a beautiful saint pierced through with arrows that still stuck from his sides. Blood ran down his pale body, and his face was turned up toward the sky in a pose of ecstatic suffering.

So, a woman's room and probably a vampire's. Someone who wasn't using it and wasn't going to use it. Elisabet. This had to be Elisabet's room, Elisabet's painting and jewels and dresses. Lucien had let Tana be chained up in the bedroom of the vampire he'd loved and also murdered.

It was a creepy discovery, made creepier by the feeling that she'd somehow replaced Elisabet. As though one girl chained to a bed was much the same as another girl sleeping in one. And however she felt around Gavriel, she would be stupid, no matter what he said or she felt, to count on his kindness. He was crazy and changeable, not to mention bloodthirsty.

Climbing up onto her knees and ignoring the rush of light-headedness, she pulled on the cuff, squeezing her thumb in tight against her palm to see if she could pull through the metal loop. She pushed with the other hand, hoping that whoever had locked it around her wrist had done so carelessly.

No luck. She was still held tight.

Regrouping, she felt along the chain and around the bracelet of the cuff with her free hand, checking to make sure there was no mechanism to take them off, the way there were on joke cuffs. Nothing. She thought that idea was a long shot, but she figured she'd have felt pretty stupid if there had been one and she hadn't at least tried.

Then she considered the brass headboard. Now that she was sitting up, she might be able to slide off the bed and land on her feet, so long as she shoved the bedside table over a bit. And from there, she could use her free hand to twist the ball off one pole and slide the cuff from the bed without bothering to remove it. At least she could try.

The night table slid over easily, only a few books slipping to the floor. Then her bare feet followed. She took a moment to catch her balance, then, bracing herself, threw her weight against the brass ball, attempting to unscrew it. It came off with a whine of metal grinding against metal.

Then, hopping up onto the frame of the bed, Tana was able to lift the other cuff off the end of the tall brass pole. She was still caught by the plastic tubing that connected her IV to the bag on the wall. Looking it over, she then decided the only thing she knew how to do was unscrew the piece that connected the tube to the crook of her arm. As soon as she did, it began to leak saline onto the bed, dripping over the wooden planks of the floor.

Staggering to the lion-headed purse, she opened it and found the marker. Then, reaching for the garnet locket around her neck, she jammed the quarter-size metal inside, pressing the locket closed around it. At least she wouldn't lose it again.

As she crouched down over her bag, she saw a polished wooden box under the bed. Pulling it toward her, she realized there was no lid. The box was lined in blue velvet and held a crossbow and several daggers with wooden blades. Basically stakes. Stakes with hilts. The smell of rose oil floated up from them. Elizabet must not have trusted any of the other vampires she lived with any more than they deserved. It was tempting to take one, but if she snuck around with one of those in her hand, she was unlikely to be able to explain it. Tana pushed herself to her feet.

She tried not to slip in the widening puddle as she walked over to the door. Dizziness flooded her, and she looked down to see that her new white dress was covered in dirt and dried blood. Her sandals were gone.

It was almost funny, the way she couldn't wear a single outfit without ruining it.

It was almost funny, but not quite.

Looking at the knob and the lock, Tana realized with surprise that although Gavriel had turned a key on the outside, the locking mechanism was on the inside. All she had to do was turn the bolt and the door opened. Which made sense, since this had been Elisabet's room. She might have locked herself in at night, but no one would have imprisoned her here. Which meant that Gavriel never meant to imprison Tana; if anything, the lock was to keep other things out.

With that thought in mind, she stepped into the hallway.

Dimmed daylight streamed in through the heavily tinted windows—it looked like the same glass at the top of the Eternal Ball, the kind that filtered light safely for vampires. The party had mostly died down, although there were some humans left, sleeping on the steps or against a bench. Tana walked past them, and the few who were awake didn't even blink at the sight of her gore-smeared clothes.

Her stomach lurched. She could smell rich, dark blood pumping under human skin, could feel the heat rising off people as she passed. She drew in a breath and shuddered with hunger.

✦ CHAPTER 30 ✦

On this side of the grave we are
exiles, on that citizens.
—Henry Ward Beecher

Once upon a time there was a little girl, and she told a lie to her friend's brother so that her friend's brother drove her to the bus station.

She brought with her a bottle of orange soda, fifty dollars (half in change), sparkly slippers, and her cell phone.

He thought he was helping.

So did she.

CHAPTER 31

For I know that Death is a guest divine,

Who shall drink my blood as I drink

this wine.

—William Winter

Walking through Lucien Moreau's house reminded Tana unnervingly of the morning after Lance's party. Like then, she was the only one moving. Music was still playing somewhere, distant as the television had been that day. And looking at all of the sleeping bodies brought to mind the corpses of the kids from her school arranged on the floor. But these kids were just passed out, and now she was the monster walking among them.

She found her way through the ballroom with the high glass ceiling, where food was still lying out on a table, rotting in the shadowed sunlight. The remains of cakes and half a tart covered with glistening fruit. Sliced cuts of meat and spiky baguettes, half-peeled oranges buzzing with flies. Overturned bowls of sugared rose petals. Although she had not eaten for many hours, the sight of it made her feel sick.

As she leaned against the wall, a shiver rolled through her. Ice crystallizing inside her.

Was Valentina still here? She remembered waking to Valentina's voice, remembered cold concrete beneath her and steel against her fingertips. A basement, she'd thought. But was that a real memory?

Tana kept moving, stumbling through rooms. There were parlors and toilets, a kitchen with gleaming appliances and a butler's pantry full of old-fashioned weapons. Then she found an alcove with a door that led to a staircase spiraling downward.

The stone steps were cold on her bare feet. She felt that chill rising up through her legs to freeze her belly, to rime her throat with a frost that would never melt.

She found herself in a vast basement. Wooden racks held bottle after bottle of wine on one wall. On the other were twelve cells. They were large and they smelled of sweat and heat and blood. In them were boys and girls, all of them lovely and none older than twenty.

Most were sleeping on the stone floor, wrapped in blankets, their heads pillowed on rolled-up clothes or backpacks. Some, isolated from the others, wore muzzles. A few had saline drips like the one hanging from a nail in Elisabet's room, two flights of stairs up. Three girls were awake, one weeping quietly near a makeshift toilet, while another two played dice.

Tana thought of the Cold girls and boys who had been chained to the walls the night before. At first, when she'd seen the kids in the cages, she'd thought they were a fresh batch and the others were dead. But now, she realized Lucien must keep them here for weeks, months, however long he could. Any blood supply was too precious to waste. The infected must be the muzzled ones, drugged into sleeping away each day in restless, red-soaked dreams.

It took a moment to realize that one of the sleeping girls was Valentina.

Tana walked closer. She could almost see the warmth radiating off all of them, shimmering above them the way heat bends the light above a hot stretch of road. The two girls playing dice seemed to have come from the party and still wore their party frocks, but their hair was dull and their eyes were sunken. Both had shunts in their arms, the skin around them dark with bruising. One had a sore nearby, yellow at the center with an outer circle of green and black scabbing. To Tana in that moment, though, they all seemed heart-stoppingly beautiful. The scent of their blood welled up from underneath their skin, making her veins sing with need.

The weeping girl looked up and saw Tana. Her eyes went wide, and she sniffled noisily, wiping her nose on her sleeve. Then she stood and came to the edge of the bars. Up close, Tana could see her long black hair and dark skin. "How did you get away from him?" the girl asked. "He's got cameras everywhere."

Tana crossed the room without really deciding to, drawn to the girl. She told herself that she only wanted to free Valentina. She told herself that she would never hurt any of them, while her mind supplied her with images of biting, ripping, rending.

"I was here?" she asked, a little dazed.

The girl nodded, wiping her wet cheeks. "You were so pale, and there was so much blood on your dress that we thought you were done for. Then one of the vampires came for you, and we were *sure* you were done for."

Tana wondered which one of them it had been. Had Gavriel been down here? "Did something happen? You're crying."

"I'm *scared*," the girl snapped. "Most of them want to be here, but not me. He recruits kids off the street, offers them food and a place to sleep, says they can earn eternal life. My friend Violet went with him a month ago, and I haven't seen her since. I came to the party to see if there was something on his recordings about what happened to her, but then they caught me in the recording room."

Which made it seem as if Lucien didn't usually grab people from his parties. As if he had taken Valentina for a reason—because she'd come in with Tana, who'd murdered a vampire? Because she'd been somewhere she wasn't supposed to be, like the girl? Tana looked up, into the eye of the lens. Then she turned her back to it, leaning toward the bars.

"Is there a key?" she mouthed. "How can I get you both out?"

The dark-haired girl came closer. One of her cheeks was smudged with dirt. She waved Tana in, whispering so she couldn't be heard on the recording. "There's two keys," she said, her breath warm on Tana's icy cheek. "One that fits in the lock on the cage and another one that unlocks the hinges so the door swings. But you're not going to find them in time."

It would be such a little thing to grab the girl's wrist and pull it through the bars of her cage. To sink her dull teeth into yielding flesh. Tana's fingers gripped the chilled metal, winding around it as if it were what she desired.

"Right," Tana said, forcing herself to focus. Two locks. Two keys. Eight people locked in a cage. Eighty-eight days of hunger, all of them worse than this. "I'll be back. I'll find some way to get you out. I promise. Tell Valentina that I promise."

At the sound of her name, Valentina stirred, turning in sleep. Tana wasn't sure what she'd think if she woke, if she'd be angry to find Tana on one side of the cage and herself on the other.

"I don't know who has them," the dark-haired girl whispered. "Other than Elisabet. She comes down here sometimes and just looks at us. It's creepy."

Tana made herself back away from the cage and the girl, hoping that her expression wasn't too like Elisabet's. Creepy. Hungry.

"I hate to say this," the dark-haired girl told her softly. "But you should get out of here while you can."

"Don't worry about me," Tana said, hoping that would be answer enough.

She thought about going up to Elisabet's room and searching it for the two keys, but maybe she didn't need them. Maybe there were bolt cutters. Or maybe there was an ax sharp and sure enough to cut right through the lock. She walked around the basement, finding a door she couldn't open and then another that led to a closet. Inside were an assortment of moth-eaten blankets, a broken chair, and a few tools. She bent down to take a closer look when someone grabbed her by the arm. She had time to lunge for the handle of a long screw-driver before she was hauled to her feet.

A vampire stood in front of her, his red eyes dim in the gloom. He had on a tuxedo shirt, although the jacket was missing and the bow tie hung loose around his neck, just wrinkled cloth. But even though he was dead, she could smell the blood inside him, magical and strange.

She thought of Midnight, out on the dark lawn. *Tana, is that you?*

"How did you get down here?" His nose wrinkled, and he took another look at her, at her neck. "You're *infected*—you're not supposed to—"

Tana didn't wait for him to finish, and she didn't try to answer. She slammed the screwdriver deep into his chest with all the force she could muster, hoping against hope that she'd be lucky enough to strike his heart. The ferocity of her attack drove him back against the wall. She ripped free the screwdriver, feeling it drag against the bones of his ribs, and then stabbed him with it again.

This time she stabbed him straight through the throat. He made a choked noise. His hands scrabbled to pull her to him, jaw working to bite the air, the light already going out of his eyes. She had him. She brought down the screwdriver like it was a dagger, over and over, until he stopped moving, until his head was at an odd angle, hanging from flesh, the bones of his neck shattered.

Blood bubbled up, the smell of it entrancing her, even through her panic. She was already operating on instinct, so she barely thought before she brought her head down. Bending over him as if to pray, she knelt and lapped at the pool of red collecting in what was left of the hollow of his throat. Tiny hairs tickled her nose as she bit down. His blood was chill and thick, sliding down her throat like honey, the taste sparking on her tongue as though she were gulping light.

Her skin felt as if it had caught fire. She'd turned into lit paper, already blistering and about to blaze up into black smoke and ash.

His blood was shady afternoons and metal filings running-thrumming through the fat roots of veins to drip syrup slow, spurting across mouth, teeth, chin.

She licked his skin, bit him, ripped with her blunt teeth, and licked again.

Time passed as if in a dream, moments blurring together. When she came back to herself, the first sound she heard was a gasp from behind her. She turned toward the cage. The people within—Valentina, the dark-haired girl, and most of the others—were huddled together on the far side. Valentina took a half step toward her and then shrank back again, her courage failing.

Tana reached up a sticky hand to touch her face. It was coated with blood, making a half mask.

She must look awful. An animal-girl.

But then Valentina did come forward, walking to the bars, widening her eyes and jerking her chin. It was a subtle but clear signal. *Look over there*, it said.

Tana turned toward the shadows and saw the shine of eyes. She stumbled back, reaching again for the slippery handle of the screwdriver, before she saw it was Gavriel. He was sitting on the floor, legs crossed. She had no idea how long he'd been sitting there, but at her astonished look he raised both eyebrows. An amused smile pulled at his lips.

"I'm a very bad host, forcing you to throw together supper for yourself," he said finally. He stood and stuck out a hand, as if to help her to her feet—as if she were some fancy lady who'd fallen from a coach into a mud puddle.

One of her hands reached for the guard's keys, the other reached up for Gavriel, letting him pull her to her feet.

Her fingers were wet with blood, but he didn't seem to notice.

She almost laughed, but she couldn't quite. She didn't feel enough like herself to trust that she wouldn't start sobbing instead.

"Were you looking for me?" she asked, to fill the silence.

"I was watching the screens in one of Lucien's video rooms. So many exits and entrances and a citadel in need of storming. And then you." She couldn't put her finger on what was different in his voice, but for the first time she thought that he was being deliberately obscure. His face was placid, though, showing nothing.

"*Tana*," Valentina whispered, her fingers reaching out through the bars to point. "He's—"

Looking up, Tana saw Lucien Moreau coming down the stairs. He was dressed all in cream, his jacket the color of ivory. Silver buttons ran over the front and down the cuffs. His shoes came to sharp points. He looked ageless, ancient and youthful in the same moment. His skin was pale, but his mouth was almost a vulgar red. He was beautiful the way the devil might have been, just before he fell.

She was sure he'd looked through one of his cameras as Gavriel had, that he'd overheard what she'd whispered to the girl in the basement and seen her kill yet another vampire. Her heart pounded.

"What have you done?" he demanded, sweeping his arm toward

the body. He wasn't looking at Tana, though, but rather at Gavriel. His voice was scolding in the manner of someone who discovered their dog chewing up the carpet. "What exactly happened here?"

"Oh, hello," said Gavriel. "Don't be angry. So she got hungry and killed someone? The city is full of humans desperate to be turned. Just choose another."

Tana was horrified by how callous he sounded, even in her defense.

Lucien shook his head. "Don't be ridiculous. She didn't kill him. You did."

A wide grin stretched across Gavriel's face, making his fangs gleam. "You're right. I killed him and then I tried to pin it on her, because I thought it would be funny. And it was funny, wasn't it?"

"Cages and cages full of humans and you kill a vampire," Lucien said, clearly exasperated. "I guess that's what you're used to, but it seems cruel to feed the girl cold blood." He turned toward Tana. "Come with me, my dear. First, let's get you cleaned up, and then I think we should talk."

He looked back at Gavriel. "You don't mind, do you?"

Gavriel was no longer smiling. "If the enemy of my enemy is my friend, then surely you should be friend to my friend."

Which didn't make sense. Not even the odd sense that he usually made, where the words came together like a riddle or a puzzle. Tana frowned. No, this was off, as though he was playacting some exaggerated version of himself.

"He wasn't always like that." Lucien rolled his eyes and extended his arm to her. It was a courtly gesture, as though she was used to

Gavriel making it, and it reminded her that they'd been friends once and maybe, despite everything Lucien had done, they'd be friends again. She thought of Elisabet and of Lance's party and how all those deaths were Lucien's doing. She put her hand on his arm, smearing sticky, half-dried blood on his shirtsleeve with great satisfaction.

He curled his lip as they went up the stairs together.

"You're awake early," Tana said, pointing up at the glass ceiling of the ballroom. The blue sky was turned ashen by the tinted windows, but the glow of the sun was bright enough to make her flinch. She wondered how Lucien stood it, when she longed to cover her eyes. She wondered if the Colder she got, the worse her aversion to sunlight would become.

"I slept restlessly," he said, surprisingly confessional. "All my dreams were of Elisabet."

Then he waved over a vampire girl who seemed to be waiting for them by the large wooden staircase to the second floor. She had mahogany-brown hair and black leather pants with a deconstructed suit jacket, sections of it sewn inside out with big red stitches. A leather jabot was tied at her throat, and her boots had knives where heels should have been. On her finger was a silver ring with a tooth set in it. As the woman got closer, she wiped the edges of her mouth, bringing up her hand, and Tana saw the tooth was a human molar.

"Marisol," he said, and the woman nodded slightly in acknowledgment. "Get the girl cleaned up. Then I want you to bring her to me in my sitting room. She can wear anything of *hers*, just make her less ghoulish."

The woman looked at Tana and gestured toward the steps. They went to Elisabet's room together, Tana walking beside Marisol obediently. Her skin felt tight and her teeth sore. "The bathroom is through there. Just leave your ruined dress on the floor. I'll find something for you in her closet." Marisol pointedly didn't mention the ball missing from the brass headboard or the pool of saline on the floor. She smiled with a closed mouth, like she was trying not to frighten Tana.

Tana looked down at the length of the silk gown she wore—grass stains and blood, so much blood. She sighed and picked up her clutch from beside the bed as casually as she could, then went into the attached bathroom.

The mirror above the sinks reflected her in horrific detail. Dark red gore soiled her face and stained her hands so that she seemed to be wearing smeary opera gloves. She choked back a sob. She didn't look human—she looked like a creature lurching from a grave.

She thought of the three vampires she'd seen in Suicide Square and of Aidan sitting alone in the room on Wormwood Court, mourning what he'd done and afraid of what he might do. She wondered if this was what they saw reflected in the mirror, over and over, drunks after a bender swearing never to let themselves get so out of control again. Drunks who were still thirsty.

The memory of her hand driving the screwdriver into the vampire's skin over and over rose up, making her stomach churn. She'd been lost in a haze of panic and then in a frenzy of hunger, and now, remembering, it felt as if surely another person had been moving her hand. That couldn't have been her squatting over the vampire's body, tearing his ruined throat with her teeth. That couldn't be her reflected in the mirror, her haunted blue eyes in a mask of gore.

Turning on the taps in the shower, she let the water run as hot as she could get it. Then she went to the small covered window. The pane was the same gray glass that covered the ceiling in the ballroom, but when she pushed on it, the frame slid up, revealing a stretch of roof and letting a sliver of yellow light into the room. Tana set down on the sink counter the keys she'd taken from the vampire she'd killed, rested her solar charger out on the slate, and plugged the cord into her phone.

In the shower stall, she watched the brown water spiral around the drain. She scrubbed her skin with Elisabet's lavender-scented soap, even washed the soap over her tongue, hoping to get rid of the heady, dark flavor that remained in her mouth, reminding her that she would want it again.

When she got out and toweled off, she saw that the screen of her phone was alive. She had eighty texts. One from Pearl, some from Pauline or kids at her school, and lots from numbers she didn't know.

From Pearl, with a picture of their dad asleep at the kitchen table: *Everything weird and boring here. U better have fun fun fun and send pix so i can be jealous.*

From a girl who'd graduated the year before: *This is your # right? Was my brother at the party? Is he with you? Did you see his body? No one will tell us anything.*

From a number she didn't know: *You shudda died w the rest.*

From another: *We're interested in exclusive interview with you and/or your friend aidan. 5k is on the table if you don't talk to any other reporters.*

Tana turned on the sink faucets to make some noise. First she called Jameson's phone. It went to voice mail again, and she started to wonder if he'd lost it. Pressing her fingers against her eyes, she tried to think.

Then she pressed a few buttons and called Pauline. The sound of the familiar ring on the other end made her chest ache.

Please have your phone with you, Tana mouthed. *Please.*

Moments later, there was a clicking sound as someone picked up.

"I am going to kill you if you're not already undead," Pauline said, her voice making Tana grin despite everything. "Are you okay? Tell me you're okay."

"Sort of," Tana said, keeping her voice low. "I'm sorry I didn't call. A lot's been going on, and I forgot to charge my phone."

"*A lot's been going on?*" Pauline repeated, yelling. "Yeah, I'll say. I saw the video of you last night. With the vampire girl that bit you and—oh my god, Tana. Oh my god. I can't believe you're really calling me and I'm shouting at you."

"I screwed up." Tana looked at her shiny, clean face in the mirror. That was the problem with monsters. Sometimes they looked just like everybody else. But her skin felt wrong, tight like it got after a sunburn. "I really screwed up, and now I'm—"

"You did not screw up," Pauline said. "Listen to me. You survived. You did whatever you had to do to survive. Just tell me—are you a vampire?"

"No," Tana said, leaning against the marble counter of the vanity. "I mean, not yet."

"So, you're Cold? You sound okay."

"For now. I'm trapped in a fancy bathroom in Lucien Moreau's house and I need to get out of here. Which is why I called. I need you to get a message to someone."

"What?" Pauline sounded completely confused.

"This guy Jameson. He has a girlfriend who's a vampire and she lives at Lucien's. I don't know her name, but I could really use her help—and his. I'm going to give you a number. Can you please just call it until you get him? He's got to pick up eventually. Tell him they got Valentina and she's locked up—"

"Hold on," Pauline said. "I've got to find a pen."

Tana held her breath, listening to the rustling sounds from the other end of the line. It was so normal, so totally normal to call Pauline to get her to do some dumb thing, to call a boy or give her a pep talk, or get advice, that Tana couldn't help feeling that the familiarity was what made the moment seem extra surreal now.

She stared at her reflection, but this time she seemed to see herself through a fun-house mirror, distorting her face and making the shape of it waver. It took her a moment to realize that was because she was looking through the tears in her eyes.

"I found a pen," Pauline said. "Go."

Tana read Jameson's number off her own phone. "That's *Jameson*. Tell him Valentina is locked up in the basement of Lucien's and I am going to try to get her out tonight, just after dark. If, during the day, he could possibly take some bolt cutters to the side fence at Lucien's so we can slip through there, that would be amazing. And if he can't, tell him not to worry. We'll figure it out."

"Tell him not to worry?" Pauline repeated back.

From the other side of the wall, Marisol called, "Lucien's waiting. Time to get dressed."

"I've got to go," Tana said. "Tell Pearl I love her."

"*I* love *you*," said Pauline. "So stay safe, okay?"

"Hey, so what's the status of you and David?" Tana asked.

"Oh, shut up." Pauline laughed and then her voice wobbled. "Don't die and I'll tell you the whole story."

Smiling, Tana hit the End button on her phone and put it back on the sill. Then she glanced at herself in the mirror. To her horror, her front teeth were scarlet. She ran her tongue over her gums, tasting the salt of her own blood.

Maybe she'd bitten her tongue?

Leaning over the sink and cupping her shaking hands, she scooped up water from the faucet, took a mouthful, swished it around, and spat red. Then she snarled at the mirror. And with the blood gone, she could see that her gums were bleeding because her canines had grown longer. They weren't as thin or sharp as vampire teeth, but they were no longer quite human teeth, either.

"Marisol," she called in a high, scared voice she didn't even recognize as her own.

Aidan had drunk Gavriel's blood and nothing had happened to him. What was happening to her?

A moment later, the vampire came into the room, her nostrils flaring at the smell of blood. Her red eyes studied Tana's reflection in the mirror. "What now?"

"Look at my teeth," Tana said in a quavering voice, pulling the towel around herself more tightly.

The vampire grabbed Tana's head, tilting it back and then reaching into her mouth to press a finger against the points of her teeth. Marisol stepped back and shook her head. "Someone gave you a bellyful of vampire blood, I'll wager. You're going to be fine. It's the way vampires used to be turned, before the world fell. They'd be fed on vampire blood until they were ready. Sometimes it would take weeks to get to the stage you're at—you must have drunk quite a lot."

She had.

"But what does it mean?" Tana asked, her fingers going to her teeth unconsciously. "Am I going to die? Am I going to turn?"

"No," Marisol said. "It just means that you're *ready* to die. You'll be stronger once you're turned."

Tana nodded, trying to calm herself. Nothing was wrong. She wasn't going to wake up a vampire. Not today, anyway. It was just a symptom of infection. A symptom she'd never heard of before, admittedly, but a symptom all the same. *More toxins*, she remembered, from the speaker at school. *An accumulation of toxins.*

"Okay," Tana said, taking a deep breath and walking past Marisol into the bedroom. She couldn't let herself seem weak. "Forget about it. I'm fine. Let's go show off my new teeth to Lucien Moreau."

A few minutes later, not having liked anything Marisol picked out, Tana dressed in the least formal thing she managed to find—a dark red, sleeveless leather dress—and followed Marisol through the halls. Not a single one of Elisabet's shoes fit even a little, for which she was obscurely glad. It was creepy enough that her clothing fit so well. The leather dress hugged her skin, stretching tight across her hips. Tana's black hair was pulled back into a high ponytail, and Gavriel's necklace still sparkled on her collarbone. As she walked, her tongue traced the points of her longer canines.

Marisol turned the knob of a lacquered black door and indicated Tana should enter, but she didn't move to follow. The door closed behind Tana as she padded across the floor as lightly as she could in bare feet. Heavy drapes covered the windows. Lucien walked toward her as though he saw perfectly, even through the gloom. In the room were two big black leather chairs and a desk carved with griffins at each of the four corners. Tana spotted a key ring of bone, scrimshawed with an image she couldn't make out, resting atop it. Three keys hung from the ring.

She'd gotten only two keys from the vampire she killed; she hoped they were the right two.

"You clean up nicely," Lucien said. "But you're younger than I thought. How old *are* you exactly?"

Tana wasn't sure if she should thank him or not. She decided not. "Seventeen."

"I didn't believe you at first," he went on. "When you told me Gavriel had given you the garnets. I was baffled as to why he would have given them to a mortal girl. Did he tell you about it—the necklace?"

"He said it belonged to his sister," said Tana. She walked over to one of the chairs but didn't sit. Lucien frightened her and fascinated her, too. She was a guest in his house, but she was also a prisoner.

Lucien snorted. "Yes, it certainly did. But that's when I knew—

when I saw the necklace around your throat. He came here to die. He must have. That's the only reason I could think of that he would give it away, to anyone, even to someone for whom he has such an inexplicable fondness. Did you know his sister was wearing it the night she decided her brother was dead? She believed Gavriel to be some kind of demon, a fetch who'd stolen his face. She tried to run away from him and he grabbed for her, but all he caught was the necklace. It broke and he never saw his sister again."

"That's sad," Tana said.

"It was a little bit funny, actually," said Lucien. "I mean, they were shouting at each other like they were idiot children, and then a man came to defend her honor. I think he was a cabbie, but he had several friends right behind him. Imagine, a vampire giving up in the face of a few dirty men on a street. It was as if Gavriel had entirely forgotten what he was."

Tana had no idea what to say to that. "And he never tried to find her?" she asked, finally.

Lucien smiled, all teeth. "I found her first, you see. It's an old story, but you might as well hear it. I thought I could make things right between them, that once she'd turned, Gavriel would be entirely happy. Katya was clever and capable—she'd made it out of Russia all on her own. So, anyway, I brought over one of my footmen. Six foot and fair of face, perfect for a lady. I sent up my card and she agreed to see me. She had one of those older, destitute spinsters who hired themselves out as chaperones. I killed her immediately."

Tana took a breath and let it out slowly, trying to find some way to accept that he'd cheerfully announced murdering an innocent woman a hundred years ago. Dizzily, she sat down in one of the chairs, deciding that she no longer cared about manners.

Lucien grinned down at her. He appeared to be enjoying himself, as though this was a favorite story that he seldom got to tell.

"Katya was upset, of course, and even more upset when I grabbed her and sank my teeth into her throat. When I let her go, she started more of her babbling about demons, but whatever she thought was going to happen, I'll wager she never imagined the hunger that would overtake her half a day later. She never guessed how she would take a letter opener to my poor, ruined footman's throat. And do you know what she did after that? The stupid girl walked right out into the sun as soon as she rose from the dead."

"She killed herself?" Gavriel had smiled when he'd talked about Katya in Paris. Surely he wouldn't have happily reminisced about circumstances that led to her death, if he'd known. But if Gavriel didn't know, why would Lucien tell Tana?

"Gavriel was quite put out by it when he discovered what I'd done, even though I had arranged the whole thing for him—it was going to be a nice surprise, a family reunion." Lucien shook his head regretfully. "She really was a pistol, his sister. Stubborn like him and just as melodramatic."

"He's not…" Tana began, but she let the sentence trail off. He *was* melodramatic sometimes, and it wasn't as if Lucien hadn't known him for a very long while, certainly long enough to make statements like that.

"Ah," said Lucien. "How sweet. I have been terribly curious— how did you manage to catch his eye? Ladies tried, but he was so often distracted, always busy putting down outbreaks and sharpening his knives. All that hunting made him a little jittery, I think. Rather off-putting for all but the most dauntless ladies. Are you dauntless, my dear?"

Tana did not know what to say to that. "I have no idea."

It's all some wicked game to him, she realized. Getting under her skin. Passing on a story to her that might or might not be true, but would rattle her and keep her off balance. Lucien liked to be the endless drip of water wearing on someone's soul. Lucien liked to watch people snap.

"I suppose it doesn't matter." He threw himself into the chair opposite Tana. "What matters is that you managed to make him care about you. And now you're going to get everything you ever dreamed of—becoming a vampire, becoming famous. Not bad. For an opportunistic little slut, you sure landed in clover."

Tana flinched at the casual way the insult rolled off his tongue.

"Oh, no. I congratulate you. Truly. If I had a drink in my hand, I would toast my admiration."

"Good thing I don't have one," said Tana. "Because I'd throw it in your face."

He tossed back his head and laughed. "I just love mortals."

"I bet," she told him.

He acknowledged her words with a nod. "It's such a relief not to have to hide anymore. Before the infection spread, we were already known by our mistakes. *Vampyr* in the Netherlands, *upir* in the Ukraine, *vrykolaka* in the Balkan region, *penangglan* on the Malay Peninsula. If we'd been better at hiding, there would have been no words for us, but there is a word for *vampire* in every corner of the world."

"And no black cloaks with red linings—well, maybe still those, but definitely not the kind with stand-up collars." Tana should probably stop talking like that, but she needed to prove to both of them that she wasn't scared, even if she was.

He ignored her, unwilling to be baited and definitely unsmiling. "And now the world sees our true faces. It is remade by us into something glorious, something where men aspire to be immortal. I like this world and I would keep it moving forward, unlike the ancient vampires. Their dream of returning to the old ways is like the Romanovs' dream of a return to power. It won't happen, no matter how much they cackle about it in their crypts and catacombs. But with the Spider nearly to my gates, our interests align."

"What do you mean?" she asked.

"Whatever the Spider did to Gavriel seems to have unhinged his mind. What they used to call *manie sans délire*—insanity without delusion. He's broken and we are without the time to put him back together. Help me control him and I will help you. No more making you drink cold, dead blood in front of a cage full of delicious girls and boys. I'll turn you, Tana. I'll show you how to be a vampire the likes of which the world has seldom known."

"You will?" she asked, thinking of her newly sharp teeth, of the way her dizzying hunger had deserted her since she'd fed. Lucien must know what was happening to her, how the vampire's blood was making her stronger, but he was obviously pretending he didn't. *Cold, dead, yucky blood, don't drink any more of that!* Sabotage disguised as kindness.

"In Paris, there was once a legendary delicacy, now outlawed,"

Lucien was saying. "A bird called an ortolan, an unremarkable-looking creature with a grayish-green head and a yellow body, is caught alive and force-fed millet until it grows fat. Then it's drowned in Armagnac. Finally, the bird is roasted and eaten whole, bones and beak and all, while the diner wears a napkin over his head. Some say that's to keep in the aroma of the dish; others say it's to hide the diner's face—and his shame—from heaven."

"That's cruel," Tana said.

"Yes," said Lucien. "Truly. And yet even that is nothing to the fineness of human blood. Do you know what it is to drink it down, hot and metallic, pumped into your mouth by the frantic heartbeats of a quivering body? It's half like spitting in the face of God, half like being him."

Tana shook her head, hunger rising despite herself. "You make it sound pretty good."

"Well," Lucien said, with a small smile. "If there's anything that spits in the face of God, I'm generally for it."

"What do I have to do?" she asked.

"Just make sure Gavriel sticks to the plan—*remembers* the plan, even. Decides he'll live after all. Continues to recall that the Spider is our enemy and that I am his ally. Do you understand? You may not believe me, but I have loved him in my way. What happened to him is my fault. I bear that responsibility, but it will be easier to bear with the Spider dead. And it will be easier for him to bear what's happened to him with you at our side. Since I want his happiness, I also must want yours."

Tana nodded slowly. "I'll do what I can," she told him.

He was standing closer than she'd expected; Tana hadn't heard him move. She shuddered as his hand came up to cup her cheek. His fingers curled against her, tips pressing against the bone hard enough to bruise. "Good, good. We never know what we're capable of until we try."

✦ CHAPTER 32 ✦

The devil tempts us not;

'tis we who tempt him,

Beckoning his skill with opportunity.

—George Eliot

Eight years before, Gavriel came apart.

First, the Spider cut open his belly.

Then he took out his guts and knotted them around the bars of his cage.

Ropy blue garlands.

They gouged out his pomegranate-seed eyes.

They fed him fouled blood and bile and his own skin.

They cut him with knives, flogged him with razor-tipped whips, and drove rusty nails into the soles of his feet.

When he healed, they did it again.

Until everything hurt all the time forever.

Pain so vast and terrible and huge it blotted out thought.

And so when he came back to himself, his memories were disjointed.

He'd ripped out someone's throat, but he was no longer sure whose.

There'd been blood everywhere; he'd slipped in it, clotted like soured milk.

There was hair, too, a nest of it in a drain.

And he remembered who had urged on his tormentors, the face of the creature who smiled down at him.

I could tell you, Gavriel thought. *I could give you someone else in my place.*

Someone you'd like better.

Someone you'd hurt worse.

But no. They'd taken every other piece of him.

He would hold on to revenge.

It would be his fairy story, his lullaby, sung softly by flayed lips.

Off-key and deranged.

CHAPTER 33

A thinking woman sleeps with monsters.
—Adrienne Rich

Tana walked down the hallway behind Lucien, past the oil paintings of landscapes in the French countryside and gory handprints. They came to a heavy oaken door. Lucien was reaching for the knob when the door opened wide.

Gavriel was framed in the opening. He had on the black jeans and black shirt he'd worn on their road trip, although they had a softness to them that suggested they'd been freshly laundered. His feet were bare. Stepping back, he waved them inside.

"See, I returned her," Lucien said, giving Tana a push against the small of her back, so she was forced to stumble into the room. "Unharmed. Undebauched."

Tana scowled. "You really are from another time, aren't you?"

Ignoring her, Lucien crossed the threshold, closing the door behind him. "We need to talk, my dear."

"All three of us?" Gavriel asked archly.

"She's your guest. We should entertain her—and keep an eye on her. According to you, she's killed two vampires in the span of a single day. Really, I should never have been left alone with her. She must be very dangerous." Lucien's smile didn't reach his eyes. He drew out from a pocket a folding knife with a handle of bone and began to pick underneath his fingernails with the point, scraping out flakes of dried blood and bits of tissue. She noticed there was something wrong with the way his nails curved, as though his fingers were tapering into claws.

"You're right. I never should have," Gavriel said, turning to Tana with a half smile just for her.

More dangerous than daybreak. She wondered if he remembered that he'd said those words. But right then, she didn't feel dangerous at all. She felt revolted and very, very afraid.

She looked around the room, trying to get her bearings. The windows were the same gray glass and the sun still blazed outside, making them glow, although she no longer had a sense of time. It might have been late afternoon or early evening. On the floor, beside the bed, was a leather duffel, several knives spilling out of it. She wondered where Gavriel had stashed it before his confrontation with Lucien.

The room was large enough for the four-poster bed at its center and the settee along one wall, its upholstery a shining black patent leather. Above it hung a painting, a meticulous study of a human heart crawling with maggots on a silver plate. It reminded Tana of her art teacher, and she wondered suddenly if it could be one of his pieces.

She should take a picture and text it to Mr. Olson, she thought. But that just made her imagine Lucien and Gavriel posing on either side of it, glowering at each other, and from there, hysteria threatened to crawl up her throat and force a giggle out of her.

That was the worst part. She could plan and she could make herself keep going, but she couldn't control when her brain overloaded on horror and threatened to shut down spectacularly, in a sputter of hysterical laughter. She felt as if she was teetering at the very edge of what she could handle; and if she started laughing now, she wouldn't stop.

Lucien crossed the room and flopped down on the settee, sprawling out, showing exactly how comfortable he was in Gavriel's bedroom. Which made sense, since they were, after all, in his home. He continued carving the underside of his nails with the knife, picking loose the last of what darkened them. The more she looked at him, the more she realized that some of his blond hair was stained with blood, too—toward the back of his head, where he probably couldn't see it. On the cameras, it would read as nothing, a blur.

She wanted to laugh again, which was ridiculous, because none of this was funny.

Tana perched on the corner of the mattress. When Gavriel looked over at her, she couldn't quite meet his gaze. She remembered how he'd watched her with the vampire in the basement, seen her stained mouth and her red teeth. What had he thought of her? She'd fallen a long way from the nice girl who offered him a ride in the trunk of her car.

No, not funny in the least.

"So," said Lucien. "The Spider's advance guard—his *Corps des Ténèbres*—is coming tonight at dusk. The Spider himself will come later in the evening when everything has been arranged for him. We don't have much time for preparations and only one chance for this plan to work."

The casual way he spoke of the Spider's arrival, as though coming and going from Coldtown for vampires like the Spider or Lucien or Elisabet was as simple as crossing any other border, was alarming. She wondered if the only creatures really stuck inside the city were humans. No, she thought, humans and vampires created after Caspar.

Gavriel ran pale fingers through the mess of his black hair, an oddly human habit. He cut his gaze toward Tana and then back to Lucien. "Just let me get close enough and I'll kill him. Don't doubt that."

"The chains would have to be real," Lucien said. "He, above all others, knows what will hold you and what won't—I'll have to use heavy steel, but we can loosen a few links. Understand? It will all have to seem very, very real."

"Yes," Gavriel said, so softly that it was almost an exhalation of breath. "And there must be some sign of struggle. Marks on my body and face, as though we really fought."

Lucien's lips pulled back from his teeth in an expression that was half smile and half snarl.

"What is the plan, exactly?" Tana asked. Lucien glanced at her in annoyance, before his face very deliberately smoothed out. Maybe he'd realized that she couldn't help Gavriel stick to a plan she didn't understand. Or maybe he'd remembered he was trying to make her like him.

"It's simple, really," he said, waving a hand in Gavriel's direction.

"The Spider is going to come pick up his prize. We're going to truss up Gavriel, and when the Spider gets close enough—and he will, he won't be able to resist gloating—Gavriel will pull free from the restraints and kill him."

Gavriel nodded his agreement. "And then Lucien's people will fall upon his *Corps*."

"And thus will the new world triumph over the old," finished Lucien.

"Nice," Tana said, feeling as though she ought to say something, but also as though everything she thought of seemed insufficient. That odd feeling of the surreal descended on her again.

Some vampires were going to murder some other vampires.

Lucien and Gavriel, best vampire frenemies, were going to murder some other vampires.

She put her hand in front of her mouth, smothering a smile.

Once upon a time, she and Pauline had had a big falling out over a leather jacket that Tana had borrowed and their mutual friend Ana puked on. There'd been a huge screaming fight and then avoiding each other for a week, eating lunch at different tables and upsetting their mutual friends with their endless snarking. But then Pauline got cast as a lead in a play and turned up at Tana's house to run lines. The fight was over, just like that.

Could Gavriel feel that way about Lucien, though? Was it possible to forgive someone who caused the death of his sister, whose necklace he'd carried with him for more than a century? Was it possible to forgive someone whose fault it was that he'd been locked in a cell and lost his mind?

Lucien stood up and started toward the door.

Quietly, Gavriel spoke, mouth curling up at one corner. "There is one more thing I would say to you."

Lucien turned, and something about Gavriel froze him in place.

"You won't betray me," Gavriel said. "But can you tell me the reason why?"

"Because I know you can kill him and I want him dead." Lucien frowned, speaking slowly, as if to a child. "You specialize in killing our own kind. And I want the Spider gone—he hates vampires who display themselves before mortals, vampires like me, who've become celebrities—so you're giving me what I want at a very small cost to myself. Besides which, you are my progeny, of which I am most proud."

Gavriel smiled. "No, you won't betray me, because if you do, I will tell the Spider your secret. I know why you gave me over to him so swiftly. I didn't realize at first, but being in a cage for a decade gives one a long time to think."

Lucien glanced up at the wall, above a painting, and then back. It was only a moment's change of gaze, but when Tana followed it, she saw the tiny glare of a camera lens.

Of course he was recording Gavriel. Of course.

It couldn't be part of the live feed, though, not if Lucien was casually discussing secrets. Unless Lucien was betraying Gavriel in the most obvious way possible—literally broadcasting their plan to the Spider. But even though the footage was likely to be hidden away in Lucien's vault somewhere, he looked nervous, as though he didn't want whatever Gavriel was about to say on a recording of any kind.

Gavriel turned toward Tana and directed the next part to her. He sounded chillingly sane. "Long ago, no new vampires could be turned without the approval of a small number of very old vampires. They pretended that they were worried about the spread of vampirism, but what they mostly worried about was one of their own progeny making an army and moving against them. As a Thorn, I hunted any progeny that stepped out of line. But what I mostly hunted were mistakes.

"Some vampires are foolish or sloppy. Some are interrupted in the middle of feeding, surprised by sunlight, or even fought off by the person being attacked. That victim goes Cold, turns, then, not knowing any better, feeds without killing. She probably *tries* to feed without killing. But in the process, she makes more vampires and soon, it's an outbreak."

Tana couldn't help imagining Gavriel being interrupted by some frantic vampire, waving around her hands, trying to explain the terrible errors he'd just made.

A laugh threatened to bubble up Tana's throat again.

"Caspar Morales was different," said Gavriel. At his name, Lucien stiffened. "He didn't remember who turned him, only that he'd had a feeling of being followed and then was surprised, alone in an alley. He woke up in his own house, with the shades drawn. On the wall, in blood, someone had written 'tell death hello.'

"It was as though someone turned him for a prank."

Lucien stayed very still. "Who would do that?" he asked finally, his tone flat.

Gavriel turned back to her, and Tana suddenly realized that she was playing the role of the jury.

"I killed five black-haired and dark-eyed vampires in the month before, all of them with something in their features that made them look, from a distance, as though they could have been kin to me. Three women and two men. All of them with an odd story about how they were turned, all with faces that spoke to me of my brother. My sister. And the clothes they wore—oddly antique, as though someone had set the outfits out for them. The jewelry, too. It was uncanny. One of the boys even had a useless old dueling pistol.

"Tedium is the worst enemy of those that live forever. We all have ways to amuse ourselves. And Lucien's are often—how shall I say it—*petty*."

Tana shivered. The chill of infection was creeping back into her skin, but she could still ignore it.

"All right," Lucien said. "Enough."

"It was like murdering ghosts, over and over again," Gavriel said. "I couldn't do it that last time.

"I let Caspar go. I let him go, but I was not the one who turned him. You did that, Lucien. You turned all of them, to see what I would do. Because it made you laugh to be cruel. And the reason you won't betray me, Lucien, is that if you do, I will tell my story to the Spider and you will spend the next decade in a cage by my side."

Tana looked at them both and for a moment the enormity of what Gavriel had said went washing over her. He was saying that the end of the world wasn't an accident; it was a joke.

"You have no proof," Lucien said. "Only a story."

Gavriel shrugged.

"If you really believed that, why would you have kept this secret for so long?" Lucien's body vibrated with manic suppressed energy. His arrogant mouth trembled.

He was afraid, Tana realized. Afraid of what the Spider would do to him if he knew, maybe afraid of all the other ancient vampires, cheated out of their old world, banding together and ripping him apart as they had done to Caspar Morales. Maybe even afraid of humans, or at least human governments finally having one person to blame.

No wonder Lucien had praised Gavriel for changing the world. Every time Lucien praised him, he was really praising himself.

But being afraid made him dangerous. Tana could see the repressed violence in his face, could see the fresh hate glittering in his red eyes. If Gavriel thought that showing Lucien the power he had over him would ensure his loyalty, Gavriel was wrong.

"I kept your secret because I liked the thought of you free," Gavriel said.

Lucien crossed the room abruptly, as if he could not bear to hear any more. He opened the door to the hall. "After tonight, we'll both be free. We'll be free forever, so long as you don't screw it up."

He slammed his way out, making the wall shake.

Gavriel flopped down on the settee and put both his hands over his face. Then he looked at her with his strange eyes. "Lord, but you must despise me."

She slid off the mattress, shaking her head.

"I'm better now," he said. "Sometimes I am, anyway. Before, it was like being in a dream. I couldn't put everything straight. It got muddled and messy, and now I—now I see how horrifying it must have been. How horrifying it must all be."

"What was it you said—*it would take a river of blood to wash away all my wounds*? I saw a video of you the other night. You appeared to be taking all your medicine at once. So I guess that helped. I'm glad." She remembered him bent over the girl's throat, balancing his knee on the edge of her chair, covering her body with his. A shudder went through her that wasn't fear.

"I really said that?" he asked. "It sounds a bit mad."

Tana laughed, perching on the arm of the settee. He reached out with cold fingers and dragged her down next to him in a surprisingly human gesture. She let herself slip onto the cushion, her head falling against his shoulder.

"How are you?" he asked softly.

"Well," Tana said, "every new outfit I get, I manage to ruin within a few hours."

His grin was immediate, his gaze going to her dress and then away. "Leather wipes down."

Resting there, smiling, his arm around her, felt a little like being out on a very dangerous date. She thought about the way he'd kissed her, with blood in her mouth and the sun rising behind her, and wondered if he wanted to kiss her again.

"So, you think this plan is going to work?" she asked suddenly, desperately needing to fill the silence. "You really trust Lucien?"

"How do you get a cat to bat at a string?" Gavriel whispered against her hair.

"I don't know," she said, shivering. "Drag it past really slow."

"Exactly," he told her, his cool fingers running over the arc of her cheek. He watched his own hand in fascination, as though he was surprised by what it was doing. "And if that doesn't work, drag the string *over* the cat. You don't show what you can really do with the string. You don't start with jerking it up into the air or moving incredibly fast. That comes later. First, you let the cat catch it. And if the cat gets it once, the cat wants to get it again."

"Like you're going to let the Spider think he's caught you?" Her voice came out a bit breathless.

He shrugged. "It's funny to watch them when the string is in the air and they're hanging on, paws off the ground. It's funny to watch them dance. They'll run right into walls to get that string back."

Tana pulled away from him a moment, regarding him seriously. He was all lush mouth and drowning eyes, all pretty monster reclining on leather cushions, but she'd seen the expression on his face before Lucien left. "He's been messing with your head a long time. Aren't you worried that he's manipulating you, Gavriel?"

She glanced up at the shining spot where the camera was. They were directly beneath it, which might mean that they might not show up on the film, but she was sure her voice would. If Lucien heard it, he'd know she never had any intention of helping him.

"I'm not sure it matters anymore. But will you do this one thing for me—will you lock your door tonight and stay inside until dawn? No matter what you hear?"

Tana took a shaky breath. That was the one thing that she couldn't promise him, not if she wanted to help Valentina. Not if she wanted Jameson's help. "Okay," she lied.

He looked worryingly relieved. "Then let me tell you a story while we wait for dusk to fall. When I was a boy, there was a woman who looked after my brother and me—she told us tales of firebirds and witches, and about the warrior-princess called Marya Morevna whom Prince Ivan married. Ivan was all alone, since he'd given his blessing for his first sister to marry a falcon, his second sister to marry an eagle, and the third to marry a raven."

"They married birds?" Tana echoed, not really so much for the answer as to show she was listening—and to make him smile.

"Birds who were sometimes men," Gavriel told her. "When Ivan saw Marya Morevna's fierceness in battle and her beauty, he fell instantly in love. They were married soon after. But warrior-princesses are very busy, so soon Marya Morevna had to invade somewhere or battle somebody and left Ivan in charge of her kingdom. He had piles of gold and very good caviar and everything anyone could want, except for one thing—she implored him never to go into a single chamber under the palace."

Tana thought of her own feet on the dusty steps leading down to her basement and to her mother, waiting in the dark. "He did, though, didn't he?" Leaning in, she rested her head against his chest, closing her eyes.

"He couldn't resist." Gavriel's accent deepened as he spoke. "And there, chained with twelve strong chains, was Koschei the Deathless. And Koschei said, 'Please, I am so thirsty. Pity me and give me some water. I have been locked away here for ten years, suffering torments you cannot imagine. My throat is so dry.'"

"Is this a real story?" Tana interrupted, thinking of Gavriel's own decade of torment, of his own thirst.

But the vampire only laughed. "A very famous one, I swear it.

Anyway, Ivan is a kindly soul and brings Koschei water, but his thirst could not be quenched with a single bucketful, nor with a second bucketful. But when Ivan brought Koschei the third bucketful of water, Koschei was restored to his full strength and broke his chains."

"The sin of mercy," Tana said.

Gavriel looked a little embarrassed and a little pleased that she'd remembered. "Yes," he said softly, cool fingers resting against the skin of her bare shoulder, distracting her. "Ivan was merciful, and all the rest of the story is how he paid for it. Koschei kidnapped Marya Morevna and took her away to his own palace, leaving Ivan to chase after them. Three times he was able to find Marya Morevna and three times was able to run away with her, but Koschei had a magical horse faster than the wind. The first time Koschei caught Ivan, out of gratitude for the water he'd been given, he let Ivan go with a warning that if he was caught again, he'd be chopped into pieces. The second time Koschei caught Ivan, he let him go with the same fearsome warning.

"The third time Koschei caught Ivan, he made good on his threats. He chopped Ivan into thirteen pieces with his sword, put the pieces into a tarred barrel, and threw the barrel into the sea. But the falcon, the eagle, and the raven who had married Ivan's sisters fished it out again. They took the pieces of Ivan's body and laid them on the ground, like a puzzle. Once they'd put him back together, they sprinkled his body with water and he woke up again, as from a deep sleep."

"So he was undead?" Tana asked. "Like a vampire?"

"Something like that. He woke up smarter, too, because this time he went to the witch Baba Yaga and won a horse as fine and fast as

Koschei's. With it, he ran away with Marya Morevna one final time. Koschei chased them on his magical horse, but this time when he caught up, Ivan's horse struck Koschei a mighty blow, smashing his skull. Then Ivan and Marya Morevna built a pyre and burned Koschei until he was ash. And then they lived happily, visiting each of Ivan's sisters and their bird-husbands, all of whom declared that Ivan did the right thing to risk so much for a woman as beautiful and fierce as Marya Morevna."

"If she was so fierce, how come she didn't just save herself?" Tana asked.

"But that's the interesting thing about the story, don't you think?" Gavriel asked with an intensity that belied it just being a story to him. "I loved it when I was a child, but as I got older I started to wonder—was it fair for Marya Morevna to lock away Koschei for ten long years without even water? And if it was fair for her, wasn't it just as fair for him to spirit her away to his castle? But Ivan—he's *good*. He's *kind*. He'd give a prisoner water. And he might not know how to save his wife, but he manages to do the impossible purely by not giving up. He is the chaotic part of the story, because he doesn't do what everyone expects of him.

"When I was a child, I thought of myself as like Ivan, but no— you are more like Ivan than I ever was. You expected me to be good, and because of you, I tried." He closed his eyes. "In the end, though, we both know I will be Koschei in this story. And that's why you should get away from me as fast as you can and keep going. Even my love is monstrous, Tana. I will keep on frightening you and—"

"You're not some fairy-tale character." She caught his chin and turned his face toward her, so that when he opened his otherworldly eyes again, she could look into them without flinching. So she could show him she meant it. "And I'm not—I'm not even sure what I am. But I know *you*. Maybe I didn't spend decades with you like Lucien did, but I bet I can make you laugh faster than he could."

"Oh, really?" He tilted his head to one side, and it was hard for her not to stare too long at the softness of his mouth. She wanted to trace the swell of it.

She leaned close, heart hammering, and licked his cheek instead. For a moment, he looked startled and then he did laugh, real, honest, helpless laughter at the sheer ridiculousness of what she'd done.

"You're yourself," Tana said, grinning. "More purely yourself than anyone I know. And if you can't see who that is anymore, then see yourself the way I see you."

Gavriel shook his head. "You can't know what I am—"

She interrupted him, talking fast. "When I was about to turn fourteen, my dad sent me to sleepaway camp. Maybe you don't know what that is, but it's usually for a couple of weeks in the summer and you—"

He pressed his hand to his chest in mock affront. "I've been locked away for ten years, not *ten thousand*."

"Fine, well okay," she said. "Anyway, I had these ideas about who I was when I left. I had about a hundred stuffed animals that my grand-parents had given me over the years, all of them piled up on my bed. And I had two best friends, Nicole and Amber. Amber lived down the street from me, and we'd been friends since basically forever. Nicole had moved to town later and gotten really close to Amber when I was in the hospital. So it was always the three of us, and we'd ride our bikes around town together and watch movies in one another's rooms.

"In friendships, everybody has roles. I was the one who worried we'd get in trouble if we markered up the Macy's bathroom in the mall or stole a pair of feather earrings from a Claire's Boutique. The one who always did what she was told. The shy one. The scared one. The goody-goody. That was the way I'd been at nine and ten and eleven and twelve, so I never noticed that it wasn't the way I was anymore at thirteen."

He ran cool fingers over the scarred skin of her arm, and for a moment she was too spellbound to go on. "I think you had a reason to be scared," he said.

"Maybe. But the thing is that when I got to that camp, no one knew me. And by the time I went home, I saw myself differently. There, I had been the first one to swim all the way across the lake. When the sink backed up, I took apart the pipes and fixed it. I nearly killed some poor kid from the boys' cabins who tried to scare us by pretending to be a vampire."

"I'll bet," Gavriel said drily.

"Laugh it up," she told him, "but the thing is, I hadn't known myself at all until I went away. I knew how Nicole and Amber saw me. And Lucien and the Spider and all the others—they're afraid of you, so they figure you must be pretty awful indeed. They think you can't feel anything, because they've forgotten how. You're very, very dangerous, I get that, and you're prone to some very theatrical brooding, but don't let yourself mistake that for some kind of inner corruption. They see themselves in you and are blinded."

He leaned toward her, gazing into her face as though some great secret swam in her eyes, his hands drawing her closer, his mouth parting slightly, showing the very tips of his canines as he bent toward her, eyes hooded. "And what do you see?"

A shudder went through her, the chill of infection racing through her veins.

He pulled back, as though he'd been scorched. His lips were still apart and there was a wildness in the way he looked at her, as though he were a trapped animal expecting the lash of a whip.

"No," she said. "I'm just Cold. It's the sickness."

He looked as if he wasn't sure whether to believe her. "You didn't drink enough blood," he said, and lifted his wrist to his mouth, biting down.

Red staining his teeth and the inside of his lower lip, he held his hand out to her.

"I can't," she said softly, pulling away, the smell of his blood making her dizzy. "Something's wrong with me already."

He frowned, studying her face. Her eyes went to his red wrist. She wanted to kiss it, to drag her tongue across it, to sink her sharp teeth past his skin. And another part of her was screaming that she couldn't do that, that she wasn't like that.

She opened her mouth, letting him see the new points of her new fangs.

"*Oh*," he said, clearly surprised, but not *that* surprised.

"Please just tell me if it's really bad. Marisol said—oh, forget what she said. Just explain."

"I'll try," Gavriel began, ignoring his bleeding wrist. "Long ago, we visited humans we wanted to turn, night after night, taking their blood and giving them our own. When they were ready—after they'd become something not quite human—we let them taste human blood and become vampires. You've, er, hastened the process by drinking so much vampire blood on your own."

His explanation was like Marisol's, except that he'd obviously seen it done. *No, you idiot,* she thought suddenly, *he had it done to him.*

"What now?" Tana asked, the words *something not quite human* echoing in her head.

Gavriel shrugged. "A vampire who's been fed on vampire blood is stronger, that's all. Most vampires turned after everything went Cold are weak, with weak blood. They're what we used to call by-blows, accidents. Mistakes."

Tana's tongue ran over the points of her teeth. Gavriel's blood was running down his arm in three lines, and she found it hard to tear her gaze away. It looked like strawberry-blueberry syrup, just as in her little-kid dream. "I'm still just Cold, though, right? In eighty-eight days, if I don't drink any more—I'll get better, won't I?"

The look on his face told her more than his words. "I've never seen anyone go backward once the physical transformation began, but that doesn't mean it's not possible."

"So it's also possible that I could be Cold forever?" she asked, her heart pounding. "Hungry, *forever and ever?*"

He was silent for a long moment, which was answer enough. Then he reached for a scarf to bind his wrist.

If she stayed Cold forever and ever, that would make her a living vampire. A living vampire that could never have what it craved.

Just when you think you've sunk as far as it's possible to sink, there's always a lower place. There's always something worse to be scared about. Wasn't that some saying? Some rule?

I don't care, she decided. *Just this once, for a little while, I'm not going to worry and I'm not going to care.* She caught Gavriel's arm and when he looked a question at her, surprised, she couldn't bring herself to answer. She didn't want to explain the recklessness, the pleasure of making the bad choice, the glory of at least this once, picking her own path to damnation. So instead of speaking, she brought her mouth down on his wounded wrist, newly sharp teeth piercing his skin and making him—even him—gasp.

She swallowed his blood, a dark vintage from some forgotten cellar. She felt like Persephone in Hades, pomegranate seeds bursting against her teeth, juice rolling on her tongue, and the more she had, the more she hungered. Her skin felt as if it were lit from the inside, her whole body shuddering with delicious sensation. He made a few soft sounds before he brought his free hand up to smother them, pressing his fingers against his own mouth. She drew harder on his wrist.

Finally, she forced herself to pull back and gaze up at him unsteadily. She felt drunk. He didn't look particularly sober, either, watching her with slightly unfocused eyes, his lips apart when he drew his hand away from them, a shiver going through his body like some low electric current.

It occurred to her that Gavriel was going to fight a very old vampire in a matter of hours and that giving up even a portion of his strength was a terrible idea. He didn't look as if he cared, though, head tipped back and eyes falling half closed. She wondered if she'd taken too much already.

"Gavriel," she said, her tongue feeling clumsy in her mouth.

"Yes?" He blinked a few times, as though he was trying to focus on her.

"You can bite me," she said. "If you want."

That seemed to snap him out of his daze. He pulled back, eyes going wide.

She crawled closer, going up on her knees and straddling one of his legs, balancing herself with her hands on his shoulders. Her heart hammered in her chest. "I'm already Cold. I'm already doomed. It won't matter."

"Tana…" he protested, looking stunned. He wanted to, though, she could tell. He bent toward her throat as though the thrum of her pulse was beating in his ears, inhaling the scent of her skin.

She squinched her eyes closed, braced for the sharp stab of fangs.

"Tana," he said again, whispering against her skin. "Tana."

"Just do it," she told him. "I'm scared enough as it is. Don't let me chicken out and—"

She felt the press of his cold lips again and then the pressure of teeth on her jugular.

Fear choked a low sob out of her. He brought his bloody wrist to her mouth, and as her teeth found the fresh wound, he bit down on her neck. It felt like twin shards of ice slid into her throat.

She groaned against his skin. Pain raced along her nerves. She felt the pull of his teeth, the rush of everything warm inside of her pouring out. She felt the race of her heart, thudding faster and faster with fear. The taste of his blood was on her tongue, and cold pinpricks raced over her spine. Her lips felt numb.

Her body was pressed against his, one of his hands against the small of her back, nerves she'd never been aware of before clenched in sudden euphoria. Pleasure unfolded inside her, sinister and seductive. It was hard to remember to breathe, hard to remember to do more than bite down on his wrist and drown in looping rapture.

She moved against him, as though she could crawl inside his skin.

Then he pushed her away, moving to the other side of the settee. Her neck stung and she gasped for air, the room coming into focus again. His eyes were closed, long sooty lashes brushing cheeks pink with her blood, black curls hanging in his face, mouth painted red. He was every bit the debauched angel, far from heaven.

Her lips parted, eager to taste, before she remembered herself.

Out the window, the sky was dark. She stood shakily.

He opened red eyes.

She wanted to tell him about Valentina and how she had to go, how she'd promised she'd help, and how she would help, except that right then she didn't want to help anyone so much as to kiss him and maybe bite him again, too, but mostly kiss him and do all the things that came after kissing.

She wanted to tell him all of that, except then the camera above the painting, the one that recorded everything they did, would record her words, too.

At the thought of Lucien watching, her gaze flickered to it, before she could make herself look away.

"I've got to get back to my room," she said, not quite able to meet his gaze. She wanted him, wanted to stay and blot out all her fear with desire. She forced herself to take a step toward the door.

He looked as if he wanted to say something that would stop her, but he only stood, putting his hand against the wall to steady himself. Dark, bluish blood ran from his wrist.

Good-bye, she thought. *Good-bye, good-bye, good-bye.*

"It's nearly over," Gavriel told her, his voice low, a mad smile pulling up one corner of his mouth. "Time for us to read the day's entrails and prophesy a glorious future."

→ CHAPTER 34 ←

Death did not come to my mother
Like an old friend.
—Josephine Miles

When Tana was little, she hadn't liked it when her mother went to parties.

She'd loved watching her get ready: loved the chiffon and silk dresses, the velvet jackets, even the crisp, just-back-from-the-dry-cleaner suits with safety pins attached; the glittering earrings and necklaces and brooches; the magic of rouging cheeks, outlining lips, and darkening eyes with shadow, then liner and mascara; the spray of perfume hanging over everything like a sweet, musky cloud, clinging to her mother's skin and hair, giving her a cool, remote elegance.

"Should I wear the pearls tonight or the gold dangles?" her mother had asked her, holding them up.

Lying on top of the duvet on her parents' bed, Tana studied her mother very carefully before choosing. You couldn't ask Pearl questions like that, because she picked the pearls every time, for her name. This time, though, Tana picked the pearls, too. They looked pretty with Mom's dress.

But as her mother's high heels clacked on the parquet wood floor, Tana got nervous about the night ahead. Her mother might not be back before bedtime, and Dad didn't understand that Tana was allowed to keep her light on for an extra half hour if she was in the middle of a really good book, plus he flatly refused to check the closet for monsters. The milky tea they had before bed was never quite sweet enough, and when he read to Pearl, he didn't do the voices. Since he didn't know how to do all those things right, bedtime went all wrong.

At ten years old, she was supposed to be a big girl. Dad would tell her that she was too grown up for night-lights and worrying about monsters under the bed. When she tried to explain that it was the *closet* she worried about, he smiled as if she'd told a joke.

But if you didn't believe in monsters, then how were you going to be able to keep safe from them?

That's how Tana wound up staying awake, waiting for her mother to come home. After an hour, tossing and turning in the dark, she snuck downstairs and sat at the kitchen table, with a single lamp on, eating dry saltines. For a while that was fine, but then, with shadows closing in and Dad and Pearl sleeping all the way upstairs, she got scared. The wood of the house creaked slightly and the pipes groaned. Outside the window the wind shivered through the bushes, and her gaze kept darting to the movement as she wondered if something was there. She kept thinking of the news programs and the attacks that all the grown-ups didn't want her to know about.

By the time the headlights of Mom's car swept over the lawn, Tana had completely freaked herself out, but she made a vow that she wouldn't let Mom see it. She was a big girl, as Dad said.

What she didn't expect was the way her mother looked when she walked in—ashen-faced, her mascara smeared as though she'd been rubbing her eyes or crying. For a moment, she just stared at Tana, her face haunted. Then she smiled a sickly, forced, horrible smile.

"Oh, did you stay up, waiting for me, my good girl?" her mother asked.

"Mommy," Tana said, crossing the kitchen to throw her arms around her, calling her something she hadn't called her for years. "Mommy, what's wrong?"

"Nothing, sweetheart, peanut, lamb chop," her mother said, and even her voice sounded strange. "Time to go to bed."

They walked up the stairs. Tana yawned. She was glad her mother was back, even though something bad must have happened, something that she felt inadequate to the task of understanding.

At the landing, her mother crouched down and took Tana by the shoulders, staring at her with a blazing intensity.

"I love you," she said. "You and your sister. I love you both so much, and nothing is ever going to change that."

Tana nodded, thoroughly frightened.

"I would do anything to protect you," her mother told her, eyes gleaming in the dim light. "Anything to get to stay with you both and watch you grow up. Anything, okay?"

"Okay," Tana said.

But as her mother tucked her into bed, leaning over and pressing her cool mouth against Tana's cheek, with the odor of perfume wafting all around them and locks of her mother's black hair hanging loose from her bobby pins, forming a curtain, Tana decided that she didn't *want* to grow up. She didn't want to be a big girl too stupid to check the closet for monsters, and she didn't want to go to parties where awful things happened that you had to pretend about, not even if it meant you got to wear pretty dresses and glittering jewels.

She didn't want to grow up, and yet there was not a single thing she could do to stop it.

CHAPTER 35

To the living we owe respect, but to the dead we owe only the truth.

—Voltaire

Tana made her way dizzily down the hallway, her heartbeat loud in her ears, the scent of her own blood in her nose, a metallic taste in her mouth. Sounds came from rooms below as the household woke, crawling from their chambers, ravenous, the night stretching out in front of them with its glittering carpet of stars.

Tana didn't want to be creeping down the hall alone, didn't want to be sneaking out of Lucien's terrifying manor without saying one last good-bye to Gavriel, but there was no safe way to say anything without being overheard. Better to leave him with the memory of his teeth against her throat and her teeth on his wrist. Better to leave him with the memory of their being a pair of monsters, wrapped in each other's arms.

And after tonight—after tonight, she'd have to chain herself up behind a sturdy door and hope for the best. Self-quarantine was dangerous, and, even without the borrowed trouble of an excess of vampire blood chilling her veins, there was a good chance she wouldn't survive.

You're not even really human anymore, some part of her sneered, sounding a lot like Winter's voice. *Give it up. Just die already. It'll be just like the dream you had—blood and forests and snow, girls with raven's-wing hair and rose-red lips and sharp teeth as white as milk.*

It worried her that it had gotten harder and harder to remember what it felt like to live her old life, even though she'd been living it mere days ago. Every memory had drowned in a sea of red.

She opened the door to Elisabet's bedroom, intent on grabbing her phone and cash, then stopped abruptly when she saw Marisol waiting for her. The vampire was sitting on the high bed, one dagger-heeled boot against the brass footboard, twisting her silver tooth ring in her fingers, clearly bored.

"You took your time getting back," Marisol said. Tana looked beyond her, to see the curtains in one corner of the room fluttering. The window was open and the white crow perched on the sill, looking in at her, its wicked curved beak opening to cry once. Something was attached to its leg—a little metal fastener where a piece of paper might fit if it was rolled up tight.

"What does Lucien want now?" Tana asked, forcing her gaze to Marisol. The vampire must have noticed the bird. *Why was she acting so nonchalant about it?*

"You don't have to worry." Marisol slid off the bed with a sigh. "Lucien's not the one that sent me."

The taste of Gavriel's blood was still in Tana's mouth, and she didn't feel entirely sober. "Jameson," she realized, speaking his name out loud. "You're his—"

"Mother." Marisol smiled, a cat with a canary it was resisting batting around. "He asked me to help you save some girl, so here I am, *helping.*"

"Oh," Tana said, realizing what he hadn't said when he'd talked about growing up in Coldtown—nothing about his mother, nothing about his parents at all. And then she couldn't help thinking of her own mother, of how her mother could have been very like this. "*Oh.*"

Valentina was going to be so happy. Maybe happy enough to eventually forget the way Tana had ripped open a vampire's throat with a screwdriver and blunt teeth right in front of her.

"Go ahead," Marisol said. "The message on the bird's leg is for you."

Tana walked over to Gremlin. The bird was still, not pecking her fingers, letting her pull the thin piece of paper from the steel casing attached to its leg.

Trust her, it said. *Trust me.*

Tana sighed.

"There's one other thing." Marisol hopped off the bed, moving with unnatural grace. Her scarlet eyes gazed past Tana, taking in the room, as though looking for cameras. "Your friend wanted Jameson to pass on a message. Some girl from your hometown is here in Coldtown. Pearl. Does that mean anything to you?"

The world wavered in place. Blackness flooded the edges of

Tana's vision. She felt as if she were falling, as if she were falling and falling and would never stop falling.

No, it couldn't be. No.

"I think her name was Pearl. Or Jewel? Some other friend of yours is trying to find her." Marisol made a vague gesture of exasperation. "I don't know. I don't know why any of you come here."

"That's my little sister," Tana said, some of her fury—at the universe, at herself, at Pearl—leaking into her voice. "She's twelve. She came here because—"

She came here because of me. Because of that stupid message I sent her.

She came here because Lucien convinced her he was harmless and excitingly dangerous at the same time.

She came here because she wanted to be a part of the show.

Marisol looked momentarily taken aback at the mention of Pearl's age and then resentful, as though Tana had forced her to feel something she didn't want to feel.

Ignoring the vampire, Tana headed toward the bathroom for her phone, the pale crow hopping after her. Checking her texts, she saw a new one from Pauline: *Jesus. Yr sister not home. She texted yr dad 1 hour ago says goigin to live with u & b on tv. I called her 16x but didt pick up. Phoned all ur friends. Gone.*

Frantically, her hands shaking, Tana hit the button to call her sister. The phone didn't even ring; it went straight to voice mail. Closing her eyes, she counted her breaths in and out, trying to find some way to calm herself.

WHERE R U RIGHT NOW???? Tana texted her sister, but time slid by with no immediate reply. Shoving her phone into her borrowed bra, where she could feel the vibration against her skin if something came in, she resisted the urge to pound her fists against the counter.

If Mom had been alive and in Coldtown, I might have come looking for her, too.

"I'm just helping you and the girl, Valentina, understand?" Marisol called. "None of the guards or staff are going to be in their usual places tonight, but that doesn't mean we can be stupid."

"We're freeing every prisoner down there who's willing to come." Tana wasn't sure she recognized her own voice, all iron filings and ice. "Everyone we can find. And we're doing it fast."

Fast, fast, so that she could make it out and get to her sister.

"I'm risking a lot for you already," Marisol said. "You will do exactly what I tell you or else I'll—"

"You're not *my* mother," Tana interrupted, walking to the bed. Picking up her purse, she dumped everything out onto the blankets. She tucked cash into her bra beside her cell and abandoned the rest. "And you don't have to help, if this is too much for you. I'll tell Jameson that you were awesome. He doesn't need to know that you couldn't be bothered."

Marisol's gaze sharpened. "I wasn't always—I wasn't a very good mother. So if my son asks me to do something, I do it, no matter how stupid it seems to me. Jameson says to help get out this girl he likes, so I'll help. Jameson says meet by the gate, so that's where we'll meet. If we get separated, he suggests we meet at the Eternal Ball, and that's fine by me, too. He thinks that we can blend into the crowd and that the cameras will keep Lucien's people from being too awful."

Marisol didn't sound as if she agreed with him, but the words passed through Tana without really mattering. Her thoughts had drifted back to Pearl wandering through the nighttime streets. For a single, hopeful moment, she recalled a day in third grade, when her whole class had sat in the grass just beyond the jungle gym and Ms. Lee had whispered, "It'll be time for lunch later," to Rachel, who'd whispered to Lance, who'd whispered to Courtney, who'd whispered to Pauline, who'd whispered to Marcus, who'd whispered to Tana. "It's time lambs ate hair," Marcus had said, his breath smelling of spearmint gum, and Tana had been proud, because she was sure she passed it on perfectly. By the time it got to the other end, though, it was even more garbled.

Maybe that was what happened. The message got confused. Marisol had misunderstood. Pearl wasn't really here.

But in her heart, Tana knew she was.

The white crow cawed, looking over with sinister eyes. *Find Pearl*, Tana wanted to command, but she knew Gremlin wouldn't understand and, anyway, he'd only listen to Jameson. No, she was going to have to get away from Lucien first, then figure out what to do from there.

What will you do? she chided herself. *Are you going to find her and then, hungry as you're going to get, what next? Drink her blood quick, before someone else does?*

Tana's eyes burned as she knelt down and reached for the box under Elisabet's bed. She strapped one of the wooden knives to her thigh, tying it down with two boot laces. Then she tucked the guard's keys into the fist of one of her hands and picked up a crossbow from the locker underneath Elisabet's bed—each bolt made of polished rosewood and thorn—for Marisol. "Okay, you point that thing at me, and hopefully everyone will think I'm some prisoner you're marching through the estate."

It really said something about what it must be like to live with Lucien Moreau that all of Elisabet's weapons were the sort one used against other vampires. This must be a very different place when all the cameras were off.

And for some reason that thought made her realize, with horrible certainty, that she knew where Pearl would be headed once she crossed the threshold into Coldtown. She'd go right to Lucien. He was Pearl's favorite celebrity vampire, after all, and she'd said she was going to be on TV. Tana closed her eyes, and for the first time since she'd woken up among corpses in Lance's farmhouse, for the first time since the scrape of teeth against her leg, she let go of the hope that she was going to make it. Maybe she could find Pearl in time and give her the marker, but there was no way out for Tana.

There was only what she did before she died.

Marisol gave her an appraising look, as though something in Tana's whole manner had changed. Frowning, Marisol walked to the door, her movements fluid as she turned the ornate knob. Barefoot, Tana padded down the stairs with Marisol.

The scent of blood and sweat was sharp in her nose and sharper still once the door to the basement opened. No one seemed to notice them passing, especially when Marisol's hand clamped tight around Tana's upper arm. "Act like a prisoner," the vampire said, hauling her along like a piece of baggage, a crossbow bolt pressed into her back in a way that suddenly felt all too realistic.

At the bottom of the stairs, she saw the cages, lit by a dim bulb in the center of the room. Valentina sat against the back wall, next to a boy in smudged white pants and black suspenders over no shirt, and the dark-haired girl Tana had spoken with before. They pushed themselves to their feet. Valentina slipped her fingers around the bars, squinting into the gloom. Tana could see perfectly. She could hear the prisoners' hearts speed, too, could hear the warm tide of their blood lapping against the edges of her mind. She thought of the crowd of people standing in the theater in front of Gavriel, all the people he'd bitten, and wondered if hunger like hers could ever be sated.

"Tana, you found her!" said Valentina, looking at Marisol. "It's *her*! How did you—"

"This is Jameson's *mom*," Tana said quickly, ignoring her red vision, ignoring the answering drum of her own heart. "And she's going to help get us out of here."

Marisol frowned, clearly confused by the emphasis Tana had put on the word *mom*.

Valentina stared at Marisol and couldn't seem to stop staring.

Tana knelt down and slid one of the keys into each lock, jiggling it around. After a moment, it turned with a heavy metallic clank.

"Hey," one of the prisoners, a hollow-chested boy, said. "What are you doing? You're not supposed to do that!"

As Tana fumbled to fit the second key in, someone started down the stairs.

"Who's there?" a guard called. "What's going on?"

"They're letting us out," called one of the girls before Valentina grabbed hold of her, pressing a hand against her mouth.

Tana leaned back against the wall, slipping Elisabet's long wooden dagger into her hand. She could picture the way it would sink into the guard's skin if he came down the stairs, the way she would rip it through his heart. Killing Midnight had been hard, but she thought of the other vampire she'd stabbed in this very place and wasn't sure it would ever be hard again. Her lips pulled back from her teeth in a silent snarl.

Marisol gazed up the stairs at him, tossing back her hair and smiling. "I'm taking a few of the prisoners out back to hose them down. You can't expect Lucien to serve them up covered in dirt."

Tana looked at Marisol's smile. She was disturbingly good at faking her feelings. Tana wondered what had happened that had made Marisol abandon her son years before? Was it that she was afraid she'd drain him? Turn him? Was it easier to glut herself on blood and give up on everything else?

I have a friend who lives in Lucien's house, Jameson had said. He hadn't called her his mother, not once, not even in the note telling Tana to trust her.

They're not human, Tana reminded herself. *I am not wholly human anymore.*

The guard seemed to swallow the explanation, but he took another step closer. "Need some help?" he called to Marisol.

Tana braced to swing. She tried to concentrate on the place to one side of his breastbone where his heart would be.

"No," Marisol said. "But find me someplace to put them upstairs. Couches or—I don't know—a table that's long enough to display them lying across it."

"Sure, okay," he said. "But we're supposed to be out of here before the Spider arrives. Lucien wants just a skeleton crew—servers and a guard or two. Charles is going to be the only one manning the cameras. So, if you're going to get them ready, you don't have a lot of time."

"Time is the only thing any of us do have," Marisol said with a shrug.

"Suit yourself," the guard told her, and Tana heard his footsteps retreating. *A skeleton crew?* Lucien had promised Gavriel that his people would be there to take down the Spider's *Corps des Ténèbres*. Not only must he have been lying, but it seemed clear that everyone in the house knew Gavriel was being set up. Even Marisol must have known it.

Tana wanted to slam the wooden knife into Lucien's heart, wanted to watch the bubbling of deep blue blood. How was she going to warn Gavriel?

And what was Gavriel thinking, letting Lucien chain him and drag him back before the monster who'd imprisoned him for a decade? Did he think that nothing could touch him now? Did he believe in the power of his own madness to carry him through? Was his head so foggy with poems and plans that he had no room for doubts?

She had to tell him before the Spider got there, before it was too late.

Marisol turned the second key, swinging open the door and regarding the prisoners, smiling a fanged smile. "You'll come with me like good little boys and girls, won't you?"

The humans looked at one another with shadowed eyes.

"Come along," Marisol told the prisoners. "That was just a story I made up for the big bad guard. Anyway, wouldn't it be easier to escape from outside? Don't you want to come with me?"

"No," one of them said, the thin boy with his ribs sticking out and liquid eyes the color of weak tea. "I knew you were lying. Lucien is keeping us safe. We're earning our place."

Marisol shrugged thin shoulders and smiled in Tana's direction. "We offered. You can't ask for more than that."

Tana gripped the cold flesh of the vampire's shoulder. "Wait." She turned to the boy. "Please—please come with us. You've got to know this is a prison. You must know he's never going to—"

"Shut up," the boy said, folding his arms.

"Let them be," Marisol told her, smug. "They made their choice."

But a few, shamefaced, shuffled out. Others stayed put with the boy, resolute.

Only the muzzled girls and boys didn't move. They slumbered away, barely stirring. Valentina shook one, but his lashes only fluttered. His eyes didn't even open.

"I think they're drugged," said Valentina.

Marisol raised both her brows. "Satisfied?"

"There's nothing else we can do, Tana." Valentina glanced toward the stairs.

"Yeah," said the dark-haired girl. "Time to cut and run. Jesus, I didn't think we'd even get this far."

Tana knew they were right. She couldn't worry about the people they were leaving behind, not now. Not with Pearl out there somewhere. Not with Gavriel about to be betrayed.

"What's wrong with your mouth?" the boy with the suspenders asked her. "Are you okay?"

Tana touched her lip and realized that her newly sharp teeth must have broken the skin. She hadn't even noticed.

Valentina leaned heavily on Tana's arm as she left the cage, clearly stiff and sore. The heat of her skin made Tana flinch with pleasure.

Marisol led them up the stairs and through a series of elaborately furnished rooms. There were a few vampires there, talking together. None looked armed for a fight with an ancient vampire's minions. As Marisol and the others moved cautiously through the glass-domed banquet hall, Tana heard a vampire's voice echo off the walls. "You, there! Stop! Stop where you are!"

At that, the prisoners ran for the door, wrenching it open and running across the dew-covered lawn under the moonlight. They scattered, with Tana, Valentina, and Marisol racing after. The moon was high in the sky, bright and full, like an overripe piece of fruit grown too heavy for its branch.

Only a single guard was stationed by the gate. He came running to intercept the boy in suspenders, calling for him to stop. Marisol shot him with the crossbow, dropping him onto the lawn with a single bolt. Tana stopped running, stunned.

You killed two of them! she yelled at herself. *You're not allowed to be shocked by death.*

Behind her, another vampire exited the house, running after them. Marisol swung the crossbow around.

"Come on!" Valentina shouted, frantic, pushing her toward a hole cut in the iron fence, the bars snapped out.

Jameson was on the other side, holding a weathered-looking flamethrower pointed toward the house and waving the other prisoners through.

Tana went after, Valentina right behind her.

Jameson grabbed Valentina by the shoulder as soon as she was away from the fence, gripping her tightly and looking at her with a devouring gaze. "I would have gone for you," he said, not quite making sense. "You should have told me and I would have done it instead, whatever it was."

"It wasn't like that," Valentina said, clearly not sure what he thought had happened.

For a moment, Tana thought that Jameson would kiss Valentina, but he dropped his hand, turning toward his mother as she ducked between the bars and swinging the flamethrower off his shoulder.

"Thanks," he said. "So, let me guess, you're going straight back to Lucien?"

"Not tonight," said his mother, glancing back at the house. It glowed with dark light. "Tonight I'm sticking with you, kid."

Over their heads, the white crow was circling.

Tana thought of Pearl, on the lawn one late summer day, her pale hair tangled because she'd cry if anyone tried to brush it, spinning around and around until she got so dizzy she fell in a pile of bare feet and dandelions and sundress.

Pearl, who was probably coming straight to the place Tana was running from. If Tana went out, scouring the streets, calling Pearl's name while Pearl went straight to Lucien, if something bad happened, Tana would hate herself forever.

She remembered a late-night episode of one of those shows on the

History Channel with a bunch of professors talking about monsters. It was one of those memories that came with the feeling of the scratchy afghan over Tana's legs as she sat on the couch; the smell of microwave popcorn; and Pearl stretched out on the old rug, stacking up LEGOs. *The monster is bigger than human. It represents abundance—overabundance*, the white-haired man had said, pushing his glasses up higher on his nose. *It has lots of eyes, extra arms, too many teeth. Everything about it is too many and too much.*

That was how she felt, right then. As if there was too much of her, as if her skin was tight with muchness. She felt ripe to bursting.

And she remembered what Gavriel had said when she'd woken up handcuffed to a bed. *Being infected, being a vampire, it's always you. Maybe it's more you than ever before. It's you as you always were, deep down inside.*

Maybe this was who she always was. Always shoving all that muchness down deep inside her where no one had to see.

And once she'd found Pearl, how long before she became the monster her mother was? How long before the infection sank so deep down into her blood that all she could think of was how to get warm again? How long before Pearl was just soft skin and a beating heart? She might be herself still, but she'd be herself hungry, a self she didn't know yet. Herself with the brake lines cut. A self she didn't trust to do anything but kill.

"Give me the crossbow," Tana said as calmly as she could. "I'm going back inside."

"What?" Valentina spun toward her. "No!"

"I have to." Tana pulled out her phone, opening her photographs and flipping to one of her little sister a year before, hair in pigtails. "Pearl's on her way here; this is what she looks like. I need you guys to do me one last favor. Please, find her."

Marisol started to object, but Jameson just nodded. "Yeah, of course. Your friend Pauline says that Pearl couldn't have made it inside before today. She might not even be through the gate yet. We've got this. Finding strays is my specialty."

Tana handed him the phone. "Please, please keep her safe."

He nodded, looking sidelong at his mother. Then he took his own cell from his back pocket, handing it to Tana. "Here, I'll call as soon as we know something."

She tucked it into her bra, overwhelmed with gratitude.

Valentina looked back at the house. "Just don't take any chances in there," she said. "The ancient, insane vampire doesn't need your help."

But what if he did?

Never again, Tana had promised herself. *No matter what, she was never going to let anyone get the better of her ever again. No more mistakes.*

"I'm through believing things will work out on their own. I'm going to kill Lucien Moreau myself," Tana said, taking the crossbow with the wooden bolts from Marisol's hands and setting it down on the ground, so that she could unclasp Gavriel's garnet necklace from around her throat, the token for leaving Coldtown safely inside. "When you find my sister, give her this for me."

Valentina took the necklace and promised that she would.

Tana hefted the crossbow, tracing her thumb over the smooth

wood and cold metal as she watched them leave, Marisol gliding into the shadows as though made of shadow herself.

I'm going to kill Lucien Moreau myself, Tana repeated, and this time she allowed herself to finish the thought. *I'm going to kill Lucien Moreau myself or I'm going to die trying.*

→ CHAPTER 36 ←

Dead men bite not.

—Theodotus

When Pearl got off the bus, she took a cab, and when the taxi let her off—past a checkpoint with an obnoxious guard—the driver took a long look at her.

"How about I drive you back, kid?" the woman asked, leaning out the window. She had big hair, dark and braided in a way that made it appear as if she wore a crown. "No charge. Now that you've seen it, you don't need to stick around a place like that. They'll eat a little thing like you and still be hungry."

"No, thanks," Pearl said, and went inside the building. She'd already ignored a bunch of calls from home, so she wasn't going to let a stranger rattle her.

She didn't feel nervous until she was sitting on a rough concrete bench, signing forms that had words like *waive all rights* and *national threat*. Once she'd said that she was infected, they'd hustled her right through the building as if she were a bomb about to go off. No one tried to convince her this was a bad decision. No one even looked at the marks she'd made on her inner arm in preparation.

But it wasn't until she was hanging above the city in an iron cage that she began to think that maybe she'd made a mistake.

Coldtown didn't look the way Pearl had expected. In all the videos, it had seemed as if it would be an endless party, full of beautiful and well-dressed people, but the streets were mostly empty and lined with garbage. And it was big, really big, with buildings stretching out toward the far walls. Pearl started to wonder if maybe it wasn't going to be as easy to find her way as she'd figured.

After Pearl had seen Tana's fight with the blue-haired girl at Lucien Moreau's, after she'd watched the girl sink her fangs into Tana's neck, Pearl had gone straight onto the fan message boards. There were lots of gross boys being perverts, chatting back and forth about how much they liked watching the girls wrestle. She ignored them and wrote her own post, asking if her sister was okay. For a tense hour, she didn't hear anything.

As she sat on her bed refreshing her browser, she kept thinking about what her grandma and grandpa had said, about how it was her job to look after Tana. She couldn't do that if they didn't live in the same place. If she'd gone to Coldtown with Tana, they could have stayed in one of the old warehouses by the water. They'd have hung out with Aidan and gone to parties instead of school, and what happened to Tana would never have happened, because Pearl would have told her that girl was bad news. But maybe now it was too late to do anything.

Then, finally, one of the board moderators private-messaged her. His name was Nicholas, and he said her sister was doing okay, but if she came to Coldtown, Lucien was interested in meeting her. *Don't tell anyone*, he wrote her. *Think of how surprised your sister will be.*

And that was what she thought of the whole ride there. All she had to do was find her way to Lucien Moreau's house. She'd imagined that would be easy; she figured she'd just ask people and they'd show her the way.

As she walked through the streets, though, no one looked safe enough to approach. A group of thin and dirty strangers stood around a burning trash can, cooking something on long, shaved sticks that looked a lot like bugs. They seemed more likely to steal her stuff than help her.

She'd seen lots of feeds from Lucien's, though, and some of them had exterior shots. All she had to do was find the part of Springfield where the big old mansions were. She was sure she'd know the house when she saw it. Invigorated by this idea, Pearl started marching toward the area of the city with the brightest lights.

"Hey," a voice said, and she spun around. A girl with curly blond hair and a tatty sundress was leaned against a brick wall, bag slung over her shoulder, smoking a cigarette that stank of some spice. "You need a place to stay?"

"Not exactly," Pearl said, feeling shy. "I'm looking for my sister and—"

"I've got a friend who knows a lot of people," she said, peeling herself off the wall. "It's not safe on the streets around here. We all travel in a big group. Runaways, just like you, right? You should come with me."

Pearl hadn't really thought of herself as a runaway. After all, it wasn't like she didn't know where she was going. It wasn't like she was going to be by herself. And there was something scary about the girl, something not right about the way she spoke, as though all the words were rehearsed.

"Thanks," Pearl said, "but I've got to find my sister."

"My friend would really like you," said the girl, smiling a smile that seemed a little too wide to be real. "Come have dinner with us. You've got to be hungry, right?"

"No, I—" Pearl started when the blond girl caught hold of her arm, fingers digging in.

"Okay, enough with being nice." The girl started dragging her toward an alley. "You're coming with me."

Pearl tried to jerk free, scrabbling at the girl's fingers. The girl reached into her bag and came up with a knife in her other hand, the kind that chopped vegetables, that was normally in kitchens. "I *said* I wasn't going to be nice."

Pearl screamed.

The people by the trash can glanced up briefly, but none of them moved.

The girl pointed her knife at Pearl's chest, making her go abruptly quiet.

"Come on," the girl said. "Don't be such a baby."

"What's going to happen to me?" Pearl asked quietly, her voice shaking.

The blond girl didn't answer. She was looking past Pearl, her eyes widening. Suddenly, she dropped Pearl's arm and started to run.

Pearl hadn't thought it was possible to be more scared, but anything that had terrified that girl had to be really, really bad. She felt light-headed with fear, as though she was going to pass out if she turned around.

She pressed her eyes shut. Then, taking a deep breath, she whirled and opened them, poised to scream, her throat hoarse from all the screaming she'd done already.

Aidan was smiling at her, his floppy brown hair falling over his ruby eyes, his sharp teeth evident, as he crossed the patchy asphalt.

"I've been looking all over for you," he said.

Behind him, from the shadows, came a second vampire.

✦ CHAPTER 37 ✦

They do neither plight nor wed

In the city of the dead,

In the city where they sleep away the hours.

—Richard Eugene Burton

Holding the crossbow to her chest, Tana crept back across the lawn. The house looked empty without the noisy partygoers spilling out the doors, but the smoked glass windows of the estate glowed with light. As she climbed the steps to the side door on the long wraparound porch, she saw a camera swinging slowly to take in the empty yard. The light on it glowed red; it wasn't recording.

She ducked under it anyway. Sucking in her breath, she turned the handle on the door and crept inside.

All the vampire hunters must have started out like this, with barely any supplies and a serious grudge. She thought of Pearl, some-where in this bleak walled city, and was determined to hold that grudge as tightly as any of them ever had.

At ten, Pearl had started watching the vampire-hunting shows obsessively after a spate of nightmares so bad that she'd woken screaming. Watching Lucien came later. He must have seemed safe, trapped behind the high gates of Coldtown, seen only through a computer screen. Pause him and he stops. Hit Play and he smiles. Watch him look through the screen as if he could see all the way down to your tiny, bruised soul.

We all wind up drawn to what we're afraid of, drawn to try to find a way to make ourselves safe from a thing by crawling inside of it, by loving it, by becoming it. But the real Lucien was the reason why the world had fallen, the cause of the deaths of everyone at the farmhouse, and was about to hand Gavriel over to some ancient and terrible creature. The only way anyone would be safe from him was if someone made him dead.

Creeping through the empty rooms, all she saw moving were cameras mounted high on the silk-covered walls, all of them with red blinking lights.

Finally she heard voices, echoing through the corridors. They were coming from the massive glass-ceilinged ballroom. She crept closer, crouching down outside the double doors and peering in. Three of Lucien's people were there, all dressed in black robes, setting up a large table in the middle of the room, along with two chairs. Behind it was Gavriel, stripped to the waist, his arms and legs spread apart by silver bars and coiled with heavy chains. Long bluish-red marks crisscrossed his chest. His dark blood had dried in a pattern, like a map, across his belly.

It will all seem very real.

Lucien paced back and forth, dressed in cream and white, his pale gold hair pushed back from his face. "What possessed you to free those prisoners?" he yelled suddenly.

Gavriel looked at him, his face unreadable. "I freed no one, more's the pity. Even when I freed myself, I found new chains."

"Just like you didn't kill that guard. Your girl did this, too, I suppose. And *where is she now*?" Lucien wiped a bloody hand against his trouser leg, not seeming to notice the stain.

Gavriel said nothing.

"The Spider has been sending people after me, you know— assassins. Craven, just-turned fools, not even a decade old. After *me*. Because of the show. Because he thinks it's an embarrassment to parade around in front of the humans, as if being a vampire is being the citizen of some blood-drenched country and he's the minister of propaganda. Well, now everyone's going to see how I cleaned up his little mess."

"Is that what I am?" Gavriel asked, his voice soft. "His mess?"

Lucien looked up at him in surprise, as though he hadn't remembered that Gavriel was there. "No. You're mine," Lucien said after a moment's pause. "I made you and you're mine. My mess."

Tana wasn't sure what that meant, but it was creepy as hell. She pressed her shoulder against the back of the door. Her heart slammed against her chest and she tried to work up her nerve.

Every plan is a house of cards. Change one thing, one variable, and the whole thing comes tumbling down. So suppose Tana shoots Lucien. Then what? Lucien's people try to catch her, Gavriel tries to get free of his chains, and maybe they both make it or one of them makes it or they don't make it at all.

There's no way out, she reminded herself. *There's only what you do before you die.*

Tana's fingers itched on the trigger of the crossbow.

"They're here," said one of Lucien's people. "The Spider's *Corps des Ténèbres* are here."

Tana's hand was steadier than it should have been, and the bow felt light in her arms, with the vampire blood running through her. She thought about all those hours she'd played darts with Pauline in the bowling alley, thought about how she'd learned to aim them just right.

"Turn on the cameras!" Lucien yelled, lifting one hand as if he were conducting an orchestra. All around the room, the red lights were turning green. "I want the world to see this."

She pictured where the bolt was supposed to go. Saw it in her mind. Then all she had to do was steady herself and pivot. Shoot. Then push herself to her feet and run.

Don't stay to see if he got hit. Don't stay to see if he fell, and certainly don't stay to see if the wooden shaft struck his heart and killed him. Don't stay to gloat or to glory or for the satisfaction of knowing you wiped that smug expression off his face. Steady. Pivot. Aim. Shoot. Run.

She looked at Gavriel, blood still caked on his wrist where she'd bitten him, head turned to one side so that she could see his face only in profile—cheekbones, tumbling hair, and downcast red eyes. He hung from silvery chains looped around his limbs. Maybe she was saving him. Maybe.

Her chance was now.

She sucked in her breath and swung around the corner, lifting the crossbow. She took two steps toward Lucien, braced herself, and shot.

The bolt flew. She had a moment to see Gavriel's head come up, eyes going wide. She had a moment to see Lucien turn, a sneer curling on his mouth. The guards started toward her, inhumanly fast, and she forgot everything she'd told herself. She stood frozen, sucking in her breath and waiting to see if she'd hit.

Lucien's arm came up to swat the bolt out of the air, but he was too slow. The bolt sliced through the cloth of his sleeve to strike him in the chest. His fanged mouth opened in a shout of almost comical surprise. Staggering back, he stumbled to one knee. Dark blood soaked his white shirt.

She nearly laughed out loud.

His three black-clad guards were almost to her.

Finally, seconds too late, much too late, she turned and ran, her bare feet slamming on the polished wooden floor, a devouring pulse thrumming inside her. She could hear the guards right behind her, their robes flapping like curtains in a strong wind. Racing for the front door, she steeled herself to throw her shoulder against it, when a hand caught the back of her dress. She was jerked backward.

Tana whipped around, slamming the crossbow against the closest vampire like a club. It struck a woman's face, and she laughed, fangs long and sharp and very white against red lipstick. She threaded her fingers through Tana's hair, nails sinking into her head as she marched her across the room and then slammed her into a door frame.

The world went blurry.

Tana looked around at the other two guards, circling her like sharks.

From the other room, a voice was calling out for them to stop immediately. It sounded like Gavriel's voice, but it must have been Lucien speaking. Fumbling, Tana tried to reload her crossbow until it was jerked out of her hand. The metal-and-wood blade was within reaching distance, strapped to her thigh, but she didn't want to go for it until her head cleared.

"Give her to me," said a gray-clad vampire. She had a thick German accent that made the words hard to understand. One of the Spider's *Corps*. They were milling in around her, all dressed in the same loose gray uniform.

Lucien's guard unhanded her, and two of the Spider's people grabbed hold. Their fingers were cool against her bare arms.

"Oh, this is rich," Lucien said as she was dragged back into the glass-domed ballroom. "You stupid, sad, demented girl."

"He's going to betray you!" she shouted to Gavriel.

Gavriel watched her with impassive red eyes and didn't speak. One of his arms was free from the chains, as though he'd tried to get to her in time. She hoped that didn't put him in more danger. After a moment, his gaze went to the German-accented woman holding her arm. Something passed between them that Tana couldn't follow.

Lucien pulled the wooden arrow out of his chest and tossed it onto the marble tiles, spattering them dark red. "Truly, a delight. Let her go, won't you?"

She felt hands releasing her, and without their support, she was ashamed to find that she swayed alarmingly.

"Come here, my deluded dear," said Lucien. "Did Gavriel put you up to this? Maybe he doesn't like you very much after all."

"No one needed to put me up to it," Tana said, staying where she was. "I wanted to kill you all on my own."

Lucien spread his arms wide, laughing. "Well, come on, then. Do it. Or no, let's wait until the Spider gets here and we can do a little gladiatorial show for him. Do you think he'd like that? Waiting would give you a moment or two to get your bearings again."

Tana took an unsteady step toward him. Her head spun.

The guards moved forward, too.

She'd seen Gavriel rip free of the heavy chains that bound him in the farmhouse guest room, tear free from the metal trunk of her car. And if Lucien was his maker, that meant he was older and more powerful than Gavriel. She couldn't possibly fight him in hand-to-hand combat. Even throwing her knife would be futile. He wasn't going to be surprised, not when she was standing right in front of him, and would have ample time to dodge.

"Lucien," Gavriel said, "if you're proposing a duel, I believe she gets to pick the weapon. I hope she picks me."

Tana looked up and saw, all over again, that one of his hands was free from the chains. Despite her muzzy head and the fear that clutched her chest, she couldn't help thinking there was something off, if only she could figure out what.

The chains. That was the problem. Lucien had *sent* Elisabet out to get Gavriel, had sent her with chains that were definitely and absolutely supposed to imprison him. Except they hadn't. He'd been weak after they escaped from Lance's farmhouse; he'd been hungry and burned by the sun. But he'd still pulled apart those iron chains, had still torn her trunk as if the metal were only thick paper.

Lucien should have known how strong Gavriel was, if Lucien was stronger.

The chains were rigged tonight, but they weren't rigged then.

"You really didn't know she was coming, did you? To *save* you," Lucien said, whirling on Gavriel. He reached into the folds of his jacket and removed a slender blade, as bright as the scales of a fish. "Did you see? She almost shot me in the heart."

"Then you were completely safe," Gavriel said. "Since you don't have one."

"It *hurt*," Lucien said petulantly, stabbing Gavriel's stomach and then again, the knife making a horrible sound as it scraped a rib. "See? It *hurts*."

Gavriel made a soft choking noise. Blood stained his mouth. Lucien must have hit a lung.

"But there's nothing you like better than when it hurts a little, is there?" Lucien asked.

Gavriel's bloody mouth lifted in a voluptuous smile. "Sure there is. I like it when it hurts a lot."

Lucien stabbed him again, twisting the blade around in Gavriel's guts. Gavriel moaned. "This is what you get, coming back here, thinking you're going to have revenge on me. On *me*, your *maker*!"

"The nerve," Gavriel whispered, that mad light bright in his eyes, blood dripping from a corner of his mouth.

Drawing him off her, Tana realized. Gavriel had gotten Lucien's attention and drawn his anger deliberately. But what was he doing? Lucien had said that the Spider had sent assassins after him. Could the Spider have decided to free Gavriel and let him work off his debt by killing Lucien? But then why would the Spider come? Why not stay in Paris and let the work be completed without any danger to himself?

Her head spun. There was something she was missing. She felt it the way you can feel a word on the tip of your tongue.

Lucien left his knife where it was, shoved in Gavriel's belly all the way to the hilt, and he paced back and forth across the marble floor. He looked transcendent with fury, lit up from the inside.

One of the gray-clad guards, a vampire with dark skin and broad cheekbones, stepped forward. "The Spider is nearly at your door," he reported. "I suggest you ready yourself."

Lucien looked at them as though he'd forgotten the audience of guards, forgotten the imminent arrival of an ancient vampire, forgotten any bargains.

Gavriel reached for the hilt of the knife embedded in his own stomach and pulled it out. Then he glanced at Tana and grinned an odd, conspiratorial grin, as though they were sharing some secret. "Tana, go."

And just like that, all the pieces came together in Tana's mind. She started to laugh, the nervous, crazy laughter she felt she'd been holding back since she'd woken up in a bathtub to find a house full of corpses. The lunatic laughter of someone who'd been in over her head from the start.

Lucien looked at her with a furrowed brow. She was laughing so hard that Lucien himself started to smile uncomfortably.

"The Spider is here," she managed to spit out, calming finally. "He's already here, isn't he? He's been here the whole time."

With a heave, Gavriel pulled his left arm free from the chains, the manacles hanging around his wrist like a bracelet. He brought up the dagger, stained with his own blood, and ran his tongue over the blade. "She's far cleverer than you."

"How did you...?" Lucien asked. "What is she talking about with this 'Spider is here' business?"

"The Spider's dead," Gavriel said, his mouth curving into a wide, terrifying grin. "He's been dead. Dead for weeks. Dead when I left Paris. That's how I escaped. I killed him."

Lucien shook his head, looking at Gavriel with blank incomprehension. "No. That's not possible. He's ancient. You can't have killed him. You're just—you're—"

"I'm the Spider now," Gavriel said.

The gray-clad *Corps* grabbed Lucien's three robed guards. Quickly and efficiently, wooden blades were thrust into their hearts. They dropped, one after another, with sickly thuds.

"It took ten years for my opportunity to come. And he left me a mighty legacy—his secrets, repeated in front of me, his vaults and bank accounts and all the things that made him the Spider, operating from behind the scenes.

"But the greatest legacy he left me was his blood. I'm much stronger than you remember. Much, much, much stronger."

Lucien looked at him, the full horror finally breaking across his face. He looked around his ballroom, empty except for enemy guards and the video cameras looking down on him. The video cameras that were recording all of this.

"When did you know?" Gavriel asked Tana conversationally.

"Just now, really," she said.

"Did I ever tell you how I met her?" Gavriel asked Lucien, his chest a mess of dark blood. He seemed to barely notice the wounds, didn't even wince as he took a few steps across the marble floor. She thought of what Jameson had said about crows letting ants sting their wings because they'd grown addicted to the burn of acid. She wondered if you could be hurt so often that you might miss it.

Lucien hadn't answered, but the arrogance was gone from his face.

Gavriel smiled, gesturing casually with his hands as he spoke, the knife he held cutting through the air. "After the Spider was dead, I still wasn't myself for a long time. I seemed to wake, lying on the cold floor, surrounded by what remained of my captors. And I realized that with the Spider dead, I commanded all his resources. And then I thought of you, Lucien.

"I landed in the Boston Harbor without letting myself heal, half mad and half starved. I looked very much like I was truly on the run, I think. And you sent Elisabet after me immediately once you heard I'd arrived, didn't you? Right around the time you sent a letter to the Spider vowing to recapture me.

"Elisabet and her churls caught up with me by the side of the Blackstone River. I'd forgotten how beautiful she was." He smiled with the memory. "She trapped me easily. I was exhausted and I had no reason to fight very hard—after all, she intended to bring me right to your side. In fact, wrapped in steel chains, thrown in the back of their black-windowed limousine, I slept as I had not slept in a decade.

"When I woke, they were dragging me toward a farmhouse. They hadn't been out of Coldtown in so long that they decided to have a feast. Elisabet and the others were drunk with blood, bloated and slow, laughing over what they'd done. And they brought me into the back room, hungry as I was, to show me a boy, already bitten. They'd tied him to the bed and chained me so that he was just out of reach. She said that if I was good, I could have him in the morning. So I sat and watched him writhe.

" 'Is it still you in there?' she'd asked me, tapping her knuckles against my head, before she went to ground in the basement. 'Do you remember all the good times we had?'

"I didn't reply.

"They covered the windows and left me there, the smell of the boy's blood filling my thoughts. I watched him, reminding myself why I needed to wait for dark, but the reasons made less and less sense in my addled mind. Then Tana came in." He looked over at her. "And she made a plan to save the boy—and to save me. Can you imagine that, Lucien? Who in the world would allow me to be saved?"

"No one with any sense," said Lucien. "But why did you go? You were being brought directly to me by Elisabet. That was your plan, wasn't it? Why go on some circuitous road trip with a pair of teenagers?"

Gavriel shrugged, grinning a wide and terrible grin. "I liked the way they looked at me. I liked driving. And I wanted to see what would happen."

"You're mad," Lucien said. "You really are insane."

"I really am," Gavriel said. "And I really am here to avenge myself on you. I just took the long way."

"So kill me, then." Lucien pulled open his shirt, showing pale white skin. "Do it."

Gavriel took a step closer and hesitated.

Lucien was his maker, the keeper of memories of people and places long gone, the monster who'd seen in Gavriel a talent for monstrousness. Tana thought about what Lucien had said the last time they'd stood in this room, weapons drawn. *Every hero is the villain of his own story.* She bet that right then, about to kill his maker, Gavriel felt pretty villainous.

And in that half second of hesitation, Lucien lunged for Tana. He got hold of her throat, lifting her high off the ground. She was choking, panicked, lashing the air. She'd seen people do this before in movies, but she'd never guessed how painful it was. She couldn't breathe, her windpipe crushing inward. Lucien grinned.

"Throw that knife and I break her neck," Lucien said slowly. "Any of your people move and I break her neck. Say something clever and I break her neck."

Gavriel nodded, pressing his hands together as if in prayer. "What would you have me do?"

No, she thought, but couldn't choke out. *Don't let him go. My sister. My sister isn't safe.*

Tana could feel her eyes bulging, her limbs kicking. He raised her higher, his smile cruel as she scrambled for the dagger at her thigh, her hand closing around the hilt.

Lucien was watching Gavriel with great satisfaction. "Take your people and get out of my house. All of you, if you want this mewling creature back. Get out!"

"We'll leave," Gavriel said, waving to his gray-clad *Corps*. They began moving toward the double doors. "But put her down. She's human. Their throats are fragile, and if she dies, you won't have much to bargain with."

Lucien set Tana's feet against the floor, his hand still at her neck. She only had the one chance. He didn't know how much vampire blood was inside her. He didn't know how fast she was or how strong.

Tana sucked in a single breath of air at the same moment she shoved the knife in through his chest, up under his rib. It made a sound going in, like ripping paper.

Lucien's eyes went wide. "Please," he said, the word so soft that it felt more like breath. "Stop. I can feel the point at the edge of my heart." In that moment, he sounded like the young man he must have been once. Just a little older than her and afraid. "Please. I will give you anything."

"Tell them what you did," Tana said, nodding with her chin toward the cameras. "Tell the world what you've done."

Lucien closed his eyes and spoke. "Caspar Morales. It was me. I turned him." Then he opened his ruby eyes and fixed his gaze on her. He looked at her as though she was the only thing that mattered in all the world, the only thing he'd ever loved. "Forgive me and I will make every single impossible dream you've ever had come true. You think no one can know what you want, but I know it already. There are those you love that you're afraid for. There are those who you love who are undeserving. And no one has seen how incredibly special you are, how you glow like a bright flame."

She felt as though her hand were on the knob of the cellar door, her feet ready to descend dusty steps again. She thought of Gavriel, driving her car through the warm summer night, wind in his hair as she told him that mercy could never be evil and his saying: *This is the world I remade with my terrible mercy.* She thought of her father lifting a shovel.

She thought of all those things as she drove the wooden knife into Lucien Moreau's heart.

Black fissures appeared on his face, spreading over him, and a moment later, his skin cracked apart like wet stone.

⟡ CHAPTER 38 ⟡

This will be the last blog post on Bill Story's journal. He was drained by two newborn vampires only hours after this went up. Because I'm his friend, he trusted me with his password in the eventuality that he didn't make it back one day. He'd never intended to be a war zone journalist, but he took up the mantle with enthusiasm and dedication after he was trapped inside Springfield's Coldtown. And although his death is a terrible tragedy, I believe he would have been glad that he died as he lived—in pursuit of a story. Bill will truly be missed by his friends, by the community of truth-seekers to which he belonged, and by the world.—MG

Tomorrow I should have some really interesting footage to post. One of my neighbors, a young woman going by the name Christobel (perhaps for Coleridge's poem *Christabel*, although the different spelling makes me doubt she knows it), asked to borrow some equipment. She has some new guests staying with her, including another young woman, calling herself Midnight, who wants to record her own transformation into a vampire. If I loan her what she needs and show her how to set everything up, she has promised that I can be one of the witnesses and even tape some footage myself. It's a rare opportunity—one that I'm surprised to find dropped in my lap after years of trying to find someone willing to let me record this very thing.

Why do I want to do it? For one thing, because there's very little footage of the change in the public sphere—although I am sure there are reels and reels hidden away in government labs. And, of course, it's likely to get this blog a lot of traffic. But I have to admit to myself (and to you, because I am a confessional sort of journalist) that what I am eager to try to see is the exact moment of change—the spark, if you will, of transformation. And I am eager to see it with my own eyes.

The big question of vampires, the question that haunts governments and individuals alike, the question that bugs me every night when I see their red eyes watching the citizens of Coldtown the way hungry cats watch fish in a bucket is: *What are they?* Are they diseased or demonic? Are they humans who have become ill, deserving hospitals and care, as some have argued? Or are they the bodies of our loved ones animated by some dark force that we ought to seek to destroy? Living here in Coldtown, I've tried to observe and document our new world, but I have failed to be able to answer this one basic question. I have even failed to decide for myself.

Maybe it's crazy to think that I'm going to be able to tell anything significant just from watching a human girl become a vampire. After all, I will be far from the first to see it. Scientists have observed vampirism, even undergone it. But I still want to be able to look at this woman in the eye when she rises from the dead. I want to use something entirely different from instruments and monitors; I want to use my instincts. I want to see whether I believe I am looking into the same person's eyes.

There's something easy about the idea that vampirism is some kind of disease—then they can't help it that they attack us, that they commit murders and atrocities, that they can only control themselves sometimes. They're sick; it's not their fault. And there's something even easier about the idea of demonic invasion, *something* forcing our loved ones to do all manner of terrible things. Still not their fault, only now we can destroy them. But the third option, the possibility that there's something monstrous inside of us that can be unleashed, is the most disturbing of all. Maybe it's just us, us with a raging hunger, us with a couple of accidental murders under our belt. Humanity, with the training wheels off the bike, careening down a steep hill. Humanity, freed from the constraints of consequence and gifted with power. Humanity, grown away from all things human.

And so, dear readers, the answer I hope to have for you tomorrow will not be a scientific one. I hope to be able to decide for myself—when we turn, is there something shoved inside of us or is it more that something inside of us has been released?

CHAPTER 39

Death is a very dull, dreary affair, and
my advice to you is to have nothing whatever
to do with it.

—W. Somerset Maugham

Tana walked out of the hall, pushing past *Corps des Ténèbres* guards and heading for the front door. She turned back once, to look at Gavriel standing in the center of the floor like a marble statue painted with red, but her head was pounding and her neck was sore and when she opened her mouth to speak, she found herself struck dumb. It was all too much. She had glutted herself on horror, and all she could do was stumble out of the house and fumble inside her leather dress for Jameson's cell phone.

Cool air brushed over her skin.

Pearl. She had to find her sister, but if her sister saw her now, she'd scream and scream and scream.

Blood was so sticky.

Gavriel hadn't called out to her, hadn't moved.

But then, she'd nearly ruined his revenge before she'd stolen it for herself; maybe he was glad she'd gone.

Come to the Eternal Ball, Jameson's phone said. *We got her.* Tana walked through the streets of Coldtown and felt nothing.

It was easy to find, even as disoriented as she was. People didn't mind giving directions, apparently not bothered that her face was spattered with blood, not minding that her hands were dark with it. Their casual demeanor was horrifying, but not as horrifying as how easy it had been to push a knife into a begging vampire's heart.

She found the place, the domed church with stained-glass windows painted black along the first few floors. Strobe lights lit the panes on the dome. The door, papered with pink-stenciled posters, was painted the same tarry black as the windows. Music thrummed from within, and a few people sat on the steps, smoking and talking. A girl with green hair in a dozen braids held up a video camera to interview an elderly woman with long white hair and gleaming red eyes. Tana recognized her with a dull pang of surprise as the old lady from the Last Stop.

The doorman pulled aside the velvet rope, waving Tana ahead of a small line of people waiting to pay the cover charge, not even bothering to take her pulse. Maybe the rules were different for people accessorizing their red dresses with a large quantity of bluish-red blood.

Then she was inside, among the dancing throng. Music pounded the air, and a carpet of people filled the hall, twirling and shaking to the music. Girls and boys danced in cages that rose and fell from the ceiling in sudden, heart-stopping, roller-coaster jerks, making everyone scream. And above it all, cameras like the ones she'd seen on Suicide Square, like the ones in Lucien Moreau's house, watching everything with their pitiless eyes, broadcasting the whole thing live.

There was a bar all along one wall that served alcohol from copper distilling vats. It spilled into mismatched mugs. On the outer edges, a few kids passed joints to one another, the heavy odor of hashish competing with a whiff of rot to spice the air.

In one corner sat the remainder of an old confessional; kids waited in line to sit in it, draw their curtains, and tell their sins anonymously to a camera. A girl stood in line, tears running over her cheeks. Behind her, the dance floor was full of people thrashing and jumping and whirling. The cavernous Eternal Ball was oddly familiar; Tana had seen it before on the screens of friends' computers and on posters in lockers. Now, moving with the crowd, it felt unreal, like being on the set of a movie.

She suspected that Pearl must love it.

A shiver went through her body, then a second one. She scanned the crowd, trying to pick out her sister. Her gaze snagged on a familiar figure, his back pressed against the staircase support beams. For a long moment, she studied his navy military jacket with the arms torn off, his garter belt with opaque white stockings and big black boots, his glittering blue eyeliner. He had something taped to his arm that looked like a shunt. It was Rufus, she realized, sweat tracing its way down his neck as he danced. As far as she could tell, he was alone. A red-eyed boy and a blond girl knelt in front of him, taking turns drinking from the tubing attached to his arm. Tana's stomach lurched, half with disgust and half with hunger.

She staggered to lean against the rail of corrugated metal stairs leading to a cordoned-off second floor, taking breath after breath until she was sure she wasn't going to be sick or attack anyone. She had to find Pearl, had to keep herself together long enough to take her back to the gate.

And horribly, in that moment, she thought of Gavriel watching her leave the glass ballroom. Gavriel, who had seemed utterly mad but who'd known exactly what he was doing the whole time. Gavriel, who'd put aside revenge for a little while to go on an adventure with her.

She shook her head, which was a mistake. It made her head throb worse than ever.

"Tana," someone said, and then Valentina was there, beside her, pressing a mug into her hand. She'd changed her clothes, pulled back her hair, and washed off all her makeup. "Oh holy hell, Tana, you're okay. You came back."

She drank automatically, the alcohol burning down her sore throat.

"Look who we found," Valentina said, and Aidan swung into view, smiling his innocent, fanged smile. Pearl was sitting on his shoulders, as though she were much younger, her gangly twelve-year-old legs dangling over his chest. Around her throat was the heavy garnet locket. She grinned at Tana, her expression dimming when she saw the blood staining her face and darkening the red of her dress.

"Hey, peanut," Tana said softly, just as their mother used to.

"Don't call me that," Pearl said, dignity clearly offended. She was wearing a sparkly black shirt, jeans, and her favorite pair of blue cowboy boots. Her eyes were lined in black pencil.

Tana turned to Valentina, taking her hand and pressing it. "Thank you. I can't thank you enough—"

The girl shook her head. "No, wait. It was Aidan who found her."

"Aidan?" Tana looked up at him, disbelieving.

"I spotted her not far from the gates," Aidan said. "She was pretty freaked out."

Pearl gave him a look of deep betrayal. "I had a plan—"

"Aidan was the only one of us who knew what she looked like in person," Valentina put in. "And the only one who wasn't a stranger."

Tana nodded, reaching for Pearl and staring at Aidan. "Thank you."

"When Pauline called me, I figured I owed you one. Maybe more than one." Aidan bent down, so Pearl could climb off his shoulders. She came into Tana's arms, hugging her tight. Tana could hear the bird-wing beat of her heart and smell the sweetness of the blood under her skin, but if Aidan could bear it then so could she. She pressed her mouth to Pearl's hair and drank in the scent of her, memorizing it.

"I just wanted to be here with you," Pearl said. Her thin shoulders shook. "I wanted to help. I didn't know—"

"It's okay," Tana whispered, hugging her even more tightly. "It's going to be okay."

"We saw you," Aidan said, pointing to one of the screens suspended from metal girders. "I mean, not all of it, probably, but—with Lucien, at the end."

She looked over at them. "You saw what happened?"

"Lucien Moreau's dead," said Valentina, over the music. "We saw *that*. We couldn't hear everything, but it looked like he went crazy."

"*You* looked awesome, though," Aidan said, and for the first time, when he smiled, his red eyes and sharp teeth seemed like a normal part of him. "Nice dress."

"I'm sorry, Tana," Pearl said, her fingers digging into Tana's arm. "I thought he—I really didn't know."

"Of course you didn't." Tana pulled her sister off to one side so she could talk to her with some privacy. "I didn't know, either. And that's why you have to leave Coldtown. I can get you out, but you have to promise never to come back. Never ever."

"But no one leaves," Pearl said wonderingly.

"Well, you're going to," Tana said. "Right now."

Pearl gave her a long look. "Aidan promised we could have fun tonight. If I can leave, can I still leave in the morning?"

Tana flashed Aidan her most vicious look. He shrugged elaborately.

"What could I do?" he asked, as though he was something other than a fearsome vampire. "Anyway, don't you think it's a bit unfair for her to come all this way and not have a story to tell all her little friends? You know I'm a pushover for a cute girl with big, begging eyes."

Pearl snickered.

Tana didn't quite trust herself to speak. For a long moment, she looked at the swings where brightly painted girls and boys dangled above the crowd, at the flashing lights, and at the cracked dome far above them. It was beautiful, in its way.

"Fine," Tana said. "But you go back to the gate just before dawn. Promise? We'll walk you there."

Pearl nodded. "Can I dance with Aidan some more? He'll protect me from any other vampires."

He smiled his charming smile. A face like a wicked cherub, that was what she'd thought before he'd ever turned, and it was even more true now. He might be a monster, but he was Aidan, too, and Aidan wouldn't hurt Pearl. "Sure," she said. "Just don't tire him out."

"I am the undead," he informed her. "I am indefatigable."

Tana watched them spin off into the crowd, Pearl's hair flying behind her like a dark banner.

"You okay?" Valentina asked.

Tana shook her head, trying to smile to take the sting out of it, but the smile felt as if it came out a bit sickly. It was odd for everything to be over and to be both the same as before and utterly changed.

It was odd to think that, like it or not, this was her new home.

"I'm going to go to the bar," Tana said. "See if I can wipe off my face with a wet napkin or something. That'll make me feel a little more human."

Valentina nodded, and Tana pushed her way through the crowd. Twice, someone stopped her to give her a high five or to offer a round of drinks in her honor. Once, someone stopped her to offer a drink from their shunt. She pushed away from them dizzily. She supposed that Lucien wasn't nearly as popular in Coldtown as he'd been on television.

Spotting Jameson sitting at one end of the bar, she headed in his direction. He saluted her with his cup when she got close enough to lean against the concrete top.

"Congratulations," he said, signaling to the bartender. A moment later, Tana had another mug set in front of her, handed over by a woman with candy-apple-red dreads who clearly didn't care about ID.

Tana hopped up on a stool.

He clinked his mug against hers and announced, "You're famous. You know that, right? And you're going to be even more famous after tonight."

She downed most of the contents of the cup, wincing. Then she poured the rest over her face. It stung, but she figured that meant the alcohol was disinfecting as it was supposed to. "You have any kind of tissue?" she asked.

He reached into his pockets and came up with an old-fashioned folded-up men's handkerchief. She took it and wiped her face, turning it a very dark red. "Sorry about ruining this thing."

"That's what it's for. Look, I'm serious about you being famous. One of only two survivors of what they're calling the Sundown Tragedy," he said, not sounding very sober. "The girl who drove an infected friend and a vampire all the way to Coldtown and turned them in. The girl who killed a vampire on camera. Oh, yeah, video of you has been all over the news and the blogs—the footage of you wrestling around in the dirt next to the garbage cans with that girl,

Midnight, is particularly popular. And now—you killed Lucien Moreau. You should charge for interviews."

"I was worried Pearl was going to be mad," Tana said. "She loved Lucien's show."

Jameson laughed.

"You've got to lock me up," she said. *Lock me up and throw away the key.*

"What about your sister?" he asked.

"She's going home, and if I ever want to see her again, I know what I've got to do."

He gave her an appraising look that reminded her alarmingly of his mother. "I know a place. We can go in the morning." Then he hesitated. "Are you sure about this? You sure you don't want to be a vampire? You're here in a sea of people who'll give you their blood. Hell, I'll give you mine if you want to turn."

"You think I should?" she asked, resting her head on the bar top. The air was hot with the heat of pumping hearts and racing blood, rising up off human skin. Just inhaling made her feel dizzy. It was tempting. Give in. Give up.

"It's hard not to want that around here. They're the top of the food chain. Apex predators."

"So why don't you turn? Get your mom to bring you over?"

"I'm contrary," he said with a snort, looking out onto the dance floor. She followed his gaze and saw that he was watching Valentina as she talked with a boy in a long leather coat. Aidan and Pearl were still spinning in mad circles. "Sometimes I don't know what I want."

Tana liked the feeling of the cool concrete under her cheek. It was rough and smooth at the same time, like the way she imagined a dragon's scales might feel. "She's pretty."

He sighed. "Yeah."

"She told me how great you were—saving her and her friend and all."

Now he grinned a rueful grin and shook his head. "Oh, now I see where you're going with this. Save your breath."

"You don't like her?" Tana asked, and then wished she hadn't, because if he said something awful about Valentina, she was going to hate him.

"Of course I like her," he said, as though it was hard for him to imagine how anyone wouldn't. "And if you tell her, I am going to make you very sorry you opened your mouth. Look, Valentina is...it's hard to explain. She's here for one reason and one reason only, the same reason most people give up their safe, normal lives to come here—to be vampires. She isn't looking for somebody like me. She might bring home a regular guy sometimes, if she's lonely, but she's not serious about any of them. She's looking for someone like your friend out there."

Boys were so stupid, Tana thought. "You should dance with her."

He winced, as though she suggested he stab himself in the foot. "I don't really dance, and she was just *imprisoned*—maybe she's not really up for dancing."

Tana shrugged, sliding off the stool. "Let's go ask her."

"Absolutely not," said Jameson.

"Oh, so you're just going to sit here in the shadows, watching her like a crazy person," Tana said. "Making sure she doesn't get in any more trouble."

"If she does, there's not much I can do, is there?" He took another gulp from the mug in front of him. It had a blue band around it and a crack down one side, which appeared to have been glued hastily, because there was still a line of hardened clear material like a badly healed scar.

"She thought your mom was your girlfriend," Tana said. She made a gesture to Valentina, vague enough to mean anything, and then pointed to Jameson. He looked alarmed. "And she wanted to save her, because it was something she could do for you. That's how she wound up imprisoned at Lucien's. I bet she didn't tell you that."

"What are you doing?" he asked, grabbing her arm hard enough to hurt.

"If you knew what kind of week I've had and what kind of week I'm about to have, then you'd know you better just go along with me." With that, she dragged him up off the stool and out into the crowd.

He gave her a murderous look, but he let himself be pulled. Valentina saw them coming and looked, if anything, more terrified than he did. Pearl ran toward Tana, though, eager for more dancing, waving up at the cameras overhead as though she was waving to all her friends back home.

"This isn't going to change anything," he said under his breath.

And then they were dancing together, all five of them, sweat slicking their limbs and the music buzzing in their heads. Even Jameson was smiling as Valentina spun around him, his fingers lingering a moment too long on her hips and his gaze slanting down, shyness coloring his cheeks. Aidan whirled Pearl in his arms, lifting her into the air and making her laugh.

Tana danced until the pain in her head faded away, until her bare feet hurt from being pounded against the floor, until her body was gloriously exhausted and with every move she knew she'd won the day because she'd survived it. Valentina somehow persuaded Jameson to stay on the dance floor. He had his hands circling her waist and her head was bent toward him like a flower bends toward the sun. And Tana finally understood how the wildness of the Eternal Ball was the wildness of grief, the intoxicating dance of carnival, where one leaves oneself at home and becomes something else for a night, hoping that the old skin will still fit when one comes back to it in the morning.

The way they arranged things was that Pauline agreed to take off from camp, drive to the gate, and pick up Pearl on the outside. Tana and Aidan walked Pearl there, through the winding streets and the refuse, past the bodies and the swarms of roaches. Dawn didn't yet blaze on the horizon, but the air had already changed, the wind bringing the warm smells of day before the daylight itself.

Tana held Pearl's hand in hers. Her sister was getting sleepy, stumbling a little, eyelids drooping as the excitement of the night wore off.

"It's my fault that you're going to be stuck here forever," Pearl said in a hushed voice. "I messed up everything."

Tana took a deep breath and then shook her head. "I might not make it out of here, but that's because I might not beat being Cold. And if that happens, then I got to say good-bye to you in person. And if I get better, then I'll figure something out, okay?"

Pearl looked very skeptical, but she nodded. "Okay."

"And you're going to say good-bye to Pauline for me. Give her a big hug and make her believe that I'm doing fine."

"She's going to see clips from the feed," Pearl said, in the tone of someone who felt honor-bound to point out the obvious.

"Well, then," Tana said, realizing that her sister was right, "it's going to be even more important that you convince her that I'm fine. Don't I seem fine?"

"I *guess,*" Pearl said.

Tana shoved her shoulder, making her grin.

They walked awhile in silence. Then, as they passed the hand-drawn sign for A Shot of Depresso, Pearl looked up at Tana and blinked. "There was a vampire boy at the Eternal Ball who said he knew you."

"What boy?" Tana asked.

Pearl shook her head, touching the garnet necklace. "He said, 'It's an honor and a delight to meet you and a tragedy you're here'—he had a weird way of talking, but he seemed nice. He started giving me a message for you, but he changed his mind."

Tana tried to convince herself that Gavriel's deciding not to pass along a message didn't mean anything, but since he hadn't spoken to her himself, that was hard to believe.

Aidan raised his eyebrows at Tana, but he kept his mouth shut.

Then it was time to lean down and hug Pearl again, to tell her that she loved her, to drink in the warmth of her skin and listen to the thunder of her heart, before letting her go at last.

Watching Pearl walk into one of the swinging iron cages alone was the hardest thing Tana had ever done. But she did. And she made herself a new promise.

She was the girl who went back to try to do the impossible thing. Outside Lance's farmhouse when all she wanted to do was run, she'd forced herself to go back through that broken window. When she'd managed to escape from the room with the skylight, she'd still gone back for Aidan. She'd even gone back and killed Lucien Moreau. And if she could go back and do all those crazy, impossible things, then maybe she could be crazy enough to go forward and save herself, too.

The next morning, Jameson locked her in the root cellar of an abandoned Victorian house, along with plastic milk jugs full of boiled water, some cans of food, a can opener, aspirin, a bunch of blankets, and whatever was left of the stuff she'd bought inside the walls. She'd attached a handcuff to one of her wrists and run the other through a chain she'd bolted to a pipe. When she handed over the key to the cuffs to Jameson, she was on the verge of telling him to forget the whole thing, to let her out, except that she was sure he'd break his promises and do it.

Eighty-eight days. Three locks on the door. Fifty-three links in the chain. One bare bulb swinging from the ceiling.

She slept for a while, fitfully, in her nest of blankets. Then she ate cold beans with a plastic spoon. Finally, she decided it was time she set up the camera before she wasn't able to. Her hands were already shaking as she shoved the first of the battery packs into the back of Midnight's old video camera. By the time she set it up on the tripod and plugged in the Livebox she'd bought off some kid Jameson knew, she needed to cut the heel of her hand with the jagged edge of a can and suck a little of her blood to steady herself for what came next. Then she turned on the camera and sat down, cross-legged, on the ground.

Looking up into the shining black lens, she started. "Hi, I'm Tana Bach. I'm seventeen, and a few days ago there was a party and—no, never mind that, if you're watching this then you've probably already heard about what happened there. Look, I just want to thank everybody for all the nice e-mails and wall posts and stuff. Thanks, too, mysterious and maybe even legit production company that wants to film me killing vampires, but this is what I'm going to be doing for twelve and a half weeks, so if you want to broadcast something, broadcast this.

"And, Dad, if you're watching, don't be too mad at Pearl, okay? It's pretty glamorous to be a vampire. It makes sense that anyone would want that. So give her a break, okay? You've only got one daughter left. And Pauline, thanks for saving my sorry ass. I should have called you back sooner.

"And for everyone else, I thought I would show you something other than the glamour. This is what it's like to sweat out an infection. I've got a bunch of water and some cans of creamed corn and I'm going to scream and beg and puke my guts up. The chains holding me are pretty good—"

Tana was drawing breath to say something else when she heard the unmistakable sound of one of the bolts on the door turning.

"Hey," she called. "Who's there?"

The second bolt turned, echoing in the empty space.

"Jameson?"

Her heart thudded and she pulled against her chain, realizing the vulnerability of her position.

"Well," she said to the camera. "Someone is coming to visit me in the secret room where I'm supposed to be holed up alone for everyone's safety. Hopefully they're not going to—"

The door opened and Gavriel stepped into the room. He looked around, taking in his surroundings. He was wearing black jeans and a black shirt, almost exactly what he was wearing when she met him. The only differences were that he wore heavy silver rings, shining with lapis and hematite, on his fingers and a leather bag slung across his body. He looked as strangely beautiful as ever, his features a touch too large for his face. Walking across the room, he switched off her video camera.

"Hi," she said, unable to quite manage more than that.

He closed the door and sat in the dirt beside her. "I heard that you gave away your marker."

She shrugged, trying to seem casual, as if she weren't chained to the wall of a room, as if he wasn't the scariest guy in the city, as if she hadn't killed his maker. "I figure that I have to be realistic about my chances. You know how many people make it through self-quarantine? The numbers are low. I might cut up my skin so bad to drink my own blood that the cuts go septic. Or I might forget to eat regular food and starve. Or I might spill all my water while I'm having a fit. Better to give the marker to some little kid, right?"

"Your sister," he said.

Tana nodded. "My sister."

Gavriel closed his eyes, sooty lashes brushing his cheek. "I'll stay with you."

"What? No," she said automatically. "No! That's crazy."

"I'm crazy," he reminded her.

He'd said it perfectly matter-of-factly, and it almost startled a laugh out of her. She took a deep breath to cover the impulse. "Look, do you get what I'm going to be like? I'm going to be puking and probably pissing my pants, not to mention screaming." Her hands started to shake again, but she pressed them together between her knees, hoping to hide just how sick she was. "I don't want you seeing me like that."

"Tana, when you left last night, I thought that I had no right to go after you, no right to even beg your forgiveness. And I still think it—so I am not here to ask to be forgiven for my arrogance or for what happened because of it, although I will ever be profoundly repentant. But let me sit with you through the long night. Here is a thing I can do." He reached into the bag and drew out an odd array of manga, ripped paperbacks of books both classic and modern, and a small stack of crumpled magazines. "See, I even brought some things to read aloud. I wasn't sure what you'd like, so there's a bit of everything."

"*Why?*" she demanded, because of all the things he could be doing, it made no sense that he would come here, to do this. Lucien was dead, and she knew that for some vampires, there were ways in and out of Coldtown. Gavriel could be on his way to a chateau in the Alps and drinking from girls half drowned in red wine. "I thought you were probably pissed off. I mean, you came a long way to kill Lucien and because of me, you didn't get to."

"No, Tana. Truly, though it must grieve you to have done it, your striking that blow certainly didn't grieve me." He paused, seeming to steel himself and then began to speak very quickly. "I love you, you see—and I fear I have no way to say or show it that isn't terrible, except coming here. I would kill everyone in the world for you, if you wanted." He seemed to notice the look that passed over her face, before rushing on. "Or not, obviously. But I thought you might rather have me read aloud"—he picked up an old issue of *Rolling Stone* from the stack, lifting it vaguely—"and sit with you. Like a normal person who loved you might, if you had a normal illness. And since you don't, I'm just right for what you do have."

She started to giggle, unable to help herself. He never said anything she expected, ever, and this was no different. Clearing her throat, she tried to find the right words. "I'd rather you didn't kill everyone in the world, yes, that's true. And I have feelings for you, too. Big, weird, crazy feelings. It's a rare enough thing to find someone who can see me the way I am, no less to peer down into dark parts of my heart, the parts of me even I don't want to look at. You did that and you laughed at my jokes, too. So I'm scared, because you're not just not *human*, you're not like *anyone*—there's nobody like you in all the world and it's you I want. I want you and I hate wanting things and I especially hate admitting I want them."

His mouth curved into a happy, hopeful smile. "So I can stay?"

Panic filled her. "No, no, no, you can't stay. If you stay, you'll let me out. I'll beg and beg and you'll let me out."

"I won't," he said, shifting closer to her. "You didn't ask me to let you out of Elisabet's room, when you were cuffed to her bed. You broke out yourself instead of simply asking me. Remember that? You didn't think I would free you then."

"This is different. Besides, I was probably wrong."

"Hush, Tana," he said, petting her hair. "Oh, my sweet Tana. Remember that I'm still a monster. I can listen to you scream and cry and beg and I still won't let you out."

His voice made her shiver with a delicious combination of nerves and calm. She remembered the footage she'd seen of him long before they'd met, imprisoned and insane underneath a cemetery in Paris, drenched in blood and cut in a thousand places. If anyone knew what it was like to be alone and in pain, it was him. For the first time since he walked into the room, she began to believe she might not have to go through all this alone. "You can't let me drink your blood. You can't bite me. Even if I beg you, even if I plead and threaten and lie. You have to promise. It's the only way I'm going to get better."

"I swear it." His red eyes held hers. "Solemnly, do I swear."

She relaxed against him, inhaling the scent of smoke and bleach and the faint trace of gore. His shoulder was very solid against her cheek, the brush of his inky hair very fine. "You really won't let me out?"

"Allow me to explain how my whole life has prepared me for this moment. I am used to girls screaming, and your screams—your screams will be sweeter than another's cries of love."

She nearly laughed, because that was as perfect a thing to say as it was perfectly awful.

"Okay," she said, drowsy and cold, feeling the shakes starting to return. "You can stay. I want you to stay. Please stay." She closed her eyes and asked the one question she'd been afraid to ask all this long while. "And if I never change back? If I'm not human enough anymore?"

He smiled; she could feel it against her skin. "Then we'll go hunt vampires together and you'll drink their blood."

"The Lady or The Tiger," she said, thinking of the drinking game she'd played at the farmhouse, thinking of the story that never ended, of a coin spinning without falling on heads or tails.

"My lady, the tiger," he told her, and got up to turn the camera back on.

✦ ACKNOWLEDGMENTS ✦

This book is a love letter to all the vampire books I read over and over growing up. To Les Daniels for his Don Sebastian de Villanueva series; Anne Rice for her Vampire Chronicles; Tanith Lee for *Sabella, or the Blood Stone*; Poppy Z. Brite for *Lost Souls*; Nancy A. Collins for *Sunglasses After Dark*; Sheridan Le Fanu for *Carmilla*; and Suzy McKee Charnas for *The Vampire Tapestry*. Thanks also to Dudley Wright's *Vampires and Vampirism*, which I got out of the library and was one of the first folklore books I read.

Thanks to Sarah Rees Brennan, Robin Wasserman, and Cassie Clare for reading through the beginning of this book while we were all in Goult together. There is nothing quite like beginning a book in the South of France for feeling decadent.

Thanks to dinner companions Holly Post, Jeffrey Rowland, Jeph Jacques, Cristi Jacques, Elka Cloke, Eric Churchill, Elias Churchill, and

Jonah Churchill for coming up with an excellent turn to the story—and also paying for my meal—despite my being late to the restaurant.

Thanks to Chris Cotter for making the Internet in Coldtown work.

Thanks to Bill Willingham for his generosity.

Thanks to the Clarion Class of 2012 (Carmen, Christopher, Danica, Daniel, Deborah, Eliza, Emma, Eric, Jonathan, Joseph, Lara, Lisa, Luke, Pierre, Ruby, Sadie, Sam, and Sarah) for putting up with my writing the end of this book while being half of their final two-week anchor team. Thanks also for that bottle of whiskey, buzzer, and octopus finger. I found them very useful during my own workshop.

Which brings me to thanking my workshoppers. Thank you, Kelly Link, Gavin Grant, Ellen Kushner, Delia Sherman, Sarah Smith, Cassie Clare (yes, she had to read it again), and Josh Lewis for giving me the confidence to show the thing I made to the world.

Thanks to Steve Berman for reading all of *Coldtown* in a single night so that he could talk to me about the ending the next morning.

Thanks to my fabulous editor, Alvina Ling, and her fabulous assistant, Bethany Strout, for catching all the things I thought I could get away with and for their insight into plenty of things I hadn't considered at all.

Thanks to my agent, Barry Goldblatt, for believing in this book.

Thanks to a handful of participants in the Nevada SCBWI mentor retreat for letting me read the first few chapters to them.

And, finally, thanks to my husband for letting me read the whole entire thing to him out loud. He said that ever since he met me, he figured I would eventually write a vampire book. Apparently he was entirely correct.

→ TURN THE PAGE FOR A SNEAK PEEK OF ←

COMING JANUARY 2015!

✦ CHAPTER 1 ✦

Down a path worn into the woods, past a stream and a hollowed-out log full of pill bugs and termites, was a glass coffin. It rested right on the ground, and in it slept a boy with horns on his head and ears as pointed as knives.

As far as Hazel Evans knew, from what her parents said to her and from what their parents said to them, he'd always been there. And no matter what anyone did, he never, ever woke up.

He didn't wake up during the long summers, when Hazel and her brother, Ben, stretched out on the full length of the coffin, staring down through the crystalline panes, fogging them up with their breath, and scheming glorious schemes. He didn't wake up when tourists came to gape or debunkers came to swear he wasn't real. He didn't wake up on autumn weekends, when girls danced right on top of him, gyrating to the tinny sounds coming from nearby iPod speakers, didn't notice when Leonie Wallace lifted her beer high over her head, as if she were saluting the whole haunted forest. He didn't so much as stir when Ben's best friend, Jack Gordon, wrote IN CASE OF EMERGENCY, BREAK GLASS in Sharpie along one side—or when Lloyd Lindblad took a sledgehammer and actually tried. No matter how many parties had been held around the horned boy—generations of parties, so that the grass sparkled with decades of broken bottles in green and amber, so that the bushes shone with crushed aluminum cans in silver and gold and rust—and no matter what happened at those parties, nothing could wake the boy inside the glass coffin.

When they were little, Ben and Hazel made him flower crowns and told him stories about how they would rescue him. Back then, they were going to save everyone who needed saving in Fairfold. Once Hazel got older, though, she mostly visited the coffin only at night, in crowds, but she still felt something tighten in her chest when she looked down at the boy's strange and beautiful face.

She hadn't saved him, and she hadn't saved Fairfold, either.

"Hey, Hazel," Leonie called, dancing to one side to make room in case Hazel wanted to join her atop the horned boy's casket. Doris Alvaro was already up there, still in her cheerleader outfit from the game their school lost earlier that night, shining chestnut ponytail whipping through the air. They both looked flushed with alcohol and good cheer.

Waving a hello to Leonie, Hazel didn't get up on the coffin, although she was tempted. Instead she threaded her way through the crowd of teenagers.

Fairfold High was a small enough school that although there were cliques (even if a few were made up of basically a single person, like how Megan Rojas was the entire Goth community), everyone had to party together if they wanted to have enough people around to party at all. But just because everyone partied together, it didn't mean they were all friends. Until a month ago, Hazel had been part of a girl posse, striding through school in heavy eyeliner and dangling, shining earrings as sharp as their smiles. Sworn in sticky, bright blood sucked from thumbs to be friends forever. She'd drifted away from them after Molly Lipscomb asked her to kiss and then jilt Molly's ex, but was furious with her once she had.

It turned out that Hazel's other friends were really just Molly's friends. Even though they'd been part of the plan, they pretended they weren't. They pretended something had happened that Hazel ought to be sorry about. They wanted Hazel to admit that she'd done it to hurt Molly.

Hazel kissed boys for all kinds of reasons—because they were cute, because she was a little drunk, because she was bored, because they let her, because it was fun, because they looked lonely, because it blotted out her fears for a while, because she wasn't sure how many kisses she had left. But she'd kissed only one boy who really belonged to someone else, and under no circumstances would she ever do it again.

At least she still had her brother to hang out with, even if he was currently on a date in the city with some guy he'd met online. And she had Ben's best friend, Jack, even if he made her nervous. And she had Leonie.

That was plenty of friends. Too many, really, considering that she was likely to disappear one of these days, leaving them all behind.

Thinking that way was how she'd wound up not asking anyone for a ride to the party that night, even though it meant walking the whole way, through the shallow edge of the woods, past farms and old tobacco barns, and then into the forest.

It was one of those early fall nights when wood smoke was in the air, along with the sweet richness of kicked-up leaf mold, and everything felt possible. She was wearing a new green sweater, her favorite brown boots, and a pair of cheap green enamel hoops. Her loose red curls still had a hint of summer gold, and when she'd looked in the mirror to smear on a little bit of tinted ChapStick before she walked out the door, she actually thought she looked pretty good.

Liz was in charge of the playlist, broadcasting from her phone through the speakers in her vintage Fiat, choosing dance music so loud it made the trees shiver. Martin Silver was chatting up Lourdes and Namiya at the same time, clearly hoping for a best-friend sandwich that was never, ever, *ever* going to happen. Molly was laughing in a half circle of girls. Stephen, in his paint-spattered shirt, was sitting on his truck with the headlights on, drinking Franklin's dad's moonshine from a flask, too busy nursing some private sorrow to care whether the stuff would make him go blind. Jack was sitting over with his brother (well, *kind of* his brother), Carter, the quarterback, on a log near the glass coffin. They were laughing, which made Hazel want to go over there and laugh with them, except that she also wanted to get up and dance, and she also wanted to run back home.

"Hazel," someone said, and she turned to see Robbie Delmonico. The smile froze on her face.

"I haven't seen you around. You look nice." He seemed resentful about it.

"Thanks." Robbie *had* to know she'd been avoiding him, which made her feel like an awful person, but ever since they'd made out at a party, he'd followed her around as though he was heartbroken, and that was even worse. She hadn't dumped him or anything like that; he'd never even asked her out. He just stared at her miserably and asked weird, leading questions, such as "What are you doing after school?" And when she told him, "Nothing, just hanging out," he never suggested anything else, never even proposed he might like to come over.

It was because of kissing boys like Robbie Delmonico that people believed Hazel would kiss *anyone.*

It really had seemed like a good idea at the time.

"Thanks," she said again, slightly more loudly, nodding. She began to turn away.

"It's new, right?" And he gave her that sad smile that seemed to say that he knew he was nice for noticing and that he knew nice guys finished last.

The funny thing was that he hadn't seemed particularly interested in her before she lunged at him. It was as though, by putting her lips to his—and, okay, allowing a certain amount of handsiness— she'd transformed herself into some kind of cruel goddess of love.

"The sweater is new," she told him, nodding. Around him, she felt as coldhearted as he clearly thought she was. "Well, I guess I'll see you around."

"Yeah," he said, letting the word linger.

And then, at the critical moment, the moment when she meant to just walk away, guilt overtook her and she said the one thing she knew she shouldn't say, the thing for which she would kick herself over and over again throughout the night. "Maybe we'll run into each other later."

Hope lit his eyes, and, too late, she realized how he'd taken it— as a promise. But by then all she could do was hightail it over to Jack and Carter.

Jack—the crush of Hazel's younger, sillier years—looked surprised when she stumbled up, which was odd, because he was almost never caught off guard. As his mother once said about him, Jack could hear the thunder before the lightning bothered to strike.

"Hazel, Hazel, blue of eye. Kissed the boys and made them cry," Carter said, because Carter could be a jerk.

Carter and Jack looked almost exactly alike, as if they were twins. Same dark, curly hair. Same amber eyes. Same deep brown skin and lush mouths and wide cheekbones that were the envy of every girl in town. They weren't twins, though. Jack was a changeling—*Carter's* changeling, left behind when Carter got stolen away by the faeries.

Fairfold was a strange place. Dead in the center of the Carling forest, the haunted forest, full of what Hazel's grandfather called Greenies and what her mother called They Themselves or the Folk of the Air. In these woods, it wasn't odd to see a black hare swimming in the creek—although rabbits don't usually much care for swimming—or to spot a deer that became a sprinting girl in the blink of an eye. Every autumn, a portion of the harvest apples was left out for the cruel and capricious Alderking. Flower garlands were threaded for him every spring. Townsfolk knew to fear the monster coiled in the heart of the forest, who lured tourists with a cry that sounded like a woman weeping. Its fingers were sticks, its hair moss. It fed on sorrow and sowed corruption. You could lure it out with a singsong chant, the kind girls dare one another to say at birthday sleepovers. Plus there was a hawthorn tree in a ring of stones where you could bargain for your heart's desire by tying a strip of your clothing to the branches under a full moon and waiting for one of the Folk to come. The year before, Jenny Eichmann had gone out there and wished herself into Princeton, promising to pay anything the faeries wanted. She'd gotten in, too, but her mother had a stroke and died the same day the letter came.

Which was why, between the wishes and the horned boy and the odd sightings, even though Fairfold was so tiny that the kids in kindergarten went to school in an adjacent building to the seniors, even though the town was so small that you had to go three towns over to buy a new washing machine or stroll through a mall, the town still got plenty of tourists. Other places had the biggest ball of twine or a very large wheel of cheese or a chair big enough for a giant. They had scenic waterfalls or shimmering caves full of jagged stalactites or bats that slept beneath a bridge. Fairfold had the boy in the glass coffin. Fairfold had the Folk.

And to the Folk, tourists were fair game.

Maybe that's what the Host had thought Carter's parents were. Carter's dad was from out of town, but Carter's mom was no tourist. It took a single night for her to realize that her baby had been stolen. And she'd known just what to do. She sent her husband out of the house for the day and invited over a bunch of neighbor ladies. They'd baked bread and chopped wood and filled an old earthenware bowl with salt. Then, when everything was done, Carter's mom heated a poker in the fireplace.

First it turned red, but she did nothing. It was only once the metal glowed white that she pressed the very tip of the poker against the changeling's shoulder.

It shrieked with pain, its voice spiraling so high that both kitchen windows shattered.

There'd been a smell like when you toss fresh grass onto a fire, and the baby's skin turned bright, bubbling red. The burn left a scar, too. Hazel had seen it when she and Jack and Ben and Carter went swimming last summer—stretched out by growing, but still there.

Burning a changeling summons its mother. She arrived on the threshold moments later, a swaddled bundle in her arms. According to the stories, she was thin and tall, her hair the brown of autumn leaves, her skin the color of bark, with eyes that changed from moment to moment, molten silver to owl gold to dull and gray as stone. There was no mistaking her for human.

"You don't take our children," said Carter's mother—or at least that's how the story Hazel heard went, and she'd heard the story a lot. "You don't spirit us away or make us sick. That's how things have worked around here for generations, and that's how things are going to keep on working."

The faerie woman seemed to shrink back a little. As if in answer, she silently held out the child she'd brought, wrapped up in blankets, sleeping as peacefully as if he were in his own bed. "Take him," she said.

Carter's mother crushed him to her, drinking in the rightness of his sour-milk smell. She said that was the one thing the Folk of the Air couldn't fake. The other baby just hadn't smelled like Carter.

Then the faerie woman had reached out her arms for her own wailing child, but the neighbor woman holding him stepped back. Carter's mother blocked the way.

"You can't have him," said Carter's mother, passing her own baby to her sister and picking up iron filings and red berries and salt, protection against the faerie woman's magic. "If you were willing to trade him away, even for an hour, then you don't deserve him. I'll keep them both to raise as my own and let that be our judgment on you for breaking oath with us."

At that, the elf woman spoke in a voice like wind and rain and brittle leaves snapping underfoot. "You do not have the lessoning of us. You have no power, no claim. Give me my child and I will place a blessing on your house, but if you keep him, you will come to regret it."

"Damn the consequences and damn you, too," said Carter's mom, according to everyone who has ever told this story. "Get the hell out."

And so, even though some of the neighbor ladies grumbled about Carter's mother borrowing trouble, that was how Jack came to live with Carter's family and to become Carter's brother and Ben's best friend. That's how they all got so used to Jack that no one was surprised anymore by how his ears tapered to small points or how his eyes shone silver sometimes, or the way he could predict the weather better than any weatherman on the news.

"So do you think Ben's having a better time than we are?" Jack asked her, forcing her thoughts away from his past and his scar and his handsome face.

If Hazel took kissing boys too lightly, then Ben never took it lightly enough. He wanted to be in love, was all too willing to give away his still-beating heart. Ben had always been like that, even when it cost him more than she wanted to think about.

However, even he didn't have much luck online.

"I think Ben's date will be boring." Hazel took the beer can from Jack's hand and swigged. It tasted sour. "Most of them are boring, even the liars. Especially the liars. I don't know why he bothers."

Carter shrugged. "Sex?"

"He likes stories," Jack said, with a conspiratorial grin in her direction.

Hazel licked the foam off her upper lip, some of her previous good cheer returning. "Yeah, I guess."

Carter stood, eyeing Megan Rojas, who'd just arrived with freshly purpled hair, carrying a bottle of cinnamon schnapps, the pointed heels of her spiderweb-stitched boots sinking into the soft earth. "I'm going to get another beer. You want something?"

"Hazel stole mine," Jack said, nodding toward her. The thick silver hoops in his ears glinted in the moonlight. "So grab another round for us both?"

"Try not to break any hearts while I'm gone," Carter told Hazel, as if he was joking, but his tone wasn't entirely friendly.

Hazel sat down on the part of the log that Carter vacated, looking at the girls dancing and the other kids drinking. She felt outside of it all, purposeless and adrift. Once, she'd had a quest, one she'd been willing to give up everything for, but it turned out that some quests couldn't be won just by giving things up.

"Don't listen to him," Jack told her as soon as his brother was safely on the other side of the casket and out of hearing range. "You didn't do anything wrong with Rob. Anyone who offers up their heart on a silver platter deserves what they get."

Hazel thought of Ben and wondered if that was true.

"I just keep making the same mistake," she said. "I go to a party and I kiss some guy that I would never think of kissing at school. Guys I don't even really like. It's as though out here, in the woods, they're going to reveal some secret side of themselves. But they're always just the same."

"It's just kissing." He grinned at her; his mouth twisted up on one side, and something twisted inside her in response. His smiles and Carter's smiles were nothing alike. "It's fun. You're not hurting anybody. It's not like you're *stabbing* boys just to make something happen around here."

That surprised a laugh out of her. "Maybe you should tell that to Carter."

She didn't explain that she wasn't so much wanting something to happen as not wanting to be the only one with a secret self to reveal.

Jack draped an arm over her shoulder, pretend-flirting. It was friendly, funny. "He's my brother, so I can tell you definitively that he's an idiot. You must amuse yourself however you can among the dull folk of Fairfold."

She shook her head, smiling, and then turned toward him. He stopped speaking, and she realized how close their faces had become.

Close enough that she could feel the warmth of his breath against her cheek. Close enough to watch the dark fringe of his eyelashes turn gold in the reflected light and to see the soft bow of his mouth.

Hazel's heart started pounding, her ten-year-old self's crush coming back with a vengeance. It made her feel just as vulnerable and silly as she'd felt back then. She hated that feeling. She was the one who broke hearts now, not the other way around.

Anyone who offers up their heart on a silver platter deserves what they get.

There was only one way to get over a boy. Only one way that ever worked.

Jack's gaze was slightly unfocused, his lips slightly apart. It seemed exactly right to close the distance between them, to shut her eyes and press her mouth to his. Warm and gentle, he pressed back for a single shared exchange of breath.

Then he pulled away, blinking. "Hazel, I didn't mean for you—"

"No," she said, leaping up, her cheeks hot. He was her friend, her brother's *best* friend. He mattered. It would never be okay to kiss him, even if he wanted her to, which he clearly did not, and which made everything much worse. "Of course not. Sorry. Sorry! I told you I shouldn't go around kissing people, and here I am doing it again."

She backed away.

"Wait," he started, reaching to catch her arm, but she didn't want to stay around while he tried to find the right words to let her down easy.

Hazel fled, passing Carter with her head down, so she didn't have to see his knowing told-you-so look. She felt stupid and, worse, like she deserved to be rejected. Like it served her right. It was the kind of karmic justice that didn't usually happen in real life, or at least didn't usually happen so fast.

Hazel headed straight for Franklin. "Can I have some of that?" she asked him, pointing to the metal flask.

He looked at her blearily through bloodshot eyes and held the flask out. "You won't like it."

She didn't. The moonshine burned all the way down her throat. But she slugged back two more swallows, hoping that she could forget everything that had happened since she'd arrived at the party. Hoping that Jack would never tell Ben what she'd done. Hoping Jack would pretend it hadn't happened. She just wished she could undo everything, unravel time like yarn from a sweater.

Across the clearing, illuminated by Stephen's headlights, Tom Mullins, linebacker and general rageaholic, leaped up onto the glass coffin suddenly enough to make the girls hop off. He looked completely wasted, face flushed and hair sticking up with sweat.

"Hey," he shouted, jumping up and down, stomping like he was trying to crack the glass. "Hey, wakey, wakey, eggs and bakey. Come on, you ancient fuck, get up!"

"Quit it," said Martin, waving for Tom to get down. "Remember what happened to Lloyd?"

Lloyd was the kind of bad kid who liked to start fires, who carried a knife to school, and who, when teachers were taking attendance, they were hard pressed to remember whether he wasn't there because he was cutting class or because he was suspended. One night last spring Lloyd had taken a sledgehammer to the glass coffin. It didn't shatter, but the next time Lloyd set a fire, he got burned. He was still in a hospital in Philadelphia, where they had to graft skin from his ass onto his face.

Some people said the horned boy had done that to Lloyd because he didn't like it when people messed with his coffin. Others said that whoever cursed the horned boy cursed the glass, too. So if anyone tried to break it, that person would bring bad luck on themselves. Though Tom Mullins knew all that, he didn't seem to care.

Hazel knew just how he felt.

"Get up!" he yelled, kicking and stomping and jumping. "Hey, lazybones, time to waaaaaaake up!"

Carter grabbed his arm. "Tom, come on. We're going to do shots. You don't want to miss this."

Tom looked unsure.

"Come *on*," Carter repeated. "Unless you're too drunk already."

"Yeah," said Martin, trying to sound convincing. "Maybe you can't hold your booze, Tom."

That did it. Tom scrambled down, lumbering away from the coffin, protesting that he could drink more than the both of them combined.

"So," Franklin said to Hazel. "Just another dull night in Fairfold, where everyone's a lunatic or an elf."

She took one more drink from the silver flask. She was starting to get used to the feeling that her esophagus was on fire. "Pretty much."

He grinned, red-rimmed eyes dancing. "Want to make out?"

From the look of him, he was as miserable as Hazel was. Franklin, who'd barely spoken for the first three years of grammar school and who everyone was sure ate roadkill for dinner sometimes. Franklin, who wouldn't thank her if she asked him what was bothering him, since she'd wager he had almost as much to forget as she did.

Hazel felt a little bit light-headed and a lot reckless. "Okay."

As they walked away from the truck and into the woods, she glanced back at the party in the grove. Jack was watching her with an unreadable expression on his face. She turned away. Passing under an oak tree, Franklin's hand in hers, Hazel thought she saw the branches shift above her, like fingers, but when she looked again, all she saw were shadows.